DETECTIVES 2

DETECTIVES 2

AVERAGE JONES

SAMUEL HOPKINS ADAMS

DR. FURNIVALL, PHYSICIAN-DETECTIVE

GEORGE F. BUTLER, M. D.

COACHWHIP PUBLICATIONS

Landisville, Pennsylvania

2 Detectives: Average Jones / Dr. Furnivall, Physician-Detective
Average Jones, by Samuel Hopkins Adams (1871-1958), first published 1911.
The Exploits of a Physician Detective, by Geo. F. Butler (1857-1921), first published 1908.
Copyright © 2011 Coachwhip Publications
No claims made on public domain material.

ISBN 1-61646-098-9
ISBN-13 978-1-61646-098-3

CoachwhipBooks.com

CONTENTS

AVERAGE JONES

DR. FURNIVALL, PHYSICIAN-DETECTIVE

AVERAGE JONES

THE B-FLAT TROMBONE

Three men sat in the Cosmic Club discussing the question: "What's the matter with Jones?" Waldemar, the oldest of the conferees, was the owner, and at times the operator, of an important and decent newspaper. His heavy face wore the expression of good-humored power, characteristic of the experienced and successful journalist. Beside him sat Robert Bertram, the club idler, slender and languidly elegant. The third member of the conference was Jones himself.

Average Jones had come by his nickname inevitably. His parents had foredoomed him to it when they furnished him with the initials A. V. R. E. as preface to his birthright of J for Jones. His character apparently justified the chance concomitance. He was, so to speak, a composite photograph of any thousand well-conditioned, clean-living Americans between the ages of twenty-five and thirty. Happily, his otherwise commonplace face was relieved by the one unfailing characteristic of composite photographs, large, deep-set and thoughtful eyes. Otherwise he would have passed in any crowd, and nobody would have noticed him pass. Now, at twenty-seven, he looked back over the five years since his graduation from college and wondered what he had done with them; and at the four previous years of undergraduate life and wondered how he had done so well with those and why he had not in some manner justified the parting words of his favorite professor.

"You have one rare faculty, Jones. You can, when you choose, sharpen the pencil of your mind to a very fine point. Specialize, my boy, specialize."

If the recipient of this admonition had specialized in anything, it was in life. Having twenty-five thousand a year of his own he might have continued in that path indefinitely, but for two influences. One was an irruptive craving within him to take some part in the dynamic activities of the surrounding world. The other was the "freak" will of his late and little-lamented uncle, from whom he had his present income, and his future expectations of some ten millions. Adrian Van Reypen Egerton had, as Waldemar once put it, "—gone into the mayor's chair with a good name and come out with a block of ice stock." In a will whose cynical humor was the topic of its day, Mr. Egerton jeered posthumously at the public which he had despoiled, and promised restitution, of a sort, through his heir.

"Therefore," he had written, "I give and bequeath to the said Adrian Van Reypen Egerton Jones, the residue of my property, the principal to be taken over by him at such time as he shall have completed five years of continuous residence in New York City. After such time the virus of the metropolis will have worked through his entire being. He will squander his unearned and undeserved fortune, thus completing the vicious circle, and returning the millions acquired by my political activities, in a poisoned shower upon the city, for which, having bossed, bullied and looted it, I feel no sentiment other than contempt."

"And now," remarked Waldemar in his heavy, rumbling voice, "you aspire to disappoint that good old man."

"It's only human nature, you know," said Average Jones. "When a man puts a ten-million-dollar curse on you and suggests that you haven't the backbone of a shrimp, you—you—"

"—naturally yearn to prove him a liar," supplied Bertram.

"Exactly. Anyway, I've no taste for dissipation, either moral or financial. I want action; something to do. I'm bored in this infernal city."

"The wail of the unslaked romanticist," commented Bertram.

"Romanticist nothing!" protested the other. "My ambitions are practical enough if I could only get 'em stirred up."

"Exactly. Boredom is simply romanticism with a morning-after thirst. You're panting for romance, for something bizarre. Egypt and St. Petersburg and Buenos Ayres and Samoa have all become commonplace to you. You've overdone them. That's why you're back here in New York waiting with stretched nerves for the Adventure of Life to cat-creep up from behind and toss the lariat of rainbow dreams over your shoulders."

Waldemar laughed. "Not a bad diagnosis. Why don't you take up a hobby, Mr. Jones?"

"What kind of a hobby?"

"Any kind. The club is full of hobby-riders. Of all people that I know, they have the keenest appetite for life. Look at old Denechaud; he was a misanthrope until he took to gathering scarabs. Fenton, over there, has the finest collection of circus posters in the world. Bellerding's house is a museum of obsolete musical instruments. De Gay collects venomous insects from all over the world; no harmless ones need apply. Terriberry has a mania for old railroad tickets. Some are really very curious. I've often wished I had the time to be a crank. It's a happy life."

"What line would you choose?" asked Bertram languidly.

"Nobody has gone in for queer advertisements yet, I believe," replied the older man. "If one could take the time to follow them up—but it would mean all one's leisure."

"Would it be so demanding a career?" said Average Jones, smiling.

"Decidedly. I once knew a man who gave away twenty dollars daily on clues from the day's news. *He* wasn't bored for lack of occupation."

"But the ordinary run of advertising is nothing more than an effort to sell something by yelling in print," objected Average Jones.

"Is it? Well perhaps you don't look in the right place."

Waldemar reached for the morning's copy of the *Universal* and ran his eye down the columns of "classified" matter. "Hark to this," he said, and read:

"Is there any work on God's green earth for a man who has just *got* to have it?"

"Or this:

"WANTED—A venerable looking man with white beard and medical degree. Good pay to right applicant."

"What's that?" asked Average Jones with awakened interest.

"Only a quack medical concern looking for a stall to impress their come-ons," explained Waldemar.

Average Jones leaned over to scan the paper in his turn.

"Here's one," said he, and read:

"WANTED—Performer on B-flat trombone. Can use at once. Apply with instrument, after 1 p.m. 300 East 100th Street."

"That seems ordinary enough," said Waldemar.

"What's it doing in a daily paper? There must be—er—technical publications—er—journals, you know, for this sort of demand."

"When Average's words come slow, you've got him interested," commented Bertram. "Sure sign."

"Nevertheless, he's right," said Waldemar. "It is rather misplaced."

"How is this for one that says what it means?" said Bertram.

"WANTED—At once, a brass howitzer and a man who isn't afraid to handle it. Mrs. Anne Cullen, Pier 49½ East River."

"The woman who is fighting the barge combine," explained Waldemar. "Not so good as it looks. She's bluffing."

"Anyway, I'd like a shy at this business," declared Average Jones with sudden conviction. "It looks to me like something to do."

"Make it a business, then," advised Waldemar. "If you care really to go in for it, my newspaper would be glad to pay for information such as you might collect. We haven't time, for example, to trace down fraudulent advertisers. If you could start an enterprise of that sort, you'd certainly find it amusing, and, at times, perhaps, even adventurous."

"I wouldn't know how to establish it," objected Average Jones.

The newspaper owner drew a rough diagram on a sheet of paper and filled it in with writing, crossing out and revising liberally. Divided, upon his pattern, into lines, the final draft read:

Have
You
Been
Stung?

Thousands have.
Thousands will be.
They're Laying for
You.
Who?
The Advertising
Crooks.

A. Jones
Ad-Visor

Can Protect You
Against Them.

Before Spending Your
Money Call on Him.
Advice on all Subjects
Connected with News-
paper, Magazine or
Display Advertising.
Free Consultation to
Persons Unable to Pay.
Call or Write, Enclos-
ing Postage. *This Is
On The Level.*
Jones, Ad-Visor.

"Ad-Visor! Do you expect me to blight my budding career by a
poisonous pun like that?" demanded Average Jones with a wry face.

"It may be a poisonous pun, but it's an arresting catch-word,"
said Waldemar, unmoved. "Single column, about fifty lines will do
it in nice, open style. Caps and lower case, and black-faced type
for the name and title. Insert twice a week in every New York and
Brooklyn paper."

"Isn't it—er—a little blatant?" suggested Bertram, with lifted
eyebrows.

"Blatant?" repeated its inventor. "It's more than that. It's howl-
ingly vulgar. It's a riot of glaring yellow. How else would you expect to catch the public?"

"Suppose, then, I do burst into flame to this effect?" queried
the prospective "Ad-Visor." "*Et après?* as we proudly say after
spending a week in Paris."

"*Aprés?* Oh, plenty of things. You hire an office, a clerk, two stenographers and a clipping expert, and prepare to take care of the work that comes in. You'll be flooded," promised Waldemar.

"And between times I'm to go skipping about, chasing long white whiskers and brass howitzers and B-flat trombones, I suppose."

"Until you get your work systematized you'll have no time for skipping. Within six months, if you're not sandbagged or jailed on fake libel suits, you'll have a unique bibliography of swindles. Then I'll begin to come and buy your knowledge to keep my own columns clean."

The speaker looked up to meet the gaze of an iron-gray man with a harsh, sallow face.

"Excuse my interrupting," said the new-comer. "Just one question, Waldemar. Who's going to be the nominee?"

"Linder."

"Linder? Surely not! Why, his name hasn't been heard."

"It will be."

"His Federal job?"

"He resigns in two weeks."

"His record will kill him."

"What record? You and I know he's a grafter. But can we prove anything? His clerk has always handled all the money."

"Wasn't there an old scandal—a woman case?" asked the questioner vaguely.

"That Washington man's wife? Too old. Linder would deny it flatly, and there would be no witnesses. The woman is dead—killed by his brutal treatment of her, they say. But the whole thing was hushed up at the time by Linder's pull, and when the husband threatened to kill him Linder quietly set a commissioner of insanity on the case and had the man put away. He's never appeared since. No, that wouldn't be politically effective."

The gray man nodded, and walked away, musing.

"Egbert, the traction boss," explained Waldemar. "We're generally on opposite sides, but this time we're both against Linder. Egbert wants a cheaper man for mayor. I want a straighter one.

And I could get him this year if Linder wasn't so well fortified. However, to get back to our project, Mr. Jones—"

Get back to it they did with such absorption that when the group broke up, several hours later, Average Jones was committed, by plan and rote, to the new and hopeful adventure of Life.

In the great human hunt which ever has been and ever shall be till "the last bird flies into the last light"—some call it business, some call it art, some call it love, and a very few know it for what it is, the very mainspring of existence—the path of the pursuer and the prey often run obscurely parallel. What time the Honorable William Linder matured his designs on the mayoralty, Average Jones sat in a suite of offices in Astor Court, a location which Waldemar had advised as being central, expensive, and inspirational of confidence, and considered, with a whirling brain, the minor woes of humanity. Other people's troubles had swarmed down upon him in answer to his advertised offer of help, as sparrows flock to scattered bread crumbs. Mostly these were of the lesser order of difficulties; but for what he gave in advice and help the Ad-Visor took payment in experience and knowledge of human nature. Still it was the hard, honest study, and the helpful toil which held him to his task, rather than the romance and adventure which he had hoped for and Waldemar had foretold—until, in a quiet street in Brooklyn, of which he had never so much as heard, there befell that which, first of many events, justified the prophetic Waldemar and gave Average Jones a part in the greater drama of the metropolis. The party of the second part was the Honorable William Linder.

Mr. Linder sat at five p.m., of an early summer day, behind lock and bolt. The third floor front room of his ornate mansion on Brooklyn's Park Slope was dedicated to peaceful thought. Sprawled in a huge and softly upholstered chair at the window, he took his ease in his house. The chair had been a recent gift from an anonymous admirer whose political necessities, the Honorable Mr. Linder idly surmised, had not yet driven him to reveal his identity. Its occupant stretched his shoeless feet, as was his custom, upon the broad window-sill, flooded by the seasonable warmth of sunshine, the while he considered the ripening mayoralty situation. He found it highly satisfactory. In the language of his inner man, it was a cinch.

Below, in Kennard Street, a solitary musician plodded. His pretzel-shaped brass rested against his shoulder. He appeared to be the "scout" of one of those prevalent and melancholious German bands, which, under Brooklyn's easy ordinances, are privileged to draw echoes of the past writhing from their forgotten recesses. The man looked slowly about him as if apprising potential returns. His gravid glance encountered the prominent feet in the third story window of the Linder mansion, and rested. He moved forward. Opposite the window he paused. He raised the mouthpiece to his lips and embarked on a perilous sea of notes from which the tutored ear might have inferred that once popular ditty, *Egypt*.

Love of music was not one of the Honorable William Linder's attributes. An irascible temper was. Of all instruments the B-flat trombone possesses the most nerve-jarring tone. The master of the mansion leaped from his restful chair. Where his feet had ornamented the coping his face now appeared. Far out he leaned, and roared at the musician below. The brass throat blared back at him, while the soloist, his eyes closed in the ecstasy of art, brought the "verse" part of his selection to an excruciating conclusion, half a tone below pitch. Before the chorus there was a brief pause for effect. In this pause, from Mr. Linder's open face a voice fell like a falling star. Although it did not cry "Excelsior," its output of vocables might have been mistaken, by a casual ear, for that clarion call. What the Honorable Mr. Linder actually shouted was:

"Getthehelloutofhere!"

The performer upturned a mild and vacant face. "What you say?" he inquired in a softly Teutonic accent.

The Honorable William Linder made urgent gestures, like a brakeman.

"Go away! Move on!"

The musician smiled reassuringly.

"I got already paid for this," he explained.

Up went the brass to his lips again. The tonal stairway which leads up to the chorus of *Egypt* rose in rasping wailfulness. It culminated in an excessive, unendurable, brazen shriek—and the Honorable William Linder experienced upon the undefended rear of his person the most violent kick of a lifetime not always devoted to the arts of peace. It projected him clear of the window-sill. His last sensible vision was the face of the musician, the mouth absurdly hollow and pursed above the suddenly removed mouthpiece. Then an awning intercepted the politician's flight. He passed through this, penetrated a second and similar stretch of canvas shading the next window below, and lay placid on his own front steps with three ribs caved in and a variegated fracture of the collar-bone. By the time the descent was ended the German musician had tucked his brass under his arm and was hurrying, in panic, down the street, his ears still ringing with the concussion which had blown the angry householder from his own front window. He was intercepted by a running policeman.

"Where was the explosion?" demanded the officer.

"Explosion? I hear a noise in the larch house on the corner," replied the musician dully.

The policeman grabbed his arm. "Come along back. You fer a witness! Come on; you an' yer horn."

"It iss not a horn," explained the German patiently, "it iss a B-flat trombone."

Along with several million other readers, Average Jones followed the Linder "bomb outrage" through the scandalized headlines of the local press. The perpetrator, declared the excited journals, had been skilful. No clue was left. The explosion had taken care of that. The police (with the characteristic stupidity of a corps of former truck-drivers and bartenders, decorated with brass buttons and shields and without further qualification dubbed "detectives") vacillated from theory to theory. Their putty-and-pasteboard fantasies did not long survive the Honorable William Linder's return to consciousness and coherence. An "inside job," they had said. The door was locked and bolted, Mr. Linder declared, and there was no possible place for an intruder to conceal himself. Clock-work, then.

"How would any human being guess what time to set it for," demanded the politician in disgust, "when I never know, myself, where I'm going to be at any given hour of any given day?"

"Then that Dutch horn-player threw the bomb," propounded the head of the "Detective Bureau" ponderously.

"Of course; tossed it right up, three stories, and kept playing his infernal trombone with the other hand all the time. You ought to be carrying a hod!"

Nevertheless, the police hung tenaciously to the theory that the musician was involved, chiefly because they had nothing else to hang to. The explosion had been very localized, the room not generally wrecked; but the chair which seemed to be the center of disturbance, and from which the Honorable William Linder had risen just in time to save his life, was blown to pieces, and a portion of the floor beneath it was much shattered. The force of the explosion had been from above the floor downward; not up through the flooring. As to murderously inclined foes, Mr. Linder disclaimed knowledge of any. The notion that the trombonist had given a signal he derided as an "Old Sleuth pipe-dream."

As time went on and "clues" came to nothing, the police had no greater concern than quietly to forget, according to custom, a problem beyond their limited powers. With the release of the German musician, who was found to be simple-minded to the verge of half-wittedness, public interest waned, and the case faded out of current print.

Average Jones, who was much occupied with a pair of blackmailers operating through faked photographs, about that time, had almost forgotten the Linder case, when, one day, a month after the explosion, Waldemar dropped in at the Astor Court offices. He found a changed Jones; much thinner and "finer" than when, eight weeks before, he had embarked on his new career, at the newspaper owner's instance. The young man's color was less pronounced, and his eyes, though alert and eager, showed rings under them.

"You have found the work interesting, I take it," remarked the visitor.

"Ra–ather," drawled Average Jones appreciatively.

"That was a good initial effort, running down the opium pill mail-order enterprise."

"It was simple enough as soon as I saw the catchword in the 'Wanted' line."

"Anything is easy to a man who sees," returned the older man sententiously. "The open eye of the open mind—that has more to do with real detective work than all the deduction and induction and analysis ever devised."

"It is the detective part that interests me most in the game, but I haven't had much of it, yet. You haven't run across any promising ads lately, have you?"

Waldemar's wide, florid brow wrinkled.

"I haven't thought or dreamed of anything for a month but this infernal bomb explosion."

"Oh, the Linder case. You're personally interested?"

"Politically. It makes Linder's nomination certain. Persecution. Attempted assassination. He becomes a near-martyr. I'm almost ready to believe that he planted a fake bomb himself."

"And fell out of a third-story window to carry out the idea? That's pushing realism rather far, isn't it?"

Waldemar laughed. "There's the weakness. Unless we suppose that he under-reckoned the charge of explosive."

"They let the musician go, didn't they?"

"Yes. There was absolutely no proof against him, except that he was in the street below. Besides, he seemed quite lacking mentally."

"Mightn't that have been a sham?"

"Alienists, of good standing examined him. They reported him just a shade better than half-witted. He was like a one-ideaed child, his whole being comprised in his ability, and ambition to play his B-flat trombone."

"Well, if I needed an accomplice," said Average Jones thoughtfully, "I wouldn't want any better one than a half-witted man. Did he play well?"

"Atrociously. And if you know what a soul-shattering blare exudes from a B-flat trombone—" Mr. Waldemar lifted expressive hands.

Within Average Jones' overstocked mind something stirred at the repetition of the words "B-flat trombone." Somewhere they had attracted his notice in print; and somehow they were connected with Waldemar. Then from amidst the hundreds of advertisements with which, in the past weeks, he had crowded his brain, one stood out clear. It voiced the desire of an unknown gentleman on the near border of Harlem for the services of a performer upon that semi-exotic instrument. One among several, it had been cut from the columns of the *Universal*, on the evening which had launched him upon his new enterprise. Average Jones made two steps to a bookcase, took down a huge scrap-book from an alphabetized row, and turned the leaves rapidly.

"Three Hundred East One Hundredth Street," said he, slamming the book shut again. "Three Hundred East One Hundredth. You won't mind, will you," he said to Waldemar, "if I leave you unceremoniously?"

"Recalled a forgotten engagement?" asked the other, rising.

"Yes. No. I mean I'm going to Harlem to hear some music. Thirty-fourth's the nearest station, isn't it? Thanks. So long."

Waldemar rubbed his head thoughtfully as the door slammed behind the speeding Ad-Visor.

"Now, what kind of a tune is he on the track of, I wonder?" he mused. "I wish it hadn't struck him until I'd had time to go over the Linder business with him."

But while Waldemar rubbed his head in cogitation and the Honorable William Linder, in his Brooklyn headquarters, breathed charily, out of respect to his creaking rib, Average Jones was following fate northward.

Three Hundred East One Hundredth Street is a house decrepit with a disease of the aged. Its windowed eyes are rheumy. It sags backward on gnarled joints. All its poor old bones creak when the winds shake it. To Average Jones' inquiring gaze on this summer day it opposed the secrecy of a senile indifference. He hesitated to pull at its bell-knob, lest by that act he should exert a disruptive force which might bring all the frail structure rattling down in ruin. When, at length, he forced himself to the summons, the merest ghost of a tinkle complained petulantly from within against his violence.

An old lady came to the door. She was sleek and placid, round and comfortable. She did not seem to belong in that house at all. Average Jones felt as if he had cracked open one of the grisly locust shells which cling lifelessly to tree trunks, and had found within a plump and prosperous beetle.

"Was an advertisement for a trombone player inserted from this house, ma'am?" he inquired.

"Long ago," said she.

"Am I too late, then?"

"Much. It was answered nearly two months since. I have never," said the old lady with conviction, "seen such a frazzled lot of folks as B-flat trombone players."

"The person who inserted the advertisement—?"

"Has left. A month since."

"Could you tell where he went?"

"Left no address."

"His name was Telford, wasn't it?" said Average Jones strategically.

"Might be," said the old lady, who had evidently formed no favorable impression of her ex-lodger. "But he *called* himself Ransom."

"He had a furnished room?"

"The whole third floor, furnished."

"Is it let now?"

"Part of it. The rear."

"I'll take the front room."

"Without even looking at it?"

"Yes."

"You're a queer young man. As to price?"

"Whatever you choose."

"You're a *very* queer young man. Are you a B-flat trombone player?"

"I collect 'em," said Average Jones.

"References?" said the old lady abruptly and with suspicion.

"All varieties," replied her prospective lodger cheerfully. "I will bring 'em to-morrow with my grip."

For five successive evenings thereafter Average Jones sat in the senile house, awaiting personal response to the following advertisement which he had inserted in the *Universal*:

> WANTED—B-flat trombonist. Must have had experience as street player. Apply between 8 and 10 p. m. R—, 300 East 100th Street.

Between the ebb and flow of applicant musicians he read exhaustively upon the unallied subjects of trombones and high explosives, or talked with his landlady, who proved to be a sociable person, not disinclined to discuss the departed guest. "Ransom," his supplanter learned, had come light and gone light. Two dress suit cases had sufficed to bring in all his belongings. He went out but little, and then, she opined with a disgustful sniff, for purposes strictly alcoholic. Parcels came for him occasionally. These were usually labeled "Glass. Handle with care." Oh! there was one other thing. A huge, easy arm-chair from Carruthers and Company, mighty luxurious for an eight-dollar lodger.

"Did he take that with him?" asked Average Jones.

"No. After he had been here a while he had a man come in and box it up. He must have sent it away, but I never saw it go."

"Was this before or after the trombone players came?"

"Long after. It was after he had picked out his man and had him up here practicing."

"Did—er—you ever—er—see this musician?" drawled Average Jones in the slow tones of his peculiar excitement.

"Bless you, yes! Talked with him."

"What was he like?"

"He was a stupid old German. I always thought he was a sort of a natural."

"Yes?" Average Jones peered out of the window. "Is this the man, coming up the street?"

"It surely is," said the old lady. "Now, *Mister* Jones, if he commences his blaring and blatting and—"

"There'll be no more music, ma'am," promised the young man, laughing, as she went out to answer the door-bell.

The musician, ushered in, looked about him, an expression of bewildered and childish surprise on his rabbit-like face.

"I am Schlichting," he murmured; "I come to play the B-flat trombone."

"Glad to see you, Mr. Schlichting," said Average Jones, leading the way up-stairs. "Sit down."

The visitor put his trombone down and shook his head with conviction.

"It iss the same room, yes," he observed. "But it iss not the same gent, no."

"You expected to find Mr. Ransom here?"

"I don't know Mr. Ransom. I know only to play the B-flat trombone."

"Mr. Ransom, the gentleman who employed you to play in the street in Brooklyn."

Mr. Schlichting made large and expansive gestures. "It iss a pleasure to play for such a gent," he said warmly. "Two dollars a day."

"You have played often in Kennard Street?"

"I don't know Kennard Street. I know only to play the B-flat trombone."

"Kennard Street. In Brooklyn. Where the fat gentleman told you to stop, and fell out of the window."

A look of fear overspread the worn and innocent face.

"I don't go there no more. The po-lice, they take there."

"But you had gone there before?"

"Not to play; no."

"Not to play? Are you sure?"

The German considered painfully. "There vass no feet in the window," he explained, brightening.

Upon that surprising phrase Average Jones pondered. "You were not to play unless there were feet the window," he said at length. "Was that it?"

The musician assented.

"It *does* look like a signal to show that Linder was in," mused the interrogator. "Do you know Linder?"

"I don't know nothing only to play the B-flat trombone," repeated the other patiently.

"Now, Schlichting," said Average Jones, "here is a dollar. Every evening you must come here. Whether I am here or not, there will be a dollar for you. Do you understand?"

By way of answer the German reached down and listed his instrument to his lips.

"No, not that," forbade Average Jones. "Put it down."

"Not to play my B-flat trombone?" asked the other, innocently hurt. "The other gent he make play here always."

"Did he?" drawled Average Jones. "And he—er—listened?"

"He listened from out there." The musician pointed to the other room.

"How long?"

"Different times," was the placid reply.

"But he was always in the other room."

"Always. And I play *Egypt*. Like this."

"No!" said Average Jones, as the other stretched out a hopeful hand.

"He liked it—*Egypt*," said the German wistfully. "He said: 'Bravo! *Encore! Bis!*' Sometimes nine, sometimes ten times over I play it, the chorus."

"And then he sent you home?"

"Then sometimes something goes 'sping-g-g-g!' like that in the back room. Then he comes out and I may go home."

"Um—m," muttered Average Jones discontentedly. "When did you begin to play in the street?"

"After a long time. He take me away to Brooklyn and tell me, 'When you see the feet iss in the window you play hard!'"

There was a long pause. Then Average Jones asked casually:

"Did you ever notice a big easy chair here?"

"I do not notice nothing. I play my B-flat trombone."

And there his limitations were established. But the old lady had something to add.

"It's all true that he said," she confirmed. "I could hear his racket in the front room and Mr. Ransom working in the back and then, after the old man was gone, Mr. Ransom sweeping up something by himself."

"Sweeping? What—er—was he—er—sweeping?"

"Glass, I think. The girl used to find little slivers of it first in one part of the room, then in another. I raised the rent for that and for the racket."

"The next thing," said Average Jones, "is to find out where that big easy chair went from here. Can you help me there?"

The old lady shook her head. "All I can do is to tell you the near-by truck men."

Canvass of the local trucking industry brought to light the conveyor of that elegant article of furniture. It had gone, Average Jones learned, not to the mansion of the Honorable William Linder, as he had fondly hoped, but to an obscure address not far from the Navy Yard in Brooklyn. To this address, having looked up and gathered in the B-flat trombonist, Average Jones led the way. The pair lurked in the neighborhood of the ramshackle house watching the entrance, until toward evening, as the door opened to let out a tremulous wreck of a man, palsied with debauch, Schlichting observed:

"That iss him. He hass been drinking again once."

Average Jones hurried the musician around the corner into concealment. "You have been here before to meet Mr. Ransom?"

"No."

"Where did he meet you to pay you your wages?"

"On some corner," said the other vaguely.

"Then he took you to the big house and left you there," urged Jones.

"No; he left me on the street corner. 'When the feet iss in the window,' he says, 'you play.'"

"It comes to this," drawled Average Jones intently, looking the employee between his vacuous eyes. "Ransom shipped the chair to Plymouth Street and from there to Linder's house. He figured out that Linder would put it in his study and do his sitting at the window in it. And you were to know when he was there by seeing his feet in the window, and give the signal when you saw him. It must have been a signal to somebody pretty far off, or he wouldn't have chosen so loud an instrument as a B-flat trombone."

"I can play the B-flat trombone louder as any man in the business," asserted Schlichting with proud conviction.

"But what gets me," pursued Average Jones, "is the purpose of the signal. Whom was it for?"

"I don't know nothing," said the other complacently. "I only know to play the B-flat trombone louder as any man in the world."

Average Jones paid him a lump sum, dismissed him and returned to the Cosmic Club, there to ponder the problem. What next? To accuse Ransom, the mysterious hirer of a B-flat trombone virtuosity, without sufficient proof upon which to base even a claim of cross-examination, would be to block his own game then and there, for Ransom could, and very likely would, go away, leaving no trace. Who was Ransom, anyway? And what relation, if any, did he bear to Linder?

Absorbed in these considerations, he failed to notice that the club was filling up beyond its wont. A hand fell on his shoulder.

"Hello, Average. Haven't seen you at a Saturday special night since you started your hobby."

It was Bertram. "What's on?" Average Jones asked him, shaking hands.

"Freak concert. Bellerding has trotted out part of his collection of mediaeval musical instruments, and some professionals are going to play them. Waldemar is at our table. Come and join us."

Conversation at the round-table was general and lively that evening, and not until the port came on—the prideful club port, served only on special occasions and in wonderful, delicate glasses—did Average Jones get an opportunity to speak to Waldemar aside.

"I've been looking into that Linder matter a little."

"Indeed. I've about given up hope."

"You spoke of an old scandal in Linder's career. What was the husband's name?"

"Arbuthnot, I believe."

"Do you know what sort of looking man he was?"

"No. I could find out from Washington."

"What was his business?"

"Government employment, I think."

"In the—er—scientific line, perhaps?" drawled Jones.

"Why, yes, I believe it was."

"Um-m. Suppose, now, Linder should drop out of the combination. Who would be the most likely nominee?"

"Marsden—the man I've been grooming for the place. A first-class, honorable, fearless man."

"Well, it's only a chance; but if I can get one dark point cleared up—" He paused as a curious, tingling note came from the platform where the musicians were tuning up.

"One of Bellerding's sweet dulcets," observed Bertram.

The performer nearest them was running a slow bass scale on a sort of two-stringed horse-fiddle of a strange shape. Average Jones' still untouched glass, almost full of the precious port, trembled and sang a little tentative response. Up—up—up mounted the thrilling notes, in crescendo force.

"What a racking sort of tone, for all its sweetness!" said Average Jones. His delicate and fragile port glass evidently shared the opinion, for, without further warning, it split and shivered.

"They used to show that experiment in the laboratory," said Bertram.

"You must have had just the accurate amount of liquid in the glass, Average. Move back, you lunatic, it's dripping all over you."

But Average Jones sat unheeding. The liquor dribbled down into his lap. He kept his fascinated gaze fixed on the shattered glass. Bertram dabbed him with a napkin.

"Tha—a—anks, Bertram," drawled the beneficiary of this attention. "Doesn't matter. Excuse me. Good night."

Leaving his surprised companions, he took hat and cane and caught a Third Avenue car. By the time he had reached Brooklyn Bridge he had his campaign mapped out. It all depended upon the opening question. Average Jones decided to hit out and hit quick.

At the house near the Navy Yard he learned that his man was out. So he sat upon the front steps while one of the highest-priced wines in New York dried into his knees. Shortly before eleven a shuffling figure paused at the steps, feeling for a key.

"Mr. Arbuthnot, otherwise Ransom?" said Average Jones blandly.

The man's chin jerked back. His jaw dropped.

"Would you like to hire another B-flat trombonist?" pursued the young man.

"Who are you?" gasped the other. "What do you want?"

"I want to know," drawled Average Jones, "how—er—you planted the glass bulb—er—the sulphuric acid bulb, you know—in the chair that you sent—er—to the Honorable William Linder, so that—er—it wouldn't be shattered by anything but the middle C note of a B-flat trombone?"

The man sat down weakly and bowed his face in his hands. Presently he looked up.

"I don't care," he said. "Come inside."

At the end of an hour's talk Arbuthnot, alias Ransom, agreed to everything that Average Jones proposed.

"Mind you," he said, "I don't promise I won't kill him later. But meantime it'll be some satisfaction to put him down and out politically. You can find me here any time you want me. You say you'll see Linder to-morrow?"

"To-morrow," said Average Jones. "Look in the next day's papers for the result."

Setting his telephone receiver down the Honorable William Linder lost himself in conjecture. He had just given an appointment to his tried and true, but quite impersonal enemy, Mr. Horace Waldemar.

"What can Waldemar want of me?" ran his thoughts. "And who is this friend, Jones, that he's bringing? Jones? Jones! Jones?!" He tried it in three different accents, without extracting any particular meaning therefrom. "Nothing much in the political game," he decided.

It was with a mingling of gruffness and dignity that he greeted Mr. Waldemar an hour later. The introduction to Average Jones he acknowledged with a curt nod.

"Want a job for this young man, Waldemar?" he grunted.

"Not at present, thank you," returned the newspaper owner. "Mr. Jones has a few arguments to present to you."

"Arguments," repeated the Honorable William Lender contemptuously. "What kind of arguments?"

"Political arguments. Mayoralty, to be specific. To be more specific still, arguments showing why you should drop out of the race."

"A pin-feather reformer, eh?"

The politician turned to meet Average Jones' steady gaze and mildly inquiring smile.

"Do you—er—know anything of submarine mines, Mr. Linder?" drawled the visitor.

"Huh?" returned the Honorable William Linder, startled.

"Submarine mines," explained the other. "Mines in the sea, if you wish words of one syllable."

The lids of the Honorable Linder contracted.

"You're in the wrong joint," he said, "this ain't the Naval College."

"Thank you. A submarine mine is a very ingenious affair. I've recently been reading somewhat extensively on the subject. The main charge is some high explosive, usually of the dynamite type. Above it is a small jar of sulphuric acid. Teeth, working on levers, surround this jar. The levers project outside the mine. When a ship strikes the mine, one or more of the levers are pressed in. The teeth crush the jar. The sulphuric acid drops upon the main charge and explodes it. Do you follow me?"

"I'll follow you as far as the front door," said the politician balefully. He rose.

"If the charge were in a chair, in the cushion of an easy chair, we'll say, on the third floor of a house in Brooklyn—"

The Honorable William Linder sat down again. He sat heavily.

"—the problem would be somewhat different. Of course, it would be easy to arrange that the first person to sit down in the chair would, by his own weight, blow himself up. But the first person might not be the right person, you know. Do you still follow me?"

The Honorable William Linder made a remark like a fish.

"Now, we have, if you will forgive my professorial method," continued Average Jones, "a chair sent to a gentleman of prominence from an anonymous source. In this chair is a charge of high explosive and above it a glass bulb containing sulphuric acid. The bulb, we will assume, is so safe-guarded as to resist any ordinary shock of moving. But when this gentleman, sitting at ease in his chair, is noticed by a trombonist, placed for that purpose in the street, below—"

"The Dutch horn-player!" cried the politician. "Then it was him; and I'll—"

"Only an innocent tool," interrupted Average Jones, in his turn. "He had no comprehension of what he was doing. He didn't understand that the vibration from his trombone on one particular note by the slide up the scale—as in the chorus of *Egypt*—would shiver that glass and set off the charge. All that he knew was to play the B-flat trombone and take his pay."

"His pay?" The question leaped to the politician's lips. "Who paid him?"

"A man—named—er—Arbuthnot," drawled Average Jones.

Linder's eyes did not drop, but a film seemed to be drawn over them.

"You once knew—er—a Mrs. Arbuthnot?"

The thick shoulders quivered a little.

"Her husband—her widower—is in Brooklyn. Shall I push the argument any further to convince you that you'd better drop out of the mayoralty race?"

Linder recovered himself a little. "What kind of a game are you ringing in on me?" he demanded.

"Don't you think," suggested Average Jones sweetly, "that considered as news, this—"

Linder caught the word out of his mouth. "News!" he roared. "A fake story ten years old, news? That ain't news! It's spite work. Even your dirty paper, Waldemar, wouldn't rake that kind of muck up after ten years. It'd be a boomerang. You'll have to put up a stronger line of blackmail and bluff than that."

"Blackmail is perhaps the correct word technically," admitted the newspaper owner, "but bluff—there you go wrong. You've forgotten one thing; that Arbuthnot's arrest and confession would make the whole story news. We stand ready to arrest Arbuthnot, and he stands ready to confess."

There was a long, tense minute of silence. Then—

"What do you want?" The straight-to-the-point question was an admission of defeat.

"Your announcement of withdrawal. I'd rather print that than the Arbuthnot story."

There was a long silence. Finally the Honorable Linder dropped his hand on the table. "You win," he declared curtly. "But you'll give me the benefit, in the announcement, of bad health caused by the shock of the explosion, to explain my quitting, Waldemar?"

"It will certainly make it more plausible," assented the newspaper owner with a smile.

Linder turned on Average Jones.

"Did you dope this out, young fellow?" he demanded.

"Yes."

"Well, you've put me in the Down-and-Out-Club, all right. And I'm just curious enough to want to know how you did it."

"By abstaining," returned Average Jones cryptically, "from the best wine that ever came out of the Cosmic Club cellar."

RED DOT

From his inner sanctum, Average Jones stared obliquely out upon the whirl of Fifth Avenue, warming itself under a late March sun.

In the outer offices a line of anxious applicants was being disposed of by his trained assistants. To the advertising expert's offices had come that day but three cases difficult enough to be referred to the Ad-Visor himself. Two were rather intricate financial lures which Average Jones was able to dispose of by a mere "Don't." The third was a Spiritualist announcement behind which lurked a shrewd plot to entrap a senile millionaire into a marriage with the medium. These having been settled, the expert was free to muse upon a paragraph which had appeared in all the important New York morning papers of the day before.

REWARD—$1,000 reward for information as to slayer of Brindle Bulldog "Rags" killed in office of Malcolm Dorr, Stengel Building, Union Square, March 29.

"That's too much money for a dog," decided Average Jones. "Particularly one that hasn't any bench record. I'll just have a glance into the thing."

Slipping on his coat he walked briskly down the avenue, and crossing over to Union Square, entered the gloomy old building which is the sole survival of the days when the Stengel estate foresaw the upward trend of business toward Fourteenth Street. Stepping from the elevator at the seventh floor, he paused underneath this sign:

Malcolm Dorr
Analytical and Consulting Chemist
Hours 10 to 4

Entering, Average Jones found a fat young man, with mild blue eyes, sitting at a desk.

"Mr. Dorr?" he asked.

"Yes," replied the fat young man nervously, "but if you are a reporter, I must—"

"I am not," interrupted the other. "I am an expert on advertising, and I want that one thousand dollars reward."

The chemist pushed his chair back and rubbed his forehead.

"You mean you have—have found out something?"

"Not yet. But I intend to."

Dorr stared at him in silence.

"You are very fond of dogs, Mr. Dorr?"

"Eh? Oh, yes. Yes, certainly," said the other mechanically.

Average Jones shot a sudden glance of surprise at him, then looked dreamily at his own finger-nails.

"I can sympathize with you. I have exhibited for some years. Your dog was perhaps a green ribboner?"

"Er—oh—yes; I believe so."

"Ah! Several of mine have been. One in particular, took medal after medal; a beautiful glossy brown bulldog, with long silky ears, and the slender splayed-out legs that are so highly prized but so seldom seen nowadays. His tail, too, had the truly Willoughby curve, from his dam, who was a famous courser."

Mr. Dorr looked puzzled. "I didn't know they used that kind of dog for coursing," he said vaguely.

Average Jones smiled with almost affectionate admiration at the crease along the knee of his carefully pressed trousers. His tone, when next he spoke, was that of a youth bored with life. Any of his intimates would have recognized in it, however, the characteristic evidence that his mind was ranging swift and far to a conclusion.

"Mr. Dorr," he drawled, "who—er—owned your—er—dog?"

"Why, I—I did," said the startled chemist.

"Who gave him to you?"

"A friend."

"Quite so. Was it that—er—friend who—er—offered the reward?"

"What makes you think that?"

"This, to be frank. A man who doesn't know a bulldog from a bed-spring isn't likely to be offering a thousand dollars to avenge the death of one. And the minute you answered my question as to whether you cared for dogs, I knew you didn't. When you fell for a green ribbon, and a splay-legged, curly-tailed medal-winner in the brindle bull class (there's no such class, by the way), I knew you were bluffing. Mr. Dorr, who—er—has been—er—threatening your life?"

The chemist swung around in his chair.

"What do you know?" he demanded.

"Nothing. I'm guessing. It's a fair guess that a reasonably valuable brindle bull isn't presented to a man who cares nothing for dogs without some reason. The most likely reason is protection. Is it in your case?"

"Yes, it is," replied the other, after some hesitation.

"And now the protection is gone. Don't you think you'd better let me in on this?"

"Let me speak to my—my legal adviser first." He called up a down-town number on the telephone and asked to be connected with Judge Elverson. "I may have to ask you to leave the office for a moment," he said to his caller.

"Very well. But if that is United States District Attorney Roger Elverson, tell him that it is A. V. R. Jones who wants to know, and remind him of the missing letter opium advertisement."

Almost immediately Average Jones was called back from the hallway, whither he had gone.

"Elverson says to tell you the whole thing," said the chemist, "in confidence, of course."

"Understood. Now, who is it that wants to get rid of you?"

"The Paragon Pressed Meat Company."

Average Jones became vitally concerned in removing an infinitesimal speck from his left cuff. "Ah," he commented, "the Canned Meat Trust. What have you been doing to them?"

"Sold them a preparation of my invention for deodorizing certain by-products used for manufacturing purposes. Several months ago I found they were using it on canned meats that had gone bad, and then selling the stuff."

"Would the meat so treated be poisonous?"

"Well—dangerous to any one eating it habitually. I wrote, warning them that they must stop."

"Did they reply?"

"A man came to see me and told me I was mistaken. He hinted that if I thought my invention was worth more than I'd received, his principals would be glad to take the matter up with me. Shortly after I heard that the Federal authorities were going after the Trust, so I called on Mr. Elverson."

"Mistake Number One. Elverson is straight, but his office is fuller of leaks than a sieve."

"That's probably why I found my private laboratory reeking of cyanide fumes a fortnight later," remarked Dorr dryly. "I got to the outer air alive, but not much more. A week later there was an explosion in the laboratory. I didn't happen to be there at the time. The odd feature of the explosion was that I hadn't any explosive drugs in the place."

"Where is this laboratory?"

"Over in Flatbush, where I live—or did live. Within a month after that, a friendly neighbor took a pot-shot at a man who was sneaking up behind me as I was going home late one night. The man shot, too, but missed me. I reported it to the police, and they told me to be sure and not let the newspapers know. Then they forgot it."

Average Jones laughed. "Of course they did. Some day New York will find out that 'the finest police force in the world' is the biggest sham outside the dime museum. Except in the case of crimes by the regular, advertised criminals, they're as helpless as babies. Didn't you take any other precautions?"

"Oh, yes. I reported the attempt to Judge Elverson. He sent a secret service man over to live with me. Then I got a commission out in Denver. When I came back, about a month ago, Judge Elverson gave me the two dogs."

"Two?"

"Yes. Rags and Tatters."

"Where's Tatters?"

"Dead. By the same road as Rags."

"Killed at your place in Flatbush?"

"No. Right here in this room."

Average Jones became suddenly very much worried about the second button of his coat. Having satisfied himself of its stability, he drawled, "Er—both of—er—them?"

"Yes. Ten days apart."

"Where were you?"

"On the spot. That is, I was here when Tatters got his death. I had gone to the wash-room at the farther end of the hall when Rags was poisoned."

"Why do you say poisoned?"

"What else could it have been? There was no wound on either of the dogs."

"Was there evidence of poison?"

"Pathological only. In Tatters case it was very marked. He was dozing in a corner near the radiator when I heard him yelp and saw him snapping at his belly. He ran across the room, lay down and began licking himself. Within fifteen minutes he began to whine. Then he stiffened out in a sort of a spasm. It was like strychnine poisoning. Before I could get a veterinary here he was dead."

"Did you make any examination?"

"I analyzed the contents of his stomach, but did not obtain positive results."

"What about the other dog?"

"Rags? That was the day before yesterday. We had just come over from Flatbush and Rags was nosing around in the corner—"

"Was it the same corner where Tatters was attacked?"

"Yes, near the radiator. He seemed to be interested in something there when I left the room. I was gone not more than two minutes."

"Lock the door after you?"

"It has a special spring lock which I had put on it."

Average Jones crossed over and looked at the contrivance. Then his glance fell to a huge, old-fashioned keyhole below the new fastening. "You didn't use that larger lock?"

"No. I haven't for months. The key is lost, I think."

Retracing his steps the investigator sighted the hole from the radiator, and shook his head.

"It's not in range," he said. "Go on."

"As I reached the door on my return, I heard Rags yelp. You may believe I got to him quickly. He was pawing wildly at his nose. I called up the nearest veterinary. Within ten minutes the convulsions came on. The veterinary was here when Rags died, which was within fifteen minutes of the first spasm. He didn't believe it was strychnine. Said the attacks were different. Whatever it was, I couldn't find any trace of it in the stomach. The veterinary took the body away and made a complete autopsy."

"Did he discover anything?"

"Yes. The blood was coagulated and on the upper lip he found a circle of small pustules. He agreed that both dogs probably swallowed something that was left in my office, though I don't see how it could have got there."

"That won't do," returned Average Jones positively. "A dog doesn't cry out when he swallows poison, unless it's some corrosive."

"It was no corrosive. I examined the mouth."

"What about the radiator?" asked Average Jones, getting down on his knees beside that antiquated contrivance. "It seems to have been the center of disturbance."

"If you're thinking of fumes," replied the chemist. "I tested for that. It isn't possible."

"No; I suppose not. And yet, there's the curious feature that the fatal influence seems to have emanated from the corner which is the most remote from both windows and door. Are your windows left open at night?"

"The windows, sometimes. The transom is kept double-bolted."

"Do they face any other windows near by?"

"You can see for yourself that they don't."

"There's no fire-escape and it's too far up for anything to come in from the street." Average examined the walls with attention and returned to the big keyhole, through which he peeped.

"Do you ever chew gum?" he asked suddenly.

The Chemist stared at him. "It isn't a habit of mine to," he said.

"But you wouldn't have any objection to my sending for some, in satisfaction of a sudden irresistible craving?"

"Any particular brand? I'll phone the corner drug store."

"Any sort will suit, thank you."

When the gum arrived, Average Jones, after politely offering some to his host, chewed up a single stick thoroughly. This he rolled out to an extremely tenuous consistency and spread it deftly across the unused keyhole, which it completely though thinly, veiled.

"Now, what's that for?" inquired the chemist, eying the improvised closure with some contempt.

"Don't know, exactly, yet," replied the deviser, cheerfully. "But when queer and fatal things happen in a room and there's only one opening, it's just as well to keep your eye on that, no matter how small it is. Better still, perhaps, if you'd shift your office."

The fat young chemist pushed his hair back, looked out of the window, and then turned to Average Jones. The rather flabby lines of his face had abruptly hardened over the firm contour below.

"No. I'm hanged if I will," he said simply.

An amiable grin overspread Average Jones' face.

"You've got more nerve than prudence," he observed. "But I don't say you aren't right. Since you're going to stick to the ship, keep your eye on that gum. If it lets go its hold, wire me."

"All right," agreed young Mr. Dorr. "Whatever your little game is, I'll play it. Give me your address in case you leave town."

"As I may do. I am going to hire a press-clipping bureau on special order to dig through the files of the local and neighboring city newspapers for recent items concerning dog-poisoning cases. If our unknown has devised a new method of canicide, it's quite possible he may have worked it somewhere else, too. Good-bye, and if you can't be wise, be careful."

Dog-poisoning seemed to Average Jones to have become a popular pastime in and around New York, judging from the succession of news items which poured in upon him from the clipping bureau. Several days were exhausted by false clues. Then one morning there arrived, among other data, an article from the Bridgeport *Morning Delineator* which caused the Ad-Visor to sit up with a jerk. It detailed the poisoning of several dogs under peculiar circumstances. Three hours later he was in the bustling Connecticut city. There he took carriage for the house of Mr. Curtis Fleming, whose valuable Great Dane dog had been the last victim.

Mr. Curtis Fleming revealed himself as an elderly, gentleman all grown to a point: pointed white nose, eyes that were pin-points of irascible gleam, and a most pointed manner of speech.

"Who are you?" he demanded rancidly, as his visitor was ushered in.

Average Jones recognized the type. He knew of but one way to deal with it.

"Jones!" he retorted with such astounding emphasis that the monosyllable fairly exploded in the other's face.

"Well, well, well," said the elder man, his aspect suddenly mollified. "Don't bite me. What kind of a Jones are you, and what do you want of me?"

"Ordinary variety of Jones. I want to know about your dog."

"Reporter?"

"No."

"Glad of it. They're no good. Had my reporters on this case. Found nothing."

"Your reporters?"

"I own the Bridgeport *Delineator*."

"What about the dog?"

"Good boy!" approved the old martinet. "Sticks to his point. Dog was out walking with me day before yesterday. Crossing a vacant lot on next square. Chased a rat. Rat ran into a heap of old timber. Dog nosed around. Gave a yelp and came back to me. Had spasm. Died in fifteen minutes. And hang me, sir," cried the old man, bringing his fist down on Average Jones' knee, "if I see how the poison got him, for he was muzzled to the snout, sir!"

"Muzzled? Then—er—why do, you—er—suggest poison?" drawled the young man.

"Fourth dog to go the same way in the last week."

"All in this locality?"

"Yes, all on Golden Hill."

"Any suspicions?"

"Suspicions? Certainly, young man, certainly. Look at this."

Average Jones took the smutted newspaper proof which his host extended, and read:

> WARNING—Residents of the Golden Hill neighbor-
> hood are earnestly cautioned against unguarded
> handling of timber about woodpiles or outbuildings
> until further notice. Danger!"

"When was this published?"

"Wasn't published. *Delineator* refused it. Thought it was a case of insanity."

"Who offered it?"

"Professor Moseley. Tenant of mine. Frame house on the next corner with old-fashioned conservatory."

"How long ago?"

"About a week."

"All the dogs you speak of died since then?"

"Yes."

"Did he give any explanation of the advertisement?"

"No. Acted half-crazy when he brought it to the office, the business manager said. Wouldn't sign his name to the thing. Wouldn't say anything about it. Begged the manager to let him have the weather reports in advance, every day. The manager put the advertisement in type, decided not to run it, and returned the money."

"Weather reports, eh?" Average Jones mused a moment. "How long was the ad to run?"

"Until the first hard frost."

"Has there—er—been a—er—frost since?" drawled Average Jones.

"No."

"Who is this Moseley?"

"Don't know much about him. Scientific experimenter of some kind, I believe. Very exclusive," added Mr. Curtis Fleming, with a grin. "Never associated with any of us neighbors. Rent on the nail, though. Insane, too, I think. Writes letters to himself with nothing in them."

"How's that?" inquired Average Jones.

The other took an envelope from his pocket and handed it over. "It got enclosed by mistake with the copy for the advertisement. The handwriting on the envelope is his own. Look inside."

A glance had shown Average Jones that the letter, had been mailed in New York on March twenty-fifth. He took out the enclosure. It was a small slip of paper. The date was stamped on with a rubber stamp. There was no writing of any kind. Near the center of the sheet were three dots. They seemed to have been made with red ink.

"You're sure the address is in Professor Moseley's writing?"

"I'd swear to it."

"It doesn't follow that he mailed it to himself. In fact, I should judge that it was sent by someone who was particularly anxious not to have any specimen of his handwriting lying about for identification.

"Perhaps. What's your interest in all this, anyway my mysterious young friend?"

"Two dogs in New York poisoned in something the same way as yours."

"Well, I've got *my* man. He confessed."

"Confessed?" echoed Average Jones.

"Practically. I've kept the point of the story to the last. Professor Moseley committed suicide this morning."

If Mr. Curtis Fleming had designed to make an impression on his visitor, his ambition was fulfilled. Average Jones got to his feet slowly, walked over to the window, returned, picked up the strange proof with its message of suggested peril, studied it, returned to the window, and stared out into the day.

"Cut his throat about nine o'clock this morning," pursued the other. "Dead when they found him."

"Do you mind not talking to me for a minute?" said Average Jones curtly.

"Told to hold my tongue in my own house by uninvited stripling," cackled the other. "You're a singular young man. Have it your own way."

After a five minutes' silence the visitor turned from the window and spoke. "There has been a deadly danger loose about here for which Professor Moseley felt himself responsible. He has killed himself. Why?"

"Because I was on his trail," declared Mr. Curtis Fleming. "Afraid to face me."

"Nonsense. I believe some human being has been killed by this thing, whatever it may be, and that the horror of it drove Moseley to suicide."

"Prove it."

"Give me a morning paper."

His host handed him the current issue of the *Delineator*.

Average Jones studied the local page.

"Where's Galvin's Alley?" he asked presently.

"Two short blocks from here."

"In the Golden Hill section?"

"Yes."

"Read that."

Mr. Curtis Fleming took the paper. His eyes were directed to a paragraph telling of the death of an Italian child living in Galvin's Alley. Cause, convulsions.

"By Jove!" said he, somewhat awed. "You can reason, young man."

"I've got to reason a lot further, if I'm to get anywhere in this affair," said Average Jones with conviction. "Do you care to come to Galvin's Alley with me?"

Together they went down the hill to a poor little house, marked by white crepe. The occupants were Italians who spoke some English. They said that four-year-old Pietro had been playing around a woodpile the afternoon before, when he was taken sick and came home, staggering. The doctor could do nothing. The little one passed from spasm into spasm, and died in an hour.

"Was there a mark like a ring anywhere on the hand or face?" asked Average Jones.

The dead child's father looked surprised. That, he said, was what the strange gentleman who had come that very morning asked, a queer, bent little gentlemen, very bald and with big eyeglasses, who was kind, and wept with them and gave them money to bury the "bambino."

"Moseley, by the Lord Harry!" exclaimed Mr. Curtis Fleming. "But what was the death-agent?"

Average Jones shook his head. "Too early to do more than guess. Will you take me to Professor Moseley's place?"

The old house stood four-square, with a patched-up conservatory on one wing. In the front room they found the recluse's body decently disposed, with an undertaker's assistant in charge. From the greenhouse came a subdued hissing.

"What's that?" asked Jones.

"Fumigating the conservatory. There was a note found near the body insisting on its being done. 'For safety,' it said, so I ordered it looked to."

"You're in charge, then?"

"It's my house. And there are no relatives so far as I know. Come and look at his papers. You won't find much."

In the old-fashioned desk was a heap of undecipherable matter, interspersed with dates, apparently bearing upon scientific experiments; a package of letters from the Denny Research Laboratories of St. Louis, mentioning enclosure of checks; and three self-addressed envelopes bearing New York postmarks, of dates respectively, March 12, March 14 and March 20. Each contained a date-stamped sheet of paper, similar to that which Mr. Curtis Fleming had shown to Average Jones. The one of earliest date bore two red dots; the second, three red dots, and the third, two. All the envelopes were endorsed in Professor Moseley's handwriting; the first with the one word "Filled." The second writing was "Held for warmer weather." The last was inscribed "One in poor condition."

Of these Average Jones made careful note, as well as of the laboratory address. By this time the hissing of the fumigating apparatus had ceased. The two men went to the conservatory and gazed in upon a ruin of limp leaves and flaccid petals, killed by the powerful gases. Suddenly, with an exclamation of astonishment, the investigator stooped and lifted from the floor a marvel of ermine body and pale green wings. The moth, spreading nearly a foot, was quite dead.

"Here's the mate, sir," said the fumigating expert, handing him another specimen, a trifle smaller. "The place was crowded with all kinds of pretty ones. All gone where the good bugs go now."

Average Jones took the pair of moths to the desk, measured them and laid them carefully away in a drawer.

"The rest must wait," he said. "I have to send a telegram."

With the interested Mr. Curtis Fleming in attendance, he went to the telegraph office, where he wrote out a dispatch.

"Mr. A. V. R. Jones?" said the operator. "There's a message here for you."

Average Jones took the leaflet and read:

> "*Found gum on floor this morning when I arrived.*
>
> Malcolm Dorr."

Then he recalled his own blank, tore it up, and substituted the following, which he ordered "rushed":

> MALCOLM DORR,
> STENGEL BUILDING, NEW YORK CITY:
> "*Leave office immediately. Do not return until it has been fumigated thoroughly. Imperative.*
> A. V. R. Jones."

"And now," said Average Jones to Mr. Fleming, "I'm going back to New York. If any collectors come chasing to you for luna moths, don't deal with them. Refer them to me, please. Here is my card."

"Your orders shall be obeyed," said the older man, his beady eyes twinkling. "But why, in the name of all that's unheard of, should collectors come bothering me about luna moths?"

"Because of an announcement to this effect which will appear in the next number of the *National Science Weekly*, and in coming issues of the New York *Evening Register*."

He handed out a rough draft of this advertisement:

"FOR SALE—Two largest known specimens of *Tropaea luna*, unmounted; respectively 10 and 11 inches spread. Also various other specimens from collection of late Gerald Moseley, of Conn. Write for particulars. Jones, Room 222 Astor Court Temple, New York."

"What about further danger here?" inquired Mr. Fleming, as Average Jones bade him good-bye. "Would we better run that warning of poor Moseley's, after all?"

For reply Jones pointed out the window. A late season whirl of snow enveloped the streets.

"I see," said the old man. "The frost. Well Mr. Mysterious Jones, I don't know what you're up to, but you've given me an interesting day. Let me know what comes of it."

On the train back to New York, Average Jones Wrote two letters. One was to the Denny Research Laboratories in St. Louis, the other to the Department of Agriculture at Washington. On the following morning he went to Dorr's office. That young chemist was in a recalcitrant frame of mind.

"I've done about ten dollars' worth of fumigating and a hundred dollars' worth of damage," he said, "and now, I'd like to have a Missouri sign. In other words, I want to be shown. What did some skunk want to kill my dogs for?"

"He didn't."

"But they're dead, aren't they?"

"Accident."

"What kind of an accident?"

"The kind in which the innocent bystander gets the worst of it. You're the one it was meant for."

"Me?"

"Certainly. You'd probably have got it if the dog hadn't."

The speaker examined the keyhole, then walked over to the radiator and looked over, under and through it minutely. "Nothing there," he observed; and, after extending his examination to the windows, book-shelf and desk, added:

"I guess we might have spared the fumigation. However, the safest side is the best."

"What is it? Some new game in projective germs?" demanded the chemist.

"Oh, disinfectants will kill other things besides germs," returned Average Jones. "Luna moths, for instance. Wait a few days and I'll have some mail to show you on that subject. In the meantime, have a plumber solder up that keyhole so tight that nothing short of dynamite can get through it."

Collectors of *lepidoptera* rose in shoals to the printed offer of luna moths measuring ten and eleven inches across the wings. Letters came in by, every mail, responding variously with fervor, suspicion, yearning eagerness, and bitter skepticism to Average Jones' advertisement. All of these he put aside, except such as bore a New York postmark. And each day he compared the new names signed to the New York letters with the directory of occupants of the Stengel Building. Less than a week after the luna moth advertisement appeared, Average Jones walked into Malcolm Dorr's office with a twinkle in his eye.

"Do you know a man named Marcus L. Ross?" he asked the chemist.

"Never heard of him."

"Marcus L. Ross is interested, not only in luna moths, but in the rest of the Moseley collection. He writes from the Delamater Apartments, where he lives, to tell me so. Also he has an office in this building. Likewise he works frequently at night. Finally, he is one of the confidential lobbyists of the Paragon Pressed Meat Company. Do you see?"

"I begin," replied young Mr. Dorr.

"It would be very easy for Mr. Ross, whose office is on the floor above, to stop at this door on his way, down-stairs after quitting work late at night when the elevator had stopped running and—let us say—peep through the keyhole."

Malcolm Dorr got up and stretched himself slowly. The sharp, clean lines of his face suddenly stood out again under the creasy flesh.

"I don't know what *you're* going to do to Mr. Ross," he said, "but I want to see him first."

"I'm not going to do anything to him," returned Average Jones, "because, in the first place, I suspect that he is far, far away, having noted, doubtless, the plugged keyhole and suffered a crisis of the nerves. It's strange how nervous your scientific murderer is. Anyway, Ross is only an agent. I'm going to aim higher."

"As how?"

"Well, I expect to do three things. First, I expect to scare a peaceful but murderous trust multimillionaire almost out of his senses; second, I expect to dispatch a costly yacht to unknown seas; and third, I expect to raise the street selling price of the evening 'yellow' journals, temporarily, about one thousand per cent. What's the answer? The answer is 'Buy to-night's papers.'"

New York, that afternoon, saw something new in advertising. That it really was advertising was shown by the "Adv." sign, large and plain, in both the papers which carried it. The favored journals were the only two which indulged in "fudge" editions; that is, editions with glaring red-typed inserts of "special" news. On the front page of each, stretching narrowly across three columns, was a device showing a tiny mapped outline in black marked Bridgeport, Conn., and a large skeleton draft of Manhattan Island showing the principal streets. From the Connecticut city downward ran a line of dots in red. The dots entered New York from the north, passed down Fourth Avenue to the south side of Union Square, turned west and terminated. Beneath this map was the legend, also in red:

WATCH THE LINE ADVANCE IN LATER EDITIONS

It was the first time in the records of journalism that the "fudge" device had been used in advertising.

Great was the rejoicing of the "newsies" when public curiosity made a "run" upon these papers. Greater it grew when the "afternoon edition" appeared, and with their keen business instinct, the urchins saw that they could run the price upward, which they promptly did, in some cases even to a nickel. This edition carried the same "fudge" advertisement, but now the red dots crossed over to Fifth Avenue and turned northward as far as Twenty-third Street. The inscription was:

UPWARD AND ONWARD
SEE NEXT EXTRA

For the "Night Extra" people paid five, ten, even fifteen cents. Rumor ran wild. Other papers, even, look the matter up as news, and commented upon the meaning of the extraordinary advertisement. This time, the red-dotted line went as far up Fifth Avenue as Fiftieth Street. And the legend was ominous:

WHEN I TURN, I STRIKE

That was all that evening. The dotted line did not turn.

Keen as newspaper conjecture is, it failed to connect the "red-line maps," with the fame of which the city was raging, with an item of shipping news printed in the evening papers of the following day:

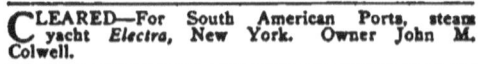

And not until the following morning did the papers announce that President Colwell, of the Canned Meat Trust, having been ordered by his physician on a long sea voyage to refurbish his depleted nerves, after closing his house on West Fifty-first Street, had sailed in his own yacht. The same issue carried a few lines about the "freak ads." which had so sensationally blazed and so suddenly waned from the "yellows." The opinion was offered that they represented the exploitation of some new brand of whisky which would announce itself later. But that announcement never came, and President Colwell sailed to far seas, and Mr. Curtis Fleming came to New York, keen for explanations, for he, too, had seen the "fudge" and marveled. Hence, Average Jones had him, together with young Mr. Dorr, at a private room luncheon at the Cosmic Club, where he offered an explanation and elucidation.

"The whole affair," he said, "was a problem in the connecting up of loose ends. At the New York terminus we had two deaths in the office of a man with powerful and subtle enemies, that office being practically sealed against intrusion except for a very large keyhole. Some deadly thing is introduced through that keyhole; so much is practically proven by the breaking out of the chewing gum with which I coated it. Probably the scheme was carried out in the evening when the building was nearly deserted. The killing influence reaches a corner far out of the direct line of the keyhole. Being near the radiator, that corner represents the attraction of warmth. Therefore, the invading force was some sentient creature."

Dorr shuddered. "Some kind of venomous snake," he surmised.

"Not a bad guess. But a snake, however small, would have been instantly noticed by the dogs. Now, let's look at the Bridgeport end. Here, again, we have a deadly influence loosed; this time by accident. A scientific experimentalist is the innocent cause of the disaster. Here, too, the peril is somewhat dependent upon warmth, since we know, from Professor Moseley's agonized eagerness for a frost, that cold weather would have put an end to it. The cold weather fails to come. Dogs are killed. Finally a child falls victim, and on that child is found a circular mark, similar to the mark on Mr. Dorr's dog's lip. You see the striking points of analogy?"

"Do you mean us to believe poor old Moseley a cold-blooded murderer?" demanded Mr. Curtis Fleming.

"Far from it. At worst an unhappy victim of his own carelessness in loosing a peril upon his neighborhood. You're forgetting a connecting link; the secretive red-dot communications from New

York City addressed by Moseley to himself on behalf of some customer who ordered simply by a code of ink dots. He was the man I had to find. The giant luna moths helped to do it."

"I don't see where they come in at all," declared Dorr bluntly. "A moth a foot wide couldn't crawl through a keyhole."

"No; nor do any damage if it did. The luna is as harmless as it is lovely. In this case the moths weren't active agents. They were important only as clues—and bait. Their enormous size showed Professor Moseley's line of work; the selective breeding of certain forms of life to two or three times the normal proportions. Very well; I had to ascertain some creature which, if magnified several times, would be deadly, and which would still be capable of entering a large keyhole. Having determined that—"

"You found what it was?" cried Dorr.

"One moment. Having determined that, I had still to get in touch with Professor Moseley's mysterious New York correspondent. I figured that he must be interested in Professor Moseley's particular branch of research or he never could have devised his murderous scheme. So I constructed the luna moth advertisement to draw him, and when I got a reply from Mr. Ross, who is a fellow-tenant of Mr. Dorr's, the chain was complete. Now, you see where the luna moths were useful. If I had advertised, instead of them, the *lathrodectus*, he might have suspected and refrained from answering."

"What's the *lathrodectus*?" demanded both the hearers at once.

For answer Average Jones took a letter from his pocket and read:

BUREAU OF ENTOMOLOGY,

U. S. DEPARTMENT OF AGRICULTURE,

WASHINGTON, D. C., *April 7*

Mr. A. V. R. Jones,

ASTOR COURT TEMPLE, NEW YORK CITY.

Dear Sir,

Replying to your letter of inquiry, the only insect answering your specifications is a small spider *Lathrodectus mactans*, sometimes popularly called the Red Dot, from a bright red mark upon the back. Rare cases are known where death has been caused by the bite of this insect. Fortunately its fangs are so weak that they can penetrate only very tender skin, otherwise death from its bite would be more common, as the venom, drop for drop, is perhaps the most virulent known to science.

This Bureau knows nothing of any experiments in breeding the *Lathrodectus* for size. Your surmise that specimens of two or three times the normal size would be dangerous to life is undoubtedly correct, and selected breeding to that end should be conducted only under adequate scientific safeguards. A *Lathrodectus mactans* with fangs large enough to penetrate the skin of the hand, and a double or triple supply of venom, would be, perhaps, more deadly than a cobra.

The symptoms of poisoning by this species are spasms, similar to those of trismus, and agonizing general pains. There are no local symptoms, except, in some cases, a circle of small pustules about the bitten spot.

Commercially, the *Lathrodectus* has value, in that the poison is used in certain affections of the heart. For details, I would refer you to the Denny Laboratories of St. Louis, Mo., which are purchasers of the venom.

The species is very susceptible to cold, and would hardly survive a severe frost. It frequents woodpiles and outhouses. Yours truly,

L. O. Howard, Chief of Bureau.

"Then Ross was sneaking down here at night and putting the spiders which he had got from Professor Moseley through my keyhole, in the hope that sooner or later one of them would get me," said Dorr.

"A very reasonable expectation, too. *Vide*, the dogs," returned Average Jones.

"And now," said Mr. Curtis Fleming, "will some one kindly explain to me what this Ross fiend had against our friend, Mr. Dorr?"

"Nothing," replied Average Jones.

"Nothing? Was he coursing with spiders merely for sport?"

"Oh, no. You see Mr. Dorr was interfering with the machinery of one of our ruling institutions, the Canned Meat Trust. He possessed information which would have indicted all the officials. Therefore it was desirable—even essential—that he should be removed from the pathway of progress."

"Nonsense! Socialistic nonsense!" snapped Mr. Curtis Fleming. "Trusts may be unprincipled, but they don't commit individual crimes."

"Don't they?" returned Average Jones, smiling amiably at his own boot-tip. "Did you ever hear of Mr. Adel Meyer's little corset steel which he invented to stick in the customs scales and rob the government for the profit of his Syrup Trust? Or of the individual oil refineries which mysteriously disappeared in fire and smoke at a time when they became annoying to the Combination Oil Trust? Or of the Traction Trust's two plots to murder Prosecutor Henry in San Francisco? I'm just mentioning a few cases from memory. Why, when a criminal trust faces only loss it will commit forgery, theft or arson. When it faces jail, it will commit murder just as determinedly. Self-defense, you know. As for the case of Mr. Dorr—" and he proceeded to detail the various attempts on the young chemist's life.

"But why so roundabout a method?" asked Dorr skeptically.

"Well, they tried the ordinary methods of murder on you through agents. That didn't work. It was up to the Trust to put one of its own confidential men on it. Ross is an amateur entomologist. He devised a means that looked to be pretty safe and, in the long run, sure."

"And would have been but for your skill, young Jones," declared Mr. Curtis Fleming, with emphasis.

"Don't forget the fortunate coincidences," replied Average Jones modestly. "They're about half of it. In fact, detective work, for all that is said on the other side, is mostly the ability to recognize and connect coincidences. The coincidence of the escape of the Red Dots from Professor Moseley's breeding cages; the coincidence of the death of the dogs on Golden Hill, followed by the death of the child; the coincidence of poor Moseley's having left the red dot letters on the desk instead of destroying them; the coincidence of Dorr's dogs being bitten, when it might easily have been himself had he gone to turn on the radiator and disturbed the savage little spider—"

"And the chief coincidence of your having become interested in the advertisement which Judge Elverson had me insert, really more to scare off further attempts than anything else," put in Dorr. "What became of the spiders that were slipped through my key-hole, anyway?"

"Two of them, as you know, were probably killed by the dogs. The others may well have died of cold. At night when the heat was off and the windows open. The cleaning woman wouldn't have been likely to notice them when she swept the bodies out. And, sooner or later, if Ross had continued to insert Red Dots through the key-hole one of them would have bitten you, Dorr, and the Canned Meat Trust would have gone on its way rejoicing."

"Well, you've certainly saved my life," declared Dorr, "and it's a case of sheer force of reasoning."

Average Jones shook his head. "You might give some of the credit to Providence," he said. "Just one little event would have meant the saving of the Italian child, and of Professor Moseley, and the death of yourself, instead of the other way around."

"And that event?" asked Mr. Curtis Fleming.

"Five degrees of frost in Bridgeport," replied Average Jones.

OPEN TRAIL

"Not good enough," said Average Jones, laying aside a sheet of paper upon which was pasted a newspaper clipping. "We can't afford luxuries, Simpson."

The confidential clerk rubbed his high, pale forehead indeterminately. "But five thousand dollars, Mr. Jones," he protested.

"Would pay a year's office rent, you're thinking. True. Nevertheless I can't see the missing Mr. Hoff as a sound professional proposition."

"So you think it would be impossible to find him?"

"Now, why should I think any such absurd thing? I think, if you choose, that he wouldn't be worth the amount, when found, to loser."

"The ad says different, sir." Simpson raised the paper and read:

"FIVE THOUSAND DOLLARS—The aforesaid sum will be paid without question to anyone furnishing information which leads to the discovery of Roderick Hoff, twenty-four years old, who left his home in Toledo, O., on April 12. Communicate with Dr. Conrad Hoff, Toledo.

"Surely Doctor Hoff is good for the amount."

"Oh, he's good for millions, thanks to his much advertised quack 'Catarrh-Killer.' The point is, from what I can discover, Mr. Roderick Hoff isn't worth retrieving at any price above one dime."

"Was the information about him that you wished, in the telegram?" asked the confidential clerk.

"Yes; all I wanted. Thanks for looking after it. Have the Toledo reporter, who sent it, forward his bill. And if the old inventor who's been haunted by disembodied voices comes again, bring him to me."

"Yes, sir," said Simpson, going out.

Left to himself, Average Jones again ran over the dispatches, conveying the information as to the lost Toledo youth. They had given a fairly complete sketch of young Hoff's life and character. At twenty-four, it appeared, Roderick Hoff had achieved a career. Emerging, by the propulsive method, from college, in the first term of his freshman year, he had taken a post-graduate course in the cigarette ward of a polite retreat for nervous wrecks. He had subsequently endured two breach-of-promise suits, had broken the state automobile record for number of speed violation arrests, had been buncoed, badgered, paneled, blackmailed and short-carded out of sums varying between one hundred and ten thousand dollars; and now, in the year of grace, 19—, was the horror of the pulpit and the delight of the press of the city which he called his home. For the rest, he was a large, mild, good-humored, pulpy individual, with a fixed delusion that the human organism can absorb a quart of alcoholic miscellany per day and be none the worse for it. The major premise of his proposition was perfectly correct. He proved it daily. The minor premise was an error. Bets were even in the Toledo clubs as to whether delirium tremens or paresis would win the event around young Mr. Hoff's kite-shaped race-track of a brain.

With his tastes the income of twenty-five thousand dollars per annum which his father allowed him from the profits of "Dr. Hoff's Catarrh-Killer," proved sadly insufficient to his needs. He mentioned this fact to his father, so Average Jones' information ran, early in April, and suggested an increase, only to be refused with some acerbity.

"Oh, very well," said he, "I'll go and make it myself."

The amazement inspired in Doctor Hoff's mind by this pronouncement was augmented in the next few days by the fact that Roderick was very busy about town in his motor-car, and was changed to vivid alarm immediately thereafter by the young man's disappearance. To all intents and appearances, Roderick Hoff had dropped off the earth on or about April twelfth. By April fifteenth New York, Pittsburg, Chicago, Washington and other clearing-houses for the distribution of the unspent increment were apprised of the elder Hoff's five thousand-dollar anxiety through the medium of the daily press. This advertisement it was, upon the practical merits of which Average Jones and his confidential clerk had differed.

"If there were any chance of sport in it," mused Average Jones, "I'd go in. But to follow the trail of a spurious young sport from bar-room to brothel and from brothel to gambling hell—" He shook his head. "Not good enough," he repeated.

Simpson's face appeared at the door. His blond forehead was wrinkled with excitement.

"Doctor Hoff is here, Mr. Jones. I told him you couldn't see him, but he wouldn't take no. Says he was recommended to you by a former client."

Following the word, there burst into Average Jones' private sanctum a gross old man, silk-hatted and bediamonded, whose side-whiskers bristled whitely with perturbed self-importance. In his hand was a patchy bundle.

"They tried to stop me!" he sputtered. "Me! I'm worth ten million dollars, an' a ten-dollar-a-week office toad tries to hold me up when I come here myself person'ly, from Toledo to see you."

Analysis of advertising in all its forms had inspired Average Jones with a profound contempt and dislike for the cruelest of all forms of swindling medical quackery. And this swollen, smug-faced intruder looked a particularly offensive specimen of his kind. Therefore the Ad-Visor said curtly:

"I can't take your case. Good day—"

"Not take it! Did you read the reward?"

"Yes. It is interesting as showing the patent medicine faker's touching confidence in the power of advertising. Otherwise it doesn't interest me. Get some one else to find your young hopeful."

"It ain't no case of findin' now. The boy's dead." His strident voice quavered and broke, but rose again to a snarl. "And, by God, I'll spend a million to get the dogs that murdered him."

At the word "murdered" Average Jones' clean cut, agreeable, but rather stolidly neutral face underwent a subtle transformation. Another personality looked out from the deep-set, somnolent, gray eyes; a personality resolute, forceful and quietly alert. It was apparently belied by the hesitant drawl, which, as all who had ever seen the Ad-Visor at his chosen pursuits well knew, signified awakened or intensified interest in the matter in hand.

"Where—er—is—the—er—body"

"I don't know. It ain't been found."

"Then how do you know he's dead?"

The other tore open the bundle he carried, and spread before Average Jones a white stained shirt with ominous brown splotches.

"It's his shirt. There's the initials. Mailed to my house and got there just after I left. My secretary brought it on, with the note that come pinned to it. Here it is."

He produced a bit of coarse wrapping-paper upon which was this message in rough capital letters:

TWO DAGOES SHOT HIM DASSENT SAY NO MORE FROM A FRIEND IN CINCINNATI

Average Jones examined the wrapper. It was postmarked Cincinnati. He next smoothed out the creased silk and studied minutely the blotches, which were heaviest about the left breast and shoulder.

To the surprise of Doctor Hoff, the young man's glance roved the big desk before him, settling with satisfaction upon a sponge-cup for moistening stamps. Applying this to one of the spots on the shirt, he rubbed the wetted portion vigorously on a sheet of paper which lay near at hand. His lips pursed. He whistled very softly and meditatively. He scratched his chin with a slow movement.

"Is that all?" he shot out suddenly at the older man.

"All! Ain't it enough? He's been murdered; murdered, I tell you, an' you set there an' whistle!"

Average Jones directed a dreamy smile toward a far corner of the room.

"I don't see anything so far," he observed, "to indicate that your son is not alive and well at this moment."

Doctor Hoff struck his fist down heavily on the desk. "What's this you're givin' me? Can't you read? Look at that note there, an' the blood on the shirt."

"Would you mind moderating your voice? My outside office is full of more or less excitable clients," said the Ad-Visor mildly. "Moreover, it's not blood anyway."

"What is it, then?"

"That's beside the question. Dried blood rubs off a faint buff color." He picked up the sheet of paper from his desk. A deep brownish streak showed where he had applied the moistened cloth. "It's the rawest kind of a blind. Why, the idiot who sent the shirt didn't even have the sense to fake bullet holes. Enough to make one lose all interest in the case," he added disgustedly.

Doctor Hoff began tugging at his side-whiskers. "Don't do nothing like that," he pleaded. "Come with me to Cincinnati. If he ain't dead they've kidnapped him for a ransom."

"Then Cincinnati is the last place on the map to look, because there's where they want you to think he is. But it doesn't look like a case of ransom to me. Let's see. Was he particularly drunk the day before he disappeared?"

"No. He was sober."

"Unusually sober, maybe?" suggested the other.

"Yes, he was. Been sober for a week. An' he was studyin', too."

"Ah! Studying what?"

"Spanish."

"Spanish, eh? Ever exhibit any interest in foreign tongues before?"

"Not enough to get him through one term in college," returned the other grimly.

"How did you know about his studying?"

"Seen the perfessor in the house."

"Some one you knew?"

"No. I asked him. Roddy was sore because I found out what he was up to."

Upon that point Average Jones meditated a moment.

"Did you see this Spanish professor again?" he inquired presently.

"Now that you speak of it, I didn't see him but the once."

"Can you leave for Toledo on to-night's train?"

"You're goin' to take the case, then?" the quack clawed nervously at his professional white whiskers. "What's your terms?" he demanded.

"That I'm to have full control and that you're to take orders and not give them."

Doctor Hoff swallowed that with a gulp. "You're on," he said finally.

On the train Doctor Hoff regaled his companion with a strictly paternal view of his son's character and pursuits as he knew them. This served, at least, to enlarge his auditor's ideas as to the average American father's vast and profound ignorance of the life, habits, manners and customs of that common but variable species, the Offspring. Beyond this it had little value. Average Jones gave its author a few specific instructions as to minor lines of home investigation, and retired to map out a tentative campaign.

His first call, on arriving at Toledo, was at the business office of the *Daily Saw*, in which he inserted the following paragraph on a repeat-until-stopped order:

WANTED—Instructor in Spanish. One with recent experience preferred. Apply between 9 and 10 A. M. Doctor Hoff, 360 Fairfield Avenue.

Thence he climbed the stairs to the den of the city editor, to whom he stated his errand openly, being too wise in his day and generation to attempt concealment or evasion with a newspaper man from whom he wanted information. The city editor obligingly furnished further details regarding "Rickey" Hoff, as he called the young man, which, while differing in important respects from Doctor Hoff's, bore the ear-marks of superior accuracy.

"The worst of it is," said the newspaper man, "that there are elements of decency about the young cub, if he'd keep sober. He won't go into the old boy's business, because he hates it. Says it's all rot and lies. He's dead right, of course. But there's nothing else for him to do, so he just fights booze. Better make a few inquiries at Silent Charley's."

"What's that?"

"Quiet little bar kept by a talkative Swede. 'Rickey' Hoff hung out there a lot. Charley even had a room fixed up for him to lay off in when he was too pickled to go home."

"Would—er—young Hoff—er—perhaps keep a few—er—extra clothes there?" asked Average Jones, seemingly struggling with a yawn.

The city editor stared. "Oh, I dare say. He used to end his sprees pretty much mussed up."

"That would perhaps explain where the shirt came from," murmured the Ad-Visor. "Much obliged for the suggestion. I'll just step around."

"Silent Charley" he found ready, even eager to talk. Yes; "Rickey" Hoff had been in his place right along. Drunk? No; not even drinking much lately. Two other gentlemen had met him there quite often. They sat in the back room and talked. No, neither of them was Spanish. One was big and clean-shaven and wore a silk hat. They called him "Colonel." A swell dresser. The other man drank gin, and a lot of it. His name was Fred. He was very tanned. One day there had been a hot discussion over a sheet of paper that lay on the table in front of the three men in the back room. "Rickey" had called a messenger boy and sent him out for a geography. "I told you there wasn't any such thing there," the saloon-keeper heard him say triumphantly, when the geography arrived. Then Fred replied: "To h–ll with you and your schoolbook! I tell you I've waded across it." The colonel smoothed things over and it ended in a magnum of champagne being ordered.

"For which the colonel paid?" asked Average Jones.

"Why, yes, he did," assented the saloon man. "He said, 'Well, it's a go, then. Here's luck to us!' He was a good spender, the colonel."

"And you haven't seen any of them since, I suppose?"

"Nary a one."

On his return to the Hoff mansion the investigator found the head thereof in a state of great excitement.

"Say, I've found out something," he cried. "Roddy's gone to Yurrup."

"Where did you find that out?" asked Average Jones with a smile.

"I been going through his papers like you told me. He's been outfitting for a trip. Bought lots of truck the last few days and I found the duplicate sale-checks that come in the packages. There's stubs for a steamer rug and for a dope for seasickness and for a compass," he concluded triumphantly.

"Compass, eh?" observed Average Jones thoughtfully. "Ship's compass is good enough for most of us going to Europe. Anything else?"

"Lot of clothes."

"What kind of clothes?"

"Cheap stuff mostly. Khaki riding-pants, neglyjee shirts and such-like."

"Not much suggestion of Europe there. What more?"

Doctor Hoff consulted a list. "Colored glasses."

"That looks like desert travel."

"Aneroid barometer."

"Mountain climbing."

"Permanganate of potash outfit."

"Snake country," commented the other.

"Patent water-still."

Average Jones leaned forward. "How big?"

"Don't know. Cost twenty dollars."

"Little one, then. That means about three people. Taken with the compass, it means a small-boat trip on salt water."

"Small boat nothin'!" retorted the other. "His doctor met me this morning an' told me Roddy had sent for him and ast him a lot of questions about eatin' aboard ship and which way to have his berth made up, and all that."

"A small-boat trip following a sea trip, then. What else have you found?"

"Nothin' much. Mosquito nettin', pills, surgeon's plaster and odds and ends of drugs."

"Let me see the drug list."

He ran his eye down the paper. Then he looked at Doctor Hoff with a half smile.

"You didn't notice anything peculiar about this list?"

"Don't know as I did."

"Not the—er—nitric acid, for instance?"

"Nope. What of it?"

"Mr. Hoff, your son has been caught by one of the oldest tricks in the whole bunco list—the lost Spanish mine swindle. That acid, together with the rest of the outfit, means a gold-hunt as plain as if it were spelled out. And the Spanish professor was sent for, not to give lessons, but to translate the fake letter. Where does your son bank?"

"Fifth National."

"Telephone there and find out how much he drew."

Doctor Hoff sat down at the 'phone. "Five hundred dollars," he said presently.

"Is that all?" asked the other, disappointed.

"Yes. Wait. He had six checks certified aggregating ten thousand dollars."

"Then it isn't South America or the West Indies. He'd want a letter of credit there. Must be some part of the United States, or just across the border. Well, we've done a good day's work, and I've got a hard evening's thinking before me. We might be able to head off the colonel's personally conducted expedition yet, if we could locate it."

The evening's thinking formulated itself into a telegram to Average Jones' club, the Cosmic. It was one among the many distinctions of the modest little club in Gramercy Park, that its membership pretty well comprised the range of available information on any topic. Under the "favored applications clause," a person whose knowledge of any particular subject was unique and authoritative, whether the topic were Esperanto or fistiana, went to the head of the waiting-list automatically and had his initiation fee remitted. Hence, Average Jones was confident of a helpful reply to his message of inquiry, which summed up his conclusions and surmises thus far:

"Cosmic Club, New York City:
Refer following to geographical expert: Where is large, shallow, unmapped body of salt water in United States, or near border, surrounded by hot, snake-infested desert and mountainous country, reputed to contain gold? Spanish associations indicated. Wire details and name of best guide, if obtainable.   Jones."

The reply was disappointing:

"Cyrus C. Allen absent from town. Will forward your wire.
                                 "Cosmic Club."

Well poised as Average Jones normally was, he chafed over the ensuing delay of four days, each of which gave the colonel's expedition just so much start upon its unknown course. The only relief was a call from the Spanish instructor who answered Jones' advertisement. He was the same who had served young Hoff. As the Ad-Visor surmised, his former employment had been merely the translation of a letter. The letter was in base Spanish, he said. He didn't remember much of it, but there was something about a lost gold mine. Yes; there was reference to a map. No; no geographical names were mentioned, but in several places the capital letters B. C. seemed to indicate a locality. He hadn't noted the date or the signature. That was all he could tell.

Doctor Hoff, who had been ramping with impatience over the man's lack of definite memory, now rushed to the atlas and began to study the maps.

"You needn't trouble," said Average Jones coolly. "You won't find it there."

"I'll find that B. C. if I have to go over every map in the geography."

"Then you'll have to get a Spanish edition. For a guess, B. C. is Baja California, the Mexican peninsula of California."

Jones sent a supplementary wire to this effect to Cyrus C. Allen, of the Cosmic Club, and within a few hours received a reply from that eminent cartographer, who had been located in a remote part of Connecticut:

> "Probably Laguna Salada, not on map. Seventy miles long; four to eight wide. Between Cocopah and Sierra Gigantica ranges. Country very wild and arid. Can be reached by water from Yuma, or pack train from Calexico. White, who has hunted there, says Captain Funcke, Calexico, best guide.
>
> "Allen."

Average Jones tossed this over to the father.

"As I figure it," he said, "your son's two friends had this all mapped out beforehand for him. One went west direct. He was the imbecile who stopped in Cincinnati and mailed you the bloody shirt to throw you off the scent. Meantime the colonel took Roderick around by a sea route, probably New York and New Orleans."

"That'd explain the steamer rug and the seasickness," admitted Doctor Hoff; "but I don't know what he'd want to go that long way for."

"Simple enough, when you reckon with this colonel person as having brains in his head. He would foresee a hue and cry as soon as the young man disappeared. So he cooks up this trip to keep his prey out of touch with the newspapers for the few days when the news of the disappearance would be fresh enough to be spread abroad in the Associated Press dispatches. From New Orleans they'd go on west by train."

"What I don't see is how they caught Roddy on such an old game. He's easy, but I didn't s'pose he was that easy."

"To do him justice, he isn't—quite. They put it up on him rather cleverly. In the period of waiting to hear from the geographical expert I've put in some fairly hard work, going over your son's effects. And, in the room over Silent Charley's bar, I found a newspaper with this in it."

He handed to Doctor Hoff a thin clipping, marked "Daily Saw, March 29":

> LOST—Spanish letter and map. Of no value except to owner. Return to No. 16, this office, and receive heartfelt thanks.

"Well," said Doctor Hoff, after reading it over twice, "that don't tell me nothing."

"No? Yet it's pretty plain. The two crooks 'planted' the letter and map on your son. Probably slipped them into a pocket of his coat while he was drunk. Then they inserted their little ad, waited until he had time to find the letter, and casually called the advertisement to his attention. The rest would be easy. But I'll have something to say to my clerk, who failed to clip that ad."

"You're workin' for *me*, now," half blustered, half whined the old quack. "Whatche goin' to do next?"

"Pack for the night train."

"Where to?"

"Yuma or Calexico. Don't know which till I get a reply to two telegrams. I'll need five hundred dollars expense money."

"Say, you don't want much, do ye?" snarled the quack, his avaricious soul in revolt at the prospect of immediate outlay. "When I hire a man I expect him to pay his own expenses and send me the bill."

"Quite so," agreed the other blandly. "But, you see, you aren't hiring me. I'm doing this on spec. And I don't propose to invest anything in a dubious proposition, myself. It isn't too late to call it off, you know."

"No, I do' wanta do that," said the other with contorted face. "I'll get the five hundred here for you in an hour."

"And about the five thousand dollars reward? I think I'd better have a word of writing on that."

"You mean you don't trust me?" snapped the other. "I'm good for five million dollars to-morrow in this town."

"I know you are—in writing," agreed the other equably. "That's why I want your valued signature. You see, to be quite frank, I haven't the fullest confidence in gentlemen in your line of business."

"I'll have my lawyer draw up a form of contract and mail it after you to-morrow," promised the quack with a crafty look.

"No, you wo—" began Average Jones; but he broke off with a smile. "Very well," he amended. "If things work out as I figure them, that will do. And," he added, dropping into his significant drawl and looking the quack flatly in the eye, "don't you—er—bank on my—er—not understanding your offer—and—er—you."

Uncomfortably pondering this reply, Doctor Hoff set about the matter of the expense money. Meantime a telegram came which settled the matter of immediate destination. It apprised Average Jones that, a fortnight previous, this paragraph had appeared in the paid columns of the Yuma Yucca:

> WANTED—Small, flat-bottomed sailboat. Centerboard type preferred. Hasty, care this office.

Average Jones bought a ticket for Yuma.

Disembarking at the Yuma station three days later, Average Jones blinked in the harsh sunlight at a small, compactly built, keen-eyed man, roughly dressed for the trail.

"I'm Captain Funcke," said the stranger. His speech was gentle, slow, even hesitant; but there was something competent and reliable in his bearing which satisfied the shrewd young reader of men's characters from the outset. "Your wire got me two days since and I came right up."

"Any trace?"

"Left here two days ago."

"Three of them?"

"Yes. Flat-bottomed, narrow-beamed boat, sloop-rigged pretty light."

"Know anything of the men?"

"Only the big one. Calls himself Colonel Richford. Had a fake copper outfit in the mountains east of Alamo."

"Where do you think they're headed for?"

"Probably the wildest country they can find, if they want to get rid of young Hoff," said the other, who had been apprised of the main points of the situation. "That would likely be the Pinto range, to the southwest of the Laguna. Richford knows that country a little. He was in there two years ago."

"They would probably want to get rid of him without obvious murder;" said Average Jones. "You see, his money is in certified checks which they'd have to get cashed. If some one should find his body with a bullet-hole in it, they'd have some explaining to do."

"Nobody'd be likely to find it. Only about two parties a year get down there. Still, somebody might trail him. And I guess old Richford is too foxy to do any killing when he turns the trick just as well without it."

"Suppose it's the Pintos, then. How do we get there?"

"Hard-ash breeze," returned the other succinctly. "Our rowboat is outfitted and waiting."

"Good work!" said Jones heartily. "How far is it?"

"Sixty miles to the turn of the Laguna. There's a four-mile current to help. They've a scant two days' start, and we'll catch up some, for their boat is heavier and their sail is no good with the wind in this direction. If we don't catch up some," he added grimly, "I wouldn't want to insure our young friend's life. So it's all aboard, if you're ready."

For the first time since embarking upon the strange seas of advertising in his quest of the Adventure of Life, Average Jones now met the experience of grilling physical toil. All that day and all the night the two men swung at the oars; swung until every muscle in the young Easterner's back had turned to live nerve-fiber, and the flesh had begun to strip from the palms of his hands. Even so, the hardy captain had done most of the work. Aided by the current, they turned the shoulder of the Cocopah range as the dawn shone lurid in the east, and the captain swung the boat's head to the southern shore of the lake. Meantime, between spells at the oars, Average Jones had outlined the case in full to Funcke. He could have found no better coadjutor.

By nature and equipment every really expert hunter and tracker is a detective. The subtleties of the trail sharpen both physical and mental sensibility. Captain Funcke was, by instinct, a student of that continuous logic which constitutes the science of the chase, whether the prize of pursuit be a mountain sheep's horns or the scholar's need of praise for the interpreting of some half-obliterated inscription on a pre-Hittite tomb. After long and silent consideration the captain gave his views.

"It isn't bunco. It's a hold-up. If Richford had wanted to stick young Hoff, he'd never have brought him here. There isn't 'color' enough within eighty miles to gild a cigar band. It looks to me like the scheme is this: They get him off in the mountains, out of sight of the lake, so he'll have no landmark to go by. Then they scare him into signing co-partnership papers, and make him turn over those certified checks to them. With the papers to show for it, they go out by Calexico and cash the checks in Los Angeles. They could put up the bluff that their partner was guarding the mine while they bought machinery and outfitted. That'd be good enough to cash certified checks by."

"Yes; that's about the way I figure it out. You spoke of Richford's being able to get rid of young Hoff effectually, without actual murder."

"All he'd have to do would be to quit the boy while he was asleep. A tenderfoot would die of thirst over there in a short time."

"Is there no water?"

"There's a *tenaja* they're depending on. But I doubt if they find any water there now. It's been an extra dry season."

"A *tenaja*?" queried the Ad-Visor.

"Rock-basin holding rainwater," explained the hunter. "There's been no rainfall since August. If they find the *tenaja* empty they'll have barely enough in the canteens they pack to get them to the next water, the Tenaja Poquita, around behind the mountains and across the desert into the next range."

"What's the next water to that?"

"The Stream of Palms. That's a day and a half on foot."

For the space of a hundred oar-strokes Average Jones ruminated.

"Suppose—er—they didn't—er—find any water in the Tenaja Poquita, either?" he drawled.

"Then they *would* be up against it."

"And there's no other water in the Pintos?"

"Yes, there is," said the captain. "There's a *tenaja* that's so high up and so hidden that it's only known to one other man besides me, and he's an Indian. It's less than an hour from the *tenaja* that Richford will take his party to. And we're sure of finding water there. It never dries up this early."

"Get me to young Hoff, then, Captain. You're in command from the moment we land."

It was broad day when the keel pushed softly into the muddy bottom of a long, shallow arm of the lake. Captain Funcke rose, stretched the kinks out of his back, and jumped ashore.

"You say I'm in command?" he inquired.

"Absolute."

"Then you roll up under that *mesquite* and fall asleep. I'm going to cast about for their trail."

To the worn-out oarsman, it seemed only a few moments later that an insistent grip on his shoulder aroused him. But the overhead sun, whose direct rays were fairly boiling the sweat out of him, harshly corrected this impression.

"I've found their boat," said Captain Funcke. "The trail heads for the Pintos. They're traveling heavy. I don't believe they're twenty-four hours ahead of us."

Average Jones stumbled to his feet. "I'm ready," he said.

"It's a case of travel light." The hunter handed over a small bag of food and a large canteen full of water. He himself packed a much larger load, including two canteens and a powerful field-glass. Taking a shotgun from the boat, he shouldered it, and set out at a long, easy stride.

To Average Jones the memory of that day has never been wholly clear. Sodden with weariness, dazzled and muddled by the savage sun-glare, he followed, with eyes fixed, the rhythmically, monotonously moving feet of his leader, through an interminable desert of soft, clogging sand; a desert which dropped away into parched *arroyos*, and rose to scorched *mesas* whereon fierce cacti thrust at him with thorns and spikes; a desert dead and mummified in the dreadful heat; a lifeless Inferno wherein moved neither beast, bird nor insect. He remembers, dimly, lying as he fell, when the indefatigable captain called a halt, and being wakened in the chill breeze of evening, to see a wall of mountains blocking the advance. Food brought him to his normal self again, and in the crisp air of night he set his face to the task of climbing. Severe as this was upon his unaccustomed muscles, the firm rocks were still a welcome relief after the racking looseness of sand that interminably sank away from foothold. At midnight the wearied pursuers dropped down from a high plateau to a narrow *arroyo*. Here again was sand. Fortunately, this time, for in it footprints stood out clear, illuminated by the white moonlight. They led direct to a side *barranca*. There the pursuers found the camp. It was deserted.

Like a hound on the trail, Captain Funcke cast about him.

"Here's where they came in. No—yes—this is it. Confound the cross-tracks! . . . Here one of them cuts across the ridge to the *tenaja* for water. . . . Wait! . . . What's this? Coyote trail? Yes, but . . . Trail brushed over, by thunder! They didn't do it carefully enough . . . Straight for the rocky *mesa*. . . . That's it! They made their sneak while Hoff was asleep, probably covering trail behind them, and struck out for the inside desert route to the Tenaja Poquita." He took a quick look about the camp and picked up an empty canteen. "Of course, they wouldn't leave him any water."

"Then he's gone to hunt it," suggested Average Jones. "Which way?"

"You can't tell which way a tenderfoot will go," said the hunter philosophically. "If he had any savvy at all he'd follow the old beaten track around by the *arroyo* to the water-hole. We'll try it."

On the way, Average Jones noticed his companion stop frequently to examine the sand for something which he evidently didn't find.

"These are fresh footsteps we're following, aren't they?" he asked.

"Yes. It isn't that. He went this way all right. But the *tenaja's* gone dry."

"How can you tell that?"

"No fresh sign of animals going this way. Must have been dry for weeks. Our mining friends have taken what little water there was and left young Hoff to die of thirst," said the other grimly. "Well, that explains the empty canteen all right."

He turned and renewed his quick progress, leaping from boulder to boulder, between narrowing walls of gray-white rock. Just as Average Jones was spent and almost ready to collapse the leader checked.

"Hark!" he whispered.

Above the beating of the blood in his ears, Jones heard an irregular, insistent scuffing sound. He crouched in silence while the captain crept up to a ledge and cautiously peered over, then went forward in response to the other's urgent beckoning. They looked down into a rock-basin of wild and curious beauty. To this day Average Jones remembers the luminous grace and splendor of a Matilija poppy, which, rooted between two boulders, swayed gently in the white moonlight above a figure of dread. The figure, naked from the waist up, huddled upon the hard-baked mud, digging madly at the earth. A sharp exclamation broke from Average Jones. The digger half-rose, turned, collapsed to his knees, and pointed with bleeding fingers to his open mouth, in which the tongue showed black and swollen.

They went down to him.

An hour later, "Rickey" Hoff was sleeping the sleep of utter exhaustion in camp. Average Jones felt amply qualified to join him. But it was not in the Ad-Visor's character to quit an enterprise before it was wholly completed. So long as the two bandits were on their way to cash the young spendthrift's checks—Jones had heard from the victim a brief account of the extortion—success was not fully won.

"We've got to get that money back," he said to Captain Funcke with conviction.

The hunter made no reply in words. He merely leaned his shotgun against his thigh, reached around beneath his coat and produced a forty-five caliber revolver. This he held out toward Jones.

"Good thing to have," conceded the other. "But—well, no; not in this case. They got the booty with a show of legality, since Hoff signed the copartnership agreement and turned over the checks. It was under duress and threats, it's true, but who's to prove that, they being two to one, and this being Mexico? No; they're within the law, and I've a notion that we can get the swag back by straight sale and barter. Provided, always, we can catch them in time."

"They'll want to make pretty good time to the Tenaja Poquita," pointed out the captain. "They're shy on water."

"On wind, too. They've traveled hard, and they can't be in the pink of condition. According to Hoff, they deserted him while he was taking a nap, about four o'clock in the afternoon. It's a fair bet they'd camp for the night, as you say it's an eight hour hike to the *tenaja*."

"Eight, the way they'd go."

"Then—er—there's a—er—shorter way?" drawled Average Jones, removing some sand from a wrinkle in his scarified and soiled trousers as carefully as if that were the one immediate and important consideration in life.

"Yes. Across the Padre Cliffs. It cuts off about four hours, and it takes us almost to the secret *tenaja* I spoke of. We can fill up there. But it's not what you'd call safe, even in daylight."

"But to a hunter, wouldn't it be well worth the risk for a record pair of horns—even if they were only tin horns?" queried Average Jones suggestively.

Captain Funcke relaxed into a grin. He nodded.

"What'll we do with *him*?" he asked, jerking his head toward the sleeper.

"Leave him water, food and a note. Now, about this Tenaja Poquita we're headed for. How much water do you think there is in it?"

"If there's a hundred gallons it's doing well, this dry season."

Average Jones got painfully to his feet. Looking carefully over the scattered camp outfit, he selected from it a collapsible pail.

Captain Funcke glanced at it with curiosity, but characteristically forebore to ask any questions. He himself shouldered the largest canteen.

"This'll be enough for both until we reach the supply," he said. "Don't need so much water at night."

But the tenderfoot hung upon his own shoulder, not only the smallest of their three canteens, but also the empty one which they had found in the camp. Their own third tin, almost full, they left beside Hoff, with a note.

"I've a notion," said Jones, "that I'll need all these receptacles for water in my own peculiar business."

"All right," assented the other patiently. He took one of them and the pail from Jones and skillfully disposed them on his own back. "Ready? Hike, then."

Two hours of the roughest kind of climbing brought them to a landslide. These sudden shiftings of the slopes are a frequent feature of travel in the Lower California mountains, often obliterating trails and costing the wayfarer painful and perilous search for a new path. On the Padre Cliffs, however, had occurred that rare phenomenon, a benevolent avalanche, piling up a safe and feasible embankment around the angle of an impracticable precipice, and thus saving an hour of the most ticklish going of the journey. Thanks to this dispensation, the two men reached the Tenaja Poquita before dawn. Scouting ahead, the captain reported no fresh trail except coyotes and mule deer, and not more than seventy-five gallons of water in the basin. Of this they both drank deeply. Then after they had filled all the canteens, Average Jones unfolded his scheme to the captain.

"If any one caught us at it," commented that experienced hunter, "we'd be shot without warning. However, the water would be evaporated in a few days anyhow, and I'll post notices at the next water-camps. I'm with you."

Taking turn and turn about with the pail, they bailed out the rock-basin, scattering the water upon the greedy sand. What little moisture remained in the sticky mud at the bottom they blotted up with more sand. They then rolled in boulders. Average Jones looked down into the hollow with satisfaction, and moved his full canteens into a grotto.

"This company," he said, "is now open for business."

At eight o'clock there was a clatter of boots upon the rocks and two men came staggering up the defile. Colonel Richford and his partner did not look to be in good repair. The colonel's face was drawn and sun-blotched. His companion, the "Fred" of Silent Charley's bar, was bloated and shaken with liquor. Both panted with the hard, dry, open-lipped breath of the first stage of thirst-exhaustion. The colonel, who was in the lead, checked and started upon discovering astride of a rock a pleasant visaged young man of a familiar American type, whose appearance was in nowise remarkable except as to locality. With a grunt that might have been greeting, but was more probably surprise, the newcomer passed the seated man. Captain Funcke he did not see at all. That astute hunter had dropped behind a boulder.

At the brink of the *tenaja* the colonel stopped dead. Then with an outburst of flaming language, he leaped in, burrowing among the rocks.

"Dry!" he yelled, lifting a furious and appalled face to his companion.

Fred stood staring from Average Jones to his three canteens. There was a murderous look on his sinister face.

"Got water?" he growled.

"Yes," replied the young man.

"Here, Colonel," said Fred. "Here's drink for us."

"For sale," added Average Jones calmly.

"People don't *buy* water in this country."

"You're not people," returned Average Jones cheerfully. "You're a corporation; a soulless corporation. The North Pinto Gold Mining Company."

"What's that!" cried the colonel thickly.

His hand flew back to his belt. Then it dropped, limp at his side, for he was gazing into the two barrels of a shotgun, which, materializing over a rock, were pointing accurately and disconcertingly at the pit of his stomach. From behind the gun Captain Funcke's quiet voice remarked:

"I wouldn't, Colonel. As for you," he added, turning to the other wayfarer, who carried a rifle, "you want to remember that a shotgun has two barrels, usually both loaded."

Stepping forward, Average Jones "lifted" the financier's weapon. Then he deprived Fred of his rifle amid a surprisingly brilliant outburst of verbal pyrotechnics.

"Now we can talk business comfortably," he observed.

"I can't talk at all pretty quick if I don't git a moistener," said Fred piteously.

Pouring out a scant cupful of water into his hat, Average Jones handed it over. "Drink slowly," he advised. "You've got about a hundred dollars' worth there at present quotations."

Colonel Richford's head went up with a jerk.

"Hundred dollars' worth!" he croaked, his eyes fiery with suspicion. "Are you going to hold up two men dying of thirst?"

"There's been only one man in danger of that death around here. His name is Hoff."

The redoubtable colonel gasped, and leaned back against a rock.

"You'll be relieved to learn that he's safe. Now, to answer your question: No, I don't propose to hold up two men for anything. I propose to deal with the president and treasurer of the North Pinto Gold Mining Company. As a practical mining man you will appreciate the absolute necessity of water in your operations. The nearest available supply is some ten hours distant. Before you could reach it I fear that—er—your company would—er—have gone out of existence. Therefore I am fortunate in being able to offer you a small supply which I will put on the market at the low rate of ten thousand dollars. I may add that—er—certified checks will—er—be accepted."

For two hours the colonel, with the occasional objurgatory assistance of his partner, talked, begged argued, threatened, and even wept. By the end of that time his tongue was making sounds like a muffled castanet, and his resolution was scorched out of him.

"You've got us," he croaked. "Here's your checks. Give me the water."

"In proper and legal form, please," said Average Jones.

He produced a contract and a fountain-pen. The contract was duly signed and witnessed. It provided for the transfer of the water, in consideration of one revolver and ten thousand dollars in checks. These checks were endorsed over to A. V. R. E. Jones, whereupon he turned over the pail of water and the largest canteen to the parched miners. Then, sorting out the checks, he pocketed two aggregating five thousand dollars, tore up three, and holding the other in his hand, turned to Captain Funcke.

"Will five hundred dollars pay you for keeping young Hoff down here a couple of months and making the beginning of a man of him?" he asked.

"Yes, and more," replied the captain.

"It's a go," said Average Jones. "I'd like to make the job complete."

Then, courteously bidding the North Pinto Gold Mining Company farewell, the two water-dealers clambered up the rocks and disappeared beyond the abrupt sky-line.

Once again Doctor Conrad Hoff sat in the private office of Average Jones, Ad-Visor. The young man was thinner, browner and harder of fiber than the Jones of two weeks previous. Doctor Hoff looked him over with shrewd eyes.

"Say, your trip ain't done you no harm, has it?" he exclaimed with a boisterous and false good nature. "You look like' a fightin'-cock. Hope the boy comes out as good. You say he's all right?"

"You've got his letter, in which he says so himself. That's enough proof, isn't it?"

"Oh, I've got the letter all right. An' it's enough as far as it goes. But it ain't proof; not the kind of proof a man pays out reward money on," he added, cunningly. "You say you left Roddy down there with that Funcke feller, hey?"

"Yes. It'll make a man of him, if anything will. I threw that in as an extra."

"Yes; but what about them two crooks that goldbricked him? What's become of them?"

"On their way to Alaska or Bolivia or Corea, or anywhere else, for all I know—or care," said Average Jones indifferently.

"Is *that* so?" The quack's voice had taken on a sneering intonation. "You come back here with your job not half done, with the guilty fellers loose an' runnin', an' you expect me to pay over, the five thousand dollars to you. Huh!"

"No, I—er—don't expect—er—anything of the sort," said Average Jones slowly.

Doctor Hoff's little, restless eyes puckered at the corners. He was puzzled. What did the young fellow mean?

"Don't, eh?" he said, groping in his mind for a solution.

"No. You forgot to send me that promised form of agreement, didn't you? Thought you'd fooled me, perhaps. Well, I wouldn't be so foolish as to expect anything in the way of fair and honorable dealing when I contract to do up a mining swindler for the benefit of the only meaner creature on God's earth—a patent medicine poisoner. So I took precautions."

"Say, be careful of what you say, young man," blustered the quack.

"I am—quite particular. And, before you leave, wouldn't you like to hear about the five thousand dollars I got for my little job?"

Doctor Hoff blinked rapidly.

"What didje say?" he finally inquired.

"Five—er—thousand—er—dollars."

"You got it?"

"In the bank."

"Where dje get it?"

"From you, through your son's check, duly certified."

Doctor Hoff blinked more rapidly and moistened his lips with an effortful tongue. "H–h–how dje work it?" he asked in a die-away voice.

"By a forced sale of water rights to the North Pinto Gold Mining Company, dissolved, in which Mr. Roderick Hoff was vice-president and silent partner," replied Average Jones with an amiable smile, as he opened the door significantly.

THE MERCY SIGN—ONE

"Want a job, Average?"

Bertram, his elegance undimmed by the first really trying weather of the early summer, drifted to the coolest spot in the Ad-Visor's sanctum and spread his languid length along a wicker settee.

"Give a man breathing space, can't you?" returned Average Jones. "This is hotter than Baja California."

"Why, I assumed that your quest of the quack's scion would have trained you down fit for anything."

"Haven't even caught up with the clippings that Simpson floods me with, since I came back," confessed the other. "What have you got up your faultlessly creased sleeve? It's got to be something different to rouse me from a well-earned lethargy."

"Because a man buncoes a loving father out of five thousand dollars"—Average Jones snorted gently— "is no reason why he should unanimously elect himself a life member of the Sons of Idleness," murmured Bertram.

He cast an eye around the uniquely decorated walls, upon which hung, here, the shrieking prospectus of a mythical gold-mine; there a small but venomous political placard, and on all sides examples of the uncouth or unusual in paid print; exploitations of grotesque quackeries; appeals, business-like, absurd, or even passionate, in the form of "Wants;" threats thinly disguised as "Personals;" dim suggestions of crime, of fraud, of hope, of tragedy, of mania, all decorated with the stars of "paid matter" or designated by the *Adv.*

sign, and each representing some case brought to A. Jones, Ad-Visor—to quote his hybrid and expressive doorplate—by some one of his numerous and incongruous clients.

"Something different?" repeated the visitor, reverting to Average Jones' last observation. "Well, yes; I think so. Where is Bellair Street?"

"Ask a directory. How should I know?" retorted the other lazily. "Sounds like old Greenwich Village."

Bertram reached over with a cane of some pale, translucent green wood, selected to match his pale green tie and the marvelous green opal which held it in place, and prodded his friend severely in the ribs. "Double-up Lucy; the sun is in the sky!" he proclaimed with unwonted energy. "Listen. I cut this out of yesterday's *Evening Register*. With my own fair hands I did it, to rouse you from your shameless sloth. With your kind attention, ladies and gentlemen—" He read:

"WANTED—A young man, unattached, competent to act as assistant in outdoor scientific work. Manual skill as desirable as experience. Emolument for one month's work generous. Man without family insisted upon. Apply after 8:30 P. M. in proper person. Smith, 74 Bellair Street."

Slowly whirling in his chair, Average Jones held out a hand, received the clipping, read it through with attention, laid it on the desk, and yawned.

"Is that all?" said the indignant Bertram. "Do you notice that 'unattached' in the opening sentence? And the specification that the applicant must be without family? Doesn't that inspire any notion above a yawn in your palsied processes of mind?"

"It does; several notions. I yawned," explained Average Jones with dignity, "because I perceive with pain that I shall have to go to work. What do you make of the thing, yourself?"

"Well, this man Smith—"

"What man Smith?"

"Smith, of 74 Bellair Street, who signs the ad."

Average Jones laughed, "There isn't any Smith," he said.

"What do you know about it?" demanded Bertram, sitting up.

"Only what the advertisement tells me. It was written by a foreigner; that's too obvious for argument. 'Emolument generous.' 'Apply in proper person.' Did a Smith ever write that? No. A Borgrevsky might have, or a Greiffenhauser, or even a Mavronovoupoulos. But never Smith."

"Well, it's nothing to me what his name is. Only I thought you might be the aspiring young scientist he was yearning for."

"Wouldn't wonder if I were, thank you. Let's see. Bellair Street? Where's the directory? Thanks. Yes, it is Greenwich Village. Well, I think I'll just stroll down that way and have a look after dinner."

Thus it was that Mr. Adrian Van Reypen Egerton Jones found himself on a hot May evening pursuing the Adventure of Life into the vestibule of a rather dingy old house which had once been the abode of solemn prosperity if not actual aristocracy in the olden days of New York City. Almost immediately the telegraphic click of the lock apprised him that he might enter, and as he stepped into the hallway the door of the right-hand ground-floor apartment opened to him.

"You will please come in," said a voice.

The tone was gentle and measured. Also it was, by its accent, alien to any rightful Smith. The visitor stepped into a passageway which was dim until he entered it and the door swung behind him. Then it became pitch black.

"You will pardon this," said the voice. "A severe affection of the eyes compels me."

"You are Mr. Smith?" asked Average Jones.

"Yes. Your hand if you please."

The visitor, groping, brushed with his fingers the back of a hand which felt strangely hot and pulpy. Immediately the hand turned and closed, and he was led forward to an inner room and seated in a chair. The gentle, hot clasp relaxed and left his wrist free. A door facing him, if his ears could be trusted, opened and shut.

"You will find matches at your elbow," said the voice, coming dulled, from a further apartment. "Doubtless you would be more comfortable with a light."

"Thank you," returned Average Jones, enormously entertained by the dime-novel setting which his host had provided for him.

He lighted the gas and looked about a sparsely furnished room without a single distinguishing feature, unless a high and odd-shaped traveling-bag which stood on a chair near by could be so regarded. The voice interrupted his survey.

"You have come in answer to my advertisement?"

"Yes, sir."

"You are, then, of scientific pursuit?"

"Of scientific ambition, at least. I hope to meet your requirements."

"Your name, if you please."

"Jones; A. Jones, of New York City."

"You live with your family?"

"I have no family or near relatives."

"That is well. I will not conceal from you that there are risks. But the pay is high. Can you endure exposure? Laboring in all weathers? Subsisting on rough fare and sleeping as you may?"

"I have camped in the northern forests."

"Yes," mused the voice. "You look hardy."

Average Jones arose. "You—er—are spying upon me, then," he drawled quietly. "I might have—er—suspected a peep-hole."

He advanced slowly toward the door whence the voice came. A chair blocked his way. Without lowering his gaze he shoved at the obstacle with his foot.

"Have a care!" warned the voice.

The chair toppled and overturned. From it fell, with a light shock, the strange valise, which, striking the floor, flew open, disclosing a small cardboard cabinet. Across the front of the cabinet was a strip of white paper labeled in handwriting, each letter being individual, with what looked to the young man like the word "MERCY." He stooped to replace the bag.

"Do not touch it," ordered the voice peremptorily.

Average Jones straightened up to face the door again.

"I will apologize for my clumsiness," he said slowly, "when you explain why you have tried to trick me."

There was a pause. Then:

"Presently," said the voice. "Meantime, after what you have accidentally seen, you will perhaps appreciate that the employment is not without its peril!"

Average Jones stared from the door to the floored cabinet and back again in stupefaction.

"Perhaps I'm stupid," he said, "but a misshapen valise containing a cabinet with a girl's name on it doesn't seem calculated to scare an able-bodied man to death. It isn't full of dynamite, is it?"

"What is your branch of scientific work?" counter-questioned the other.

"Botany," replied the young man, at random.

"No other? Physics? Entomology? Astronomy? Chemistry? Biology?"

The applicant shook his head in repeated negation. "None that I've specialized on."

"Ah! I fear you will not suit my purpose."

"All right. But you haven't explained, yet, why you've been studying me through a peep-hole, when I am not allowed to see you."

After a pause of consideration the voice spoke again.

"You are right. Since I can not employ you, I owe you every courtesy for having put you to this trouble. You will observe that I am not very presentable."

The side door swung open. In the dimness of the half-disclosed apartment Average Jones saw a man huddled in a chair. He wore a black skull cap. So far as identification went he was safe. His whole face was grotesquely blotched and swollen. So, also, were the hands which rested on his knees.

"You will pardon me," said Average Jones, "but I am by nature cautious. You have touched me. Is it contagious?"

A contortion of the features, probably indicating a smile, made the changeling face more hideous than before.

"Be at peace," he said. "It is not. You can find your way out? I bid you good evening, sir."

"Now I wonder," mused Average Jones, as he jolted on the rear platform of an Eighth Avenue car, "by what lead I could have landed that job. I rather think I've missed something."

All that night, and recurrently on many nights thereafter, the poisoned and contorted face and the scrawled "MERCY" on the cabinet lurked troublously in his mind. Nor did Bertram cease to scoff him for his maladroitness until both of them temporarily forgot the strange "Smith" and his advertisement in the entrancement of a chase which led them for a time far back through the centuries to a climax that might well have cost Average Jones his life. They had returned from Baltimore and the society of the Man who spoke Latin a few days when Bertram, at the club, called up Average Jones' office.

"I'm sending Professor Paul Gehren to you," was his message. "He'll call to-day or to-morrow."

Average Jones knew Professor Gehren by sight, knew of him further by repute as an impulsive, violent, warm-hearted and learned pundit who, for a typically meager recompense, furnished sundry classes of young gentlemen with amusement, alarm and instruction, in about equal parts, through the medium of lectures at the Metropolitan University. During vacations the professor pursued, with some degree of passion, experiments which added luster and selected portions of the alphabet to his name. Twice a week he walked down-town to the Cosmic Club, where he was wont to dine and express destructive and anarchistic views upon the nature, conduct, motives and personality of the organization's governing committees.

On the day following Bertram's telephone, Professor Gehren entered Astor Court Temple, took the elevator to the ninth floor, and, following directions, found himself scanning a ground-glass window flaunting the capitalized and gilded legend,

A. JONES, AD-VISOR

"Ad-Visor," commented the professor, rancorously. "A vicious verbal monstrosity!" He read on:

ADVICE UPON ADVERTISING IN ALL FORMS
Consultation Free. Step In

"Consultation free!" repeated the educator with virulence. "A trap! A manifest pitfall! I don't know why Mr. Bertram should have sent me hither. The enterprise is patently quack," he asseverated in a rising voice.

Upon the word a young man opened the door and, emerging, received the accusation full in the face. The young man smiled.

"Quack, I said," repeated the exasperated mentor, "and I repeat it. Quack!"

"If you're suffering from the delusion that you're a duck," observed the young man mildly, "you'll find a taxidermist on the top floor."

The caller turned purple. "If you are Mr. Jones, of the Cosmic Club—"

"I am."

"—there are certain things which Mr. Bertram must explain."

"Yes; Bertram said that you were coming, but I'd almost given you up. Come in."

"Into a—a den where free advice is offered? Of all the patent and infernal rascalities, sir, the offer of free advice—"

"There, there," soothed the younger man. "I know all about the free swindles. This isn't one of them. It's just a fad of mine."

He led the perturbed scholar inside and got him settled in a chair. "Now, go ahead. Show me the advertisement and tell me how much you lost."

"I've lost my assistant. There is no advertisement about it. What I came for is advice. But upon seeing your tricky door-plate—"

"Oh, that's merely to encourage the timorous. Who is this assistant?"

"Harvey Craig, a youth, hardly more than a boy, for whom I feel a certain responsibility, as his deceased parents left him in my care."

"Yes," said Jones as the professor paused.

"He has disappeared."

"When?"

"Permanently, since ten days ago."

"Permanently?"

"Up to that time he had absented himself without reporting to me for only three or four days at a time."

"He lived with you?"

"No. He had been aiding me in certain investigations at my laboratory."

"In what line?"

"Metallurgy."

"When did he stop?"

"About four weeks ago."

"Did he give any reason?"

"He requested indefinite leave. Work had been offered him, he hinted, at a very high rate of remuneration."

"You don't know by whom?"

"No, I know nothing whatever about it."

"Have you any definite suspicions as to his absence?"

"I gravely fear that the boy has made away with himself."

"Why so?"

"After his first absence I called to see him at his room. He had obviously undergone a violent paroxysm of grief or shame."

"He told you this?"

"No. But his eyes, and, indeed, his whole face, were abnormally swollen, as with weeping."

"Ah, yes." Average Jones' voice had suddenly taken on a bored indifference. "Were—er—his hands, also?"

"His hands? Why should they?"

"Of course, why, indeed? You noted them?"

"I did not, sir."

"Did he seem depressed or morose?"

"I can not say that he did."

"Professor Gehren, what, newspaper do you take?"

The scholar stared. "The *Citizen* in the morning, the *Register* in the evening."

"Are either of them delivered to your laboratory?"

"Yes; the *Register*."

"Do you keep it on file?"

"No."

"Ah! That's a pity. Then you wouldn't know if one were missing?"

The professor reflected. "Yes, there was a copy containing a letter upon Von Studeborg's recent experiments—"

"Can you recall the date?"

"After the middle of June, I think."

Average Jones sent for a file and handed it to Professor Gehren.

"Is this it?" he asked, indicating the copy of June 18.

"That is the letter!" said that gentleman.

Average Jones turned the paper and found, upon an inside page, the strange advertisement from 74 Bellair Street.

"One more question, Professor," said he. "When did you last see Mr. Craig?"

"Nine or ten days ago. I think it was July 2."

"How did he impress you?"

"As being somewhat preoccupied. Otherwise normal."

"Was his face swollen then?"

"No."

"Where did you see him?"

"The first time at my laboratory, about eleven o'clock."

"You saw him again that day, then?"

"Yes. We met by accident at a little before two P.M. on Twenty-third Street. I was surprised, because he had told me he had to catch a noon train and return to his work."

"Then he hadn't done so?"

"Yes. He explained that he had, but that he had been sent back to buy some supplies."

"You believe he was telling the truth?"

"In an extensive experience with young men I have never known a more truthful one than he."

"Between the first day of his coming back to New York and the last, had you seen him?"

"I had talked with him over the telephone. He called up two or three times to say that he was well and working hard and that he hoped to be back in a few weeks."

"Where did he call up from?"

"As he did not volunteer the information, I am unable to say."

"Unfortunate again. Well, I think you may drop the notion of suicide. If anything of importance occurs, please notify me at once. Otherwise, I'll send you word when I have made progress."

Having dismissed the anxious pundit, Average Jones, so immersed in thought as to be oblivious to outer things, made his way to the Cosmic Club in a series of caroms from indignant pedestrian to indignant pedestrian. There, as he had foreseen, he found Robert Bertram.

"Can I detach you from your usual bridge game this evening?" he demanded of that languid gentleman.

"Very possibly. What's the inducement?"

"Chapter Second of the Bellair Street advertisement. I've told you the first chapter. You've been the god-outside-the-machine so far. Now, come on in."

Together they went to the Greenwich Village house. The name "Smith" had disappeared from the vestibule.

"As I expected," said Jones. "Our hope be in the landlord!"

The landlord turned out to be a German landlady, who knew little concerning her late ground-floor tenant and evinced no interest in the subject. The "perfessor," as she termed "Smith," had taken the flat by the month, was prompt in payment, quiet in habit, given to long and frequent absences; had been there hardly at all in the last few weeks. Where had he moved to? Hummel only knew! He had left no address. Where did his furniture go? Nowhere; he'd left it behind. Was any one in the house acquainted with him? Mrs. Marron in the other ground-floor flat had tried to be. Not much luck, she thought.

Mrs. Marron was voluble, ignorant, and a willing source of information.

"The perfessor? Sure! I knew'm. 'Twas me give'm the name. He was a Mejum. Naw! Not for money. Too swell for that. But a real-thing Mejum. A big one; one of the kind it comes to, nacheral. Spirit-rappin's! Somethin' fierce! My kitchen window is on the airshaft. So's his. Many's the time in the still evenin's I've heard the rap-rap-rappin' on his window an' on the wall, but mostly on the window. Blip! out of the dark. It'd make you just hop! And him sittin' quiet and peaceful in the front room all the time. Yep; my little girl seen him there while I was hearin' the raps."

"Did you ask him about them?" inquired Jones.

"Sure! He wouldn't have it at first. Then he kinder smiled and half owned up. And once I seen him with his materializin' wand, sittin' in the room almost dark."

"His what?"

"Materializin' wand. Spirit-rod, you know. As tall as himself and all shiny and slick. It was slim and sort o' knobby like this wood—what's the name of it, now?—they make fish poles out of. Only the real big-bugs in spiritualism use 'em. They're dangerous. You wouldn't caich me touchin' it or goin' in there even now. I says to Mrs. Kraus, I says—"

And so the stream of high-pitched, eager talk flowed until the two men escaped from it into the vacant apartment. This was much as Average Jones had seen on his former visit. Only the strange valise was missing. Going to the kitchen, which he opened through intermediate doors on a straight line with the front room, Average Jones inspected the window. The glass was thickly marked with faint, bluish blurs, being, indeed, almost opaque from them in the middle of the upper pane. There was nothing indicative below the window, unless it were a considerable amount of crumbled putty, which he fingered with puzzled curiosity.

In the front room a mass of papers had been half burned. Some of them were local journals, mostly the *Evening Register*. A few were publications in the Arabic text.

"Oriental newspapers," remarked Bertram.

Average Jones picked them up and began to fold them. From between two sheets fluttered a very small bit of paper, narrow and half curled, as if from the drying of mucilage. He lifted and read it.

"Here we are again, Bert," he remarked in his most casual tone. "The quality of this Mercy is strained, all right."

The two men bent over the slip, studying it. The word was, as Average Jones had said, in a strained, effortful handwriting, and each letter stood distinct. These were the characters:

Mε·2 cy

"Is it mathematical, do you think, possibly?" asked Average Jones.

"All alone by itself like that? Rather not! More like a label, if you ask me."

"The little sister of the label on the cabinet, then."

"*Cherchez la femme*," observed Bertram. "It sounds like perfect foolishness to me; a swollen faced outlander who rules familiar spirits with a wand, and, between investigations in the realms of science, writes a girl's name all over the place like a lovesick school-boy! Is Mercy his spirit-control, do you suppose?"

"Oh, let's get out of here," said Average Jones. "I'm getting dizzy with it all. The next step," he observed, as they walked slowly up the street, "is by train. Want to take a short trip to-morrow, Bert? Or, perhaps, several short trips?"

"Whither away, fair youth?"

"To the place where the fake 'Smith' and the lost Craig have been doing their little stunts."

"I thought you said Professor Gehren couldn't tell you where Craig had gone."

"No more he could. So I've got to find out for myself. Here's the way I figure it out: The two men have been engaged in some out-of-door work that is extra hazardous. So much we know. Harvey Craig has, I'm afraid, succumbed to it. Otherwise he'd have sent some word to Professor Gehren. He may be dead or he may only be disabled by the dangerous character of the work, whatever it was. In any case our mysterious foreign friend has probably skipped out hastily. Now, I propose to find the railroad station they passed through, coming and going, and interview the ticket agent."

"You've got a fine large contract on your hands to find it."

"Not so large, either. All we have to do is to look for a place that is very isolated and yet quite near New York."

"How do you know it is quite near New York?"

"Because Harvey Craig went there and back between noon and two o'clock, Professor Gehren says. Now, we've got to find such a place which is near a stretch of deserted, swampy ground, very badly infested with mosquitoes. I'd thought of the Hackensack Meadows, just across the river in Jersey."

"That is all very well," said Bertram; "but why mosquitoes?"

"Why, the poisoned and swollen face and hands both of them suffered from," explained Average Jones. "What else could it be?"

"I'd thought of poison-ivy or some kind of plant they'd been grubbing at."

"So had I. But I happened to think that anything of that sort, if it had poisoned them once, would keep on poisoning them, while mosquitoes they could protect themselves against, if they didn't become immune, as they most likely would. As there must have been a lot of 'skeeters' to do the kind of job that 'Smith's' face showed, I naturally figured on a swamp."

"Average," said Bertram solemnly, "there are times when I conceive a sort of respect for your commonplace and plodding intellect. Now, let me have my little inning. I used to commute—on the Jersey and Delaware Short Line. There's a station on that line, Pearlington by name, that's a combination of Mosquitoville, Lonesomehurst and Nutting Doon. It's in the mathematical center of the ghastliest marsh anywhere between Here and Somewhere else. I think that's our little summer resort, and I'm yours for the nine A. M. train to-morrow."

Dismounting from that rather casual accommodation on the following day, the two friends found Pearlington to consist of a windowed packing-box inhabited by a hermit in a brass-buttoned blue. This lonely official readily identified the subjects of Average Jones' inquiry.

"I guess I know your friends, all right. The dago was tall and thin and had white hair; almost snow-white. No, he wasn't old, neither. He talked very soft and slow. Used to stay off in the reeds three and four days at a time. No, ain't seen him for near a week; him nor his boat nor the young fellow that was with him. Sort of bugologists, or something, wasn't they."

"Have you any idea where we could find their camp?"

The railroad man laughed.

"Fine chance you got of finding anything in that swamp. There's ten square miles of it, every square just like every other square, and a hundred little islands, and a thousand creeks and rivers winding through."

"You're right," agreed Average Jones. "It would take a month to search it. You spoke of a boat."

"It's my notion they must have had a houseboat. They could a-rowed it up on the tide from the Kills—a little one. I never saw no tent with 'em. And they had to have something over their heads. The boat I seen 'em have was a rowboat. I s'pose they used it to go back and forth in."

"Thanks," said Average Jones. "That's a good idea about the houseboat."

On the following day this advertisement appeared in the newspapers of several shore towns along the New Jersey and Staten Island coast.

ADRIFT—A small houseboat lost several days ago from the Hackensack Meadows. Fifty dollars reward paid for information leading to recovery. JONES, Ad-Visor, Astor Court Temple, New York.

Two days later came a reply, locating the lost craft at Bayonne. Average Jones went thither and identified it. Within its single room was uttermost confusion, testifying to the simplest kind of housekeeping sharply terminated. Attempt had been made to burn the boat before it was given to wind and current, but certain evidences of charred wood, and the fact of a succession of furious thundershowers in the week past, suggested the reason for failure. In a heap of rubbish, where the fire had apparently started, Average Jones found, first, a Washington newspaper, which he pocketed; next, with a swelling heart, the wreck of the pasteboard cabinet, but no sign of the strange valise which had held it. The "Mercy" sign was gone from the cabinet, its place being supplied by a placard, larger, in a different handwriting, and startlingly more specific:

"DANGER! IF FOUND DESTROY AT ONCE.
Do Not Touch With Bare Hands."

There was nothing else. Gingerly, Average Jones detached the sign. The cabinet proved to be empty. He pushed a rock into it, lifted it on the end of a stick and dropped it overboard. One after another eight little fishes glinted up through the water, turned their white bellies to the sunlight and bobbed, motionless. The investigator hastily threw away the label and cast his gloves after it. But on his return to the city he was able to give a reproduction of the writing to Professor Gehren which convinced that anxious scholar that Harvey Craig had been alive and able to write not long before the time when the houseboat was set adrift.

THE MERCY SIGN—TWO

Some days after the recovery of the houseboat, Average Jones sat at breakfast, according to his custom, in the café of the Hotel Palatia. Several matters were troubling his normally serene mind. First of these was the loss of the trail which should have led to Harvey Craig. Second, as a minor issue, the Oriental papers found in the deserted Bellair Street apartment had been proved, by translation, to consist mainly of revolutionary sound and fury, signifying, to the person most concerned, nothing. As for the issue of the Washington daily, culled from the houseboat, there was, amidst the usual mélange of social, diplomatic, political and city news, no marked passage to show any reason for its having been in the possession of "Smith." Average Jones had studied and restudied the columns, both reading matter and advertising, until he knew them almost by heart. During the period of waiting for his order to be brought he was brooding over the problem, when he felt a hand-pressure on his shoulder and turned to confront Mr. Thomas Colvin McIntyre, solemn of countenance and groomed with a supernal modesty of elegance, as befitted a rising young diplomat, already Fifth Assistant Secretary of State of the United States of America.

"Hello, Tommy," said the breakfaster. "What'll you have to drink? An *entente cordiale?*"

"Don't joke," said the other. "I'm in a pale pink funk. I'm afraid to look into the morning papers."

"Hello! What have you been up to that's scandalous?"

"It isn't me," replied the diplomat ungrammatically. "It's Telfik Bey."

"Telfik Bey? Wait a minute. Let me think." The name had struck a response from some thought wire within Average Jones' perturbed brain. Presently it came to him as visualized print in small headlines, reproduced to the mind's eye from the Washington newspaper which he had so exhaustively studied.

THIS TURK A QUICK JUMPER

Telfik Bey, Guest of Turkish Embassy, Barely Escapes a Speeding Motor-Car

No arrest, it appeared, had been made. The "story," indeed, was brief, and of no intrinsic importance other than as a social note. But to Average Jones it began to glow luminously.

"Who is Telfik Bey?" he inquired.

"He isn't. Up to yesterday he was a guest of this hotel."

"Indeed! Skipped without paying his bill?"

"Yes—ah. Skipped—that is, left suddenly without paying his bill, if you choose to put it that way."

The tone was significant. Average Jones' good-natured face became grave.

"Oh, I beg your pardon, Tommy. Was he a friend of yours?"

"No. He was, in a sense, a ward of the Department, over here on invitation. This is what has almost driven me crazy."

Fumbling nervously in the pocket of his creaseless white waistcoat he brought forth a death notice.

"From the *Dial*," he said, handing it to Average Jones.

The clipping looked conventional enough.

> DIED—July 21, suddenly at the Hotel Palatia: Telfik Bey of Stamboul, Turkey. Funeral services from the Turkish Embassy, Washington, on Tuesday. Ana Alhari.

"If the newspapers ever discover—" The young diplomat stopped short before the enormity of the hypothesis.

"It looks straight enough to me as a death notice, except for the tail. What does 'Ana Alhari' mean? Sort of a *requiescat*?"

"Yes; like a mice!" said young Mr. McIntyre bitterly. "It means 'Hurrah!' That's the sort of *requiescat* it is!"

"Ah! Then they got him the second time."

"What do you mean by 'second time?'"

"The Washington incident, of course, was the first; the attempted murder—that is, the narrow escape of Telfik Bey."

Young Mr. McIntyre looked baffled. "I'm blessed if I know what you're up to, Jones," he said. "But if you *do* know anything of this case I need your help. In Washington, where they failed, we fooled the newspapers. Here, where they've succeeded—"

"Who are 'they?'" interrupted Jones.

"That's what I'm here to get at. The murderers of Telfik Bey, of course. My instructions are to find out secretly, if at all. For if it does get into the newspapers there'll be the very deuce to pay. It isn't desirable that even Telfik Bey's presence here should have been known for reasons which—ah—(here Average Jones remarked the resumption of his friend's official bearing)—which, not being for the public, I need not detail to you."

"You need not, in point of fact, tell me anything about it at all," observed Average Jones equably.

Pomposity fell away from Mr. Thomas Colvin McIntyre, leaving him palpably shivering.

"But I need your help. Need it very much. You know something about handling the newspapers, don't you?"

"I know how to get things in; not how to keep them out."

The other groaned. "It may already be too late. What newspapers have you there?"

"All of 'em. Want me to look?"

Mr. McIntyre braced himself.

"Turk dies at Palatia," read Average Jones. "Mm—heart disease . . . wealthy Stamboul merchant . . . studying American methods . . . Turkish minister notified."

"Is that all?"

"Practically."

"And the other reports?"

Average Jones ran them swiftly over. "About the same. Hold on! Here's a little something extra in the *Universal*."

"'Found on the floor . . . bell-boy who discovered the tragedy collapses . . . condition serious . . . Supposedly shock—'"

"What's that?" interrupted young Mr. McIntyre, half rising. "Shot?"

"You're nervous, Tommy. I didn't say 'shot.' Said 'shock.'"

"Oh, of course. Shock—the bell-boy, it means."

"See here; first thing you know you'll be getting me interested. Hadn't you better open up or shut up?"

Mr. McIntyre took a long breath and a resolution simultaneously.

"At any rate I can trust you," he said. "Telfik Bey is not a merchant. He is a secret, confidential agent of the Turkish government. He came over to New York from Washington in spite of warnings that he would be killed."

"You're certain he was killed?"

"I only wish I could believe anything else."

"Shot?"

"The coroner and a physician whom I sent can find no trace of a wound."

"What do they say?"

"Apoplexy."

"The refuge of the mystified medico. It doesn't satisfy you?"

"It won't satisfy the State Department."

"And possibly not the newspapers, eventually."

"Come up with me and look the place over, Average. Let me send for the manager."

That functionary came, a vision of perturbation in a pale-gray coat. Upon assurance that Average Jones was "safe" he led the way to the rooms so hastily vacated by the spirit of the Turkish guest.

"We've succeeded in keeping two recent suicides and a blackmail scheme in this hotel out of the newspapers," observed the manager morosely. "But this would be the worst of all. If I could have known, when the Turkish Embassy reserved the apartment—"

"The Turkish Embassy never reserved any apartment for Telfik Bey," put in the Fifth Assistant Secretary of State.

"Surely you are mistaken, sir," replied the hotel man. "I saw their emissary myself. He specified for rooms on the south side, either the third or fourth floor. Wouldn't have anything else."

"You gave him a definite reservation?" asked Jones.

"Yes; 335 and 336."

"Has the man been here since?"

"Not to my knowledge."

"A Turk, you think?"

"I suppose so. Foreign, anyway."

"Anything about him strike you particularly?"

"Well, he was tall and thin and looked sickly. He talked very soft, too, like a sick man."

The characterization of the Pearlington station agent recurred to the interrogator's mind. "Had he—er—white hair?" he half yawned.

"No," replied the manager, and, in the same breath, the budding diplomat demanded:

"What are you up to, Average? Why should he?"

Average Jones turned to him. "To what other hotels would the Turkish Embassy be likely to send its men?"

"Sometimes their *charge d'affaires* goes to the Nederstrom."

"Go up there and find out whether a room has been reserved for Telfik Bey, and if so—"

"They wouldn't reserve at two hotels, would they?"

"—by whom," concluded Average Jones, shaking his head at the interruption. "Find out who occupied or reserved the apartments on either side."

Mr. Thomas Colvin McIntyre lifted a wrinkling eyebrow. "Really, Jones," he observed, "you seem to be employing me rather in the capacity of a messenger boy."

"If you think a messenger boy could do it as well, ring for one," drawled Average Jones, in his mildest voice. "Meantime, I'll be in the Turk's room here."

Numbers 335 and 336, which the manager opened, after the prompt if somewhat sulky departure of Mr. McIntyre, proved to consist of a small sitting room, a bedroom and a bath, each with a large window giving on the cross-street, well back from Fifth Avenue.

"Here's where he was found." The manager indicated a spot near the wall of the sitting-room and opposite the window. "He had just pushed the button when he fell."

"How do you know that?"

"Bronson, the bell-boy on that call, answered. He knocked several times and got no answer. Then he opened the door and saw Mr. Telfik down, all in a heap."

"Where is Bronson?"

"At the hospital, unconscious."

"What from?"

"Shock, the doctors say."

"What—er—about the—er—shot?"

The manager looked startled. "Well, Bronson says that just as he opened the door he saw a bullet cross the room and strike the wall above the body."

"You can't see a bullet in flight."

"He saw this one," insisted the manager. "As soon as it struck it exploded. Three other people heard it."

"What did Bronson do?"

"Lost his head and ran out. He hadn't got halfway to the elevator when he fell, in a sort of fainting fit. He came to long enough to tell his story. Then he got terribly nauseated and went off again."

"He's sure the man had fallen before the explosion?"

"Absolutely."

"And he got no answer to his knocking?"

"No. That's why he went in. He thought something might be wrong."

"Had anybody else been in the room or past it within a few minutes?"

"Absolutely no one. The floor girl's desk is just outside. She must have seen anyone going in."

"Has she anything to add?"

"She heard the shot. And a minute or two before, she had heard and felt a jar from the room."

"Corroborative of the man having fallen before the shot," commented Jones.

"When I got here, five minutes later, he was quite dead," continued the manager.

Evidence of the explosion was slight to the investigating eye of Average Jones. The wall showed an abrasion, but, as the investigator expected, no bullet hole. Against the leg of a desk he found a small metal shell, which he laid on the table.

"There's your bullet," he observed with a smile.

"It's a cartridge, anyway," cried the hotel man. "He must have been shot, after all."

"From inside the room? Hardly! And certainly not with that. It's a very small fulminate of mercury shell, and never held lead. No. The man was down, if not dead, before that went off."

Average Jones was now at the window. Taking a piece of paper from his pocket he brushed the contents of the window-sill upon it. A dozen dead flies rolled upon the paper. He examined them thoughtfully, cast them aside and turned back to the manager.

"Who occupy the adjoining rooms?"

"Two maiden ladies *did*, on the east. They've left," said the manager bitterly. "Been coming here for ten years, and now they've quit. If the facts ever get in the newspapers—"

"What's on the west, adjoining?"

"Nothing. The corridor runs down there."

"Then it isn't probable that any one got into the room from either side."

"Impossible," said the manager.

Here Mr. Thomas Colvin McIntyre arrived with a flushed face.

"You are right, Average," he said. "The same man had reserved rooms at the Nederstrom for Telfik Bey."

"What's the location?"

"Tenth floor; north side. He had insisted on both details. Nos. 1015, 1017."

"What neighbors?"

"Bond salesman on one side, Reverend and Mrs. Salisbury, of Wilmington, on the other."

"Um-m-m. What across the street?"

"How should I know? You didn't tell me to ask."

"It's the Glenargan office building, just opened, Mr. Jones," volunteered the manager.

Average Jones turned again to the window, closed it and fastened his handkerchief in the catch. "Leave that there," he directed the manager. "Don't let any one into this room. I'm off."

Stopping to telephone, Average Jones ascertained that there were no vacant offices on the tenth floor, south side of the Glenargan apartment building, facing the Nederstrom Hotel. The last one had been let two weeks before to—this he ascertained by judicious questioning—a dark, foreign gentleman who was an expert on rugs. Well satisfied, the investigator crossed over to the skyscraper across from the Palatia. There he demanded of the superintendent a single office on the third floor, facing north. He was taken to a clean and vacant room. One glance out of the window showed him his handkerchief, not opposite, but well to the west.

"Too near Fifth Avenue," he said. "I don't like the roar of the traffic."

"There's one other room on this floor, farther along," said the superintendent, "but it isn't in order. Mr. Perkins' time isn't up till day after tomorrow, and his things are there yet. He told the janitor, though, that he was leaving town and wouldn't bother to take away the things. They aren't worth much. Here's the place."

They entered the office. In it were only a desk, two chairs and a scrap basket. The basket was crammed with newspapers. One of them was the *Hotel Register*. Average Jones found Telfik Bey's name, as he had expected, in its roster.

"I'll give fifty dollars for the furniture as it stands."

"Glad to get it," was the prompt response. "Will you want anything else, now?"

"Yes. Send the janitor here."

That worthy, upon receipt of a considerable benefaction, expressed himself ready to serve the new tenant to the best of his ability.

"Do you know when Mr. Perkins left the building?"

"Yes, sir. This morning, early."

"This morning! Sure it wasn't yesterday?"

"Am I sure? Didn't I help him to the street-car and hand him his little package? That sick he was he couldn't hardly walk alone."

Average Jones pondered a moment. "Do you think he could have passed the night here?"

"I know he did," was the prompt response. "The scrubwoman heard him when she came this morning."

"Heard him?"

"Yes, sir. Sobbing, like."

The nerves of Average Jones gave a sharp "kickback," like a mis-cranked motor-car. His trend of thought had suddenly been reversed. The devious and scientific slayer of Telfik Bey in tears? It seemed completely out of the picture.

"You may go," said he, and seating himself at the desk, proceeded to an examination of his newly acquired property. The newspapers in the scrap basket, mainly copies of the *Evening Register*, seemed to contain, upon cursory examination, nothing germane to the issue. But, scattered among them, the searcher found a number of fibrous chips. They were short and thick; such chips as might be made by cutting a bamboo pole into cross lengths, convenient for carrying.

"The 'spirit-wand,'" observed Average Jones with gusto. "That was the 'little package,' of course."

Next, he turned his attention to the desk. It was bare, except for a few scraps of paper and some writing implements. But in a crevice there shone a glimmer of glass. With a careful finger-nail Average Jones pushed out a small phial. It had evidently been sealed with lead. Nothing was in it.

Its discoverer leaned back and contemplated it with stiffened eyelids. For, upon its tiny, improvised label was scrawled the "Mercy sign;" mysterious before, now all but incredible.

For silent minutes Average Jones sat bemused. Then, turning in a messenger call, he drew to him a sheet of paper upon which he slowly and consideringly wrote a few words.

"You get a dollar extra if this reaches the advertising desk of the *Register* office within half an hour," he advised the uniformed urchin who answered the call. The modern mercury seized the paper and fled forthwith.

Punctuality was a virtue which Average Jones had cultivated to the point of a fad. Hence it was with some discountenance that his clerk was obliged to apologize for his lateness, first, at 4 p.m. of July 23, to a very dapper and spruce young gentleman in pale mauve spats, who wouldn't give his name; then at 4:05 p.m. of the same day to Professor Gehren, of the Metropolitan University; and finally at 4:30 p.m. to Mr. Robert Bertram. When, only a moment before five, the Ad-Visor entered, the manner of his apology was more absent than fervent.

Bertram held out a newspaper to him.

"Cast your eye on that," said he. "The *Register* fairly reeks with freaks lately."

Average Jones read aloud.

> SMITH-PERKINS, formerly 74 Bellair—Send
> map present location H. C. Turkish Triumph about
> smoked out. MERCY—Box 34, Office.

"Oh, I don't know about its being so freakish," said Average Jones.

"Nonsense! Look at it! Turkish Triumph—that's a cigarette, isn't it? H. C.—what's that? And signed Mercy. Why, it's the work of a lunatic!"

"It's my work," observed Average Jones blandly.

The three visitors stared a him in silence.

"Rather a forlorn hope, but sometimes a bluff will go," he continued.

"If H. C. indicates Harvey Craig, as I infer," said Professor Gehren impatiently, "are you so infantile as to suppose that his murderer will give information about him?"

Average Jones smiled, drew a letter from his pocket, glanced at it and called for a number in Hackensack.

"Take the 'phone, Professor Gehren," he said, when the reply came. "It's the Cairnside Hospital. Ask for information about Harvey Craig."

With absorbed intentness the other three listened to the one-sided conversation.

"Hello! . . . May I speak to Mr. Harvey Craig's doctor? . . . This is Professor Gehren of the Metropolitan University . . . Thank you, Doctor. How is he? . . . Very grave? . . . Ah, has been very grave. . . . Wholly out of danger? . . . What was the nature of his illness? . . . When may I see him? . . . Very well. I will visit the hospital to-morrow morning. Thank you. . . . I should have expected that you would notify me of his presence." . . . A long silence intervened, then "Good-bye."

"It is most inexplicable," declared Professor Gehren, turning to the others. "The doctor states that Harvey was brought there at night, by a foreigner who left a large sum of money to pay for his care, and certain suggestions for his treatment. One detail, carefully set down in writing, was that if reddish or purple dots appeared under Harvey's nails, he was to be told that Mr. Smith released him and advised his sending for his friends at once."

"Reddish or purple dots, eh?" repeated Average Jones. "I should like—er—to have talked with—er—that doctor before you cut off."

"And I, sir," said the professor, with the grim repression of the thinker stirred to wrath, "should like to interview this stranger."

"Perfectly feasible, I think," returned Average Jones.

A long silence.

"You don't mean that you've located him already!" cried young Mr. McIntyre.

"He was so obliging as to save me the trouble."

Average Jones held up the letter from which he had taken the Cairnside Hospital's telephone number. "The advertisement worked to a charm. Mr. Smith gives his address in this, and intimates that I may call upon him."

Young Mr. McIntyre rose.

"You're going to see him, then?"

"At once."

"Did I understand you to imply that I am at liberty to accompany you?" inquired Professor Gehren.

"If you care to take the risk."

"Think there'll be excitement?" asked Bertram languidly. "I'd like to go along."

Average Jones nodded. "One or a dozen; I fancy it will be all the same to Smith."

"You think we'll find him dead." Young Mr. McIntyre leaped to this conclusion. "Count me in on it."

"N–no; not dead."

"Perhaps his friend 'Mercy' has gone back on him, then," suggested Mr. McIntyre, unabashed.

"Yes; I rather think that's it," said Average Jones, in a curious accent. "'Mercy' has gone back on him, I believe, though I can't quite accurately place her as yet. Here's the taxi," he broke off. "All aboard that's going aboard. But it's likely to be dangerous."

Across town and far up the East Side whizzed the car, over the bridge that leads away from Manhattan Island to the north, and through quiet streets as little known to the average New Yorker as are Hong Kong and Caracas. In front of a frame house it stopped. On a side porch, over which bright roses swarmed like children clambering into a hospitable lap, sat a man with a gray face. He was tall and slender, and his hair, a dingy black, was already showing worn streaks where the color had faded. At Average Jones he gazed with unconcealed surprise.

"Ah; it is you!" he exclaimed. "You," he smiled, "are the 'Mercy' of the advertisement?"

"Yes."

"And these gentlemen?"

"Are my friends."

"You will come in?"

Average Jones examined a nodding rose with an indulgent, almost a paternal, expression.

"If you—er—think it—er—safe," he murmured.

"Assuredly."

As if exacting a pledge the young man held out his hand. The older one unhesitatingly grasped it. Average Jones turned the long fingers, which enclosed his, back upward, and glanced at them.

"Ah," he said, and nodded soberly, "so, it is that."

"Yes; it is that," assented the other. "I perceive that you have communicated with Mr. Craig. How is he?"

"Out of danger."

"That is well. A fine and manly youth. I should have sorely regretted it if—"

Professor Gehren broke in upon him. "For the peril in which you have involved him, sir, you have to answer to me, his guardian."

The foreigner raised a hand. "He was without family or ties. I told him the danger. He accepted it. Once he was careless—and one is not careless twice in that work. But he was fortunate, too. I, also, was fortunate in that the task was then so far advanced that I could complete it alone. I got him to the hospital at night; no matter how. For his danger and illness I have indemnified him in the sum of ten thousand dollars. Is it enough?"

Professor Gehren bowed.

"And you, Mr. Jones; are you a detective?"

"No; merely a follower of strange trails—by taste."

"Ah. You have set yourself to a dark one. You wish to know how Telfik Bey"—his eyes narrowed and glinted— "came to his reward. Will you enter, gentlemen?"

"I know this much," replied Average Jones as, followed by his friends, he passed through the door which their host held open. "With young Craig as an assistant, you prepared, in the loneliest part of the Hackensack Meadows, some kind of poison which, I believe, can be made with safety only in the open air."

The foreigner smiled and shook his head.

"Not with safety, even then," he said. "But go on."

"You found that your man was coming to New York. Knowing that he would probably put up at the Palatia or the Nederstrom, you reserved rooms for him at both, and took an office across from each. As it was hot weather, you calculated upon his windows being open. You watched for him. When he came you struck him down in his own room with the poison."

"But how?" It was the diplomat who interrupted.

"I think with a long blow-gun."

"By George!" said Bertram softly. "So the spirit-wand of bamboo was a blow-gun! What led you to that, Average?"

"The spirit rappings, which the talky woman in the Bellair Street apartment used to hear. That and the remnants of putty I found near the window. You see the doors opening through the whole length of the apartment gave a long range, where Mr.—er—Smith could practice. He had a sort of target on the window, and every time he blew a putty ball Mrs. Doubletongue heard the spirit. Am I right, sir?"

The host bowed.

"The fumes, whatever they were, killed swiftly?"

"They did. Instantly; mercifully. Too mercifully."

"How could you know it was fumes?" demanded Mr. Thomas Colvin McIntyre.

"By the dead flies, the effect upon the bell-boy, and the fact that no wound was found on the body. Then, too, there was the fulminate of mercury shell."

"Of what possible use was that?" asked Professor Gehren.

"A question that I've asked myself, sir, a great many times over in the last twenty-four hours. Perhaps Mr. Smith could answer that best. Though—er—I think the shell was blown through the blow-pipe to clear the deadly fumes from the room by its explosion, before any one else should suffer. Smith is, at least, not a wanton slaughterer."

"You are right, sir, and I thank you," said the foreigner. He drew himself up weakly but with pride. "Gentlemen, I am not a murderer. I am an avenger. It would have gone hard with my conscience had any innocent person met death through me. As for that Turkish dog, you shall judge for yourself whether he did not die too easily."

From among the papers in a *tiroir* against the wall he took a French journal, and read, translating fluently. The article was a bald account of the torture, outrage and massacre of Armenian women and girls, at Adana, by the Turks. The most hideous portion of it was briefly descriptive of the atrocities perpetrated by order of a high Turkish official upon a mother and two young daughters. "An Armenian prisoner, being dragged by in chains, went mad at the sight," the correspondent stated.

"I was that prisoner," said the reader. "The official was Telfik Bey. I saw my naked daughter break from the soldiers and run to him, pleading for pity, as he sat his horse; and I saw him strike his spur into her bare breast. My wife, the mother of my children—"

"Don't!" The protest came from the Fifth Assistant Secretary of State.

He had risen. His smooth-skinned face was contracted, and the sweat stood beaded on his forehead. "I—I can't stand it. I've got my duty to do. This man has made a confession."

"Your pardon," said the foreigner. "I have lived and fed on and slept with that memory, ever since. On my release I left my country. The enterprise of which I had been the head, dye-stuff manufacturing, had interested me in chemistry. I went to England to study further. Thence I came to America to wait."

"You have heard his confession, all of you," said young Mr. McIntyre, rising. "I shall have him put under arrest pending advice from Washington."

"You may save yourself the trouble, I think, Tommy," drawled Average Jones. "Mr. Smith will never be called to account in this world for the murder—execution of Telfik Bey."

"You saw the marks on my finger-nails," said the foreigner. "That is the sure sign. I may live twenty-four hours; I may live twice or three times that period. The poison does its work, once it gets into the blood, and there is no help. It matters nothing. My ambition is satisfied."

"And it is because of this that you let us find you?" asked Bertram.

"I had a curiosity to know who had so strangely traced my actions."

"But what was the poison?" asked Professor Gehren.

"I think Mr. Jones has more than a suspicion," replied the doomed man, with a smile. "You will find useful references on yonder shelf, Mr. Jones."

Moving across to the shelf, Average Jones took down a heavy volume and ran quickly over the leaves.

"Ah!" he said presently, and not noticing, in his absorption, that the host had crossed again to the *tiroir* and was quietly searching in a compartment, he read aloud:

"Little is known of cyanide of cacodyl, in its action the swiftest and most deadly of existing poisons. In the '40's, Bunsen, the German chemist, combined oxide of cacodyl with cyanogen, a radical of prussic acid, producing cyanide of cacodyl, or dimethyl arsine cyanide. As both of its components are of the deadliest description, it is extremely dangerous to make. It can be made only in the open air, and not without the most extreme precaution known to science. Mr. Lacelles Scott, of England, nearly lost his life experimenting with it in 1904. A small fraction of a grain gives off vapor sufficient to kill a human being instantly."

"Had you known about this stuff, Average?" asked Bertram.

"No, I'd never heard of it. But from its action and from the lettered cabinet, I judged that—"

"This is all very well," broke in Mr. Assistant Secretary Thomas Colvin McIntyre, "but I want this man arrested. How can we know that he isn't shamming and may not escape us, after all?"

"By this," retorted their host. He held aloft a small glass vial, lead-seated, and staggered weakly to the door.

"Stop him!" said Average Jones sharply.

The door closed on the words. There was a heavy fall without, followed by the light tinkle of glass.

Average Jones, who had half crossed the room in a leap, turned to his friends, warning them back.

"Too late. We can't go out yet. Wait for the fumes to dissipate."

They stood, the four men, rigid. Presently Average Jones, opening a rear window, leaped to the ground, followed by the others, and came around the corner of the porch. The dead man lay with peaceful face. Professor Gehren uncovered.

"God forgive him," he said. "Who shall say that he was not right?"

"Not I," said the young assistant secretary in awed tones. "I'm glad he escaped. But what am I to do? Here we are with a dead body on our hands, and a state secret to be kept from the prying police."

Average Jones stood thinking for a moment, then he entered the room and called up the coroner's office on the telephone.

"Listen, you men," he said to his companions. Then, to the official who answered: "There's a suicide at 428 Oliver Avenue, the Bronx. Four of us witnessed it. We had come to keep an appointment with the man in connection with a discovery he claimed in metallurgy, and found him dying. Yes; we will wait here. Good-bye."

Returning to the porch again, he cleared away the fragments of glass, aided by Bertram. To one of these clung a shred of paper. For all his languid self-control the club dilettante shivered a little as he thrust at it with a stick.

"Look, Average, it's the 'Mercy' sign again. What a hideous travesty!"

Average Jones shook his bead.

"It isn't 'Mercy,' Bert. It's the label that he attached, for precaution, to everything that had to do with his deadly stuff. The formula for cyanide of cacodyl is 'Me-2cy.' It was the scrawly handwriting that misled; that's all."

"So I was right when I suggested that his 'Mercy' had gone back on him," said Mr. Thomas Colvin McIntyre, with a semi-hysterical giggle.

Average Jones looked from the peaceful face of the dead to the label, fluttering in the light breeze.

"No," he said gravely. "You were wrong. It was his friend to the last."

BLUE FIRES

"Cabs for comfort; cars for company," was an apothegm which Average Jones had evolved from experience. A professed student of life, he maintained, must keep in touch with life at every feasible angle. No experience should come amiss to a detective; he should be a pundit of all knowledge. A detective he now frankly considered himself; and the real drudgery of his unique profession of Ad-Visor was supportable only because of the compensating thrill of the occasional chase, the radiance of the Adventure of Life glinting from time to time across his path.

There were few places, Average Jones held, where human nature in the rough can be studied to better advantage than in the stifling tunnels of the subway or the close-packed sardine boxes of the metropolitan surface lines. It was in pursuance of this theory that he encountered the Westerner, on Third avenue car. By custom, Average Jones picked out the most interesting or unusual human being in any assembly where he found himself, for study and analysis. This man was peculiar in that he alone was not perspiring in the sodden August humidity. The clear-browned skin and the rangy strength of the figure gave him a certain distinction. He held in his sinewy hands a doubly folded newspaper. Presently it slipped from his hold to the seat beside him. He stared at the window opposite with harassed and unseeing eyes. Abruptly he rose and went out on the platform. Average Jones picked up the paper. In the middle of the column to which it was folded was a marked advertisement:

ARE you in an embarrassing position? Anything, anywhere, any time, regardless of nature or location. Everybody's friend. Consultation at all hours. Suite 152, Owl Building, Brooklyn.

The car was nearing Brooklyn Bridge. Average Jones saw his man drop lightly off. He followed and at the bridge entrance caught him up.

"You've left your paper," he said.

The stranger whirled quickly. "Right," he said. "Thanks. Perhaps you can tell me where the Owl Building is."

"Are you going there?"

"Yes."

"I wouldn't."

A slight wrinkle of surprise appeared on the man's tanned forehead.

"Perhaps *you* wouldn't," he returned coolly.

"In other words, 'mind your business,'" said Average Jones, with a smile.

"Something of that sort," admitted the stranger.

"Nevertheless, I wouldn't consult with Everbody's Friend over in the Owl Building."

"Why?"

"Er—because—er—if I may speak plainly," drawled Average Jones, "I wouldn't risk a woman's name with a gang of blackmailers."

"You've got your nerve," retorted the stranger. The keen eyes, flattening almost to slits, fixed on the impassive face of the other.

"Well, I'll go you," he decided, after a moment. His glance swept the range of vision and settled upon a rathskeller sign. "Come over there where we can talk."

They crossed the grilling roadway, and, being wise in the heat, ordered "soft" drinks.

"Now," said the stranger, "you've declared in on my game. Make good. What's your interest?"

"None, personally. I like your looks, that's all," replied the other frankly. "And I don't like to see you run into that spider's web."

"You know them?"

"Twice in the last year I've made 'em change their place of business."

"But you don't know me. And you spoke of a woman."

"I've been studying you on the car," explained Average Jones. "You're hard as nails; yet your nerves are on edge. It isn't illness, so it must be trouble. On your watch-chain you've got a solitaire diamond ring. Not for ornament; you aren't that sort of a dresser. It's there for convenience until you can find a place to put it. When a deeply troubled man wears an engagement ring on his watch chain it's a fair inference that there's been an obstruction in the course of true love. Unless I'm mistaken, you, being a stranger newly come to town, were going to take your case to those man-eating sharks?"

"How do you know I've just come to town?"

"When you looked at your watch I noticed it was three hours slow. That must mean the Pacific coast, or near it. Therefore you've just got in from the Far West and haven't thought to rectify your time. At a venture I'd say you were a mining man from down around the Ray-Kelvin copper district in Arizona. That peculiar, translucent copper silicate in your scarf-pin comes from those mines."

"The Blue Fire? I wish it had stayed there, all of it! Anything else?"

"Yes," returned Average Jones, warming to the game. "You're an Eastern college man, I think. Anyway, your father or some older member of your family graduated from one of the older colleges."

"What's the answer?"

"The gold of your Phi Beta Kappa key is a different color from your watch-chain. It's the old metal, antedating the California gold. Did your father graduate some time in the latter forties or early fifties?"

"Hamilton, '51. I'm '89. Name, Kirby."

A gleam of pleasure appeared in Average Jones keen eyes. "That's rather a coincidence," he said. "Two of us from the Old Hill. I'm Jones of '04. Had a cousin in your class, Carl Van Reypen."

They plunged into the intimate community of interest which is the peculiar heritage and asset of the small, close-knit old college.

Presently, however, Kirby's forehead wrinkled again. He sat silent, communing with himself. At length he lifted his head like one who has taken a resolution.

"You made a good guess at a woman in the case," he, said. "And you call this a coincidence? She'd say it was a case of intuition. She's very strong on intuition and superstition generally." There was a mixture of tenderness and bitterness in his tone. "Chance brought that advertisement to her eyes. A hat-pin she'd dropped stuck through it, or something of the sort. Enough for her. Nothing would do but that I should chase over to see the Owl Building bunch. At that, maybe her hunch was right. It's brought me up against you. Perhaps you can help me. What are you? A sort of detective?"

"Only on the side." Average Jones drew a card from his pocket, and tendered it:

A. JONES, Ad-Visor

Advice upon all matters connected with
Advertising

Astor Court Temple   *2 to 5 P. M.*

"Ad-Visor, eh?" repeated the other. "Well, there's going to be an advertisement in the *Evening Truth* to-day, by me. Here's a proof of it."

Average Jones took the slip and read it.

> Lost—Necklace of curious blue stones from Hotel
> Denton, night of August 6. Reward greater than value
> of stones for return to hotel. No questions asked.

"Reward greater than value of stones," commented Average Jones. "There's a sentimental interest, then?"

"Will you take the case?" returned Kirby abruptly.

"At least I'll look into it," replied Average Jones.

"Come to the hotel, then, and lunch with me, and I'll open up the whole thing."

Across a luncheon-table, at the quiet, old-fashioned Hotel Denton, Kirby unburdened himself.

"You know all that's necessary about me. The—the other party in the matter is Mrs. Hale. She's a young widow. We've been engaged for six months; were to be married in a fortnight. Now she insists on a postponement. That's where I want your help."

Average Jones moved uneasily in his chair. "Really, Mr. Kirby, lovers' quarrels aren't in my line."

"There's been no quarrel. We're as much engaged now as ever, in spite of the return of the ring. It's only her infern—her deep-rooted superstition that's caused this trouble. One can't blame her; her father and mother were both killed in an accident after some sort of 'ghostly warning.' The first thing I gave her, after our engagement, was a necklace of these stones"—he tapped his scarf pin— "that I'd selected, one by one, myself. They're beautiful, as you see, but they're not particularly valuable; only semiprecious. The devil of it is that they're the subject of an Indian legend. The Indians and Mexicans call them "blue fires," and say they have the power to bind and loose in love. Edna has been out in that country; she's naturally high strung and responsive to that sort of thing, as I told you, and she fairly soaked in all that nonsense. To make it worse, when I sent them to her I wrote that—that—" a dull red surged up under the tan skin— "that as long as the fire in the stones burned blue for her my heart would be all hers. Now the necklace is gone. You can imagine the effect on a woman of that temperament. And you can see the result." He pointed with a face of misery to the solitaire on his watch-chain. "She insisted on giving this back. Says that a woman as careless as she proved herself can't be trusted with jewelry. And she's hysterically sure that misfortune will follow us for ever if we're married without recovering the fool necklace. So she's begged a postponement."

"Details," said Average Jones crisply.

"She's here at this hotel. Has a small suite on the third floor. Came down from her home in central New York to meet my mother, whom she had never seen. Mother's here, too, on the same floor. Night before last Mrs. Hale thought she heard a noise in her outer room. She made a look-see, but found nothing. In the morning when she got up, about ten (she's a late riser) the necklace was gone."

"Where had it been left?"

"On a stand in her sitting-room."

"Anything else taken?"

"That's the strange part of it. Her purse, with over a hundred dollars in it, which lay under the necklace, wasn't touched."

"Does she usually leave valuables around in that casual way?"

"Well, you see, she's always stayed at the Denton and she felt perfectly secure here."

"Any other thefts in the hotel?"

"Not that I can discover. But one of the guests on the same floor with Mrs. Hale saw a fellow acting queerly that same night. There he sits, yonder, at that table. I'll ask him to come over."

The guest, an elderly man, already interested in the case, was willing enough to tell all he knew.

"I was awakened by some one fumbling at my door and making a clinking noise," he explained. "I called out. Nobody answered. Almost immediately I heard a noise across the hall. I opened my door. A man was fussing at the keyhole of the room opposite. He was very clumsy. I said, 'Is that your room?' He didn't even look at me. In a moment he started down the hallway. He walked very fast, and I could hear him muttering to himself. He seemed to be carrying something in front of him with both hands. It was his keys, I suppose. Anyway I could hear it clink. At the end of the hall he stopped, turned to the door at the left and fumbled at the keyhole for quite a while. I could bear his keys clink again. This time, I suppose, he had the right room, for be unlocked it and went in. I listened for fifteen or twenty minutes. There was nothing further."

Average Jones looked at Kirby with lifted brows of inquiry. Kirby nodded, indicating that the end room was Mrs. Hales'.

"How was the man dressed?" asked Average Jones.

"Grayish dressing-gown and bed-slippers. He was tall and had gray hair."

"Many thanks. Now, Mr. Kirby, will you take me to see Mrs. Hale?"

The young widow received them in her sitting-room. She was of the slender, big-eyed, sensitive type of womanhood; her piquant face marred by the evidences of sleeplessness and tears. To Average Jones she gave her confidence at once. People usually did.

"I felt sure the advertisement would bring us help," she said wistfully. "Now, I feel surer than ever."

"Faith helps the worst case," said the young man, smiling. "Mr. Kirby tells me that the intruder awakened you."

"Yes; and I'm a very heavy sleeper. Still I can't say positively that anything definite roused me; it was rather an impression of some one's being about. I came out of my bedroom and looked around the outer room, but there was nobody there."

"You didn't think to look for the necklace?"

"No," she said with a little gasp; "if I only had!"

"And—er—you didn't happen to hear a clinking noise, did you?"

"No."

"After he'd got into the room he'd put the key up, wouldn't he?" suggested Kirby.

"You're assuming that he had a key."

"Of course he had a key. The guest across the ball saw him trying it on the other doors and heard it clink against the lock."

"If he had a key to this room why did he try it on several other doors first?" propounded Average Jones. "As for the clinking noise, in which I'm a good deal interested—may I look at your key, Mrs. Hale?"

She handed it to him. He tried it on the lock, outside, jabbing at the metal setting. The resultant sound was dull and wooden. "Not much of the clink which our friend describes as having heard, is it?" he remarked.

"Then how could he get into my room?" cried Mrs. Hale.

"Are you sure your door was locked?"

"Certain. As soon as I missed the necklace I looked at the catch."

"That was in the morning. But the night before?"

"I always slip the spring. And I know I did this time because it had been left unsprung so that Mr. Kirby's mother could come in and out of my sitting-room, and I remember springing it when she left for bed."

"Sometimes these locks don't work." Slipping the catch back, Average Jones pressed the lever down. There was a click, but the ward failed to slip. At the second attempt the lock worked. But repeated trials proved that more than half the time the door did not lock.

"So," observed Average Jones, "I think we may dismiss the key theory."

"But the locked door this morning?" cried Mrs. Hale.

"The intruder may have done that as he left."

"I don't see why," protested Kirby, in a tone which indicated a waning faith in Jones.

"By way of confusing the trail. Possibly he hoped to suggest that he'd escaped by the fire-escape. Presumably he was on the balcony when Mrs. Hale came out into this room."

As he spoke Average Jones laid a hand on the heavy net curtains which hung before the balcony window. Instead of parting them, however, he stood with upturned eyes.

"Was that curtain torn before yesterday?" he asked Mrs. Hale.

"I hardly think so. The hotel people are very, careful in the upkeep of the rooms."

Jones mounted a chair with scant respect for the upholstery, and examined the damaged drapery. Descending, he tugged tentatively at the other curtain, first with his right hand, then with his left; then with both. The fabric gave a little at the last test. Jones disappeared through the window.

When he returned, after five minutes, he held in his hand some scrapings of the rusted iron which formed the balcony railing.

"You're a mining man, Mr. Kirby," he said. "Would you say that assayed anything?"

Kirby examined the glinting particles. "Gold," he said decisively.

"Ah, then the necklace rubbed with some violence against the railing. Now, Mrs. Hale, how long were you awake?"

"Ten or fifteen minutes. I remember that a continuous rattling of wagons below kept up for a little while. And I heard one of the drivers call out something about taking the air."

"Er—really!" Average Jones became suddenly absorbed in his seal ring. He turned it around five accurate times and turned it back an equal number of revolutions. "Did he—er—get any answer?"

"Not that I heard."

The young man pondered, then drew a chair up to, Mrs. Hale's escritoire, and, with an abrupt "excuse me," helped himself to pen, ink and paper.

"There!" he said, after five minutes' work. "That'll do for a starter. You see," he added, handing the product of his toil to Mrs. Hale, "this street happens to be the regular cross-town route for the milk that comes over by one of the minor ferries. If you heard a number of wagons passing in the early morning they were the milk-vans. Hence this."

Mrs. Hale read:

"MILK-DRIVERS, ATTENTION—Delaware Central mid-town route. Who talked to man outside hotel early morning of August 7? Twenty dollars to right man. Apply personally to Jones, Ad-Visor, Astor Court Temple, New York."

"For the coming issue of the *Milk-Dealers' Journal*," explained its author. "Now, Mr. Kirby, I want you to find out for me—Mrs. Hale can help you, since she has known the hotel people for years—the names of all those who gave up rooms on this floor, or the floors above or below, yesterday morning, and ask whether they are known to the hotel people."

"You think the thief is still in the hotel?" cried Mrs. Hale.

"Hardly. But I think I see smoke from your blue fires. To make out the figure through the smoke is not—" Average Jones broke off, shaking his head. He was still shaking his head when he left the hotel.

It took three days for the milk-journal advertisement to work. On the afternoon of August tenth, a lank, husky-voiced teamster called at the office of the Ad-Visor and was passed in ahead of the waiting line.

"I'm after that twenty," he declared.

"Earn it," said Average Jones with equal brevity.

"Hotel Denton. Guy on the third floor balcony—"

"Right so far."

"Leanin' on the rail as if he was sick. I give him a hello. 'Takin' a nip of night air, Bill?' I says. He didn't say nothin'."

"Did he do anything?"

"Kinder fanned himself an' jerked his head back over his shoulder. Meanin' it was too hot to sleep inside, I reckon. It sure was hot!"

"Fanned himself? How?"

"Like this." The visitor raised his hands awkwardly, cupped them, and drew them toward his face.

"Er—with both hands?"

"Yep."

"Did you see him go in?"

"Nope."

"Here's your twenty," said Average Jones. "You're long on sense and short on words. I wish there were more like you."

"Thanks. Thanks again," said the teamster, and went out.

Meantime Kirby had sent his list of the guests who had given up their rooms on August seventh:

George M. Weaver, Jr., Utica, N. Y., well known to hotel people and vouched for by them.

Walker Parker, New Orleans, ditto.

Mr. and Mrs. Charles Hull; quiet elderly people; first visit to hotel.

Henry M. Gillespie, Locke, N. Y. Middle-aged man; new guest.

C. F. Willard, Chicago; been going to hotel for ten years; vouched for by hotel people.

Armed with the list, Average Jones went to the Hotel Denton and spent a busy morning.

"I've had a little talk with the hotel servants," said he to Kirby, when the latter called to make inquiries. "Mr. Henry M. Gillespie, of Locke, New York, had room 168. It's on the same floor with Mrs. Hale's suite, at the farther end of the hall. He had only one piece of luggage, a suitcase marked H. M. G. That information I got from the porter. He left his room in perfect order except for one thing:

one of the knobs on the headboard of the old fashioned bed was broken off short. He didn't mention the matter to the hotel people."

"What do you make of that?"

"It was a stout knob. Only a considerable effort of strength exerted in a peculiar way would have broken it as it was broken. There was something unusual going on in room 168, all right."

"Then you think Henry M. Gillespie, of Locke, New York, is our man."

"No," said Average Jones.

The Westerner's square jaw fell. "Why not?"

"Because there's no such person as Henry M. Gillespie, of Locke, New York. I've just sent there and found out."

Three stones of the fire-blue necklace returned on the current of advertised appeal. One was brought in by the night bartender of a "sporting" club. He had bought it from a man who had picked it up in a gutter; just where, the finder couldn't remember. For the second a South Brooklyn pawnbroker demanded (and received) an exorbitant reward. A florist in Greenwich, Connecticut, contributed the last. With that patient attention to detail which is the A. B. C. of detective work, Average Jones traced down these apparently incongruous wanderings of the stones and then followed them all, back to Mrs. Hale's fire-escape.

The bartender's stone offered no difficulties. The setting which the pawnbroker brought in had been found on the city refuse heap by a scavenger. It had fallen through a grating into the hotel cellar, and had been swept out with the rubbish to go to the municipal "dump." The apparent mystery of the florist was lucid when Jones found that the hotel exchanged its shop-worn plants with the Greenwich Floral Company. His roaming eye, keen for every detail, had noticed a row of tubbed azaleas within the ground enclosure of the Denton. Recalling this to mind, it was easy for the Ad-Visor to surmise that the gem had dropped from the fire-escape into a tub, which was, shortly after, shipped to the florist. Thus it was apparent that the three jewels had been stripped from the necklace by forcible contact with the iron rail of the fire-escape at the point where Average Jones had found the "color" of precious metal. The stones were identified by Kirby, from a peculiarity in the setting, as the end three, nearest the clasp at the back; a point which Jones carefully noted. But there the trail ended. No more fire-blue stones came in.

For three weeks Average Jones issued advertisements like commands. The advertisements would, perhaps, have struck the formal-minded Kirby as evidences of a wavering intellect. Indeed, they present a curious and incongruous appearance upon the page of Average Jones' scrapbook, where they now mark a successful conclusion. The first reads as follows:

> OH, YOU HOTEL MEN! Come through with the dope on H. M. G. What's he done to your place? Put a stamp on it and we'll swap dates on his past performances. A. JONES, Astor Court Temple, New York City.

This was spread abroad through the medium of *Mine Host's Weekly* and other organs of the hotel trade.

It was followed by this, of a somewhat later date:

> WANTED—Slippery Sams, Human Eels, Fetter Kings, etc. Liberal reward to artist who sold second-hand props to amateur, with instructions for use. Send full details, time and place to A. JONES, Astor Court Temple, New York City.

Variety, the *Clipper* and the *Billboard* scattered the appeal broadcast throughout "the profession." Thousands read it, and one answered it. And within a few days after receiving that answer Jones wired to Kirby:

> "Probably found. Bring Mrs. Hale to-morrow at
> 11. Answer. A. Jones."

Kirby answered. He also telegraphed voluminously to his ex-fiancée, who had returned to her home, and who replied that she would leave by the night train. Some minutes before the hour the pair were at Average Jones' office. Kirby fairly pranced with impatience while they were kept waiting in a side room. The only other occupant was a man with a large black dress-suit case, who sat at the window in a slump of dejection. He raised his head for a moment when they were summoned and let it sag down again as they left.

Average Jones greeted his guests cordially. Their first questions to him were significant of the masculine and feminine differences in point of view.

"Have you got the necklace?" cried Mrs. Hale.

"Have you got the thief?" queried Kirby.

"I haven't got the necklace and I haven't got the thief," announced Average Jones; "but I think I've got the man who's got the necklace."

"Did the thief hand it over to him?" demanded Kirby.

"Are you conversant with the Baconian system of thought, which Old Chips used to preach to us at Hamilton?" countered Average Jones.

"Forgotten it if I ever knew it," returned Kirby.

"So I infer from your repeated use of the word 'thief.' Bacon's principle—an admirable principle in detective work—is that we should learn from things and not from the names of things. You are deluding yourself with a name. Because the law, which is always rigid and sometimes stupid, says that a man who takes that which does not belong to him is a thief, you've got your mind fixed on the name 'thief,' and the idea of theft. If I had gone off on that tack I shouldn't have the interesting privilege of introducing to you Mr. Harvey M. Greene, who now sits in the outer room."

"H. M. G.," said Kirby quickly. "Is it possible that that decent-looking old boy out there is the man who stole—"

"It is *not*," interrupted Average Jones with emphasis, "and I shall ask you, whatever may occur, to guard your speech from offensive expressions of that sort while he is here."

"All right, if you say so," acquiesced the other. "But do you mind telling me how you figure out a man traveling under an alias and helping himself to other people's property on any other basis than that he's a thief?"

"A, B, C," replied Average Jones; "as thus: A—Thieves don't wander about in dressing-gowns. B—Nor take necklaces and leave purses. C—Nor strip gems violently apart and scatter them like largess from fire-escapes. The rest of the alphabet I postpone. Now for Mr. Greene."

The man from the outer room entered and nervously acknowledged his introduction to the others.

"Mr. Greene," explained Jones, "has kindly consented to help clear up the events of the night of August sixth at the Hotel Denton and"—he paused for a moment and shifted his gaze to the newcomer's narrow shoes— "and—er—the loss of—er—Mrs. Hale's jeweled necklace."

The boots retracted sharply, as under the impulse of some sudden emotion; startled surprise, for example. "What?" cried Greene, in obvious amazement. "I don't know anything about a necklace."

A twinkle of satisfaction appeared at the corners of Average Jones' eyes.

"That also is possible," he admitted. "If you'll permit the form of an examination; when you came to the Hotel Denton on August sixth, did you carry the same suitcase you now have with you, and similarly packed?"

"Ye—es. As nearly as possible."

"Thank you. You were registered under the name of Henry M. Gillespie?"

The other's voice was low and strained as he replied in the affirmative.

"For good reasons of your own?"

"Yes."

"For which same reasons you left the hotel quite early on the following morning?"

"Yes."

"Your business compels you to travel a great deal?"

"Yes."

"Do you often register under an alias?"

"Yes," returned the other, his face twitching.

"But not always?"

"No."

"In a large city and a strange hotel, for example, you'd take any name which would correspond to the initials, H. M. G., on your

dress-suit case. But in a small town where you were known, you'd
be obliged to register under your real name of Harvey M. Greene.
It was that necessity which enabled me to find you."

"I'd like to know how you did it," said the other gloomily.

From the left-hand drawer of his desk Jones produced a piece
of netting, with hooks along one end.

"Do you recognize the material, Mrs. Hale," he asked.

"Why, it's the same stuff as the Hotel Denton curtains, isn't
it?" she asked.

"Yes," said Average Jones, attaching it to the curtain rod at the
side door. "Now, will you jerk that violently with one hand?"

"It will tear loose, won't it?" she asked.

"That's just what it will do. Try it."

The fabric ripped from the hooks as she jerked.

"You remember," said Jones, "that your curtain was torn partly
across, and not ripped from the hook at all. Now see."

He caught the netting in both hands and tautened it sharply. It
began to part.

"Awkward," he said, "yet it's the only way it could have been
done. Now, here's a bedpost, exactly like the one in room 168, occupied by Mr. Greene at the Denton. Kirby, you're a powerful man.
Can you break that knob off with one hand?"

He wedged the post firmly in a chair for the trial. The bedpost
resisted.

"Could you do it with both hands?" he asked.

"Probably, if I could get a hold. But there isn't surface enough
for a good hold."

"No, there isn't. But now." Jones coiled a rope around the post
and handed the end to Kirby. He pulled sharply. The knob snapped
and rolled on the floor.

"Q. E. D.," said Kirby. "But it doesn't mean anything to me."

"Doesn't it? Let me recall some other evidence. The guest who
saw Mr. Greene in the hallway thought he was carrying something
in both hands. The milk driver who hailed him on the balcony
noticed that he gestured awkwardly with both hands. In what

circumstances would a man use both hands for action normally performed with one?"

"Too much drink," hazarded Kirby, looking dubiously at Greene, who had been following Jones' discourse with absorbed attention.

"Possibly. But it wouldn't fit this case."

"Physical weakness," suggested Mrs. Hale.

"Rather a shrewd suggestion. But no weakling broke off that bedpost in Henry M. Gillespie's room. I assumed the theory that the phenomena of that night were symptomatic rather than accidental. Therefore, I set out to find in what other places the mysterious H. M. G. had performed."

"How did you know my initials really were H. M. G.?" asked Mr. Greene.

"The porter at the Denton had seen them on 'Henry M. Gillespie's' suitcase. So I sent out loudly printed call to all hotel clerks for information about a troublesome H. M. G."

He handed the "OH, YOU HOTEL MEN" advertisement to the little group.

"Plenty of replies came. You have, if I may say it without offense, Mr. Greene, an unfortunate reputation among hotel proprietors. Small wonder that you use an alias. From the Hotel Carpathia in Boston I got a response more valuable than I had dared to hope. An H. M. G. guest—H. Morton Garson, of Pillston, Pennsylvania (Mr. Greene nodded)—had wrecked his room and left behind him this souvenir."

Leaning over, Jones pulled, clinking from the scrap-basket, a fine steel chain. It was endless and some twelve feet in total length, and had two small loops, about a foot apart. Mrs. Hale and Kirby stared at it in speechless surprise.

"Yes, that is mine," said Mr. Greene with composure. "I left it because it had ceased to be serviceable to me."

"Ah! That's very interesting," said Average Jones with a keen glance. "Of course when I examined it and found no locks, I guessed that it was a trick chain, and that there were invisible springs in the wrist loops."

"But why should any one chain Mr. Greene to his bed with a trick chain?" questioned Mrs. Hale, whose mind had been working swiftly.

"He chained himself," explained Jones, "for excellent reasons. As there is no regular trade in these things, I figured that he probably bought it from some juggler whose performance had given him the idea. So," continued Jones, producing a specimen of his advertisements in the theatrical publications, "I set out to find what professional had sold a 'prop' to an amateur. I found the sale had been made at Marsfield, Ohio, late in November of last year, by a 'Slippery Sam,' termed 'The Elusive Edwardes.' On November twenty-eighth of last year Mr. Harvey M. Greene, of Richmond, Virginia, was registered at the principal, in fact the only decent hotel, at Barsfield. I wrote to him and here he is."

"Yes; but where is my necklace?" cried Mrs. Hale.

"On my word of honor, madam, I know nothing of your necklace," asserted Greene, with a painful contraction of his features. "If this gentleman can throw any more light—"

"I think I can," said Average Jones. "Do you remember anything of that night's events after you broke off the bedpost and left your room—the meeting with a guest who questioned you in the hall, for example?"

"Nothing. Not a thing until I awoke and found myself on the fire-escape."

"Awoke?" cried Kirby. "Were you asleep all the time?"

"Certainly. I'm a confirmed sleep-walker of the worst type. That's why I go under an alias. That's why I got the trick handcuff chain and chained myself up with it, until I found it drove me fighting crazy in my sleep when I couldn't break away. That's why I slept in my dressing-gown that night at the Denton. There was a red light in the hall outside and any light, particularly a colored one, is likely to set me going. I probably dreamed I was escaping from a locomotive—that's a common delusion of mine—and sought refuge in the first door that was open."

"Wait a minute," said Average Jones. "You—er—say that you are—er—peculiarly susceptible to—er—colored light."

"Yes."

"Mrs. Hale, was the table on which the necklace lay in line with any light outside?"

"I think probably with the direct ray of an electric globe shining through the farther window."

"Then, Mr. Greene," said, Average Jones, "the glint of the fire-blue stones undoubtedly caught your eye. You seized on the necklace and carried it out on the fire-escape balcony, where the cool air or the milk-driver's hail awakened you. Have you no recollection of seeing such a thing?"

"Not the faintest, unhappily."

"Then he must have dropped it to the ground below," said Kirby.

"I don't think so," controverted Jones slowly. "Mr. Greene must have been clinging to it tenaciously when it swung and caught against the railing, stripping off the three end stones. If the whole necklace had dropped it would have broken up fine, and more than three stones would have returned to us in reply to the advertisements. And in that case, too, the chances against the end stones alone returning, out of all the thirty-six, are too unlikely to be considered. No, the fire-blue necklace never fell to the ground."

"It certainly didn't remain on the balcony," said Kirby. "It would have been discovered there."

"Quite so," assented Average Jones. "We're getting at it by the process of exclusion. The necklace didn't fall. It didn't stay. Therefore?"—he looked inquiringly at Mrs. Hale.

"It returned," she said quickly.

"With Mr. Greene," added Average Jones.

"I tell you," cried that gentleman vehemently, "I haven't set eyes on the wretched thing."

"Agreed," returned Average Jones; "which doesn't at all affect the point I wish to make. You may recall, Mr. Greene, that in my message I asked you to pack your suitcase exactly as it was when you left the hotel with it on the morning of August seventh."

"I've done so with the exception of the conjurer's chain, of course."

"Including the dressing-gown you had on, that night, I assume. Have you worn it since?"

"No. It hung in my closet until yesterday, when I folded it to pack. You see, I—I've had to give up the road on account of my unhappy failing."

"Then permit me." Average Jones stooped to, the dress-suit case, drew out the garment and thrust his hand into its one pocket. He turned to Mrs. Hale.

"Would you—er—mind—er—leaning over a bit?" he said.

She bent her dainty head, then gave a startled cry of delight as the young man, with a swift motion, looped over her shoulders a chain of living blue fires which gleamed and glinted in the sunlight.

"They were there all the time," she exclaimed; "and you knew it."

"Guessed it," he corrected, "by figuring out that they couldn't well be elsewhere—unless on the untenable hypothesis that our friend, Mr. Greene here, was a thief."

"Which only goes to prove," said Kirby soberly, "that evidence may be a mighty deceptive accuser."

"Which only goes to prove," amended Average Jones, "that there's no fire, even the bluest, without traceable smoke."

PIN-PRICKS

"The thing is a fake," declared Bertram. He slumped heavily into a chair, and scowled at Average Jones' well-littered desk, whereon he had just tossed a sheet of paper. His usually impeccable hair was tousled. His trousers evinced a distinct tendency to bag at the knees, and his coat was undeniably wrinkled. That the elegant and flawless dilettante of the Cosmic Club should have come forth, at eleven o'clock of a morning, in such a state of comparative disreputability, argued an upheaval of mind little short of phenomenal.

"A fake," he reiterated. "I've spent a night of pseudo-intellectual riot and ruin over it. You've almost destroyed a young and innocent mind with your infernal palimpsest, Average."

"You would have it," returned Average Jones with a smile. "And I seem to recall a lofty intimation on your part that there never *was* a cipher so tough but what you could rope, throw, bind, and tie a pink ribbon on its tail in record time."

"Cipher, yes," returned the other bitterly. "That thing isn't a cipher. It's an alphabetical riot. Maybe," he added hopefully, "there was some mistake in my copy?"

"Look for yourself," said Average Jones, handing him the original.

It was a singular document, this problem in letters which had come to light up the gloom of a November day for Average Jones; a stiffish sheet of paper, ornamented on one side with color prints of alluring "spinners," and on the other inscribed with an appeal, in print. Its original vehicle was an envelope, bearing a one-cent stamp, and addressed in typewriting:

Mr. William H. Robinson,
The Caronia,
Broadway and Evenside Ave.,
New York City.

The advertisement on the reverse of the sheet ran as follows:

> A NGLERS—When you are looking for "Baits That
>   Catch Fish," do you see these spinners in the
> store where you buy tackle? You will find here twelve
> baits, every one of which has a record and has liter-
> ally caught tons of fish. We call them "The 12 Surety
> Baits." We want you to try them for casting and
> trolling these next two months, because all varieties
> of bass are particularly savage in striking these baits
> late in the season.

> D EALERS—You want your customers to have these
>   12 Shoemaker "Surety Baits" that catch fish.
> This case will sell itself empty over and over again,
> for every bait is a record-breaker and they catch fish.
> We want you to put in one of these cases so that the
> anglers will not be disappointed and have to wait for
> baits to be ordered. It will be furnished FREE,
> charges prepaid, with your order for the dozen baits
> it contains.

The peculiar feature of the communication was that it was profusely be-pimpled with tiny projections, evidently made by thrusting a pin in from the side which bore the illustrations. The perforations were liberally scattered. Most, though not all of them, transfixed certain letters. Accepting this as indicative, Bertram had copied out all the letters thus distinguished, with the following cryptic result:

> b-n-r-k-n-o-n-h-t (doubtful) i (doubtful) d-o-o-n-t-r-r-h-n-
> h-r-n-l-n-r-f-i-A-i-r-l-r-o-n-n-t-t-m-n-n (doubtful) r-r-r-c-r
> (doubtful) r-r M-r-p-c (two punctures) l-r-n-n-r-o-n-r-r-r
> h-n-i l S-h-i-r-n-r-f-r-o-n-h (twice) W-r-o-n (doubtful)
> A-r-r-r-v-i-l-f-r (perforated twice) o-n-o-n-r-r-o-n-c (doubt-
> ful) m-t (perforated twice) n-o-A-n-r-f-o-n-n-o-r-t-A-i-r-r-t
> n-h-l-b (perforated three times) f-n-A-r-r-r-d-A-o-d (doubt-
> ful) r-r-h-r-b-r-n-t.

"Yes, the copy's all right," growled Bertram. "Tell me again how you came by it."

"Robinson came here twice and missed me. Yesterday I got the note from him which you've seen, with the enclosure which has so threatened your reason. You know the rest. Perhaps you'd have done well to study the note for clues to the other document."

Something in his friend's tone made Bertram glance up suspiciously.

"Let me see the note," he demanded.

Average Jones handed it to him. There was no stamp on it; it had been left by the writer. It was addressed, in rather scrawly chirography, to "A. Jones, Ad-Visor," and read:

> The Caronia, Nov. 18.
>
> Mr. A. Jones, Astor Court Temple: I have tried unsuccessfully to see you twice. Enclosed you will find the reason. Please *read through it carefully.* Then I am sure you will see and help me. Money is no object. I will call to-morrow at noon.
>
> Respectfully,
> William H. Robinson.

"Well, I see nothing out of the ordinary in that," observed Bertram.

"Nothing?" inquired Average Jones.

Bertram read the message again. "Of course the man is rattled. That's obvious in his handwriting. Also, he has inverted one sentence in his haste and said 'read through it,' instead, of 'read it through.' Otherwise, it's ordinary enough."

"It must be vanity that keeps you from eyeglasses, Bert," Average Jones observed with a sigh. "Well, I'm afraid I set you on the wrong track, myself!"

Bertram lifted an eyebrow with an effort. "Meaning, I suppose, that you're on the right one and have solved the cipher."

"Cipher be jiggered. You were right in your opening remark. There isn't any cipher. If you read Mr. Robinson's note correctly, and if you'd had the advantage of working on the original of the advertisement as I have, you'd undoubtedly have noticed at once—"

"Thank you," murmured Bertram.

"—that fully one-third of the pin-pricks don't touch any letters at all."

"Then we should have taken the letters which lie between the holes?"

"No. The letters don't count. It's the punctures. Force your eyes to consider those alone, and you will see that the holes themselves form letters and words. Read through it carefully, as Robins directed."

He held the paper up to the light. Bertram made out in straggling characters, formed in skeleton the perforations, this legend:

ALL POINTS TO
YOU TAKE THE
SHORT CUT DEATH
IS EASIER THAN
SOME THINGS.

"Whew! That's a cheery little greeting," remarked Bertram. "But why didn't friend Robinson point it out definitely in his letter?"

"Wanted to test my capacity perhaps. Or, it may have been simply that he was too frightened and rattled to know just what he was writing."

"Know anything of him?"

"Only what the directory tells, and directories don't deal in really intimate details of biography, you know. There's quite an assortment of William H. Robinsons, but the one who lives at the Caronia appears to be a commission merchant on Pearl Street. As the Caronia is one of the most elegant and quite the most enormous of those small cities within themselves which we call apartment houses, I take it that Mr. Robinson is well-to-do, and probably married. You can ask him, yourself, if you like. He's due any moment, now."

Promptly, as befitted a business man, Mr. William H. Robinson arrived on the stroke of twelve. He was a well-made, well-dressed citizen of forty-five, who would have been wholly ordinary save for one peculiarity. In a room more than temperately cool he was sweating profusely, and that, despite the fact that his light over-coat was on his arm. Not polite perspiration, be it noted, such as would have been excusable in a gentleman of his pale and sleek plumpness, but soul-wrung sweat, the globules whereof gathered in the grayish hollows under his eyes and assailed, not without effect, the glistening expanse of his tall white collar. He darted a glance at Bertram, then turned to Average Jones.

"I had hoped for a private interview," he said in a high piping voice.

"Mr. Bertram is my friend and business confidant."

"Very good. You—you have read it?"

"Yes."

"Then—then—then—" The visitor fumble with nerveless fingers, at his tightly buttoned cut-away coat. It resisted his efforts. Suddenly, with a snarl of exasperation, he dragged violently at the lapel, tearing the button outright from the cloth. "Look what I have done," he said, staring stupidly for a moment at the button which had shot across the room. Then, to the amazed consternation of the others, he burst into tears.

Average Jones pushed a chair behind him, while Bertram brought him a glass of water. He gulped out his thanks, and, mastering himself after a moment's effort, drew a paper from his inner pocket which he placed on the desk. It was a certified check for one hundred dollars, made payable to Jones.

"There's the rest of a thousand ready, if you can help me," he said.

"We'll talk of that later," said the prospective beneficiary. "Sit tight until you're able to answer questions."

"Able now," piped the other in his shrill voice. "I'm ashamed of myself, gentlemen, but the strain I've been under— When you've heard my story—"

"Just a moment, please," interrupted Average Jones, "let me get at this my own way."

"Any way you like," returned the visitor.

"Good! Now what is it that points to you?"

"I don't know any more than you."

"What are the 'some things' that are worse than death?"

Mr. Robinson shook his head. "I haven't the slightest notion in the world."

"Nor of the 'short cut' which you are advised to take?"

"I suppose it means suicide." He paused for a moment. "They can't drive me to that—unless they drive me crazy first." He wiped the sweat from under his eyes, breathing hard.

"Who are 'they?'"

Mr. Robinson shook his head. In the next question the interrogator's tone altered and became more insistent.

"Have you ever called in a doctor, Mr. Robinson?"

"Only once in five years. That was when my nerves broke down—under this."

"When you do call in a doctor, is it your habit to conceal your symptoms from him?"

"Of course not. I see what you mean. Mr. Jones, I give, you my word of honor, as I hope to be saved from this persecution, I don't know any more than yourself what it means."

"Then—er—I am—er—to believe," replied Jones, drawling, as he always did when interest, in his mind, was verging on excitement, "that a simple blind threat like this—er—without any backing from your own conscience—er—could shake you—er—as this has done? Why, Mr. Robinson, the thing—er—may be—er—only a raw practical joke."

"But the others!" cried the visitor. His face changed and fell. "I believe I am going crazy," he groaned. "I didn't tell you about the others."

Diving into his overcoat pocket he drew out a packet of letters which he placed on the desk with a sort of dismal flourish.

"Read those!" he cried.

"Presently." Average Jones ran rapidly over the eight envelopes. With one exception, each bore the imprint of some firm name made familiar by extensive advertising. All the envelopes were of softish Manila paper varying in grade and hue, under one-cent stamps.

"Which is the first of the series?" he asked.

"It isn't among those. Unfortunately it was lost, by a stupid servant's mistake, pin and all."

"Pin?"

"Yes. Where I cut open the envelope—"

"Wait a moment. You say you cut it open. All these, being one-cent postage, must have come unsealed. Was the first different?"

"Yes. It had a two-cent stamp. It was a circular announcement of the Swift-Reading Encyclopedia, in a sealed envelope. There was a pin bent over the fold of the letter so you couldn't help but notice it. Its head was stuck through the blank part of the circular. Leading from it were three very small pins arranged as a pointer to the message."

"Do you remember the message?"

"Could I forget it! It was pricked out quite small on the blank fold of the paper. It said: 'Make the most of your freedom. Your time is short. Call at General Delivery, Main P. O., for your warning.' I—"

"You went there?"

"The next day."

"And found—?"

"An ordinary sealed envelope, addressed in pinpricks connected by pencil lines. The address was scrawly, but quite plain."

"Well, what did it contain?"

"A commitment blank to an insane asylum."

Average Jones absently drew out his handkerchief, elaborately whisked from his coat sleeve an imaginary speck of dust, and smiled benignantly where the dust was supposed to have been.

"Insane asylum," he murmured. "Was—er—the blank—er—filled in?"

"Only partly. My name was pricked in, and there was a specification of dementia from drug habit, with suicidal tendencies."

With a quick signal, unseen by the visitor, Average Jones opened the way to Bertram, who, in wide range of experience and study had once specialized upon abnormal mental phenomena.

"Pardon me," that gentleman put in gently, "has there ever been any dementia in your family?"

"Not as far as I know."

"Or suicidal mania?"

"All my people have died respectably in their beds," declared the visitor with some vehemence.

"Once more, if I may venture. Have you ever been addicted to any drug?"

"Never, sir."

"Now," Average Jones took up the examination, "will you tell me of any enemy who would have reason to persecute you?"

"I haven't an enemy in the world."

"You're fortunate," returned the other smiling, "but surely, some time in your career—business rivalry—family alienation—any one of a thousand causes?"

"No," answered the harassed man. "Not for me. My business runs smoothly. My relations are mostly dead. I have no friends and no enemies. My wife and I live alone, and all we ask," he added in a sudden outburst of almost childish resentment, "is to be left alone."

The inquisitor's gaze returned to the packet of letters. "You haven't complained to the post-office authorities?"

"And risk the publicity?" returned Robinson with a shudder.

"Well, give me over night with these. Oh, and I may want to 'phone you presently. You'll be at home? Thank you. Good day."

"Now," said Average Jones to Bertram, as their caller's plump back disappeared, "this looks pretty queer to me. What did you think of our friend?"

"Scared but straight," was Bertram's verdict.

"Glad to hear it. That's my idea, too. Let's have a look at the material. We've already got the opening threat, and the General Delivery follow-up."

"Which shows, at least, that it isn't a case of somebody in the apartment house tampering with the mail."

"Not only that. It's a dodge to find out whether he got the first message. People don't always read advertisements, even when sealed, as the first message-bearing one was. Therefore, our mysterious persecutor says: 'I'll just have Robinson prove it to me, if he *did* get the first message, by calling for the second.' Then, after a lapse of time, he himself goes to the General Delivery, asks for a letter for Mr. William H. Robinson, finds it's gone, and is satisfied."

"Yes, and he'd be sure then that Robinson would go through all the mailed ads with a fine-tooth comb, after that. But why the pin-pricks? Just to disguise his hand?"

"Possibly. It's a fairly effectual disguise."

"Why didn't he address the envelope that way, then?"

"The address wouldn't be legible against the white background of the paper inside. On the other hand, if he'd addressed all his envelopes by pinpricks filled in with pencil lines, the post-office people might get curious and look into one. Sending threats through the mail is a serious matter."

Average Jones ran over the letter again. "Good man, Robinson!" he observed. "He's penciled the date of receipt on each one, like a fine young methodical business gent. Here we are: 'Rec'd July 14. Card from Goshorn & Co., Oriental Goods.' Message pricked in through the cardboard: 'You are suspected by your neighbors. Watch them.' Not bad for a follow-up, is it?"

"It would look like insanity, if it weren't that—that through the letters 'one increasing purpose runs,'" parodied Bertram.

"Here's one of July thirty-first; an advertisement of the Croiset Line tours to the Orient. Listen here, Bert: 'Whither can guilt flee that vengeance may not follow?'"

"I can't quite see Robinson in the part of guilt," mused Bertram. "What's next?"

"More veiled accusation. The medium is a church society announcement of a lecture on Japanese Feudalism. Date, August seventeenth. Inscription: 'If there is no blood on your soul, why do you not face your judges?'"

"Little anti-climactic, don't you think?"

"What about this one of September seventh, then? Direct reference back to the drug habit implied in the commitment blank. It's a testimonial booklet of one of the poisonous headache dopes, Lemona Powders. The message is pricked through the cover. 'Better these than the hell of suspense.'"

"Trying the power of suggestion, eh?"

"Quite so. The second attempt at it is even more open. An advertisement of Shackleton's Safeguard Revolvers. Date, September twenty-second. Advice, by pin: 'As well this as any other way.'"

"Drug or suicide," remarked Bertram. "The man at the other end doesn't seem particular which."

"There's the insane asylum always to fall back on. Under date of October first, comes the Latherton Soap Company's impassioned appeal to self-shaving manhood. Great Caesar! No wonder poor Robinson was upset. Listen to this: 'God himself hates you.' After that there's a three-weeks respite, for there's October twenty-second on this one, Kirkby and Dunn's offering of five percent water bonds. 'The commission has its spies watching you constantly.' Calculated to inspire confidence in the most timid soul! Now we come to the soup course: Smith and Perkins' Potted Chowder. Date of November third. Er—Bert—here's something—er—really worth while, now. Hark to the song of the pin."

He read sonorously:

> *"Animula, vagula, Bandula,*
> *Hospes, comesque corporis;*
> *Quae nunc abibis in loca?"*

"Hadrian, isn't it?" cried Bertram, in utter amazement. "Of course it is! Hadrian's terrified invocation to his own parting spirit. 'Guest and companion of my body; into what places will you now go?' Average, it's uncanny! Into what place of darkness and dread is the Demon of the Pin trying to drive poor Robinson's spirit?"

Average Jones shook his head. "'*Pailidula, nudula, rigida,*'" he completed the quatrain. "'Ghostpale, stark, and rigid.' He's got a grisly imagination, that pin-operator. I shouldn't care to have him on my trail."

"But Robinson!" protested Bertram feebly. "What has a plump, commonplace, twentieth-century, cutaway-wearing, flat-inhabiting Robinson to do with a Roman emperor's soul-questionings?"

"Perhaps the last entry of the lot will tell us. *Palmerton's Magazine's* feature announcement, received November ninth. No; it doesn't give any clue to the Latinity. It isn't bad, though. 'The darkness falls.' That's all there is to it. And enough."

"I should say the darkness did fall," confirmed Bertram. "It falls—and remains."

Average Jones pushed the collection of advertisements aside and returned to the opening phase of the problem, the fish-bait circular which Robinson had mailed him. So long after, that Bertram hardly recognized it as a response to his last remark, the investigator drawled out:

"Not such—er—impenetrable darkness. In fact,—er—Eureka, or words to that effect. Bert, when does the bass season end?"

"November first, hereabouts, I believe."

"The postmark on the envelope that carried this advertisement to our friend advises the use of the baits for 'these next two months.' Queer time to be using bass-lures, after the season is closed. Bert, it's a pity I can't waggle my ears."

"Waggle your ears! For heaven's sake, why?"

"Because then I'd be such a perfect jackass that I could win medals at a show. I ought to have guessed it at first glance, from the fact that the advertisement couldn't well have been mailed to Robinson originally, anyhow."

"Why not?"

"Because he's not in the sporting-goods business, and the advertisement is obviously addressed to the retail trade. Don't you remember: it offers a showcase, free. What does a man living in an apartment want of a show-case to keep artificial bait in? What we—er—need here is—er—steam."

A moment's manipulation of the radiator produced a small jet. In this Average Jones held the envelope. The stamp curled tip and dropped off. Beneath it were the remains of a small portion of a former postmark.

"I thought so," murmured Average Jones.

"Remailed!" exclaimed Bertram.

"Remailed," corroborated his friend. "I expect we'll find the others the same."

One by one he submitted the envelopes to the steam bath. Each of them, as the stamp was peeled off, exhibited more or less fragmentary signs of a previous cancellation.

"Careless work," criticized Average Jones. "Every bit of the mark should have been removed, instead of trusting to the second stamp to cover what little was left, by shifting it a bit toward the center of the envelope. Look; you can see on this one where the original stamp was peeled off. On this the traces of erasure are plain enough. That's why Manila paper was selected: it's easier to erase from."

"Is Robinson faking?" asked Bertram. "Or has some one been rifling his waste-basket?"

"That would mean an accomplice in the house, which would be dangerous. I think it was done at longer range. As for the question of our friend's faking in his claim of complete ignorance of all this, I propose to find that out right now."

Drawing the telephone to him, he called the Caronia apartments. Thus it was that Mr. William H. Robinson, for two unhappy minutes, profoundly feared that at last he had really lost his mind. This is the conversation in which he found himself implicated.

"Hello! Mr. Robinson? This is Mr. A. Jones. You hear me?"

"Yes, Mr. Jones. What is it?"

"*Integer vitae, scelerisque purus.*"

"I—I—beg your pardon!"

"*Non egit Mauris jaculis nec arcu.*"

"This is Mr. Robinson: Mr. William H. Rob—"

"*Nec venenatis gravida sag*—Hello! Central, don't cut off! Mr. Robinson, do you understand me?"

"God knows, I don't!"

"If he doesn't recognize the *Integer Vitae*," said Average Jones in a swift aside to Bertram, "he certainly wouldn't know the more obscure Latin of the late Mr. Hadrian."

"One more question, Mr. Robinson. Is there, in all your acquaintance, any person who never goes out without an attendant? Take time to think, now."

"Why—why—why," stuttered the appalled subject of this examination, and fell into silence. From the depths of the silence he presently exhumed the following: "I *did* have a paralytic cousin who always went out in a wheeled chair. But she's dead."

"And there's no one else?"

"No. I'm quite sure."

"That's all. Good-bye."

"Thank Heaven! Good-bye."

"What was that about an attendant?" inquired Bertram, as his friend replaced the receiver.

"Oh, I've just a hunch that the sender of those messages doesn't go out unaccompanied."

"Insane? Or semi-insane? It does rather look like delusional paranoia."

As nearly as imperfect humanity may, Average Jones appeared to be smiling indulgently at the end of his own nose.

"Dare say you're right—er—in part, Bert. But I've also a hunch that our man Robinson is himself the delusion as well as the object."

"I wish you wouldn't be cryptic, Average," said his friend pathetically. "There's been enough of that without your gratuitously adding to the sum of human bewilderment."

Average Jones scribbled a few words on a pad, considered, amended, and handed the result over to Bertram, who read:

"WANTED—Professional envelope eraser to remove marks from used envelopes. Experience essential. Apply at once—A. Jones, Advisor, Astor Court Temple."

"Would it enlighten your gloom to see that in every New York and Brooklyn paper to-morrow?" inquired its inventor.

"Not a glimmer."

"We'll give this ad a week's repetition if necessary, before trying more roundabout measures. As soon as I have heard from it I'll drop in at the club and we'll write—that is to say, compose a letter."

"To whom?"

"Oh, that I don't know yet. When I do, you'll see me."

Three days later Average Jones entered the Cosmic Club, with that twinkling up-turn of the mouth corners which, with him, indicated satisfactory accomplishment.

"Really, Bert," he remarked, seeking out his languid friend, in the laziest corner of the large divan. "You'd be surprised to know how few experienced envelope erasers there are in four millions of population. Only seven people answered that advertisement, and they were mostly tyros."

"Then you didn't get your man?"

"It was a woman. The fifth applicant. Got a pin about you?"

Bertram took a pearl from his scarf.

"That's good. It will make nice, bold, inevitable sort of letters. Come over here to this desk."

For a few moments he worked at a sheet of, paper with the pin, then threw it down in disgust.

"This sort of thing requires practice," he muttered. "Here, Bert, you're cleverer with your fingers than I. You take it, and I'll dictate."

Between them, after several failures, they produced a fair copy of the following:

"Mr. Alden Honeywell will choose between making explanation to the post-office authorities or calling at 3:30 p.m. to-morrow on A. Jones, Ad-Visor, Astor Court Temple."

This Average Jones enclosed in an envelope which he addressed in writing to Alden Honeywell, Esq., 550 West Seventy-fourth Street, City, afterward pin-pricking the letters in outline. "Just for moral effect," he explained. "In part this ought to give him a taste of the trouble he made for poor Robinson. You'll be there to-morrow, Bert?"

"Watch me!" replied that gentleman with unwonted emphasis. "But will Alden Honeywell, Esquire?"

"Surely. Also Mr. William H. Robinson, of the Caronia. Note that 'of the Caronia.' It's significant."

At three-thirty the following afternoon three men were waiting in Average Jones' inner office. Average Jones sat at his desk sedulously polishing his left-hand fore-knuckle with the tennis callous of his right palm. Bertram lounged gracefully in the big chair. Mr. Robinson fidgeted. There was an atmosphere of tension in the room. At three-forty there came a tap-tapping across the floor of the outer room, and a knock at the door brought them all to their feet. Average Jones threw the door open, took the man who stood outside by the arm, and pushing a chair toward him, seated him in it.

The new-comer was an elderly man dressed with sober elegance. In his scarf was a scarab of great value; on his left hand a superb signet ring. He carried a heavy, gold-mounted stick. His face was curiously divided against itself. The fine calm forehead and the deep setting of the widely separate eyes gave an impression of intellectual power and balance. But the lower part of the face was mere wreckage; the chin quivering and fallen, from self-indulgence, the fine lines of the nose coarsened by the spreading nostrils; the mouth showing both the soft contours of sensuality and the hard, fine line of craft and cruelty. The man's eyes were unholy. They stared straight before him, and were dead. With his entrance there was infused in the atmosphere a sense of something venomous. "Mr. Alden Honeywell?" said Average Jones.

"Yes." The voice had refinement and calm.

"I want to introduce you to Mr. William H. Robinson."

The new-comer's head turned slowly to his right shoulder then back. His eyes remained rigid.

"Why, the man's blind!" burst out Mr. Robins in his piping voice.

"Blind!" echoed Bertram. "Did you know this, Average?"

"Of course. The pin-pricks showed it. And the letter mailed to Mr. Robinson at the General Delivery, which, if you remember, had the address penciled in from pin-holes."

"When you have quite done discussing my personal misfortune," said Honeywell patiently, "perhaps you will be good enough to tell me which is William Robinson."

"I am," returned the owner of that name. "And do *you* be good enough to tell me why you hound me with your hellish threats."

"That is not William Robinson's voice!" said the blind man. "Who are you?"

"William H. Robinson."

"Not William Honeywell Robinson!"

"No; William Hunter Robinson."

"Then why am I brought here?"

"To make a statement for publication in to-morrow morning's newspaper," returned Average Jones crisply.

"Statement? Is this a yellow journal trap?"

"As a courtesy to Mr. Robinson, I'll explain. How long have you lived in the Caronia, Mr. Robinson?"

"About eight months."

"Then, some three or four months before you moved in, another William H. Robinson lived there for a short time. His middle name was Honeywell. He is a cousin, and an object of great solicitude to this gentleman here. In fact, he is, or will be, the chief witness against Mr. Honeywell in his effort to break the famous Holden Honeywell will, disposing of some ten million dollars. Am I right, Mr. Honeywell?"

"Thus far," replied the blind man composedly.

"Five years ago William Honeywell Robinson became addicted to a patent headache 'dope.' It ended, as such habits do, in insanity. He was confined two years, suffering from psychasthenia, with suicidal melancholia and delusion of persecution. Then he was released, cured, but with a supersensitive mental balance."

"Then the messages were intended to drive him out of his mind again," said Bertram in sudden enlightenment. "What a devil!"

"Either that, or to impel him, by suggestion, to suicide or to revert to the headache powders, which would have meant the asylum again. Anything to put him out of the way, or to make his testimony incompetent for the will contest. So, when the ex-lunatic returned from Europe a year ago, our friend Honeywell here, in some way located him at the Caronia. He matured his little scheme. Through a letter broker who deals with the rag and refuse collectors, he got all the second-hand mail from the Caronia. Meantime, William Honeywell Robinson had moved away, and as chance would have it, William Hunter Robinson moved in, receiving the

pinprick letters which, had they reached their goal, would probably have produced the desired effect."

"If they drove a sane man nearly crazy, what wouldn't they have
done to one whose mind wasn't quite right!" cried the wronged
Robinson.

"But since Mr. Honeywell is blind," said Bertram, "how could
he see to erase the cancellations?"

"Ah! That's what I asked myself. Obviously, he couldn't. He'd
have to get that done for him. Presumably he'd get some stranger
to do it. That's why I advertised for a professional eraser who was
experienced, judging that it would fetch the person who had done
Honeywell's work."

"Is there any such thing as a professional envelope eraser?"
asked Bertram.

"No. So a person of experience in this line would be almost
unique. I was sure to find the right one, if he or she saw my advertisement. As a matter of fact, it turned out to be an unimaginative
young woman who has told me all about her former employment
with Mr. Honeywell, apparently with no thought that there was
anything strange in erasing cancellations from hundreds of envelopes—for Honeywell was cautious enough not to confine her to
the Robinson mail alone—and then pasting on stamps to remail
them."

"You appear to have followed out my moves with some degree
of acumen, Mr.—er—Jones," said the blind schemer suavely.

"Yet I might not have solved your processes easily if you had
not made one rather—if you will pardon me—stupid mistake."

For the first time, the man's bloated lips shook. His evil pride
of intellectuality was stung.

"You lie!" he said hastily. "I do not make mistakes."

"No? Well, have it as you will. The point that you are to sign
here a statement, which I shall read to you before these witnesses,
announcing for publication the withdrawal of your contest for the
Honeywell millions."

"And if I decline?"

"The painful necessity will be mine of turning over these instructive documents to the United States postal authorities. But not before giving them to the newspapers. How would you look in court, in view of this attempt to murder a fellow man's reason?"

Mr. Honeywell had now gained his composure. "You are right," he assented. "You seem to have a singular faculty for being right. Be careful it does not fail you—sometime."

"Thank you," returned Average Jones. "Now you will listen, please, all of you."

He read the brief document, placed it before the blind man, and set a pin between his finger and thumb. "Sign there," he said.

Honeywell smiled as he pricked in his name.

"For identification, I suppose," he said. "Am I to assign no cause to the newspapers for my sudden action?"

A twinkle of malice appeared in Average Jones' eye.

"I would suggest waning mental acumen," he said.

The blind man winced palpably as he rose to his feet. "That is the second time you have taunted me on that. Kindly tell me my mistake."

Average Jones led him to the door and opened it.

"Your mistake," he drawled as he sped his parting guest into the grasp of a waiting attendant, "was—er—in not remembering that—er—you mustn't fish for bass in November."

BIG PRINT

In the Cosmic Club Mr. Algernon Spofford was a figure of distinction. Amidst the varied, curious, eccentric, brilliant, and even slightly unbalanced minds which made the organization unique, his was the only wholly stolid and stupid one. Club tradition declared that he had been admitted solely for the beneficent purpose of keeping the more egotistic members in a permanent and pleasing glow of superiority. He was very rich, but otherwise quite harmless. In an access of unappreciated cynicism, Average Jones had once suggested to him, as a device for his newly acquired coat-of-arms, "Rocks et Praeterea Nihil."

But the "praeterea nihil" was something less than fair to Mr. Spofford, with whom it was not strictly a case of "nothing further" besides his "rocks." Ambition, the vice of great souls, burned within Spofford's pigeon-breast. He longed to distinguish himself in the line of endeavor of his friend Jones and was prone to proffer suggestions, hints, and even advice, to the great tribulation of the recipient.

Hence it was with misgiving that the Ad-Visor opened the door of his sanctum to Mr. Spofford, on a harsh December noon. But the misgivings were supplanted by pleased surprise when the caller laid in his hand a clipping from a small country town paper, to this effect:

RANSOM—Lost lad from Harwick not drowned or
harmed. Retained for ransom. Safe and sound to

parents for $50,000. Write, Mortimer Morley, General Delivery, N. Y. Post-Office.

"Thought that'd catch you," chuckled Mr. Spofford, in great self-congratulation. "'Jones'll see into this,' I says to myself. 'If he don't, I'll explain.' Somethin' *to* that, ay?"

Average Jones looked from the advertisement to the vacuous smile of Mr. Algernon Spofford. "Oh, you'll explain, will you?" he said softly. "Well, the thing I'd like to have explained is—come over here to the window a minute, will you, Algy?"

Mr. Spofford came, and gazed down upon a dispiriting area of rain-swept street and bedraggled wayfarers.

"See that ten-story office building across the way?" pursued Average Jones. "What would you do if, coming in here at midnight, you were to see twenty-odd rats ooze out of that building and disperse about their business?"

"I—I'd quit," said the startled promptly.

"That's the obvious solution," retorted the other, "but my question wasn't intended to elicit a brand of music-hall humor."

Spofford contemplated the building uneasily. "I don't know what you're up to, Average," he complained. "Is it a catch?"

"No; it's a test case. What would you do?"

"I'd think it was Billy-be-dashed queer," answered Spofford with profound conviction.

"You're getting on," said Jones tartly. "And next?"

"Ay? How do I know? What're you devilin' me this way for?"

"You wouldn't call a policeman?"

"No," said Spofford, staring.

"You wouldn't hustle around and 'phone Central?"

"Bosh!"

"Yet if any one told you you hadn't the sense of a policeman, you'd resent it."

"Of course, I would!"

"Well, Jimmy McCue, the night special, who patrols past the corner, saw that very thing happen a few nights ago at the Sterriter

Building. Knowing that rats don't go out at midnight for a saunter, two dozen strong, he began to suspect."

"Suspect what?" growled Spofford.

"That there must be some abnormal cause for so abnormal a proceeding. Think, now, Algy."

"I've heard of rats leavin' a sinkin' ship. The building might have been sinkin'," suggested the visitor hopefully.

"Is that the best you can do? I'll give you one more try."

"I know," said Spofford. "A cat."

"On my soul," declared Average Jones, gazing at his club-mate with increased interest, "you're the most remarkable specimen of inverted mentality I've ever encountered. D'you think a cat habitually rounds up two dozen rats and then chivies 'em out into the street for sport? McCue didn't have any cat theory. He figured that when rats come out of a place that way the place is afire. So he turned in an alarm and saved a two hundred and fifty thousand dollar building."

"Umph!" grunted Spofford. "Well, what's that got to do with the advertisement I brought you?"

"Nothing in the world, directly. I'm merely trying to figure out, in my own way, how a mind like yours could see under the surface print into the really interesting peculiarity of this clipping. Now I know that your mind didn't do anything of the sort. Come on, now, Algy, who sent this to you?"

"Cousin of mine up in Harwick. I wish you weren't so Billy-be-dashed sharp, Average. I used to visit in Harwick, so they asked me to get you interested in Bailey Prentice's case. He's the lost boy."

"You've done it. Now tell me all you know."

Spofford produced a letter which gave the outlines of the case. Bailey Prentice's disappearance it was set forth, was the lesser of two simultaneous phenomena which violently jarred the somnolent New England village of Harwick from its wonted calm. The greater was the "Harwick meteor." At ten-fifteen on the night of December twelfth, the streets being full of people coming from the moving picture show, there was a startling concussion from the overhanging clouds and the astounded populace saw a ball of flame plunging earthward, to the northwest of the town, and waxing in intensity as it fell. Darkness succeeded. But, within a minute, a lurid radiance rose and spread in the night. The aerial bolt had gone crashing through an old barn on the Tuxall place, setting it afire.

Bailey Prentice was among the very few who did not go to the fire. Taken in connection with the fact that he was fourteen years old and very thoroughly a boy, this, in itself, was phenomenal. In the excitement of the occasion, however, his absence was not noted. But when, on the following morning, the Reverend Peter Prentice, going up to call his son, found the boy's room empty and the bed untouched, the second sensation of the day was launched. Bailey Prentice had, quite simply, vanished.

Some one offered the theory that, playing truant from the house while his father was engaged in work below stairs, he had been overwhelmed and perhaps wholly consumed by a detached fragment from the fiery visitant. This picturesque suggestion found many supporters until, on the afternoon of December fourteenth, a coat and waistcoat were found on the seashore a mile north of the village. The Reverend Mr. Prentice identified the clothes as his son's. Searching parties covered the beach for miles, looking for the body. Preparations were made for the funeral services, when a new and astonishing factor was injected into the situation. An advertisement, received by mail from New York, with stamps affixed to the "copy" to pay for its insertion, appeared in the local paper.

"And here's the advertisement," concluded Mr. Algernon Spofford, indicating the slip of paper which he had turned over to Average Jones. "And if you are going up to Harwick and need help there, why I've got time to spare."

"Thank you, Algy," replied Average Jones gravely. "But I think you'd better stay here in case anything turns up at this end. Suppose," he added with an inspiration, "you trace this Mortimer Morley through the general delivery."

"All right," agreed Spofford innocently satisfied with this wild-goose errand. "Lemme know if anything good turns up."

Average Jones took train for Harwick, and within a few hours was rubbing his hands over an open fire in the parsonage, whose stiff and cheerless aspect bespoke the lack of a woman's humanizing touch, for the Reverend Mr. Prentice was a widower. Overwrought with anxiety and strain, the clergyman, as soon as he had taken his coat, began a hurried, inconsequential narrative, broke off, tried again, fell into an inextricable confusion of words, and, dropping his head in his hands, cried:

"I can't tell you. It is all a hopeless jumble."

"Come!" said the younger man encouragingly. "Comfort yourself with the idea that your son is alive, at any rate."

"But how can I be sure, even of that?"

Average Jones glanced at a copy of the advertisement which he held. "I think we can take Mr. Morley's word so far."

"Even so; fifty thousand dollars ransom!" said the minister, and stopped with a groan.

"Nonsense!" said Average Jones heartily. "That advertisement counts for nothing. Professional kidnappers do not select the sons of impecunious ministers for their prey. Nor do they give addresses through which they may be found. You can dismiss the advertisement as a blind; the second blind, in fact."

"The second?"

"Certainly. The first was the clothing on the shore. It was put there to create the impression that your son was drowned."

"Yes; we all supposed that he must be."

"By what possible hypothesis a boy should be supposed to take off coat and waistcoat and wade off-shore into a winter sea is beyond my poor powers of conjecture," said the other. "No. Somebody 'planted' the clothes there."

"It seems far-fetched to me," said the Reverend Mr. Prentice doubtfully. "Who would have any motive for doing such a thing?"

"That is what we have to find out. What time did your son go to his room the night of his disappearance?"

"Earlier than usual, as I remember. A little before nine o'clock."

"Any special reason for his going up earlier?"

"He wanted to experiment with a new fishing outfit just given him for his birthday."

"I see. Will you take me to his room?"

They mounted to the boy's quarters, which overlooked the roof of the side porch from a window facing north. The charred ruins of a barn about, half a mile away were plainly visible through this window.

"The barn which the meteor destroyed," said the Reverend Mr. Prentice, pointing it out.

One glance was all that Average Jones bestowed upon a spot which, for a few days, had been of national interest. His concern was inside the room. A stand against the wall was littered with bits of shining mechanism. An unjointed fishing-rod lay on the bed. Near at hand were a small screw-driver and a knife with a broken blade.

"Were things in this condition when you came to call Bailey in the morning and found him gone?" asked Average Jones.

"Nothing has been touched," said the clergyman in a low voice.

Average Jones straightened up and stretched himself languidly. His voice when he spoke again took on the slow drawl of boredom. One might have thought that he had lost all interest in the case but for the thoughtful pucker of the broad forehead which belied his halting accents.

"Then—er—when Bailey left here he hadn't any idea of—er—running away."

"I don't follow you, Mr. Jones."

"Psychology," said Average Jones. "Elementary psychology. Here's your son's new reel. A normal boy doesn't abandon a brand-new fad when he runs away. It isn't in boy nature. No, he was taking this reel apart to study it when some unexpected occurrence checked him and drew him outside."

"The meteor."

"I made some inquiries in the village on my way, up. None of the hundreds of people who turned out for the fire, remembers seeing Bailey about."

"That is true."

"The meteor fell at ten-fifteen. Bailey went upstairs before nine. Allow half an hour for taking apart the reel. I don't believe he'd have been longer at it. So, it's probable that he was out of the house before the meteor fell."

"I should have heard him go out of the front door."

"That is, perhaps, why he went out of the window," observed Average Jones, indicating certain marks on the sill. Swinging his feet over, he stepped upon the roof of the porch, and peered at the ground below.

"And down the lightning rod," he added.

For a moment he stood meditating. "The ground is now frozen hard," he said presently. "Bailey's footprints where he landed are deeply marked. Therefore the soil must have been pretty soft at the time."

"Very," agreed the clergyman. "There had been a three-day downpour, up to the evening of Bailey's disappearance. About nine o'clock the wind shift to the northeast, and everything froze hard. There has been no thaw since."

"You seem very clear on these points, Mr. Prentice."

"I noted them specially, having in mind to write a paper on the meteorite for the *Congregationalist*."

"Ah! Perhaps you could tell me, then, how soon after the meteor's fall, the barn yonder was discovered to be afire?"

"Almost instantly. It was in full blaze within very short time after."

"How short? Five minutes or so?"

"Not so much. Certainly not more than two."

"H'm! Peculiar! Ra–a–a–ather peculiar." drawled Average Jones. "Particularly in view of the weather."

"In what respect?"

"In respect to a barn, water-soaked by a three-day rain bursting into flame like tinder."

"It had not occurred to me. But the friction and heat of the meteorite must have been extremely great."

"And extremely momentary except as to the lower floor, and the fire should have taken some time to spread from that. However, to turn to other matters—" He swung himself over the edge of the roof and went briskly down the lightning rod. Across the frozen ground he moved, with his eyes on the soil, and presently called up to his host:

"At any rate, he started across lots in the direction of the barn. Will you come down and let me in?"

Back in the study, Average Jones sat meditating a few moments. Presently he asked:

"Did you go to the spot where your son's clothes were found?"

"Yes. Some time after."

"Where was it?"

"On the seashore, some half a mile to the east of the Tuxall place, and a little beyond."

"Is there a roadway from the Tuxall place to the spot?"

"No; I believe not. But one could go across the fields and through the barn to the old deserted roadway."

"Ah. There's an old roadway, is there?"

"Yes. It skirts the shore to join Boston Pike about three miles up."

"And how far from this roadway were your son's clothes found?"

"Just a few feet."

"H'm. Any tracks in the roadway?"

"Yes. I recall seeing some buggy tracks and being surprised, because no one ever drives that way."

"Then it is conceivable that your son's clothes might have been tossed from a passing vehicle, to the spot where they were discovered."

"Conceivable, certainly. But I can see no grounds for such a conjecture."

"How far down the road, in this direction, did tracks run?"

"Not beyond the fence-bar opening from the Tuxall field, if that is what you mean."

"It is, exactly. Do you know this Tuxall?"

"Hardly at all. He is a recent comer among us."

"Well, I shall probably want to make his acquaintance, later."

"Have a care, then. He is very jealous of his precious meteor, and guards the ruins of the barn, where it lies, with a shot gun."

"Indeed? He promises to be an interesting study. Meantime, I'd like to look at your son's clothes."

From a closet Mr. Prentice brought out a coat and waistcoat of the "pepper-and-salt" pattern which is sold by the hundreds of thousands the whole country over. These the visitor examined carefully. The coat was caked with mud, particularly thick on one shoulder. He called the minister's attention to it.

"That would be from lying wet on the shore," said the Reverend Mr. Prentice.

"Not at all. This is mud, not sand. And it's ground or pressed in. Has any one tampered with these since they were found?"

"I went through the pockets."

Average Jones frowned. "Find anything?"

"Nothing of importance. A handkerchief, some odds and ends of string—oh, and a paper with some gibberish on it."

"What was the nature of this gibberish?"

"Why it might have been some sort of boyish secret code, though it was hardly decipherable enough to judge from. I remember some flamboyant adjectives referring to something three feet high. I threw the paper into the waste-basket."

Turning that receptacle out on the table, Average Jones discovered in the debris a sheet of cheap, ruled paper, covered with penciled words in print characters. Most of these had been crossed out in favor of other words or sentences, which in turn had been "scratched." Evidently the writer had been toilfully experimenting toward some elegance or emphasis of expression, which persistently eluded him. Amidst the wreck and ruin of rhetoric, however, one phrase stood out clear:

"Stupendous scientific sensation."

Below this was a huddle and smudge of words, from which adjectives darted out like dim flame amidst smoke. "Gigantic" showed in its entity followed by an unintelligible erasure. At the end this line was the legend "3 Feet High." "Veritable Visitor," appeared below, and beyond it, what seemed to be the word "Void." And near the foot of the sheet the student of all this chaos could make faintly but unmistakably, "Marvelous Man-l—" the rest of the word being

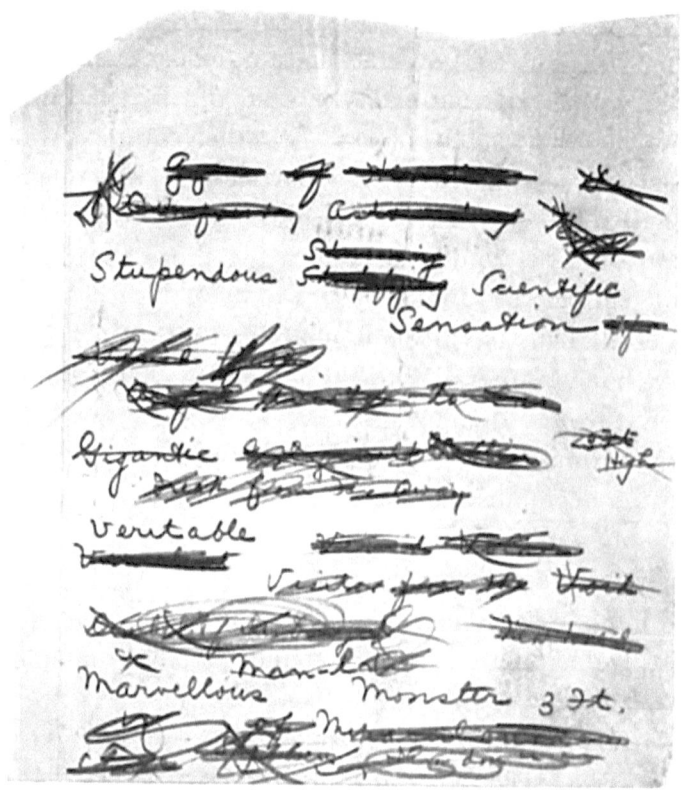

"A paper with some gibberish on it"

cut off by a broad black smear. "Monster 3 Feet." The remainder was wholly undecipherable.

Average Jones looked up from this curio, and there was a strange expression in the eyes which met the minister's.

"You—er—threw this in the—er—waste-basket." he drawled. "In which pocket was it?"

"The waistcoat. An upper one, I believe. There was a pencil there, too."

"Have you an old pair of shoes of Bailey's," asked the visitor abruptly.

"Why, I suppose so. In the attic somewhere."

"Please bring them to me."

The Reverend Mr. Prentice left the room. No sooner had the door closed after him than Average Jones jumped out of his chair stripped to his shirt, caught up the pepper-and-salt waistcoat, tried it on and buttoned it across his chest without difficulty; then thrust his arm into the coat which went with it, and wormed his way, effortfully, partly into that. He laid it aside only when he had determined that he could get it no farther on. He was clothed and in his right garments when the Reverend Mr. Prentice returned with a much-worn pair of shoes.

"Will these do?" he asked.

Average Jones hardly gave them the courtesy of a glance. "Yes," he said indifferently, and set them aside. "Have you a time-table here?"

"You're going to leave?" cried the clergyman, in sharp disappointment.

"In just half an hour," replied the visitor, holding his finger on the time-table.

"But," cried Mr. Prentice, "that is the train back to New York."

"Exactly."

"And you're not going to see Tuxall?"

"No."

"Nor to examine the place where the clothes were found?"

"Haven't time."

"Mr. Jones, are you giving up the attempt to discover what became of my boy?"

"I know what became of him."

The minister put out a hand and grasped the back of a chair for support. His lips parted. No sound came from them. Average Jones carefully folded the paper of "gibberish" and tucked it away in his card case.

"Bailey has been carried away by two people in a buggy. They were strangers to the town. He was injured and unconscious. They still have him. Incidentally, he has seriously interfered with a daring and highly ingenious enterprise. That is all I can tell you at present."

The clergyman found his voice. "In heaven, Mr. Jones," he cried, "tell me who and what these people are."

"I don't know who they are. I do know what they are. But it can do no good to tell you the one until I can find out the other. Be sure of one thing, Bailey is in no further danger. You'll hear from me as soon as I have anything definite to report."

With that the Reverend Mr. Prentice had to be content; that and a few days later, a sheet of letter-paper bearing the business imprint of the Ad-Visor, and enclosing this advertisement:

> WANTED—3 Ft. type for sensational Bill Work. Show samples. Delivery in two weeks. A. JONES, Ad-Visor, Astor Court Temple, N. Y. City.

Had the Reverend Mr. Prentice been a reader of journals devoted to the art and practice of printing he might have observed that message widely scattered to the trade. It was answered by a number of printing shops. But, as the answers came in to Average Jones, he put them aside, because none of the seekers for business was able to "show samples." Finally there came a letter from Hoke and Hollins of Rose Street. They would like Mr. Jones to call and inspect some special type upon which they were then at work. Mr. Jones called. The junior member received him.

"Quite providential, Mr. Jones," he said. "We're turning out some single-letter, hand-made type of just the size you want. Only part of the alphabet, however. Isn't that a fine piece of lettering!"

He held up an enormous M to the admiration of his visitor.

"Excellent!" approved Average Jones. "I'd like to see other letters; A, for example."

Mr. Hollins produced a symmetrical A.

"And now, an R, if you please; and perhaps a V."

Mr. Hollis looked at his visitor with suspicion. "You appear to be selecting the very letters which I have," he remarked.

"Those which—er—would make up the—er—legend, 'Marvelous Man-Like Monster," drawled Average Jones.

"Then you know the Farleys," said the print man.

"The Flying Farleys?" said Average Jones. "They used to do ascensions with firework trimmings, didn't they? No; I don't exactly know them. But I'd like to."

"That's another matter," retorted Mr. Hollins, annoyed at having betrayed himself. "This type is decidedly a private—even a secret—order. I had no right to say anything about it or the customers who ordered it."

"Still, you could see that a letter left here for them reached them, I suppose."

After some hesitation, the other agreed. Average Jones sat down to the composition of an epistle, which should be sufficiently imperative without being too alarming. Having completed this delicate task to his satisfaction he handed the result to Hollins.

"If you haven't already struck off a line, you might do so," he suggested. "I've asked the Farleys for a print of it; and I fancy they'll be sending for one."

Leaving the shop he went direct to a telegraph office, whence he dispatched two messages to Harwick. One was to the Reverend Peter Prentice, the other was to the local chief of police. On the following afternoon Mr. Prentice trembling in the anteroom of the Ad-Visor's. With the briefest word of greeting Average Jones led him into his private office, where a clear-eyed boy, with his head swathed in bandages sat waiting. As the Ad-Visor closed the door after him, he heard the breathless, boyish "Hello, father," merged in the broken cry of the Reverend Peter Prentice.

Five minutes he gave father and son. When he returned to the room, carrying a loose roll of reddish paper, he was followed by a strange couple. The woman was plumply muscular. Her attractive face was both defiant and uneasy. Behind her strode a wiry man of forty. His chief claim to notice lay in an outrageously fancy waistcoat, which was ill-matched with his sober, commonplace, "pepper-and-salt" suit.

"Mr. and Mrs. Farley, the Reverend Mr. Prentice," said Average Jones in introduction.

"The strangers in the wagon?" asked the clergyman quickly.

"The same," admitted the woman briefly.

The Reverend Mr. Prentice turned upon Farley. "Why did you want to steal my boy away?" he demanded.

"Didn't want to. Had to," replied that gentleman succinctly.

"Let's do this in order," suggested Average Jones. "The principal actor's story first. Speak up, Bailey."

"Don't know my own story," said the boy with a grin. "Only part of it. Mrs. Farley's been awful good to me, takin' care of me an' all that. But she wouldn't tell me how I got hurt or where I was when I woke up."

"Naturally. Well, we must piece it out among us. Now, Bailey, you were working over your reel the night the meteor fell, when—"

"What meteor? I don't know anything about a meteor."

"Of course you don't," said Average Jones laughing. "Stupid of me. For the moment I had forgotten that you were out of the world then. Well, about nine o'clock of the night you got the reel, you looked out of your window and saw a queer light over at the Tuxall place."

"That's right. But say, Mr. Jones, how do you know about the light?"

"What else but a light could you have seen, on a pitch-black night?" counter-questioned Average Jones with a smile. "And it must have been something unusual, or you wouldn't have dropped everything to go to it."

"That's what!" corroborated the boy. "A kind of flame shot up from the ground. Then it spread a little. Then it went out. And there were people running around it."

"Ah! Some one must have got careless with the oil," observed Average Jones.

"That fool Tuxall!" broke in Farley with an oath. "It was him gummed the whole game."

"Mr. Tuxall, I regret to say," remarked Average Jones, "has left for parts unknown, so the Harwick authorities inform me, probably foreseeing a charge of arson."

"Arson?" repeated the Reverend Mr. Prentice in astonishment.

"Of course. Only oil and matches could have made a barn flare up, after a three-days' rain, as his did. Now, Bailey, to continue. You ran across the fields to the Tuxall place and went around—let me see; the wind had shifted to the northeast—yes; to the north-east of the barn and quite a distance away. There you saw a man at work in his shirt."

"Well—I'll—be—jiggered!" said the boy in measured tones. "Where were you hiding, Mr. Jones?"

"Not behind the tree there, anyway," returned the Ad-Visor with a chuckle. "There is a tree there, I suppose?"

"Yes; and there was something alive tied up in it with a rope."

"Well, not exactly alive," returned Average Jones, "though the mistake is a natural one."

"I tell you, I *know*," persisted Bailey. "While Mr. and Mrs. Farley were workin' over some kind of a box, I shinned up the tree."

"Bold young adventurer! And what did you find?"

"One of the limbs was shakin' and thrashin'. I crawled out on it. I guess it was kind o' crazy me, but I was goin' to find out what was what if I broke my neck. There was a rope tied to it, and some big thing up above pullin' and jerkin' at it, tryin' to get away. Pretty soon, Mr. and Mrs. Farley came almost under me. He says: 'Is Tuxall all ready?' and she says: 'He thinks we ought to wait half an hour. The street'll be full of folks then. Then he says: 'Well, I hate to risk it, but maybe it's better.' Just then, the rope gave a twist and came swingin' over on me, and knocked me right off the limb. I gave a yell and then I landed. Next I knew I was in bed. And that's all."

"Now I'll take up the wondrous tale," said Average Jones. "The Farleys, naturally discomfited by Bailey's abrupt and informal ar-rival, were in a quandary. Here was an inert boy on their hands. He might be dead, which would be bad. Or, he might be alive, which would be worse, if they left him."

"How so?" asked the Reverend Mr. Prentice.

"Why, you see," explained Average Jones, "they couldn't tell how much he might have seen and heard before he made his hasty descent. He might have enough information to spoil their whole careful and elaborate plan."

"But what in the world was their plan?" demanded the minister.

"That comes later. They took off Bailey's coat and waistcoat, perhaps to see if his back was broken (Farley nodded), and finding him alive, tossed his clothes into the buggy, where Farley had left his own, and completed their necessary work. Of course, there was danger that Bailey might come to at any moment and ruin everything. So they worked at top speed, and left the final performance to Tuxall. In their excitement they forgot to find out from their accomplice who Bailey was. Consequently, they found themselves presently driving across country with an unknown and undesired white elephant of a boy on their hands. One of them conceived the idea of tossing his clothes upon the sea-beach to establish a false clue of drowning, until they could decide what was to be done with him. In carrying this out they made the mistake which lighted up the whole trail."

"Well, I don't see it at all," said Farley glumly. "How did you ever get to us?"

Average Jones mildly contemplated the mathematical center of his questioner.

"New waistcoat?" he asked.

Farley glanced down at the outrageous pattern with pride.

"Yep. Got it last week."

"Lost the one that came with the pepper-and-salt suit you're wearing?"

"Damn!" exploded Farley in sudden enlightenment.

"Just so. Your waistcoat got mixed with the boy's clothes, which are of the same common pattern, and was tossed out on the beach with his coat."

"Well, I didn't leave a card in it, did I?" retorted the other.

"Something just as good."

"The ad, Tim!" cried the woman. "Don't you remember, you couldn't find the rough draft you made while we were waiting?"

"That's right, too," he said. "It was in that vest-pocket. But it didn't have no name on it."

"Then, that," put in the Reverend Peter Prentice, "was the scrawled nonsense—"

"Which you—er—threw into the waste-basket," drawled Average Jones with a smile.

"Those were not Bailey's clothes at all?"

"The coat was his; not the waistcoat. His waistcoat may have fallen out of the buggy, or it may be there yet."

"But what does all this talk of people at work in the dark, and arson, and a mysterious creature tied in a tree lead to?"

"It leads," said Average Jones, "to a very large rock, much scorched, and with a peculiar carving on it, which now lies imbedded in the earth beneath Tuxall's barn."

"If you've seen that," said Farley, "it's all up."

"I haven't seen it. I've inferred it. But it's all up, nevertheless."

"Serves us right," said the woman disgustedly. "I wish we'd never heard of Tuxall and his line of bunk."

"Mystification upon mystification!" cried the clergyman. "Will some one please give a clue to the maze?"

"In a word," said Average Jones. "The Harwick meteor."

"What connection—"

"Pardon me, one moment. The 'live thing' in the tree was a captive balloon. The box on the ground was a battery. The wire from the battery was connected with a firework bomb, which, when Tuxall pressed the switch, exploded, releasing a flaming 'dropper.' About the time the 'dropper' reached the earth Tuxall lighted up his well-oiled barn. All Harwick, having had its attention attracted by the explosion, and seen the portent with its own eyes, believed that a huge meteor had fired the building. So Tuxall and Company had a well attested wonder from the heavens. That's the little plan which Bailey's presence threatened to wreck. Is it your opinion that the stars are inhabited, Prentice?"

"What!" cried the minister, gaping.

"Stars—inhabited—living, sentient creatures."

"How should I know!"

"You'd be interested to know, though, wouldn't you?"

"Why, certainly. Any one would."

"Exactly the point. Any one would, and almost any one would pay money to see, with his own eye the attested evidence of human, or approximately human, life in other spheres. It was a big stake that Tuxall, Farley and Company were playing for. Do you begin to see the meaning of the big print now?"

"I've heard nothing about big prints," said the puzzled clergy-man.

"Pardon me, you've heard but you haven't understood. How-ever, to go on, Tuxall and our friends here fixed up a plan on the prospects of a rich harvest from public curiosity and credulity. Tuxall planted a big rock under the barn, fixed it up appropriately with torch and chisel and sent for the Farleys, who are expert fire-work and balloon people, to counterfeit a meteor."

"Amazing!" cried the clergyman.

"Such a meteor, furthermore, as had never been dreamed of before. If you were to visit Tuxall's barn, you would undoubtedly find on the boulder underneath it a carving resembling a human form, a hoax more ambitious than the Cardiff Giant. He carted the rock in from some quarry and did the scorching and carving him-self, I suppose."

"And you discovered all that in a half-day's visit to Harwick?" asked the Reverend Mr. Prentice incredulously.

"No, but in half-minute's reading of the 'gibberish' which you threw away."

Taking from the desk the reddish roll which he had brought into the room with him, he sent the loose end of it wheeling across the floor, until it lay, fully outspread. In black letters against red, the legend glared and blared its announcement:

MARVELOUS MAN-LIKE MONSTER!

"Those letters, Mr. Prentice," pursued the Ad-Visor, "measure just three feet from top to bottom. The phrase 'three feet high' which so puzzled you, as combined with the adjectives of great size, was obviously a printer's direction. All through the smudged 'copy,' which you threw away, there run alliterative lines, 'Stupendous Scientific Sensation,' 'Veritable Visitor Void' and finally 'Marvel-ous Man-l— Monster.' Only one trade is irretrievably committed to and indubitably hall-marked by alliteration, the circus trade. You'll recall that Farley insensibly fell into the habit even in his advertisement; 'lost lad,' 'retained for ransom' and 'Mortimer

Morley.' Therefore I had the combination circus poster, an alleged meteor which burned a barn in a highly suspicious manner, and an apparently purposeless kidnapping. The inference was as simple as it was certain. The two strangers with Tuxall's aid, had prepared the fake meteor with a view to exploiting the star-man. Bailey had literally tumbled into the plot. They didn't know how much he had seen. The whole affair hinged on his being kept quiet. So they took him along. All that I had to do, then, was to find the deviser of the three-foot poster. He was sure to be Bailey's abductor."

"Say," said Farley with conviction, "I believe you're the devil's first cousin."

"When you left me in Harwick," said the Reverend Peter Prentice, before Average Jones could acknowledge this flattering surmise, "you said that strangers had done the kidnapping. How did you tell they were strangers then?"

"From the fact that they didn't know who Bailey was, and had to advertise him, indefinitely, as 'lost lad from Harwick.'"

"And that there were two of them?" pursued the minister.

"I surmised two minds: one that schemed out the 'planting' of the clothes on the shore; the other, more compassionate, that promulgated the advertisement."

"Finally, then, how could you know that Bailey was injured and unconscious?"

"If he hadn't been unconscious then and for long after, he'd have revealed his identity to his captors, wouldn't he?" explained the Ad-Visor.

There was a long pause. Then the woman said timidly:

"Well, and now what?"

"Nothing," answered Average Jones. "Tuxall has got away. Mr. Prentice has recovered his son. You and Farley have had your lesson. And I—"

"Yes, and you, Mr. Detective-man," said the woman, as he paused. "What do you get out of it?"

Average Jones cast an affectionate glance at the sprawling legend which disfigured his floor.

"A unique curio in my own special line," he replied. "An ad which never has been published and never will be. That's enough for me."

There was a double knock at the door, and Mr. Algernon Spofford burst in, wearing a face of gloom.

"Say, Average," he began, but broke off with a snort of amazement. "You've found him!" cried. "Hello, Mr. Prentice. Well, Bailey, alive and kicking, eh?"

"Yes; I've found him and them," replied Average Jones.

"You've done better than me, then. I've been through the post-office department from the information window here to the post-master-general in Washington, and nobody'll help me find Mortimer Morley."

"Then let me introduce him; Algy, this is Mortimer Morley; in less private life Mr. Tim Farley, and his wife, Mrs. Farley, Mr. Spofford."

"Well, I'll be Billy-be-dashed," exploded Mr. Spofford. "How did you work it out, Average?"

"On the previously enunciated principle," returned Average Jones with a smile, "that when rats leave a sinking ship or a burning building there's usually something behind, worth investigating."

THE MAN WHO SPOKE LATIN

Mementoes of Average Jones' exploits in his chosen field hang on the walls of his quiet sanctum. Here the favored visitor may see the two red-ink dots on a dated sheet of paper, framed in with the card of a chemist and an advertised sale of lepidopterae, which drove a famous millionaire out of the country. Near by are displayed the exploitation of a lure for black-bass, strangely perforated (a man's reason hung on those pin-pricks), and a scrawled legend which seems to spell "Mercy" (two men's lives were sacrificed to that); while below them, set in somber black, is the funeral notice of a dog worth a million dollars; facing the call for a trombone-player which made a mayor, and the mathematical formula which saved a governor. But nowhere does the observer find any record of one of the Ad-Visor's most curious cases, running back two thousand years; for its owner keeps it in his desk drawer, whence the present chronicler exhumed it, by accident, one day. Average Jones has always insisted that he scored a failure on this, because, through no possible fault of his own, he was unable to restore a document of the highest historical and literary importance. Of that, let the impartial reader judge.

It was while Average Jones was waiting for a break of that deadlock of events which, starting from the flat-dweller with the poisoned face, finally worked out the strange fate of Telfik Bey, that he sat, one morning, breakfasting late. The cool and breezy inner portico of the Cosmic Club, where small tables overlook a gracious fountain shimmering with the dart and poise of goldfish, was deserted save for himself, a summer-engagement star actor, a specialist in carbo-hydrates, and a famous adjuster of labor troubles; the four men being fairly typical of the club's catholicity of membership. Contrary to his impeccant habit, Average Jones bore the somewhat frazzled aspect of a man who has been up all night. Further indication of this inhered in the wide yawn, of which he was in mid-enjoyment, when a hand on his shoulder cut short his ecstasy.

"Sorry to interrupt so valuable an exercise," said a languid voice. "But—" and the voice stopped.

"Hello, Bert," returned the Ad-Visor, looking up at the faultlessly clad slenderness of his occasional coadjutor, Robert Bertram. "Sit down and keep me awake till the human snail who's hypothetically ministering to my wants can get me some coffee."

"What particular phase of intellectual debauchery have you been up to now?" inquired Bertram, lounging into the chair opposite.

"Trying to forget my troubles by chasing up a promising lead which failed to pan, out. 'Wanted: a Tin Nose,' sounds pretty good, eh?"

"It is music to my untutored ear," answered Bertram.

"But it turned out to be merely an error of the imbecile, or perhaps facetious printer, who sets up the *Trumpeter's* personal column. It should have read, 'Wanted—a Tea Rose.'"

"Even that seems far from commonplace."

"Only a code summons for a meeting of the Rosicrucians. I suppose you know that the order has been revived here in America."

"Not the true Rosicrucians, surely!" said Bertram.

"They pretend to be. A stupid lot who make child's play of it," said Average Jones impatiently. "Never mind them. I'd rather know what's on your mind. You made an observation when you came in, rather more interesting than your usual output of table-talk. You said 'but' and nothing further. The conjunction 'but,' in polite grammar, ordinarily has a comet-like tail to it."

"Apropos of polite grammar, do you speak Latin?" asked Bertram carelessly.

"Not enough to be gossipy in it."

"Then you wouldn't care to give a job to a man who can't speak anything else?"

"On that qualification alone?"

"No—o, not entirely. He is a good military engineer, I believe."

"So that's the other end of the 'but,' is it?" said Average Jones. "Go on. Elaborate."

Bertram laid before his friend a printed clipping in clear, large type, saying: "When I read this, I couldn't resist the notion that somehow or other it was in your line; pursuit of the adventure of life, and all that. Let's see what you make of it."

Average Jones straightened in his chair.

"Latin!" he said. "And an ad, by the look of it. Can our blind friend, J. Alden Honeywell, have taken to the public prints?"

"Hardly, I think. This is from the *Classical Weekly*, a Baltimore publication of small and select patronage."

"Hm. Looks ra—a—a—ather alluring," commented Average Jones with a prolonged drawl. "Better than the Rosicrucian fakery, anyhow."

He bent over the clipping, studying these words.

> *L. Livius M. F. Praenestinus, quodlibet in negotium non inhonestum qui victum meream locare velim. Litteratus sum; scriptum facere bene scio. Stipendia multa emeritus, scientiarum belli, praesertim muniendi, sum peritus. Hac de re pro me spondebit M. Agrippa. Latine tantum scio. Siquis me velit convenire, quovis die mane adesto in publicis hortis urbis Baltimorianae ad signum apri.*

"Can you make it out?" asked Bertram.

"Hm-m-m. Well—the general sense. Livius seems to yearn in modern print for any honest employment, but especially scrapping of the ancient variety or secretarying. Apply to Agrippa for references. Since he describes his conversation as being confined to Latin, I take it he won't find many jobs reaching out eagerly for him. Anybody who wants him can find him in the Park of the Wild Boar in Baltimore. That's about what I make of it. Now, what's his little lay, I wonder."

"Some lay of Ancient Rome, anyhow," suggested Bertram. "Association with Agrippa would put him back in the first century, B. C., wouldn't it? Besides, my informant tells me that Mr. Livius, who seems to have been an all-around sort of person, helped organize fire brigades for Crassus, and was one of the circle of minor poets who wrote rhapsodies to the fair but frail Clodia's eyebrows, ear-lobes and insteps."

"Your informant? The man's actually been seen, then?"

"Oh, Yes. He's on view as per advertisement, I understand."

Average Jones rose and stretched his well-knit frame. "Baltimore will be hotter than the Place-as-Isn't," he said plaintively. "Martyrdom by fire! However, I'm off by the five-o'clock train. I'll let you know if anything special comes of it, Bert."

Barye's splendid bronze boar couches, semi-shaded, in the center of Monument Park, Baltimore's social hill-top. There Average lounged and strolled through the longest hour of a glaring July morning. People came and went; people of all degrees and descriptions, none of whom suggested in any particular the first century, B. C. One individual only maintained any permanency of situation. He was a gaunt, powerful, freckled man of thirty who sprawled on a settee and regarded Average Jones with obvious and amused interest. In time this annoyed the Ad-Visor, who stopped short, facing the settee.

"He's gone," said the freckled man.

"Meaning Livius, the Roman?" asked Average Jones.

"Exactly. Lucius Livius, son of Marcus Praenestinus."

"Are you the representative of this rather peculiar person, may I ask?"

"It would be a dull world, except for peculiar persons," observed the man on the settee philosophically. "I've seen very many peculiar persons lately by the simple process of coming here day after day. No, I'm not Mr. Livius' representative. I'm only a town-bound and interested observer of his."

"There you've got the better of me," said Average Jones. "I was rather anxious to see him myself."

The other looked speculatively at the trim, keen-faced young man. "Yet you do not look like a Latin scholar," he observed; "if you'll pardon the comment."

"Nor do you," retorted Jones; "if the apology is returnable."

"I suppose not," owned the other with a sigh. "I've often thought that my classical capacity would gain more recognition if I didn't have a skin like Bob Fitzsimmons and hands like Ty Cobb. Nevertheless, I'm in and of the department of Latin of Johns Hopkins University. Name, Warren. Sit down."

"Thanks," said the other. "Name, Jones. Profession, advertising advisor. Object, curiosity."

"A. V. R. E. Jones; better known as Average Jones, I believe?"

"*Experto crede!* Being dog Latin for 'You seem to know all about it.'" The new-comer eyed his vis-à-vis. "Perhaps you—er—know Mr. Robert Bertram," he drawled.

"*Oculus*—the eye—*tauri*—of the bull. Bull's eye!" said the freckled one, with a grin. "I'd heard of your exploits through Bertram, and thought probably you'd follow the bait contained in my letter to him."

"Nothing wrong with your nerve-system, is there?" inquired Average Jones with mock anxiety. "Now that I'm here, where is L. Livius And-so-forth?"

"Elegantly but uncomfortably housed with Colonel Ridgway Graeme in his ancestral barrack on Carteret Street."

"Is this Colonel Graeme a friend of yours?"

"Friend and foe, tried and true. We meet twice a week, usually at his house, to squabble over his method of Latin pronunciation and his construction of the ablative case. He's got a theory of the ablative absolute," said Warren with a scowl, "fit to fetch Tacitus howling from the shades."

"A scholar, then?"

"A very fine and finished scholar, though a faddist of the rankest type. Speaks Latin as readily as he does English."

"Old?"

"Over seventy."

"Rich?"

"Not in money. Taxes on his big place keep him pinched; that and his passion for buying all kinds of old and rare books. He's got, perhaps an income of five thousand, clear, of which about three thousand goes in book auctions."

"Any family?"

"No. Lives with two ancient colored servants who look after him."

"How did our friend from B. C. connect up with him?"

"Oh, he ran to the old colonel like a chick to its hen. You see, there aren't so very many Latinists in town during the hot weather. Perhaps eighteen or twenty in all came from about here and from Washington to see the prodigy in 'the Park of the Boar,' after the advertisement appeared. He wouldn't have anything to do with any of us. Pretended he didn't understand our kind of Latin. I offered him a place, myself, at a wage of more *denarii* than I could well afford. I wanted a chance to study him. Then came the colonel and fairy grabbed him. So I sent for you—in my artless professional way."

"Why such enthusiasm on the part of Colonel Graeme?"

"Simple enough. Livius spoke Latin with in accent which bore out the old boy's contention. I believe they also agreed on the ablative absolute."

"Yes—er—naturally," drawled Average Jones. "Does our early Roman speak pretty ready Latin?"

"He's fairly fluent. Sometimes he stumbles a little on his constructions, and he's apt to be—well—monkish—rather than classical when in full course."

"Doesn't wear the *toga virilis*, I suppose."

"Oh, no. Plain American clothes. It's only his inner man that's Roman, of course. He met with a bump on the head—this is his story, and he's got a the scar to show for it—and when he came to, he'd lost ground a couple of thousand years and returned to his former existence. No English. No memory of who or what he'd been. No money connection whatsoever with the living world."

"Humph! Wonder if he's been a student of Kipling. You remember 'The Greatest Story in the World; the reincarnated galley slave?' Now as to this Colonel Graeme; has he ever published?"

"Yes. Two small pamphlets, issued by the Classicist Press, which publishes the *Classical Weekly*."

"Supporting his fads, I suppose."

"Right. He devoted one pamphlet to each."

Average Jones contemplated with absorbed attention an ant which was making a laborious spiral ascent of his cane. Not until it had gained a vantage point on the bone handle did he speak again.

"See here, Professor Warren: I'm a passionate devotee of the Latin tongue. I have my deep and dark suspicions of our present modes of pronunciation, all three of 'em. As for the ablative absolute, its reconstruction and regeneration have been the inspiring principle of my studious manhood. Humbly I have sat at the feet of Learning, enshrined in the Ridgway Graeme pamphlets. I must meet Colonel Graeme—after reading the pamphlets. I hope they're not long."

Warren frowned. "Colonel Graeme is a gentleman and my friend, Mr. Jones," he said with emphasis. "I won't have him made a butt."

"He shan't be, by me," said Average Jones quietly. "Has it perhaps struck you, as his friend, that—er—a close daily association with the psychic remnant of a Roman citizen might conceivably be non-conducive to his best interest?"

"Yes, it has. I see your point. You want to approach him on his weak side. But, have you Latin enough to sustain the part? He's shrewd as a weasel in all matters of scholarship, though a child whom any one could fool in practical affairs."

"No; I haven't," admitted Average Jones. "Therefore, I'm a mute. A shock in early childhood paralyzed my centers of speech. I talk to you by sign language, and you interpret."

"But I hardly know the deaf-mute alphabet."

"Nor I. But I'll waggle my fingers like lightning if he says anything to me requiring an answer, and you'll give the proper reply. Does Colonel Graeme implicitly credit the Romanism of his guest?"

"He does, because he wants to. To have an educated man of the classic period of the Latin tongue, a friend of Caesar, an auditor of Cicero and a contemporary of Virgil, Horace and Ovid come back and speak in the accent he's contended for, make a powerful support for his theories. He's at work on a supplementary thesis already."

"What do the other Latin men who've seen Livius, think of the metempsychosis claim?"

"They don't know. Livius explained his remote antecedents only after he had got Colonel Graeme's private ear. The colonel has kept it quiet. 'Don't want a rabble of psychologists and soul-pokers worrying him to death,' he says."

"Making it pretty plain sailing for the Roman. Well, arrange to take me there as soon as possible."

At the Graeme house, Average Jones was received with simple courtesy by a thin rosy-cheeked old gentleman with a dagger-like imperial and a dreamy eye, who, on Warren's introduction, made him free of the unkempt old place's hospitality. They conversed for a time, Average Jones maintaining his end with nods and gestures, and (ostensibly) through the digital mediumship of his sponsor.

Presently Warren said to the host:

"And where is your visitor from the past?"

"Prowling among my books," answered the old gentleman.

"Are we not going to see him?"

The colonel looked a little embarrassed. "The fact is, Professor Warren, Livius has taken rather an aversion to you."

"I'm sorry. How so?"

A twinkle of malice shone in the old scholar's eye. "He says your Latin accent frets his nerves," he explained.

"In that case," said Warren, obeying a quick signal from his accomplice, "I'll stroll in the garden, while you present Mr. Jones to Livius."

Colonel Graeme led the way to a lofty wing, once used as a drawing-room, but now the repository for thousands of books, which not only filled the shelves but were heaped up in every corner.

"I must apologize for this confusion, sir," said the host. "No one is permitted to arrange my books but myself. And my efforts, I fear, serve only to make confusion more confounded. There are four other rooms even more chaotic than this."

At the sound of his voice a man who had been seated behind a tumulus of volumes rose and stood. Average Jones looked at him keenly. He was perhaps forty-five years of age, thin and sinewy, with a close-shaven face, pale blue eyes, and a narrow forehead running high into a mop of grizzled locks. Diagonally across the front part of the scalp a scar could be dimly perceived through the hair. Average Jones glanced at the stranger's hands, to gain, if possible, some hint of his former employment. With his faculty of swift observation, he noticed that the long, slender fingers were not only mottled with dust, but also scuffed, and, in places, scarified, as if their owner had been hurriedly handling a great number of books.

Colonel Graeme presented the new-comer in formal Latin. He bowed. The scarred man made a curious gesture of the hand, addressing Average Jones in an accent which, even to the young man's long-unaccustomed ears, sounded strange and strained.

"*Di illi linguam astrinxere; mutus est*," said Colonel Graeme, indicating the younger man, and added a sentence in sonorous metrical Greek.

Average Jones recalled the Æschylean line. "Well, though 'a great ox hath stepped on my tongue,' it hasn't trodden out my eyes, praises be!" said he to himself as he caught the uneasy glance of the Roman.

By way of allaying suspicion, he scribbled upon a sheet of paper a few complimentary Latin sentences, in which Warren had sedulously coached him for the occasion, and withdrew to the front room, where he was presently joined by the Johns Hopkins man. Fortunately, the colonel gave them a few moments together.

"Arrange for me to come here daily to study in the library," whispered Jones to the Latin professor.

The other nodded.

"Now, sit tight," added Jones.

He stepped, soft-footed, on the thick old rug, across to the library door and threw it open. Just inside stood Livius, an expression of startled anger on his thin face. Quickly recovering himself, he explained, in his ready Latin, that he was about to enter and speak to his patron.

"Shows a remarkable interest in possible conversation," whispered Jones, on his withdrawal, "for a man who understands no English. Also does me the honor to suspect me. He must have been a wily chap—in the Consulship of Plancus."

Before leaving, Average Jones had received from Colonel Graeme a general invitation to spend as much time as he chose, studying among the books. The old man-servant, Saul, had orders to admit him at any hour. He returned to his hotel to write a courteous note of acknowledgment.

Many hours has Average Jones spent more tediously than those passed in the cool seclusion of Colonel Ridgway Graeme's treasure-house of print. He burrowed among quaint accumulations of forgotten classics. He dipped with astonishment into the savage and ultra-Rabelaisian satire of Von Hutter's *Epistolae Obscurorum Virorum*," which set early sixteenth century Europe a-roar with laughter at the discomfited monks; and he cleansed himself from that tainted atmosphere in the fresh air and free English of a splendid Audubon "first"—and all the time he was conscious that the Roman watched, watched, watched. More than once Livius offered aid, seeking to apprise himself of the supposed mute's line of investigation; but the other smilingly fended him off. At the end of four days, Average Jones had satisfied himself that if Livius were seeking anything in particular, he had an indefinite task before him, for the colonel's bound treasures were in indescribable confusion. Apparently he had bought from far and near, without definite theme or purpose. As he bought he read, and having read, cast aside; and where a volume fell, there it had license to lie. No cataloguer had ever sought to restore order to that bibliographic riot. To seek any given book meant a blind voyage, without compass or chart, throughout the mingled centuries.

Often Colonel Graeme spent hours in one or the other of the huge book-rooms talking with his strange protégé and making copious notes. Usually the old gentleman questioned and the other answered. But one morning the attitude seemed, to the listening Ad-Visor, to be reversed. Livius, in the far corner of the room, was speaking in a low tone. To judge from the older man's impatient manner the Roman was interrupting his host's current of queries with interrogations of his own. Average Jones made a mental note, and, in conference with Warren that evening, asked him to ascertain from Colonel Graeme whether Livius's inquiries had indicated a specific interest in any particular line of reading.

On the following day, however, an event of more immediate import occupied his mind. He had spent the morning in the upstairs library, at the unevadable suggestion of Colonel Graeme, while the colonel and his Roman collogued below. Coming down about noon, Average Jones entered the colonel's small study just in time to see Livius, who was alone in the room, turn away sharply from the desk. His elbow was held close to his ribs in a peculiar manner. He was concealing something under his coat. With a pretense of clumsiness, Average Jones stumbled against him in passing. Livius drew away, his high forehead working with suspicion. The Ad-Visor's expression of blank apology, eked out with a bow and a grimace, belied the busy-working mind within. For, in the moment's contact, he had heard the crisp rustle of paper from beneath the ill-fitting coat.

What paper had the man from B. C. taken furtively from his benefactor's table? It must be large; otherwise he could have readily thrust it into his pocket. No sooner was Livius out of the room than Average Jones scanned the desk. His face lighted with a sudden smile. Colonel Graeme never read a newspaper; boasted, in fact, that he wouldn't have one about the place. But, as Average Jones distinctly recalled, he had, himself, that very morning brought in a copy of the *Globe* and dropped it into the scrap basket near the writing-table. It was gone. Livius had taken it.

"If he's got the newspaper-reading habit," said Average Jones to himself, "I'll set a trap for him. But Warren must furnish the bait."

He went to look up his aide. The conference between them was long and exhaustive, covering the main points of the case from the beginning.

"Did you find out from Colonel Graeme," inquired Average Jones, "whether Livius affected any particular brand of literature?"

"Yes. He seems to be specializing on late seventeenth century British classicism. Apparently he considers that the flower of British scholarship of that time wrote a very inferior kind of dog-Latin."

"Late seventeenth century Latinity," commented Average Jones. "That—er—gives, us a fair start. Now as to the body-servant."

"Old Saul? I questioned him about strange callers. He said he remembered only two, besides an occasional peddler or agent. They were looking for work."

"What kind of work?"

"Inside the house. One wanted to catalogue the library."

"What did he look like?"

"Saul says he wore glasses and a worse tall hat than the colonel's and had a full beard."

"And the other?"

"Bookbinder and repairer. Wanted to fix up Colonel Graeme's collection. Youngish, smartly dressed, with a small waxed moustache."

"And our Livius is clean-shaven," murmured Average Jones. "How long apart did they call?"

"About two weeks. The second applicant came on the day of the last snowfall. I looked that up. It was March 27."

"Do you know, Warren," observed Average Jones, "I sometimes think that part of your talents, at least, are wasted in a chair of Latin."

"Certainly, there is more excitement in this hide-and-seek game, as you play it, than in the pursuits of a musty pedant," admitted the other, crackling his large knuckles. "But when are we going to spring upon friend Livius and strip him of his fake toga?"

"That's the easiest part of it. I've already caught him filling a fountain-pen as if he'd been brought up on them, and humming the spinning chorus from *The Flying Dutchman*; not to mention the lifting of my newspaper."

"*Nemo mortalium omnibus horis sapit*," murmured Warren.

"No. As you say, no fellow can be on the job all the time. But our problem is not to catch Livius, but to find out what it is he's been after for the last three months."

"Three months? You're assuming that it was he who applied for work in the library."

"Certainly. And when he failed at that he set about a very carefully developed scheme to get at Colonel Graeme's books anyway. By inquiries he found out the old gentleman's fad and proceeded to get in training for it. You don't know, perhaps, that I have a corps of assistants who clip, catalogue and file all unusual advertisements. Here is one which they turned up for me on my order to send me any queer educational advertisements: 'Wanted—Daily lessons in Latin speech from competent Spanish scholar. Write, Box 347, *Banner* office.' That is from the New York *Banner* of April third, shortly after the strange caller's second abortive attempt to get into the Graeme library."

"I suppose our Livius figured out that Colonel Graeme's theory of accent was about what a Spaniard would have. But he couldn't have learned all his Latin in four months."

"He didn't. He was a scholar already; an accomplished one, who went wrong through drink and became a crook, specializing in rare books and prints. His name is Enderby; you'll find it in the Harvard catalogue. He's supposed to be dead. My assistant traced him through his Spanish-Latin teacher, a priest."

"But even allowing for his scholarship, he must have put in a deal of work perfecting himself in readiness of speech and accent."

"So he did. Therefore the prize must be big. A man of Enderby's caliber doesn't concoct a scheme of such ingenuity, and go into bondage with it, for nothing. Do you belong to the Cosmic Club?"

The assistant professor stared. "No," he said.

"I'd like to put you up there. One advantage of membership is that its roster includes experts in every known line of erudition, from scarabs to skeeing. For example, I am now going to telegraph for aid from old Millington, who seldom misses a book auction and is a human bibliography of the wanderings of all rare volumes. I'm going to find out from him what British publication of the late seventeenth century in Latin is very valuable; also what volumes of that time have changed hands in the last six months."

"Colonel Graeme went to a big book auction in New York early in March," volunteered Warren, "but he told me he didn't pick up anything of particular value."

"Then it's something he doesn't know about and Livius does. I'm going to take advantage of our Roman's rather un-B.-C.-like habit of reading the daily papers by trying him out with this advertisement."

Average Jones wrote rapidly and tossed the result to his coadjutor who read:

"LOST—Old book printed in Latin. Buff leather binding, a little faded ('It's safe to be that,' explained Average Jones). No great value except to owner. Return to Colonel Ridgway Graeme, 11 Carteret Street, and receive reward."

The advertisement made its appearance in big type on the front pages of the Baltimore paper of the following day. That evening Average Jones met Warren, for dinner, with a puckered brow.

"Did Livius rise to the bait?" asked the scholar.

"Did he!" chuckled Average Jones. "He's been nervous as a cat all day and hardly has looked at the library. But what puzzles me is this." He exhibited a telegram from New York.

> "Millington says positively no book of that time and description any great value. Enderby at Barclay auction in March and made row over some book which he missed because it was put up out of turn in catalogue. Barclay auctioneer thinks it was one of Percival privately bound books 1680-1703. Am anonymous book of Percival library, *De Meritis Librorum Britannorum*, was sold to Colonel Graeme for $47, a good price. When do I get in on this?
>
> "(Signed), Robert Bertram."

"I know that treatise," said Warren. "It isn't particularly rare."

Average Jones stared at the telegram in silence. Finally he drawled: "There are—er—books and—er—books—and—er—things in books. Wait here for me."

Three hours later he reappeared with collar wilted, but spirits elate, and abruptly announced:

"Warren, I'm a cobbler."

"A what?"

"A cobbler. Mend your boots, you know."

"Are you in earnest?"

"Certainly. Haven't you ever remarked that a serious-minded earnestness always goes with cobbling? Though I'm not really a practical cobbler, but a proprietary one. Our friend, Bertram, will dress and act the practical part. I've wired him and he's replied, collect, accepting the job. You and I will be in the background."

"Where?"

"No. 27 Jasmine Street. Not a very savory locality. Why is it, Warren, that the beauty of a city street is generally in inverse ratio to the poetic quality of its name? There I've hired the shop and stock of Mr. Hans Fichtel for two days, at the handsome rental of ten dollars per day. Mr. Fichtel purposes to take a keg of beer a-fishing. I think two days will be enough."

"For the keg?"

"For that noble Roman, Livius. He'll be reading the papers pretty keenly now. And in to-morrow's, he'll find this advertisement."

Average Jones read from a sheet of paper which he took from his pocket:

"FOUND—Old book in foreign language, probably Latin, marked 'Percival.' Owner may recover by giving satisfactory description of peculiar and obscure feature and refunding for advertisement. Fichtel, 27 Jasmine Street."

"What is the peculiar and obscure feature, Jones?" asked Warren.

"I don't know."

"How do you know there is any?"

"Must be something peculiar about the book or Enderby wouldn't put in four months of work on the chance of stealing it. And it must be obscure, otherwise the auctioneer would have spotted it."

"Sound enough!" approved the other. "What could it be? Some interpolated page?"

"Hardly. I've a treatise in my pocket on seventeenth century book-making, which I'm going to study to-night. Be ready for an early start to meet Bertram."

That languid and elegant gentleman arrived by the first morning train. He protested mightily when he was led to the humble shoe-shop. He protested more mightily when invited to don a leather apron and smudge his face appropriately to his trade. His protests, waxing vehement and eventually profane, as he barked his daintily-kept fingers, in rehearsal for giving a correct representation of an honest artisan cobbling a boot, died away when Average Jones explained to him that on pretense of having found a rare book, he was to worm out of a cautious and probably suspicious criminal the nature of some unique and hidden feature of the volume.

"Trust me for diplomacy," said Bertram airily.

"I will because I've got to," retorted Average Jones. "Well, get to work. To you the outer shop: to Warren and me this rear room. And, remember, if you hear me whetting a knife, that means come at once."

Uncomfortably twisted into a supposedly professional posture, Bertram wrought with hammer and last, while putting off, with lame, blind and halting, excuses, such as came to call for their promised footgear. By a triumph of tact he had just disposed of a rancid-tongued female who demanded her husband's boots, a satisfactory explanation, or the arbitrament of the lists, when the bell tinkled and the two watchers in the back room heard a nervous, cultivated voice say:

"Is Mr. Fichtel here?"

"That's me," said Bertram, landing an agonizing blow on his thumb-nail.

"You advertised that you had found an old book."

"Yes, sir. Somebody left it in the post-office."

"Ah; that must have been when I went to mail some letters to New York," said the other glibly. "From the advertised description, the book is without doubt mine. Now as to the reward—"

"Excuse me, but you wouldn't expect me to give it up without any identification, sir?"

"Certainly not. It was the *De Meritis Libror*—"

"I can't read Latin, sir."

"But you could make that much out," said the visitor with rising exasperation. "Come; if it's a matter of the reward—how much?"

"I wouldn't mind having a good reward; say ten dollars. But I want to be sure it's your book. There's something about it that you could easily tell me sir, for any one could see it."

"A very observing shoemaker," commented the other with a slight sneer. "You mean the—the half split cover?"

"Swish-swish; whish-swish," sounded from the rear room.

"Excuse me," said Bertram, who had not ceased from his pretended work. "I have to get a piece of leather."

He stepped into the back room where Average Jones, his face alight, held up a piece of paper upon which he had hurriedly scrawled:

"Mss. bound into cover. Get it out of him. Tell him you've a brother who is a Latin scholar."

Bertram nodded, caught up a strip of calf-skin and returned.

"Yes, sir," he said, "the split cover and what's inside?"

The other started. "You didn't get it out?" he cried. "You didn't tear it!"

"No, sir. It's there safe enough. But some of it can be made out."

"You said you didn't read Latin."

"No, sir; but I have a brother that went through the Academy. He reads a little." This was thin ice, but Bertram went forward with assumed assurance. "He thinks the manuscript is quite rare. Oh, Fritz! Come in."

"Any letter of Bacon's is rare, of course," returned the other impatiently. "Therefore, I purpose offering you fifty dollars reward."

He looked up as Average Jones entered. The young man's sleeves were rolled up, his face was generously smudged, and a strip of cobbler's wax beneath the tipper lip, puffed and distorted the firm line of his mouth. Further, his head was louting low on his neck, so that the visitor got no view sufficient for recognition.

"Lord Bacon's letter—er—must be pretty rare, Mister," he drawled thickly. "But a letter—er—from Lord Bacon—er—about Shakespeare—*that* ought to be worth a lot of money."

Average Jones had taken his opening with his customary incisive shrewdness. The mention of Bacon had settled it, to his mind. Only one imaginable character of manuscript from the philosopher scholar-politician could have value enough to tempt a thief of Enderby's calibre. Enderby's expression told that the shot was a true one. As for Bertram, he had dropped his shoemaker's knife and his shoemaker's role.

"Bacon on Shakespeare! Shades of the departed glory of Ignatius Donnelly!"

The visitor drew back. Warren's gaunt frame appeared in the doorway. Jones' head lifted.

"It ought to be as—er—unique," he drawled, "as an—er—Ancient Roman speaking perfect English."

Like a flash, the false Livius caught up the knife from the bench where the false cobbler had dropped it and swung toward Average Jones. At the moment the ample hand of Professor Warren, bunched into a highly competent fist, flicked across and caught the assailant under the ear. Enderby, alias Livius, fell as if smitten by a cestus. As his arm touched the floor, Average Jones kicked unerringly at the wrist and the knife flew and tinkled in a far corner. Bertram, with a bound, landed on the fallen man's chest and pinned him.

"Did he get you, Average?" he cried.

"Not—er—this time. Pretty good—er—team work," drawled the Ad-Visor. "We've got our man for felonious assault, at least."

Enderby, panting under Bertram's solid knee, blinked and struggled.

"No use, Livius," said Average Jones. "Might as well quiet down and confess. Ease up a little on him, Bert. Take a look at that scar of his first though."

"Superficial cut treated with make-up paint; a clever job," pronounced Bertram after a quick examination.

"As I supposed," said Average Jones.

"Let me in on the deal," pleaded Livius. "That letter is worth ten thousand, twelve thousand, fifteen thousand dollars—anything you want to ask, if you find the right purchaser. And you can't manage it without me. Let me in."

"Thinks we're crooks, too?" remarked Average Jones. "Exactly what's in this wonderful letter?"

"It's from Bacon to the author of the book, who wrote about 1610. Bacon prophesies that Shakespeare, 'this vagabond and humble mummer' would outshine and outlive in fame all the genius of his time. That's all I could make out by loosening the stitches."

"Well, that *is* worth anything one could demand," said Warren in a somewhat awed tone.

"Why didn't you get the letter when you were examining it at the auction room?" inquired Average Jones.

"Some fool of a binder had overlooked the double cover, and sewed it in. I noticed it at the auction, gummed the opening together while no one was watching, and had gone to get cash to buy the book; but the auctioneer put it up out of turn and old Graeme got it. Bring it to me and I'll show you the 'pursed' cover. Many of the Percival books were bound that way."

"We've never had it, nor seen it," replied Average Jones. "The advertisement was only a trap into which you stepped."

Enderby's jaw dropped. "Then it's still at the Graeme house," he cried, beating on the floor with his free hand. "Take me back there!"

"Oh, we'll take you," said Warren grimly.

Close-packed among them in a cab, they drove him back to Carteret Street. Colonel Ridgway Graeme was at home and greeted them courteously.

"You've found Livius," he said, with relief. "I had begun to fear for him."

"Colonel Graeme," began Average Jones, "you have—"

"What! Speech!" cried the old gentleman. "And you a mute! What does this mean?"

"Never mind him," broke in Enderby Livius. "There's something more important."

But the colonel had shrunk back. "English from you, Livius!" he cried, setting his hand to his brow.

"All will be explained in time, Colonel," Warren assured him. "Meanwhile, you have a document of the utmost importance and value. Do you remember buying one of the Percival volumes at the Barclay auction?"

The collector drew his brows down in an effort to remember.

"An octavo, in fairly good condition?" he asked.

"Yes, yes!" cried Enderby eagerly. "Where is it? What did you do with it?"

"It was in Latin—very false Latin." The four men leaned forward, breathless. "Oh, I remember. It slipped from my pocket and fell into the river as I was crossing the ferry to Jersey."

There was a dead, flat, stricken silence. Then Average Jones turned hollow eyes upon Warren.

"Professor," he said, with a rueful attempt at a smile, "what's the past participle, passive, plural, of the Latin verb, 'to sting'?"

THE ONE BEST BET

"Morrison has jammed the Personal Liberty bill through," said Waldemar, scrawling a head on his completed editorial, with one eye on the clock, which pointed to midnight.

"That was to be expected, wasn't it?" asked Average Jones.

"Oh, yes," replied the editor-owner of the *Universal* in his heavy bass. "And now the governor announces he will veto it."

"Thereby bringing the whole power of the gambling ring down on him like an avalanche."

"Naturally. Morrison has declared open war against 'Pharisee Phil,' as he calls Governor Arthur. Says he'll pass the bill over his veto. In his heart he knows he can't do it. Still, he's a hard fighter."

Average Jones tipped his chair back against the wall of the editorial sanctum. "What do you suppose," he inquired with an air of philosophic speculation, "that the devil will do with Carroll Morrison's soul when he gets it? Deodorize it?"

"Harsh words, young sir! Harsh words and treasonable against one of our leading citizens; multimillionaire philanthropist, social leader, director of banks, insurance companies and railroads, and emperor of the race-track, the sport of kings."

"The sport of kings—maintained on the spoils of clerks," retorted Average Jones. "'To improve the breed of horses,' if you please! To make thieves of men and harlots of women, because Carroll Morrison must have his gambling-game dividends! And now he has our 'representative' legislature working for him to that honorable end!"

"Man to see you, Mr. Waldemar," said an office boy, appearing at the door.

"Too late," grunted the editor.

"He says it's very particular, sir, and to tell you it's something Mr. Morrison is interested in."

"Morrison, eh? All right. Just step into the inner office, will you, Jones? Leave the door open. There might be something interesting."

Hardly had Average Jones found a chair in the darkened office when the late caller appeared. He was middle-aged, pursy, and dressed with slap-dash ostentation. His face was bloated and seared with excesses. But it was not intoxication that sweated on his forehead and quivered in his jaw. It was terror. He slumped into the waiting chair and mouthed mutely at the editor.

"Well?" The bullet-like snap of the interrogation stung the man into babbling speech.

"'S like this, Misser Wald'mar. 'S like this. Y—y—yuh see, 's like this. Fer Gawsake, kill out an ad for me!"

"What? In to-morrow's paper? Nonsense! You're too late, even if I wished to do it."

The visitor stood up and dug both hands into his side pockets. He produced, first a binocular, which, with a snarl, he flung upon the floor. Before it had stopped bumping, there fluttered down upon the seat of his chair a handful of greenbacks. Another followed, and another, and another. The bills toppled and spread, and some of them slid to the floor. Still the man delved.

"There!" he panted at last. "Money talks. There's the stuff. Count it. Eighteen hundred if there's a dollar. More likely two thou. If that ain't enough, make your own price. I don't care what it is. Make it, Misser. Put a price on it."

There was something loathsome and obscene in the creature's gibbering flux of words. The editor leaned forward.

"Bribery, eh?" he inquired softly.

The man flinched from the tone. "It ain't bribery, is it, to ast you to rout out jus' one line from an ad an' pay you for the trouble.

My own ad, too. If it runs, it's my finish. I was nutty when I wrote it. Fer Gawsake, Misser—"

"Stop it! You say Morrison sent you here?"

"No, sir. Not exac'ly. 'S like this, M' Wald'mar. I hadda get to you some way. It's important to Misser Morrison, too. But he don't know I come. He don't know nothing about it. Oh, Gaw! If he finds out—"

"Put that money back in your pockets."

With an ashen face of despair, the man obeyed. As he finished, he began to sag at the joints. Slowly he slackened down until he was on his knees, an abject spectacle of disgust.

"Stand up," ordered Waldemar.

"Liss'n; liss'n t' me," moaned the man. "I'll make it three thousand. Fi' thou—"

"Stand *up!*"

The editor's hearty grip on his coat collar heaved the creature to his feet. For a moment he struggled, panting, then spun, helpless and headlong from the room, striking heavily against the passage wall outside. There was a half-choked groan; then his footsteps slumped away into silence.

"Ugh!" grunted Waldemar. "Come back, Jones."

Average Jones reentered. "Have you no curiosity in your composition?" he asked.

"Not much—having been reared in the newspaper business."

Stooping, Average Jones picked up the glasses which the man had thrown on the floor and examined them carefully. "Rather a fine instrument," he observed. "Marked N. K. I think I'll follow up the owner."

"You'll never find him now. He has too much start."

"Not at all. When a man is in his state of abject funk, it's ten to one he lands at the nearest bar. Wait for me."

In fifteen minutes Average Jones was back. There was a curious expression on his face as he nodded an assent to his friend's inquiring eyebrows.

"Where?" asked Waldemar.

"On the floor of a Park Row saloon."

"Dead drunk, eh?"

"No—er; not—er—drunk. Dead."

Waldemar stiffened in his chair. "Dead!" he repeated.

"Poison, probably. The ad was his finish, as he said. The next thing is to find it."

"The first edition will be down any minute now. But it'll take some finding. Why, counting 'classified,' we're carrying fifteen hundred ads in every issue. With no clue to the character of this one—"

"Plenty of clue," said Average Jones suavely. "You'll find it on the sporting page, I think."

"Judging from the man's appearance? Rather far-fetched, isn't it?"

"Judging from a pair of very fine binoculars, a mention of Carroll Morrison's name, and, principally, some two thousand dollars in a huge heap."

"I don't quite see where that leads."

"No? The bills must have been mostly ones and twos. Those are a book-maker's takings. The binocular is a racing-man's glass. Our late friend used the language of the track. I think we'll find him on page nine."

"Try," said Waldemar, handing him a paper still spicy with the keen odor of printer's ink.

Swiftly the Ad-Visor's practiced eye ran over the column. It checked at the "offer" of a notorious firm of tipsters who advertised to sell "inside information" on the races to their patrons. As a special lure, they were, on this day, letting the public in on a few particularly "good things" free.

"There you are," said Average Jones, pointing out the advertisement.

To his astonishment, Waldemar noted that his friend's indicatory finger shook a little. Normally, Average Jones was the coolest and most controlled of men.

"Noble and Gale's form ad," he observed. "I see nothing unusual in that."

"Yet—er—I fancy it's quite important—er—in its way."

The editor stared. "When you talk like a bored Britisher, Average," he remarked, "there's sure to be something in the air. What is it?"

"Look at the last line."

Again Waldemar turned to the paper. "'One Best Bet,'" he read. "'That the Pharisee will never finish.' Well?"

"That the Pharisee will never finish," repeated Average Jones. "If the Pharisee is a horse, the line becomes absurd at once. How could any one know that a horse would fail to finish in a race? But if it—er—referred—er—to a man, an official known—er—as Pharisee Phil—"

"Wait!" Waldemar had jumped to his feet. A thrill, increasing and pulsating through the floor beneath them, shook the building. The editor jumped for the telephone.

"Composing room; quick! Give me the foreman. Hello! That you, Corrigan? Stop the presses. . . . I don't care if we miss every train in the country. . . . Don't answer back. This is Mr. Waldemar. Stop the presses!"

The thrill waned and ceased. At the telephone, Waldemar continued: "Look up the Noble and Gale tip ad, page nine, column six. Kill the last line, the One Best Bet... Don't ask *me* how. Chisel it out. Burn it out. Dynamite it out. But kill it. After that's done, print . . . . Hello; Dan? Send the sporting editor in here in a hurry."

"Good work," said Average Jones. "They'll never know how near their idea of removing Governor Arthur came to being boasted of in plain print."

Waldemar took his huge head in his hands and rocked it gently. "It's on," he said. "And right-side-before. Yet, it tries to tell me that a man, plotting to murder the governor, advertises the fact in my paper! I'll get a new head."

"Keep that one for a while," advised Average Jones. "It may be better than you think. Anyway, here's the ad. And down yonder is the dead man whom it killed when he failed to kill it. So much is real."

"And here's Bendig," said the other, as the sporting editor entered. "Any such horse as 'The Pharisee,' Bendig?"

"No, sir. I suppose you mean that Noble and Gale ad. I saw it in proof. Some of Nick Karboe's funny work, I expect."

"Nick Karboe; N. K.," murmured Average Jones, laying a hand on the abandoned field glass. "Who is this man Karboe, Mr. Bendig?"

"Junior partner of Noble and Gale. He puts out their advertising."

"Any connection whatever with Mr. Carroll Morrison?"

"Why, yes. Before he went to pieces he used to be Mr. Morrison's confidential man, and lately he's been doing some lobbying for the association. I understood he'd quit it again."

"Quit what?" asked Waldemar. "Drink?"

"Worse. The white stuff. Coke."

Average Jones whistled softly. "That explains it all," he said. "A cocaine fiend on a debauch becomes a mental and moral imbecile. It would be perfectly in character that he should boast of a projected crime."

"Very well," said Waldemar, after the sporting editor had left, "but you don't really connect Morrison with this?"

"Don't I! At least I propose to try. See here, Waldemar; two months ago at a private dinner, Morrison made a speech in which he said that men who interfered with the rights of property, like Governor Arthur, were no better than anarchists and ought to be handled accordingly. Therefore, I don't think that a plan—a safe one, of course—to put 'Pharisee Phil' away would greatly disturb our friend's distorted conscience. You see, the governor has laid impious hands on Morrison's holy of holies, the dividend. By the way, where is Governor Arthur?"

"On the train for this city. He's to review the parade at the Harrisonia Centennial, and unveil the statute to-morrow night; that is, to-night, to be accurate."

"A good opportunity," murmured Average Jones.

"What! In the sight of a hundred thousand people?"

"That might be the very core of the opportunity. And at night."

"If you feel certain, it's a case for the police, isn't it?"

"Hardly! The gambling gang control the police, wholly. They would destroy the trail at once."

"Then why not warn the governor?"

"I don't know him."

"Suppose I make an appointment to take you to see him in the morning?"

This was agreed upon. At ten o'clock Governor Arthur received them at his hotel, greeting Average Jones with flattering warmth.

"You're the amateur detective who scared the Honorable William Linder out of the mayoralty nomination," said he, shaking hands. "What are you going to do to me?"

"Give you some racing news to read, Governor."

The governor took the advertisement proof and read it carefully. Characteristically, he then re-read it throughout.

"You think this is meant for me?" he asked, handing it back.

"I do. You're not exactly what one would call popular with the racing crowd, you know, Governor."

"Mr. Morrison, in the politest manner in the world, has allowed me to surmise as much," said the other, smiling broadly. "A very polished person, Mr. Morrison. He can make threats of extinction—political, of course—more delicately than any other subtle blackmailer I have ever met. And I have met several in my time."

"If this were merely political extinction, which I fancy you can take care of yourself, I shouldn't be taking up your time, sir."

"My dear Jones—" a friendly hand fell on the visitor's shoulder— "I gravely fear that you lack the judicial mind. It's a great thing to lack—at times." Governor Arthur's eyes twinkled again, and his visitor wondered whence had come his reputation as a dry, unhumorous man. "As to assassination," he pursued, "I'm a sort of Christian Scientist. The best protection is a profound conviction that you're safe. That reacts on the mind of any would-be assassin. To my mind, my best chance of safety lies in never thinking of danger."

"Then," said Waldemar, "any attempt to persuade you against appearing at Harrisonia to-night would be time wasted."

"Absolutely, my dear Waldemar. But don't think that I'm not appreciative of your thoughtfulness and that of Mr. Jones."

"What is the program of the day, Governor?" asked Average Jones.

"Rather a theatrical one. I'm to ride along Harrison Avenue to the reviewing stand, in the old coach-of-state of the Harrison family, a lofty old ark, high as a circus wagon, which has been patched up for the occasion. Just before I reach the reviewing stand, a silk cord is to be handed to me and I am to pull the veil from the great civic statue with that, as, I move on."

"Then I think that Mr. Waldemar and I will look the ground over. Could we get you by telephone, sir, if necessary?"

"Any time up to seven o'clock."

"What do you think of the chance of their passing the bill over your veto?" asked Waldemar.

"They are spending money as it has never been spent before," replied Governor Arthur. "I'll admit to you, Waldemar, that if I could find any legitimate method of calling Morrison off, I would not scruple to use it. It is, of course, Morrison's money that we are fighting."

"Possibly—er—that, too—er—might be done," drawled Average Jones.

The governor looked at him sharply. "After the Linder affair, Mr. Jones," said he, "I would follow you far. Call my secretary at any time, if you want me."

"Now to look over the line of parade," said Average Jones as he and Waldemar emerged from the hotel.

Half an hour's ride brought them to the lively suburban city of Harrisonia, gay with flags and bunting. From the railroad station, where the guest of honor was to be met by the old coach, to the spot where the civic statue awaited its unveiling at his hands, was about half a mile along Harrison Avenue, the principal street. The walk along this street developed nothing of interest to Average Jones until they reached the statue. Here he paused to look curiously at a number of square platforms built out from windows in the business blocks.

"For flash-light outfits," explained Waldemar. "One of them is our paper's."

"Flash-lights, eh?" said Average Jones. "And there'll be fireworks and the air will be full of light and noise, under cover of which almost anything might be done. I don't like it! Hello! What's here?"

He turned to the glass front of a prosperous-looking cigar store on the south side of the avenue and pointed to a shattered hole in the window. Behind it a bullet swung on a thread from the ceiling, and this agent of disaster the proprietor had ingeniously turned to account in advertising, by the following placard:

```
+---------------------------------------------+
|                 AIM LOWER                    |
|   If you expect to shoot holes in our prices.|
|         WE CHALLENGE COMPETITION.            |
+---------------------------------------------+
```

"Not bad," approved Average Jones. "I feel a great yearning to smoke—"

They entered the store and were served by the proprietor. As he was making change, Average Jones asked:

"When was the bombardment?"

"Night before last, some time," replied the man.

"Done by a deflected bullet, wasn't it?"

"Haven't any idea how it was done or why. I got here in the morning and there she was. What makes you think it was a deflected bullet?"

"Because it was whirling end-over. Normally, a bullet bores a pretty clean hole in plate glass."

"That's so, too," agreed the man with some interest.

Average Jones handed a cigar to Waldemar and lighted one himself. Puffing at it as he walked to the door, he gazed casually around and finally centered his attention on a telegraph pole standing on the edge of the sidewalk. He even walked out and around the pole. Returning, he remarked to the tobacconist:

"Very good cigars, these. Ever advertise 'em?"

"Sure." The man displayed a tin square vaunting the virtues of his "Camarados."

"Outside the shop, I meant. Why wouldn't one of those signs look good on that telegraph pole?"

"It would look good to me," said the vendor, "but it wouldn't look good to the telegraph people. They'd have it down."

"Oh, I don't know. Give me one, lend me a ladder, and I'll make the experiment."

The tobacconist stared. "All right," he said. "Go as far as you like." And he got the required articles for his customer.

With silent curiosity Waldemar watched Average Jones place the ladder against the outside of the pole, mount, nail up the sign, drop a plumb-line, improvised from a key and a length of string, to the ground, set a careful knot in the string and return to earth.

"What did you find?" asked the editor.

"Four holes that you could cover with a silver dollar. Some gunnery, that!"

"Then how did the other shot happen to go so far wrong?"

"Do you see that steel work over there?"

Average Jones pointed across to the north side of the street, just opposite, where a number of buildings had been torn down to permit of the erection of a new one. The frame had risen three stories, and through the open spaces in the gaunt skeleton the rear of the houses facing on the street next northward could be seen. Waldemar indicated that he did see the edifice pointed out by Average Jones.

"The bullet came from back of that—perhaps from the next street. They sighted by the telegraph pole. Suppose, now, a man riding in a high coach passes along this avenue between the pole and the gun operator, over yonder to the northward. Every one of the bullets which hit the pole would have gone right through his body. Probably a fixed gun. As for the wide shot, we'll see."

As he spoke, the Ad-Visor was leading the way across the street. With upturned face he carefully studied the steel joists from end to end. Presently he pointed. Following the line of his finger, Waldemar saw a raw scar on the under side of one of the joists.

"There it is," said Average Jones. "The sights were a trifle off at the first shot, and the bullet ticked the steel and deflected."

"So far, so good," approved Waldemar.

"I can approximate the height of the steel beam from the ground, close enough for a trial formula," continued Average Jones. "Now, Waldemar, I call your attention to that restaurant on the opposite corner."

Waldemar conned the designated building with attention. "Well," he said finally, "what of it? I don't see anything wrong with it."

"Precisely my point," returned the Ad-Visor with a grin. "Neither do I. Therefore, suppose you go there and order luncheon for two, while I walk down to the next block and back again. I'll be with you in four minutes."

He was somewhat better than his word. Dropping into the chair opposite his friend, he figured swiftly and briefly on the back of an envelope, which he returned to his pocket.

"I suppose you've done a vast amount of investigating since you left me," remarked the editor sardonically. "Meanwhile, the plot to murder the governor goes merrily on."

"I've done a fair amount of pacing over distance," retorted Average Jones imperturbably. "As for the governor, they can't kill him till he comes, can they? Besides, there's plenty of time for them to change their minds. As a result of my little constitutional just now, and a simple exercise in mathematics, you and I will call at a house on Spencer Street, the next street north, after luncheon."

"What house?"

"Ah! that I don't know, as yet. We'll see when we get there."

Comfortably fed, the two strolled up to Spencer Street and turned into it, Average Jones eying the upper windows of the houses. He stopped in front of an old-fashioned frame structure, which was built on a different plan of floor level from its smaller neighbors of brick. Up the low steps went Jones, followed by the editor. An aged lady, of the species commonly, conjectured as "maiden," opened the door.

"Madam," said Average Jones, "could we rent your third floor rear for this evening?"

"No, sir," said she. "It's rented."

"Perhaps I could buy the renters off," suggested Jones. "Could I see them?"

"Both out," she answered shortly. "And I don't believe you could get the room from them, for they're all fixed up to take photographs of the parade."

"Indee–ee–eed," drawled Average Jones, in accents so prolonged, even for him, that Waldemar's interest flamed within him. "I—er—ra–ra–aather hoped—er—when do you expect them back?"

"About four o'clock."

"Thank you. Please tell them that—er—Mr. Nick Karboe called."

"For heaven's sake, Average," rumbled Waldemar, as they regained the pavement, "why did you use the dead man's name? It gave me a shiver."

"It'll give them a worse one," replied the Ad-Visor grimly. "I want to prepare their nerves for a subsequent shock. If you'll meet me here this evening at seven, I think I can promise you a queer spectacle."

"And meantime?"

"On that point I want your advice. Shall we make a sure catch of two hired assassins who don't amount to much, or take a chance at the bigger game?"

"Meaning Morrison?"

"Meaning Morrison. Incidentally, if we get him we'll be able to kill the Personal Liberty bill so dead it will never raise its head again."

"Then I'm for that course," decided the editor, after a little consideration, "though I can't yet make myself believe that Carroll Morrison is party to a deliberate murder plot."

"How the normal mind does shrink from connecting crime with good clothes and a social position!" remarked the Ad-Visor. "Just give me a moment's time."

The moment he spent jotting down words on a bit of paper, which, after some emendation, he put away.

"That'll do for a heading," he remarked. "Now, Waldemar, I want you to get the governor on the 'phone and tell him, if he'll follow directions, we'll put the personal liberty bill where the wicked cease from troubling. Morrison is to be in the reviewing stand, isn't he?"

"Yes; there's a special place reserved for him, next the press seats."

"Good! By the way, you'd better send for two press seats for you and myself. Now, what I want: the governor to do is this: get a copy of the Harrisonia *Evening Bell*, fold it to an advertisement headed 'Offer to Photographers,' and as he passes Carroll Morrison on the stand, hold it up and say to him just this: 'Better luck next time.' For anything further, I'll see you in the reviewing stand. Do you think he'll do it?"

"It sounds as foolish as a college initiation stunt. Still, you heard what Governor Arthur said about his confidence in you. But what is this advertisement?"

"As yet, it isn't. But it will be, as soon as I can get to the office of the *Bell*. You'll meet me on this corner at seven o'clock, then?"

"Yes. Meantime, to be safe, I'll look after the reviewing stand tickets myself."

At the hour named, the editor arrived. Average Jones was already there, accompanied by a messenger boy. The boy wore the cheerful grin of one who has met with an unexpected favor of fortune.

"They've returned, both of 'em," said Average Jones as Waldemar approached. "What about the governor?"

"It took a mighty lot of persuasion, but he'll do it," replied the editor.

"Skip, son," said the Ad-Visor, handing the messenger boy a folded newspaper. "The two gentlemen on the third floor rear. And be sure you say that it's a personal, marked copy."

The boy crossed the street and entered the house. In two minutes he emerged, nodded to Average Jones and walked away. Five minutes passed. Then the front door opened cautiously and a tall, evil-looking man slunk into the vestibule. A second man followed him. They glanced eagerly from left to right. Average Jones stepped out to the curb-stone.

"Here's the message from Karboe," he called.

"My God!" gasped the tall man.

For an instant he made as if to turn back. Then, clearing the steps at one jump, he stumbled, sprawled, was up again instantly and speeding up the street, away from Average Jones, turned the corner neck and neck with his companion who, running powerfully, had overtaken him.

The door of the house stood ajar. Before Waldemar had recovered from his surprise, Average Jones was inside the house. Hesitation beset the editor. Should he follow or wait? He paused, one foot on the step. A loud crash within resolved his doubts. Up he started, when the voice of Average Jones in colloquy with the woman who had received them before, checked him. The colloquy seemed excited but peaceful. Presently Average Jones came down the steps.

"They left the ad," said he. "Have you seen it?"

"No; I hadn't time to get a paper," replied Waldemar, taking the copy extended to him and reading in large display:

OFFER TO PHOTOGRAPHERS

$1,000 Reward for Special Flash-light Photo of Governor Arthur in To-night's Pageant. Must be Taken According to Plans and Specifications Designated by the Late Nick Karboe.

Apply to A. JONES, Ad-Visor.

Astor Court Temple, New York City.

"No wonder they ran," said Waldemar with a grin, as he digested this document.

"And so must we if we're to get through the crowd and reach the reviewing stand," warned Average Jones, glancing at his watch.

Their seats, which they attained with some difficulty, were within a few feet of the governor's box. Within reach of them sat Carroll Morrison, his long, pale, black-bearded face set in that immobility to which he had schooled it. But the cold eyes roved restlessly and the little muscles at the corners of the lips twitched.

"Tell me that he isn't in on the game!" whispered Average Jones, and Waldemar nodded.

The sound of music from down the street turned all faces in that direction. A roar of cheering swept toward them and was taken up in the stands. The governor, in his high coach, came in sight. And, at that moment, terror struck into the soul of Waldemar.

"Suppose they came back!" he whispered to Average Jones. "We've left the house unguarded."

"I've fixed that," replied the Ad-Visor in the same tone. "Watch Morrison!"

Governor Arthur approached the civic statue. An official, running out to the coach, handed him a silken cord, which he secured with a turn around the wrist. The coach rolled on. The cord tautened; the swathings sundered and fell from the gleaming splendor of marble, and a blinding flash, followed by another, and a third, blotted out the scene in unbearable radiance.

Involuntarily Morrison, like thousands of others, had screened his sight with his hands after the second flash. Now, as the kindlier light returned, he half rose, rubbing his eyes furiously. A half-groan escaped him. He sank back, staring in amaze. For Governor Arthur was riding on, calm and smiling amid the shouts.

Morrison shrank. Could it be that the governor's eyes were fixed on his? He strove to shake off the delusion. He felt, rather than saw, the guest of honor descend from the coach; felt rather than saw him making straight toward himself; and he winced and quivered at the sound of his own name.

"Mr. Morrison," the governor was saying, at his elbow, "Mr. Morrison, here is a paper that may interest you. Better luck next time."

Morrison strove to reply. His voice clucked in his throat, and the hand with which he took the folded newspaper was as the hand of a paralytic.

"He's broken," whispered Average Jones.

He went straight to Governor Arthur, speaking in his ear. The governor nodded. Average Jones returned to his seat to watch Carroll Morrison who, sat, with hell-fires of fear scorching him, until the last band had blared its way into silence.

Again the governor was speaking to him.

"'Mr. Morrison, I want you to visit a house near here. Mr. Jones and Mr. Waldemar will come along; you know them, perhaps. Please don't protest. I positively will not take a refusal. We have a motor-car waiting."

Furious, but not daring to refuse, Morrison found himself whirled swiftly away, and after a few turns to shake off the crowd, into Spencer Street. With his captors, he mounted to the third floor of an old frame house. The rear room door had been broken in. Inside stood a strange instrument, resembling a large camera, which had once stood upright on a steel tripod riveted to the floor. The legs of the tripod were twisted and bent. A half-demolished chair near by suggested the agency of destruction.

"Just to render it harmless," explained Average Jones. "It formerly pointed through that window, so that a bullet from the barrel would strike that pole way yonder in Harrison Street, after first passing through any intervening body. Yours, for instance, Governor."

"Do I understand that this is a gun, Mr. Jones," asked that official.

"Of a sort," replied the Ad-Visor, opening up the camera-box and showing a large barrel superimposed on a smaller one. "This is a sighting-glass," he explained, tapping the larger barrel. "And this," tapping the smaller, "carries a small but efficient bullet. This curious sheath"—he pointed to a cylindrical jacket around part of the rifle barrel— "is a Coulomb silencer, which reduces a small-arm report almost to a whisper. Here is an electric button which was connected with yonder battery before I operated on it with the chair, and distributed its spark, part to the gun, part to the flash-light powder on this little shelf. Do you see the plan now? The instant that the governor, riding through the street yonder, is sighted through this glass, the operator presses the button, and flash-light and bullet go off instantaneously."

"But why the flash-light?" asked the governor.

"Merely a blind to fool the landlady and avert any possible suspicion. They had told her that they had a new invention to take flash-lights at a distance. Amidst the other flashes, this one wouldn't be noticed particularly. They had covered their trail well."

"Well, indeed," said the governor. "May I congratulate you, Mr. Morrison, on this interesting achievement in ballistics?"

"As there is no way of properly resenting an insult from a man in your position," said Morrison venomously, "I will reserve my answer to that outrageous suggestion."

"Meantime," put in Average Jones, "let me direct your attention to a simple mathematical formula." He drew from his pocket an envelope on which were drawn some angles, subjoined by a formula. Morrison waved it aside.

"Not interested in mathematics?" asked Average Jones solicitously. "Very well, I'll elucidate informally. Given a bullet hole in a telegraph pole at a certain distance, a bullet scar on an iron girder at a certain lesser distance, and the length of a block from here to Harrison Avenue—which I paced off while you were skillfully ordering luncheon, Waldemar—and an easy triangulation brings us direct to this room and to two fugitive gentlemen with whom I mention the hypothesis with all deference, Mr. Morrison, you are probably acquainted."

"And who may they have been?" retorted Morrison contemptuously.

"I don't know," said Average Jones.

"Then, sir," retorted the racing king, "your hypothesis is as impudent as your company is intolerable. Have you anything further to say to me?"

"Yes. It would greatly please Mr. Waldemar to publish in tomorrow's paper an authorized statement from you to the effect that the Personal Liberty bill will be withdrawn permanently."

"Mr. Waldemar may go to the devil. I have endured all the hectoring I propose to. Men in my position are targets for muckrakers and blackmailers—"

"Wait a moment," Waldemar's heavy voice broke in. "You speak of men in your position. Do you understand just what position you are in at present?"

Morrison rose. "Governor Arthur," he said with stony dignity, "I bid you good evening."

Waldemar set his bulky back against the door. The lips drew back from Morrison's strong teeth with the snarl of an animal in the fury and terror of approaching peril.

"Do you know Nick Karboe?"

Morrison whirled about to face Average Jones. But he did not answer the question. He only stared.

"Carroll Morrison," continued Average Jones in his quiet drawl, "the half-hour before he—er—committed suicide—er—Nick Karboe spent in the office of the—er—*Universal* with Mr. Waldemar and—er—myself. Catch him, Waldemar!"

For Morrison had wilted. They propped him against the wall and he, the man who had insolently defied the laws of a great commonwealth, who had bribed legislatures and bossed judges and browbeaten the public, slobbered, denied and begged. For two disgustful minutes they extracted from him his solemn promise that henceforth he would keep his hands off the laws. Then they turned him out.

"Suppose you enlighten me with the story, gentlemen," suggested the governor.

Average Jones told it, simply and modestly. At the conclusion, Governor Arthur looked from the wrecked camera-gun to the mathematical formula which had fallen to the floor.

"Mr. Jones," he said, "you've done me the service of saving my life; you've done the public the service of killing a vicious bill. I wish I could thank you more publicly than this."

"Thank you, Governor," said Average' Jones modestly. "But I owed the public something, you know, on account of, my uncle, the late Mayor Van Reypen."

Governor Arthur nodded. "The debt is paid," he said. "That knowledge must be your reward; that and the consciousness of having worked out a remarkable and original problem."

"Original?" said Average Jones, eying the diagram on the envelope's back, with his quaint smile. "Why, Governor, you're giving me too much credit. It was worked out by one of the greatest detectives of all time, some two thousand years ago. His name was Euclid."

THE MILLION-DOLLAR DOG

To this day, Average Jones maintains that he felt a distinct thrill at first sight of the advertisement. Yet Fate might well have chosen a more appropriate ambush in any one of a hundred of the strange clippings which were grist to the Ad-Visor's mill. Out of a bulky pile of the day's paragraphs, however, it was this one that leaped, significant, to his eye.

> WANTED—Ten thousand loathly black beetles, by a leaseholder who contracted to leave a house in the same condition as he found it. ACKROYD, 100 W. Sixteenth St., New York.

"Black beetles, eh?" observed Average Jones. "This Ackroyd person seems to be a merry little jester. Well, I'm feeling rather jocular, myself, this morning. How does one collect black beetles, I wonder? When in doubt, inquire of the resourceful Simpson."

He pressed a button and his confidential clerk entered.

"Good morning, Simpson," said Average Jones. "Are you acquainted with that shy but pervasive animal, the domestic black beetle?"

"Yes, sir; I board," said Simpson simply.

"I suppose there aren't ten thousand black beetles in your boarding-house, though?" inquired Average Jones.

Simpson took it under advisement. "Hardly," he decided.

"I've got to have 'em to fill an order. At least, I've got to have an installment of 'em, and to-morrow."

Being wholly without imagination, the confidential clerk was impervious to surprise or shock. This was fortunate, for otherwise, his employment as practical aide to Average Jones would probably have driven him into a madhouse. He now ran his long, thin, clerkly hands through his long, thin, clerkly hair.

"Ramson, down on Fulton Street, will have them, if any one has," he said presently. "He does business under the title of the Insect Nemesis, you know. I'll go there at once."

Returning to his routine work, Average Jones found himself unable to dislodge the advertisement from his mind. So presently he gave way to temptation, called up Bertram at the Cosmic Club, and asked him to come to the Astor Court Temple office at his convenience. Scenting more adventure, Bertram found it convenient to come promptly. Average Jones handed him the clipping. Bertram read it with ascending eyebrows.

"Hoots!" he said. "The man's mad."

"I didn't ask you here to diagnose the advertiser's trouble. That's plain enough—though you've made a bad guess. What I want of you is to tap your flow of information about old New York. What's at One Hundred West Sixteenth Street?"

"One hundred West Sixteenth; let me see. Why, of course; it's the old Feltner mansion. You must know it. It has a walled garden at the side; the only one left in the city, south of Central Park."

"Any one named Ackroyd there?"

"That must be Hawley Ackroyd. I remember, now, hearing that he had rented it. Judge Ackroyd, you know, better known as 'Oily' Ackroyd. He's a smooth old rascal."

"Indeed? What particular sort?"

"Oh, most sorts, in private. Professionally, he's a legislative crook; head lobbyist of the Consolidated."

"Ever hear of his collecting insects?"

"Never heard of his collecting anything but graft. In fact, he'd have been in jail years ago, but for his family connections. He married a Van Haltern. You remember the famous Van Haltern will case, surely; the million-dollar dog. The papers fairly, reeked of it a year ago. Sylvia Graham had to take the dog and leave the country to escape the notoriety. She's back now, I believe."

"I've heard of Miss Graham," remarked Average Jones, "through friends of mine whom she visits."

"Well, if you've only heard of her and not seen her," returned Bertram, with something as nearly resembling enthusiasm as his habitual languor permitted, "you've got something to look forward to. Sylvia Graham is a distinct asset to the Scheme of Creation."

"An asset with assets of her own, I believe," said Average Jones. "The million dollars left by her grandmother, old Mrs. Van Haltern, goes to her eventually; doesn't it?"

"Provided she carries out the terms of the will, keeps the dog in proper luxury and buries him in the grave on the family estate at Schuylkill designated by the testator. If these terms are not rigidly carried out, the fortune is to be divided, most of it going to Mrs. Hawley Ackroyd, which would mean the judge himself. I should say that the dog was as good as sausage meat if 'Oily' ever gets hold of him."

"H'm. What about Mrs. Ackroyd?"

"Poor, sickly, frightened lady! She's very fond of Sylvia Graham, who is her niece. But she's completely dominated by her husband."

"Information is your long suit, Bert. Now, if you only had intelligence to correspond—" Average Jones broke off and grinned mildly, first at his friend, then at the advertisement.

Bertram caught up the paper and studied it. "Well, what *does* it mean?" he demanded.

"It means that Ackroyd, being about to give up his rented house, intends to saddle it with a bad name. Probably he's had a row with the agent or owner, and is getting even by making the place difficult to rent again. Nobody wants to take a house with the reputation of an entomological resort."

"It would be just like Oily Ackroyd," remarked Bertram. "He's a vindictive scoundrel. Only a few days ago, he nearly killed a poor devil of a drug clerk, over some trifling dispute. He managed to keep it out of the newspapers but he had to pay a stiff fine."

"That might be worth looking up, too," ruminated Average Jones thoughtfully.

He turned to his telephone in answer to a ring. "All right, come, in, Simpson," he said.

The confidential clerk appeared. "Ramson says that regular black beetles are out of season, sir," he reported. "But he can send to the country and dig up plenty of red-and-black ones."

"That will do," returned the Ad-Visor. "Tell him to have two or three hundred here to-morrow morning."

Bertram bent a severe gaze on his friend. "Meaning that you're going to follow up this freak affair?" he inquired.

"Just that. I can't explain why, but—well, Bert, I've a hunch. At the worst, Ackroyd's face when he sees the beetles should be worth the money."

"When you frivol, Average, I wash my hands of you. But I warn you, look out for Ackroyd. He's as big as he is ugly; a tough customer."

"All right. I'll just put on some old clothes, to dress the part of a beetle-purveyor correctly, and also in case I get 'em torn in my meeting with judge 'Oily.' I'll see you later—and report, if I survive his wrath."

Thus it was that, on the morning after this dialogue, a clean-built young fellow walked along West Sixteenth Street, appreciatively sniffing the sunny crispness of the May air. He was rather shabby looking, yet his demeanor was by no means shabby. It was confident and easy. On the evidence of the bandbox which he carried, his mission should have been menial; but he bore himself wholly unlike one subdued to petty employments. His steady, gray eyes showed a glint of anticipation as he turned in at the gate of the high, broad, brown house standing back, aloof and indignant, from the roaring encroachments of trade. He set his burden down and, pulled the bell.

The door opened promptly to the deep, far-away clangor. A flashing impression of girlish freshness, vigor, and grace was disclosed to the caller against a background of interior gloom. He stared a little more patently than was polite. Whatever his expectation of amusement, this, evidently, was not the manifestation looked for. The girl glanced not at him, but at the box, and spoke a trifle impatiently.

"If it's my hat, it's very late. You should have gone to the basement."

"It isn't, miss," said the young man, in a form of address, the semi-servility of which seemed distinctly out of tone with the quietly clear and assured voice. "It's the insects."

"The *what?*"

"The bugs, miss."

He extracted from his pocket a slip of paper, looked from it to the numbered door, as one verifying an address, and handed it to her.

"From yesterday's copy of the *Banner*, miss. You're not going back on that, surely," he said somewhat reproachfully.

She read, and as she read her eyes widened to lakes of limpid brown. Then they crinkled at the corners, and her laugh rose from the mid-tone contralto, to a high, bird-like trill of joyousness. The infection of it tugged at the young man's throat, but he successfully preserved his mask of flat and respectful dullness.

"It must have been Uncle," she gasped finally. "He said he'd be quits with the real estate agent before he left. How perfectly absurd! And are those the creatures in that box?"

"The first couple of hundred of 'em, miss."

"Two hundred!" Again the access of laughter swelled the rounded bosom as the breeze fills a sail. "Where did you get them?"

"Woodpile, ash-heap, garbage-pail," said the young man stolidly. "Any particular kind preferred, Miss Ackroyd?"

The girl looked at him with suspicion, but his face was blankly innocent.

"I'm not Miss Ackroyd," she began with emphasis, when a querulous voice from an inner room called out: "Whom are you talking to, Sylvia?"

"A young man with a boxful of beetles," returned the girl, adding in brisk French: "*Il est tres amusant ce farceur. Je ne le comprends pas du tout. C'est une blague, peut-être. Si on l'invitait dans la maison pour un moment?*"

Through one of the air-holes, considerately punched in the cardboard cover of the box, a sturdy crawler had succeeded in pushing himself. He was, in the main, of a shiny and well-groomed black, but two large patches of crimson gave him the festive appearance of being garbed in a brilliant sash. As he stood rubbing his fore-legs together in self-congratulation over his exploit, his bearer addressed him in French quite as ready as the girl's:

"*Permettez-moi, Monsieur le Coléoptère, de vous presenter mes excuses pour cette demoiselle qui s'exprime en langue étrangère chez elle.*"

"Don't apologize to the beetle on my account," retorted the girl with spirit. "You're here on your own terms, you know, both of you."

Average Jones mutely held up the box in one hand and the advertisement in the other. The adventurer-bug flourished a farewell to the girl with his antennae, and retired within to advise his fellows of the charms of freedom.

"Very well," said the girl, in demure tones, though lambent mirth still flickered, golden, in the depths of the brown eyes. "If you persist, I can only suggest that you come back when Judge Ackroyd is here. You won't find him particularly amenable to humor, particularly when perpetrated by a practical joker in masquerade."

"Discovered," murmured Average Jones. "I shouldn't have vaunted my poor French. But must I really take my little friends all the way back? You suggested to the mystic voice within that I might be invited inside."

"You seem a decidedly unconventional person," began the other with dawning disfavor.

"Conventionality, like charity, begins at home," he replied quickly. "And one would hardly call this advertisement a pattern of formal etiquette."

"True enough," she admitted, dimpling, and Average Jones was congratulating himself on his diplomacy, when the querulous voice broke in again, this time too low for his ears.

"I don't ask you the real reason for your extraordinary call," pursued the girl with a glint of mischief in her eyes, after she had responded in an aside, "but auntie thinks you've come to steal my dog. She thinks that of every one lately."

"Auntie? Your dog? Then you're Sylvia Graham. I might have known it."

"I don't know how you might have known it. But I am Sylvia Graham—if you insist on introducing me to yourself."

"Miss Graham," said the visitor promptly and gravely, "let me present A.V.R.E. Jones: a friend—"

"Not the famous Average Jones!" cried the girl. "That is why your face seemed so familiar. I've seen your picture at Edna Hale's. You got her 'blue fires' back for her. But really, that hardly explains your being here, in this way, you know."

"Frankly, Miss Graham, it was just as a lark that I answered the advertisement. But now that I'm here and find you here, it looks—er—as if it might—er—be more serious."

A tinge of pink came into the girl's cheeks, but she answered lightly enough:

"Indeed, it may, for you, if uncle finds you here with those beetles."

"Never mind me or the beetles. I'd like to know about the dog that your aunt is worrying over. Is he here with you?"

The soft curve of Miss Graham's lips straightened a little. "I really think," she said with decision, "that you had better explain further before questioning."

"Nothing simpler. Once upon a time there lived a crack-brained young Don Quixote who wandered through an age of buried romance piously searching for trouble. And, twice upon a time, there dwelt in an enchanted stone castle in West Sixteenth Street an enchanting young damsel in distress—"

"I'm not a damsel in distress," interrupted Miss Graham, passing over the adjective.

The young man leaned to her. The half smile had passed from his lips, and his eyes were very grave.

"Not—er—if your dog were to—er—disappear?" he drawled quietly.

The swift unexpectedness of the counter broke down the girl's guard.

"You mean Uncle Hawley," she said.

"And your suspicions jump with mine."

"They don't!" she denied hotly. "You're very unjust and impertinent."

"I don't mean to be impertinent," he said evenly. "And I have no monopoly of injustice."

"What do you know about Uncle Hawley?"

"Your aunt—"

"I won't hear a word against my aunt."

"Not from me, be assured. Your aunt, so you have just told me, believes that your dog is in danger of being stolen. Why? Because she knows that the person most interested has been scheming against the animal, and yet she is afraid to warn you openly. Doesn't that indicate who it is?"

"Mr. Jones, I've no right even to let you talk like this to me. Have you anything definite against Judge Ackroyd?"

"In this case, only suspicion."

Her head went up. "Then I think there is nothing more to be said."

The young man flushed, but his voice was steady as he returned:

"I disagree with you. And I beg you to cut short your visit here, and return to your home at once."

In spite of herself the girl was shaken by his persistence. "I can't do that," she said uneasily. And added, with a flash of anger, "I think you had better leave this house."

"If I leave this house now I may never have any chance to see you again."

The girl regarded him with level, non-committal eyes.

"And I have every intention of seeing you again—and—again—and again. Give me a chance; a moment."

Average Jones' mind was of the emergency type. It summoned to its aid, without effort of cerebration on the part of its owner, whatever was most needed at the moment. Now it came to his rescue with the memory of judge Ackroyd's encounter with the drug clerk, as mentioned by Bertram. There was a strangely hopeful suggestion of some link between a drug-store quarrel and the arrival of a million-dollar dog, "better dead" in the hopes of his host.

"Miss Graham; I've gone rather far, I'll admit," said Jones; "but, if you'll give me the benefit of the doubt, I think I can show you some basis to work on. If I can produce something tangible, may I come back here this afternoon? I'll promise not to come unless I have good reason."

"Very well," conceded Miss Graham reluctantly, "it's a most unusual thing. But I'll agree to that."

"*Au revoir*, then," he said, and was gone.

Somewhat to her surprise and uneasiness, Sylvia Graham experienced a distinct satisfaction when, late that afternoon, she beheld her unconventional acquaintance mounting the steps with a buoyant and assured step. Upon being admitted, he went promptly to the point.

"I've got it."

"Your justification for coming back?" she asked.

"Exactly. Have you heard anything of some trouble in which judge Ackroyd was involved last week?"

"Uncle has a very violent temper," admitted the girl evasively. "But I don't see what—"

"Pardon me. You will see. That row was with a drug clerk."

"Well?"

"In an obscure drug store several blocks from here."

"Yes?"

"The drug clerk insisted—as the law requires—on judge Ackroyd registering for a certain purchase."

"Perhaps he was impertinent about it."

"Possibly. The point is that the prospective purchase was cyanide of potassium, a deadly and instantaneous poison."

"Are you sure?" asked the girl, in a low voice.

"I've just come from the store. How long have you been here at your uncle's?"

"A week."

"Then just about the time of your coming with the dog, your uncle undertook to obtain a swift and sure poison. Have I gone far enough?"

"I—I don't know."

"Well, am I still ordered out of the house?"

"N–n–no."

"Thank you for your enthusiastic hospitality," said Average Jones so dryly that a smile relaxed the girl's troubled face. "With that encouragement we'll go on. What is your uncle's attitude toward the dog?"

"Almost what you might call ingratiating. But Peter Paul—that's my dog's name, you know—doesn't take to uncle. He's a crotchety old doggie."

"He's a wise old doggie," amended the other, with emphasis. "Has your uncle taken him out, at all?"

"Once he tried to. I met them at the corner. All four of Peter Paul's poor old fat legs were braced, and he was hauling back as hard as he could against the leash."

"And the occurrence didn't strike you as peculiar?"

"Well, not then."

"When does your uncle give up this house?"

"At the end of the week. Uncle and aunt leave for Europe."

"Then let me suggest again that you and Peter Paul go at once."

Miss Graham pondered. "That would mean explanations and a quarrel, and more strain for auntie, who is nervous enough, anyway. No, I can't do that."

"Do you realize that every day Peter Paul remains here is an added opportunity for judge Ackroyd to make a million dollars, or a big share of it, by some very simple stratagem?"

"I haven't admitted yet that I believe my uncle to be a—a murderer," Miss Graham quietly reminded him.

"A strong word," said Average Jones smiling. "The law would hardly support your view. Now, Miss Graham, would it grieve you very much if Peter Paul were to die?"

"I won't have him put to death," said she quickly. "That would be cheating my grandmother's intentions."

"I supposed you wouldn't. Yet it would be the simplest way. Once dead, and buried in accordance with the terms of the will, the dog would be out of his troubles, and you would be out of yours."

"It would really be a relief. Peter Paul suffers so from asthma, poor old beastie. The vet says he can live only a month or two longer, anyway. But I've got to do as Grandmother wished, and keep Peter Paul alive as long as possible."

"Admitted." Average Jones fell into a baffled silence, studying the pattern of the rug with restless eyes. When he looked up into Miss Graham's face again it was with a changed expression.

"Miss Graham," he said slowly, "won't you try to forget, for the moment, the circumstances of our meeting, and think of me only as a friend of your friends who is very honestly eager to be a friend to you, when you most need one?"

Now, Average Jones's birth-fairy had endowed him with one priceless gift: the power of inspiring an instinctive confidence in himself. Sylvia Graham felt, suddenly, that a hand, sure and firm, had been outstretched to guide her on a dark path. In one of those rare flashes of companionship which come only when clean and honorable spirits recognize one another, all consciousness of sex was lost between them. The girl's gaze met the man's level, and was held in a long, silent regard.

"Yes," she said simply; and the heart of Average Jones rose and swore a high loyalty.

"Listen, then. I think I see a clear way. Judge Ackroyd will kill the dog if he can, and so effectually conceal the body that no funeral can be held over it, thereby rendering your grandmother's bequest to you void. He has only a few days to do it in, but I don't think that all your watchfulness can restrain him. Now, on the other hand, if the dog should die a natural death and be buried, he can still contest the will. But if he should kill Peter Paul and hide the body where we could discover it, the game would be up for him, as he then wouldn't even dare to come into court with a contest. Do you follow me?"

"Yes. But you wouldn't ask me to be a party to any such thing."

"You're a party, involuntarily, by remaining here. But do your best to save Peter Paul, if you will. And please call me up immediately at the Cosmic Club, if anything in my line turns up."

"What is your line?" asked Miss Graham, the smile returning to her lips. "Creepy, crawly bugs? Or imperiled dogs? Or rescuing prospectively distressed damsels?"

"Technically it's advertising," replied Average Jones, who had been formulating a shrewd little plan of his own. "Let me recommend to you the advertising columns of the daily press. They're often amusing. Moreover your uncle might break out in print again. Who knows?"

"Who, indeed? I'll read religiously."

"And, by the way, my beetles. I forgot and left them here. Oh, there's the box. I may have a very specific use for them later. *Au revoir*—and may it be soon!"

The two days succeeding seemed to Average Jones, haunted as he was by an importunate craving to look again into Miss Graham's limpid and changeful eyes, a dull and sodden period of probation. The messenger boy who finally brought her expected note, looked to him like a Greek godling. The note enclosed this clipping:

LOST—Pug dog answering to the name of Peter Paul. Very old and asthmatic. Last seen on West 16th Street. Liberal reward for information to ANXIOUS. Care of *Banner* office.

> *Dear Mr. Jones* (she had written):
> *Are you a prophet?* (Average Jones chuckled, at this point.) *The enclosed seems to be distinctly in our line. Could you come some time this afternoon? I'm puzzled and a little anxious.*
>
> > Sincerely yours,
> > Sylvia Graham.

Average Jones could, and did. He found Miss Graham's piquant face under the stress of excitement, distinctly more alluring than before.

"Isn't it strange?" she said, holding out a hand in welcome. "Why should any one advertise for my Peter Paul? He isn't lost."

"I am glad to hear that," said the caller gravely.

"I've kept my promise, you see," pursued the girl. "Can you do as well, and live up to your profession of aid?"

"Try me."

"Very well, do you know what that advertisement means?"

"Perfectly."

"Then you're a very extraordinary person."

"Not in the least. I wrote it."

"Wrote it! You? Well—really! Why in the world did you write it?"

"Because of an unconquerable longing to see," Average Jones paused, and his quick glance caught the storm signal in her eyes, "your uncle," he concluded calmly.

For one fleeting instant a dimple flickered at the corner of her mouth. It departed. But departing, it swept the storm before it.

"What do you want to see uncle about, if it isn't an impertinent question?"

"It is, rather," returned the young man judicially. "Particularly, as I'm not sure, myself. I may want to quarrel with him."

"You won't have the slightest difficulty in that," the girl assured him.

She rang the bell, dispatched a servant, and presently judge Ackroyd stalked into the room. As Average Jones was being presented, he took comprehensive note and estimate of the broadcheeked, thin-lipped face; the square shoulders and corded neck, and the lithe and formidable carriage of the man. Judge "Oily" Ackroyd's greeting of the guest within his gates did not bear out the *sobriquet* of his public life. It was curt to the verge of harshness.

"What is the market quotation on beetles, judge?" asked the young man, tapping the rug with his stick.

"What are you talking about?" demanded the other, drawing down his heavy brows.

"The black beetle; the humble but brisk haunter of household crevices," explained Average Jones. "You advertised for ten thousand specimens. I've got a few thousand I'd like to dispose of, if the inducements are sufficient."

"I'm in no mood for joking, young man," retorted the other, rising.

"You seldom are, I understand," replied Average Jones blandly. "Well, if you won't talk about bugs, let's talk about dogs."

"The topic does not interest me, sir," retorted the other, and the glance of his eye was baleful, but uneasy.

The tapping of the young man's cane ceased. He looked up into his host's glowering face with a seraphic and innocent smile.

"Not even if it—er—touched upon a device for guarding the street corners in case—er—Peter Paul went walking—er—once too often?"

Judge Ackroyd took one step forward. Average Jones was on his feet instantly, and, even in her alarm, Sylvia Graham noticed how swiftly and naturally his whole form "set." But the big man turned away, and abruptly left the room.

"Were you wise to anger him?" asked the girl, as the heavy tread died away on the stairs.

"Sometimes open declaration of war is the soundest strategy."

"War?" she repeated. "You make me feel like a traitor to my own family."

"That's the unfortunate part of it," he said; "but it can't be helped."

"You spoke of having some one guard the corners of the block," continued the girl, after a thoughtful silence. "Do you think I'd better arrange for that?"

"No need. There'll be a hundred people on watch."

"Have you called out the militia?" she asked, twinkling.

"Better than that. I've employed the tools of my trade."

He handed her a galley proof marked with many corrections. She ran through it with growing amazement.

HAVE YOU SEEN THE DOG?

$100—One Hundred Dollars—$100

FOR THE BEST ANSWER IN 500 WORDS

OPEN TO ALL HIGH SCHOOL BOYS

Between now and next Saturday an old Pug
Dog will come out of a big House on West 16th
Street, between 5th and 6th Avenues. It may
be by Day. It may be any hour of the Night.
Now, you Boys, get to work.

REMEMBER: $100 IN CASH

HERE ARE THE POINTS TO MIND—

1—Description of Dog.
2—Description of Person with him.
3—Description of House he Comes from.
4—Account of Where they Go.
5—Account of What they Do.

Manuscripts must be written plainly and
mailed within twenty-four hours of the discovery of the dog to

A. JONES : AD-VISOR,

ASTOR COURT TEMPLE, NEW YORK

"That will appear in every New York paper tomorrow morning," explained its deviser.

"I see," said the girl. "Any one who attempts to take Peter Paul
away will be tracked by a band of boy detectives. A stroke of genius, Mr. Average Jones."

She curtsied low to him. But Average Jones was in no mood for
playfulness now.

"That restricts the judge's endeavors to the house and garden,"
said he, "since, of course he'll see the advertisement."

"I'll see that he does," said Miss Graham maliciously.

"Good! I'll also ask you to watch the garden for any suspicious
excavating."

"Very well. But is that all?" Miss Graham's voice was wistful.

"Isn't it enough?"

"You've been so good to me," she said hesitantly. "I don't like
to think of you as setting those boys to an impossible task."

"Oh, bless you!" returned the Ad-Visor heartily; "that's all arranged for. One of my men will duly parade with a canine especially obtained for the occasion. I'm not going to swindle the youngsters."

"It didn't seem like you," returned Miss Graham warmly. "But you must let me pay for it, that and the advertising bill."

"As an unauthorized expense—" he began.

She laid a small, persuasive hand on his arm.

"You must let me pay it. Won't you?"

Average Jones was conscious of a strange sensation, starting from the point where the firm, little hand lay. It spread in his veins and thickened his speech.

"Of course," he drawled, uncertainly, "if you—er—put it—er—that way!"

The hand lifted. "Mr. Average Jones," said the owner, "do you know you haven't once disappointed me in speech or action during our short but rather eventful acquaintance?"

"I hope you'll be able to say the same ten years from now," he returned significantly.

She flushed a little at the implication. "What am I to do next?" she asked.

"Do as you would ordinarily do; only don't take Peter Paul, into the street, or you'll have a score of high-school boys trailing you. And—this is the most important—if the dog fails to answer your call at any time, and you can't readily find him by searching, telephone me, at once, at my office. Good-bye."

"I think you are a very staunch friend to those who need you," she said, gravely and sweetly, giving him her hand.

She clung in his mind like a remembered fragrance, after he had gone back to Astor Court Temple to wait. And though he plunged into an intricate scheme of political advertising which was to launch a new local party, her eyes and her voice haunted him. Nor had he banished them, when, two days later, the telephone brought him her clear accents, a little tremulous now.

"Peter Paul is gone."

"Since when?"

"Since ten this morning. The house is in an uproar."

"I'll be up in half an hour at the latest."

"Do come quickly. I'm—I'm a little frightened."

"Then you must have something to do," said Average Jones decisively. "Have you been keeping an eye on the garden?"

"Yes."

"Go through it again, looking carefully for signs of disarranged earth. I don't think you'll find it, but it's well to be sure. Let me in at the basement door at half-past one. Judge Ackroyd mustn't see me."

It was a strangely misshapen presentation of the normally spick-and-span Average Jones that gently rang the basement bell of the old house at the specified hour. All his pockets bulged with lumpy angles. Immediately, upon being admitted by Miss Graham herself, he proceeded to disenburden himself of box after box, such as elastic bands come in, all exhibiting a homogeneous peculiarity, a hole at one end thinly covered with a gelatinous substance.

"Be very careful not to let that get broken," he instructed the mystified girl. "In the course of an hour or so it will melt away itself. Did you see anything suspicious in the garden?"

"No!" replied the girl. She picked up one of the boxes. "How odd!" she cried. "Why, there's something in it that's alive!"

"Very much so. Your friends, the beetles, in fact."

"What! Again? Aren't you carrying the joke rather far?"

"It's not a joke any more. It's deadly serious. I'm quite sure," he concluded in the manner of one who picks his words carefully, "that it may turn out to be just the most serious matter in the world to me."

"As bad as that?" she queried, but the color that flamed in her cheeks belied the lightness of her tone.

"Quite. However, that must wait. Where is your uncle?"

"Up-stairs in his study."

"Do you think you could take me all through the house some-time this afternoon without his seeing me?"

"No, I'm sure I couldn't. He's been wandering like an uneasy spirit since Peter Paul disappeared. And he won't go out, because he is packing."

"So much the worse, either for him or me. Where are your rooms?"

"On the second floor."

"Very well. Now, I want one of these little boxes left in every room in the house, if possible, except on your floor, which is probably out of the reckoning. Do you think you could manage it soon?"

"I think so. I'll try."

"Do most of the rooms open into one another?"

"Yes, all through the house."

"Please see that they're all unlocked, and as far as possible, open. I'll be here at four o'clock, and will call for judge Ackroyd. You must be sure that he receives me. Tell him it is a matter of great importance. It is."

"You're putting a fearful strain on my feminine curiosity," said Miss Graham, the provocative smile quirking at the comers of her mouth.

"Doubtless," returned the other dryly. "If you strictly follow directions, I'll undertake to satisfy it in time. Four o'clock sharp, I'll be here. Don't be frightened whatever happens. You keep ready, but out of the way, until I call you. Good-bye."

With even more than his usual nicety was Average Jones attired, when, at four o'clock, he sent his card to judge Ackroyd. Small favor, however, did his appearance find, in the scowling eyes of the judge.

"What do *you* want?" he growled.

"I'll take a cigar, thank you very much," said Average Jones innocently.

"You'll take your leave, or state your business."

"It has to do with your niece."

"Then what do you take my time for, damn your impudence."

"Don't swear." Average Jones was deliberately provoking the older man to an outbreak. "Let's—er—sit down and—er—be chatty."

The drawl, actually an evidence of excitement, had all the effect of studied insolence. Judge Ackroyd's big frame shook.

"I'm going to k–k–kick you out into the street, you young p–p–p–pup," he stuttered in his rage.

His knotted fingers writhed out for a hold on the other's collar. With a sinuous movement, the visitor swerved aside and struck the other man, flat-handed, across the face. There was an answering howl of demoniac fury. Then a strange thing happened. The assailant turned and fled, not to the ready egress of the front door, but down the dark stairway to the basement. The judge thundered after, in maddened, unthinking pursuit. Average Jones ran fleetly and easily. And his running was not for the purpose of flight alone, for as he sped through the basement rooms, he kept casting swift glances from side to side, and up and down the walls. The heavy-weight pursuer could not get nearer than half a dozen paces.

From the kitchen Average Jones burst into the hallway, doubled back up the stairs and made a tour of the big drawing-rooms and living-rooms of the first floor. Here, too, his glance swept room after room, from floor to ceiling. The chase then led upward to the second floor, and by direct ascent to the third. Breathing heavily, judge Ackroyd lumbered after the more active man. In his dogged rage, he never thought to stop and block the hall-way; but trailed his quarry like a bloodhound through every room of the third floor, and upward to the fourth. Half-way up this stairway, Average Jones checked his speed and surveyed the hall above. As he started again he stumbled and sprawled. A more competent observer than the infuriated pursuer might have noticed that he fell cunningly. But judge Ackroyd gave a shout of savage triumph and increased his speed. He stretched his hand to grip the fugitive. It had almost touched him when he leaped, to his feet and resumed his flight.

"I'll get you now!" panted the judge.

The fourth floor of the old house was almost bare. In a hall-embrasure hung a full-length mirror. All along the borders of this, Average Jones' quick ranging vision had discerned small red-banded objects which moved and shifted. As the glass reflected his extended figure, it showed, almost at the same instant, the outstretched, bony hand of "Oily" Ackroyd. With a snarl, half rage, half satisfaction, the pursuer hurled himself forward—and fell, with a plunge that rattled the house's old bones. For, as he reached, Jones, trained on many a foot-ball field, had whirled and dived at his knees. Before the fallen man could gather his shaken wits, he was pinned with the most disabling grip known in the science of combat, a strangle-hold with the assailant's wrist clamped in below and behind the ear. Average Jones lifted his voice and the name that came to his lips was the name that had lurked subconsciously, in his heart, for days.

"Sylvia!" he cried. "The fourth floor! Come!"

There was a stir and a cry from two floors below. Sylvia Graham had broken from the grasp of her terrified aunt, and now came up the sharp ascent like a deer, her eyes blazing with resolve and courage.

"The mirror," said Average Jones. "Push it aside. Pull it down. Get behind it somehow. Lie quiet, Ackroyd or I'll have to choke your worthless head off."

With an effort of nervous strength, the girl lifted aside the big glass. Behind it a hundred scarlet banded insects swarmed and scampered.

"It's a panel. Open it."

She tugged at the woodwork with quick, clever fingers. A section loosened and fell outward with a bang. The red-and-black beetles fled in all directions. And now, judge Ackroyd found his voice.

"Help!" he roared. "Murder!"

The sinewy pressure of Average Jones' wrist smothered further attempts at vocality to a gurgle. He looked up into Sylvia Graham's tense, face, and jerked his head toward the opening.

"Unless my little detectives have deceived me," he said, "you'll find the body in there."

She groped, and drew forth a large box. In it was packed the body of Peter Paul. There was a cord about the fat neck.

"Strangled," whispered the girl. "Poor old doggie!" Then she whirled upon the prostrate man. "You murderer!" she said very low.

"It's not murder to put a dying brute out of the way," said the shaken man sullenly.

"But it's fraud, in this case," retorted Average Jones. "A fraud of which you're self-convicted. Get up." He himself rose and stepped back, but his eye was intent, and his muscles were in readiness.

There was no more fight in judge "Oily" Ackroyd. He slunk to the stairs and limped heavily down to his frightened and sobbing wife. Miss Graham leaned against the wall, white and spent. Average Jones, his heart in his eyes, took a step forward.

"No!" she said peremptorily. "Don't touch me. I shall be all right."

"Do you mind my saying," said he, very low, "that you are the bravest and finest human being I've met in a—a somewhat varied career."

The girl shuddered. "I could have stood it all," she said, "but for those awful, crawling, red creatures."

"Those?" said Average Jones. "Why, they were my bloodhounds, my little detectives. There's nothing very awful about those, Sylvia. They've done their work as nature gave 'em to do it. I knew that as soon as they got out, they would find the trail."

"And what are they?"

"Carrion beetles," said Average Jones. "Where the vultures of the insect kingdom are gathered together, there the quarry lies."

Sylvia Graham drew a long breath. "I'm all right now," she pronounced. "There's nothing left, I suppose, but to leave this house. And to thank you. How am I ever to thank you?" She lifted her eyes to his.

"Never mind the thanks," said Average Jones unevenly. "It was nothing."

"It was everything! It was wonderful!" cried the girl, and held out her slender hands to him.

As they clasped warmly upon his, Average Jones' reason lost its balance. He forgot that he was in that house on an equivocal footing; he forgot that he had exposed and disgraced Sylvia Graham's near relative; he forgot that this was but his third meeting with Sylvia Graham herself; he forgot everything except that the sum total of all that was sweetest and finest and most desirable in womanhood stood warm and vivid before him; and, bending over the little, clinging hands, he pressed his lips to them. Only for a moment. The hands slipped from his. There was a quick, frightened gasp, and the girl's face, all aflush with a new, sweet fearfulness and wondering confusion, vanished behind a ponderous swinging door.

The young man's knees shook a little as he walked forward and put his lips close to the lintel.

"Sylvia."

There was a faint rustle from within.

"I'm sorry. I mean, I'm glad. Gladder than of anything I've ever done in my life."

Silence from within.

"If I've frightened you, forgive me. I couldn't help it. It was stronger than I. This isn't the place where I can tell you. Sylvia, I'm going now."

No answer.

"The work is done," he continued. "You won't need me any more." Did he hear, from within, a faint indrawn breath? "Not for any help that I can give. But I—I shall need you always, and long for you. Listen, there mustn't be any misunderstanding about this, dear. If you send for me, it must be because you want me; knowing that, when I come, I shall come for you. Good-bye, dear."

"Good-bye." It was the merest whisper from behind the door. But it echoed in the tones of a thousand golden hopes and dismal fears in the whirling brain of Average Jones as he walked back to his offices.

Two days later he sat at his desk, in a murk of woe. Nor word nor sign had come to him from Miss Sylvia Graham. He frowned heavily as Simpson entered the inner sanctum with the usual packet of clippings.

"Leave them," he ordered.

"Yes, sir." The confidential clerk lingered, looking uncomfortable. "Anything from yesterday's lot, sir?"

"Haven't looked them over yet."

"Or day before's?"

"Haven't taken those up either."

"Pardon me, Mr. Jones, but—are you ill, sir?"

"No," snapped Average Jones.

"Ramson is inquiring whether he shall ship more beetles. I see in the paper that Judge Ackroyd has sailed for Europe on six hours' notice, so I suppose you won't want any more?"

Average Jones mentioned a destination for Rawson's beetles deeper than they had, ever digged for prey.

"Yes, sir," assented Simpson. "But if I might suggest, there's a very interesting advertisement in yesterday's paper repeated this morn—"

"I don't want to see it."

"No, Sir. But—but still—it—it seems to have a strange reference to the burial of the million-dollar dog, and an invitation that I thought—"

"Where is it? Give it to me!" For once in his life, high pressure of excitement had blotted out Average Jones' drawl. His employee thrust into his hand this announcement from the *Banner* of that morning:

> DIED—At 100 West 16th Street, Sept. 14, Peter Paul, a dog, for many years the faithful and fond companion of the late Amelia Van Haltern. Burial in accordance with the wish and will of Mrs. Van Haltern, at the family estate, Schuylkill, Sept. 17, at 3 o'clock. His friend, Don Quixote, is especially bidden to come, if he will.

Average Jones leaped to his feet. "My parable," he cried. "Don Quixote and the damsel in distress. Where's my hat? Where's the time-table? Get a cab! Simpson, you idiot, why didn't you make me read this before, confound you! I mean God bless you. Your salary's doubled from to-day. I'm off."

"Yes, Sir," said the bewildered Simpson, "but about Ramson's beetles?"

"Tell him, to turn 'em out to pasture and keep 'em as long as they live, at my expense," called back Average Jones as the door slammed behind him.

Miss Sylvia Graham looked down upon a slender finger ornamented with the oddest and the most appropriate of engagement
rings, a scarab beetle red-banded with three deep-hued rubies.

"But, Average," she said, and the golden laughter flickered again
in the brown depths of her eyes, "not even you could expect a girl
to accept a man through a keyhole."

"I suppose not," said Average Jones with a sigh of profoundest
content. "Some are for privacy in these matters; others for publicity. But I suppose I'm the first man in history who ever got his
heart's answer in an advertisement."

DR. FURNIVALL,
PHYSICIAN-DETECTIVE

THE HAUTOVER CASE

At 8 o'clock on an evening in late September a group of five physicians and surgeons, gathered at the home of a colleague for the purpose of comparing professional notes, sat down to dinner. Though the conversation, originally intended to be strictly confined to medicine, soon became diverted by a chance remark of the host into the channels of criminology and medicine combined, one of their number, who for some years had acted as resident physician in the state penitentiary, and whose name was famous in penology, ate in silence without apparent interest in the subjects under discussion. He had uttered scarcely a word after entering the dining-room. This taciturnity on his part was not unusual, for he was known by his colleagues to be of a thinking rather than garrulous nature, given to few remarks even on festive occasions. However, the host, Dr. Roe, in order to draw him into the conversation, finally turned to him and said:

"Did you hear that, Furnivall? Gerrish says all criminals are insane."

Dr. Furnivall raised his head slowly and looked across the table at Dr. Gerrish.

"When did you find that out," he asked.

"What?" came in a chorus from all sides. And Dr. Roe continued: "You don't mean to say you subscribe to that?"

Furnivall raised his eyebrows and waved his hand in mock deprecation. In appearance he was an ordinary man, rather good-looking, of middle age. He wore a beard, which was streaked with gray, and the only thing about him that seemed noticeable was his eyes. These in repose were ordinary enough, too, at first glance. But a closer acquaintance with them disclosed a singular quality, which one would begin to describe as color and end by declaring to be a fascination of depth. Looking steadily into them was like standing on a precipice and gazing over till the impulse comes to plunge down. Blue, of a very dark limpid tone, one would say they were on a casual view, but a blue that flickered and waved under observation between blue and dark gray, suddenly flaming to a fixed and powerful black, which seemed to bore into one's very soul, and yet at the same time resemble a bottomless well into which it would be the most pleasing and natural thing in the world for one to jump and carelessly sink. Despite the fact that they lacked any suggestion of wildness, and that the whites were no more than normally in evidence, a true psychologist would recognize these singular eyes as most peculiarly adapted to the use of hypnotism. They had, however, never been put to these uses, as far as the doctor's friends were aware.

With the lifting of his brows and the waving of his hand, Dr. Furnivall said:

"Gentlemen, the question is one largely of terminology. What is insanity? And I suppose Gerrish means that every criminal is insane, for the moment, at least, or he would never commit the crime. Probably we would say that insanity is a state of mind which impels a person to do what no sane person would do; but that doesn't seem to help us much. It resolves itself, on one side, into a matter of observance or nonobservance of custom.

"He who does a little different from the majority is called a crank, or eccentric; if he acts greatly different he is foolish, or demented, or odd, or crazed, or insane, and so forth. Now the ordinary man does not, for example, default and run away with the funds of a bank, even when he has a chance to do so. He who does so is therefore not ordinary. Maybe he is only a fool, without sense enough to know how small are his chances for escape. Maybe he is insane. But call him what you will, his is not the normal mind."

At this another chorus went up:

"But circumstances! How are you going to leave them out? Wouldn't circumstances force, sometimes, even a normal person—"

Furnivall again waved his hand as if the question were trivial.

"A man's circumstances are the man himself; are part of him. Circumstances do not force him; he forces them. He makes them. An absolutely honest man could not be made to steal, even by the thumb screws of the inquisition, any more than he could, on the physical side, be made to lift a ton with his hands. Temptation, like muscular strength, does not lie without; it lies within. What a man is is what puts him in his circumstances. I will even venture to assert that a thoroughly wise person could, if it were possible for him to know all the circumstances surrounding any man, work back to the discovery of that man's very mind and soul, and from that basis work forward and predict every thought and act of his future life."

At this the table burst into a roar of derisive, good-humored laughter, and Gerrish said:

"You ought to have been a detective, old man. As nothing but a physician and penologist with a few letters after his name, you waste and most recklessly squander a talent that should be put to some real use in the world."

"Oh," answered Furnivall, in the midst of the laughter over this brilliant sarcasm, "you forget that I am not a wise man. It is only the wise who could work this miracle. And, further, was there ever a man whose circumstances could be all known, however simple they might seem, by any other man? I think not. Still, there are undoubtedly many cases in which one could learn a sufficient number of facts to indicate with certainty—"

At this instant the door was thrown violently open and a man came whirling in, locked in a fierce mutual embrace with the butler.

"Help, help, sir—he's crazy! He's choking me!" gasped the servant.

"Let me in, then! Curse you, I tell you it's life or death with me!"

With a last spasmodic heave he threw the butler against the wall and rushed up to Dr. Furnivall.

"Jack!" exclaimed the doctor. "What the dev—"

"For God's sake, hide me, doctor, hide me!" cried the intruder, who was a sallow youth of 22 or 23. "They're after me. Tads is dead—killed—murdered—God! And they say I did it. Hide me somewhere!"

He bounded around the room frantically as if searching with blind eyes for a way of escape or concealment.

"Sit down," commanded the doctor calmly. "You act as if something were the matter. There's nothing in the world important enough to make a sane man raise such a row."

At the word "sane" the doctors, all with the same thought, looked at each other and the stranger. The coincidence of this affair with their late subject of discussion struck them speechless. Moreover, the young man was, to their experienced eyes far from sane at that moment. That such a person should develop a homicidal tendency was within the possibilities. There was commiseration in their hearts for their colleague, for if he were interested in this youth here was an opportunity to apply his theories, and these, as he had himself hinted them, pointed inevitably to the guilt of his friend. What would he do?

The stranger threw himself upon the lounge and buried his face in his hands at the doctor's words.

"Do you want me to give myself up?" he cried hysterically.

"Dr. Roe," said Furnivall, "and my friends, this is Mr. John Harwich. Jack, pull yourself together and sit up. Don't act so childishly. You're not going to be hurt. Come, gentlemen, let's finish our dinner. In the meantime our young friend will tell us his story. Roe, please order the servants to admit anybody who calls. Now, Jack."

The youth sat erect with a jerk. His face was haggard, his eyelids quivered, his hands twitched, the thumbs inside his fingers, and his whole body trembled violently. When he spoke his voice, though not loud, gave the effect of screaming.

"Tads was found dead on his bed this afternoon; that's all," he ejaculated. "And, oh—horrible!—because I am the next heir, they say I did it."

He started up, his eyes rolling in his head, and then sank back again on the couch, lolling exhausted against the wall.

"Were you in the vicinity at the time he was found?" asked the doctor. His eyes were veiled in a downward look at the tablecloth, his fingers crumbling the bread at his plate. The observant doctors waited breathlessly for the answer.

"That is the fate of it," he burst forth. "You know I hadn't been there for months, but this morning—think of it! This day of all others—I took a spin out there in the motor, and—and—"

He groaned and threw out his hands despairingly.

The doctor, his fingers still busy with the crumbs, sat a moment in silence, while the company watched him, tense, with an emotion in which sympathy bore a large part. His face, however, never changed under their gaze from an expression indicative of calm consideration of the facts.

"Were you there long? Had you any opportunity to do it?"

"Great heavens—you don't, you can't—for God's sake say you don't believe—"

"Jack," interrupted Furnivall, looking him steadily in the eye for the first time, "sit up straight and tell your story from the beginning."

"I won't," he returned doggedly, "if you are going to think I had anything to do with it. I thought that you, above everybody, would have faith in me. I know it looks bad for me. I didn't like Tads; everybody knows that. I've been there all day, but I scarcely saw him. I was alone a good deal, too, and so was he, they say. But I didn't touch him. I didn't say three words to him. He was found on his bed at 6 o'clock, stabbed in the heart, naked, and all covered with oil. I believe whoever did it meant to burn him and the house too. They say a tramp was around there in the afternoon and got something to eat from the cook. Why don't they lay it to him? I wouldn't do such a thing as that; it isn't in me."

There was a remarkable change in the narrator's manner as he went on, the doctor's eyes holding him. Between the stubborn tone in which he began and the docile conclusion there was all the difference that lies between an ugly and an amiable child.

The skilled group, watching intently, remained silent, but they sought each other with their eyes. They had recognized an instance of true hypnotism, with no hocus-pocus about it; indeed, with no chance for anything of the kind, which is a rare thing. And they were interested to the point of enthusiasm. Not a man of them now believed the youth guilty, for had he been he would have told it as unconcernedly under the influence of that compelling gaze as he had just asserted his innocence. A less self-controlled company would have shouted applause at this unostentatious yet wonderful display of pure science.

"Is your motor outside, Jack?" asked the doctor, pushing his chair back from the table.

"Yes; at the door. I came as fast as I could to your house first, and they told me you were here." He suddenly stopped and looked around "Where's that butler? I'm sorry. I should have spoken to him, but I was excited and ran by him. He must have thought—"

The doctor, who had been scribbling a prescription, interrupted by handing it to him saying:

"Take this to a drug store, get it filled, and dose yourself. Go home. Walk. I shall want your motor for the remainder of the night. Go now, for I must be off in a hurry."

He thrust the young man from the room and turned to the company.

"He isn't guilty!" they cried, as with one voice.

"I don't know. You saw his symptoms and know what he would be capable of under sufficient stimulus. I am going down to Hautover's to find out."

"Hautover!" they exclaimed. He was the richest man in the city.

"Yes. The dead boy was his only child, and Jack is his only nephew—his sister's son. His father was my dearest friend and I was the boy's guardian till his majority."

"But," objected Dr. Gerrish, "the hypnotism, the suggestion—wouldn't that have brought out his guilt if he were guilty? That young fellow spoke the truth if ever a man did. His whole manner showed that he couldn't lie. He was a perfect automaton."

Furnivall smiled and motioned for his hat and coat.

"An epileptic, you know, forgets," he said. "If my theories are correct it would be perfectly possible for Jack, who ordinarily has a good memory, to commit a crime in a flurry of hysteria and forget all about it two hours afterward, so that he would be unable to tell of it if he would. However," he continued, "I'm going to look into the case for his sake. He's a good fellow, and shan't suffer if I can help it. Should you like to go along, Gerrish?"

Dr. Gerrish eagerly signified his assent. They entered the automobile together, and in half an hour of rapid driving, during which time scarcely a word passed between them, they arrived at the country house of Jonas Hautover.

Dr. Furnivall was well known by this gentleman, and when he stated his errand to him he willingly rehearsed the facts of the tragedy, which were substantially as Harwich had stated them. He added, however, that it was the police who accused his nephew.

"For ourselves," he concluded, "we don't know what to think. It doesn't seem possible that Jack could do such a thing. And we are all too deeply distracted to reason about the terrible affair."

"May I see the body?"

The bereaved father led the way to a chamber at the door of which a woman watcher sat, motioned them to go in, and left them alone with the dead.

The body was that of a boy of five years, fair and well formed, lying on a bed with a sheet over it. They immediately saw that in addition to the stab wound in the heart there was an abrasion of the skin of the forehead, and this Dr. Furnivall examined curiously. He beckoned to the woman at the door.

"Were you his nurse?" he asked.

"Yes, sir."

"When did you last see him alive—what time?"

The woman looked frightened. She evidently was one of more than the usual intelligence, but the situation was too large and dreadful for her. She began to weep, but managed to stammer.

"I couldn't say just exactly, sir, but I think it was around 5 o'clock."

"Where was he then?"

"He was running down the back stairs, sir, laughing, for I was after him to wash him up for dinner. And he went out the door into the grounds, at the back of the house, and nobody saw him afterward."

"Then you were the last person to see him alive?"

"Yes, sir, I suppose so, sir."

"But, as I understand it, he was struck down in his room. He must have come back again. How could he do that without being seen—with the house full of people, besides the servants?"

"I don't know, oh, I don't know, sir," she sobbed, wringing her hands. "How could the murderer himself get in and nobody see him?"

Dr. Furnivall turned again to the body.

"Notice the shape of that mark on the forehead, Gerrish," he whispered, "and remember it. They poured oil over him and were going to burn him, were they?" he continued in so strange a tone that his colleague threw him a quick glance.

Never had he seen the calm and assured Dr. Furnivall show such vivacity. The blue of his eyes had become gray, his face was alight with animation, and his movements, ordinarily slow, restrained, almost apathetic, were now lightning like in their celerity. As Dr. Gerrish gazed a strange thought came to him, and the next instant he was dumfounded to hear his companion express that very thought in words.

"Do you know, Gerrish," he said, speaking so fast that his hearer could hardly realize the utterance as that of the deliberate man he had known for so many years, "when you said at dinner that I should be a detective, I believe you hit it. It was what I was thinking about that very moment. You were joking then, but I'm not now. Why, I never felt such interest in anything, so much life fluid sparkling and boiling in me, in my life as I do this instant. I'm a new man. I feel the pure, unmixed power of the cosmos itself moving me about as a champion moves chessmen on a board. If that doesn't mean to a man that he has found his vocation, what does? It's what is called genius. I know now that I've got it, along this line, at any rate, and I'm devilish sure I never had it in medicine, as well as I succeeded. That was all work, hard, hard work, and no play. But this! Why, it's joy, it's exhilaration, intoxication! Come!"

He hurried from the room and presently stood with his friend outside gazing eagerly up at the boy's window.

"Um'm!" he muttered, darting here and there, examining the wall, the ground, and the near by summer-house. "One story—no vines, no ladder, summer-house too far off, and too low; went in that window—but how, how?—ah!"

The jerky muttering suddenly ceased, and the speaker stood with mouth open in amaze, staring at his companion. The grounds were well lighted by electricity, and though there were shadows dense and large scattered all around, the two doctors could see each ether but little less plainly than they could by day-light itself.

"What is it?" Dr. Gerrish was startled at Furnivall's look.

For answer he took him by the wrist, and bringing his hand down to the grass directly under the window, rubbed it back and forth. Then he asked:

"What have you on your hand?"

"Sweet oil," answered Dr. Gerrish promptly.

"Well?" He eyed him expectantly. It was fully ten seconds before Dr. Gerrish grasped the meaning of the interrogation. When he did his own face reflected the astonishment of Furnivall's.

"Jove!" he exclaimed, and began hurriedly examining the ground. "Yes," he continued excitedly, "the grass is broken down here, and there's oil all around. They must have spilt—"

Furnivall regarded him disgustedly.

"He was *laid* here, after the oil was poured over him," he corrected.

"Ah! And therefore you mean—"

"Certainly. In short, the boy was killed and covered with oil, and then brought into his room through that window. The crime was not committed in the house."

"It's the strangest thing I ever heard of," said Dr. Gerrish, in a low tone. "I don't understand it in the least. Such a little boy, and—it's horrible! What did they cover him with oil for? And why was he laid down here?"

"Because those things were logical results of the murderer's bent of mind."

"Yes, but how much does that explain?"

"Everything—to one who knows the murderer's motive. Now," continued Furnivall, speaking with lightning speed, "I must see everybody in that house. I know the crime, I know the motive, and the only thing necessary now is to find the person who could have that motive sufficiently strong to result in the crime.

"It was somebody who passes freely about the house and grounds, for he must have been seen going in and out, and his presence was taken for granted. That disposes of the tramp theory. It was either a guest or a servant. There was only one concerned, for the body was laid here while he went to the child's room and lowered a rope from the window. It was also a woman, and that lets Jack out, for the part of the house in which the room is located is given over to the women, and a man would not only attract notice, but cause consternation there."

Dr. Furnivall paused, and gazing straight into the eyes of his friend, added, with an abrupt change of manner to slow solemnity:

"Has it occurred to you why the body was naked?"

Dr. Gerrish shuddered and shook his head, making an awed, deprecating motion with his hands.

"I give it all up," he said. "The whole thing from beginning to end is beyond me. I thought at first that I should be interested, but I fear it's too grewsome for my stomach. I never dreamed of anything like this, and shall attend strictly to medicine hereafter. To my mind work of this sort is assigned by nature to the police."

"The police! Yes, but there are moments for every man when he himself is a policeman. Where would Jack be if left to the police? Every fact in this case points to him as the guilty one—I mean every fact as far as the police can see into it. Do you realize how many different branches of science I have used already in this search, branches which the police know only by name, and some of them not even that much? Ten! Telepathy, botany, criminology, medicine, surgery, history, religion, mathematics, psychiatry, and logic. You do not see all these in it now, but you will when the thing is over. And every one of them is a necessary constituent of the solution. Without them the truth of this unique crime would look like falsehood, and infallibly the wrong person would be made to suffer."

"I have often thought a little education would do no harm to the police," said Dr. Gerrish somewhat dryly.

"It is not the job, but the man, that counts," returned Furnivall, quickly. "And we're all of us children of nature looking for truth, each according to his ability. Now, we haven't a second to lose. I wish you would—but wait."

He slipped out of his light overcoat with a quick movement, rolled it into a bundle, and placed it carefully beneath the window.

"Now," he continued, hurriedly, "you move to the left and I'll take the right. I wish to find how far away, in the present light, that bundle can be seen. We'll make a circle and meet half way."

The result was easily found to be that outside of a small area the object could not be discerned at all owing to the shrubbery and the summer-house, except in one direction. This was along a walk between a row of maples, down which it was visible for some distance.

The doctor uttered an exclamation of satisfaction.

"The body," he said, "covered with a cloth saturated with oil, was laid here at about 6 o'clock. It was not dark enough at that hour for the lights to be turned on in the park, yet it was not full daylight, and the guests and servants were all busy preparing for dinner. It could have been done at no other time. Still the criminal took terrible chances for detection, with so many persons likely to be around. She is either a fool or a dare-devil. We must take that into account in our search for her. The servants we can examine at any time, but the guests will be leaving now—Gerrish, you must think up some plan of gathering all the visitors, male and female, into one room, so that we may see them. Tell Hautover. He'll fix it. Have them rounded up as soon as possible. I'll be back in five minutes."

He started away down the maple walk as he spoke, and Dr. Gerrish, sadly reluctant, but feeling that it must be done, sought the child's sorrowing father.

Within the stipulated time Dr. Furnivall hurriedly entered the house and found that the guests were assembling in one of the drawing-rooms, where they had been asked to meet their host, as he had something to say to them regarding his affliction.

"There are eleven of them," whispered Dr. Gerrish; "seven women and four men. Three men and four women are already gone."

"Before their time?" asked Furnivall, quickly.

"Yes, on account of this—"

"Were the women married?"

"All but one, a girl of 19 or so."

"No matter, then. The indications point to a middle aged spinster. Or she might be elderly. It is barely possible that she is married, but if so, unhappily. Fanaticism, Gerrish; look for that. Watch their eyes for fanaticism. Do you begin to see?"

He peered half curiously, half banteringly, at his colleague, who only shook his head.

"Well, then," Furnivall hurried on, "don't you remember the abrasion of the forehead, the nakedness, and the oil?"

Gerrish shuddered.

"Only too well," he said.

"And they tell you nothing?"

"Yes," he returned, "they do. They tell me that somewhere in the world there is a fiend beneath the conception of the human mind."

"Well, well," said Furnivall brusquely, "it doesn't strike me as it does you. When you've seen the 'fiend' you'll open your eyes. And I think you'll see her presently. But what's all this?"

From the drawing-room came sounds of commotion, and entering in haste, they found that the task Mr. Hautover had set for himself had been too much for his state of mind and he had collapsed on the sofa.

"You look after him Gerrish," said Furnivall. "This is just my chance. I'll speak to them myself."

While the servants carried their master from the room, followed by Dr. Gerrish, Dr. Furnivall briefly addressed the guests. He said that their host had only meant to express his regret that their stay had been so calamitously shortened, and announced that the house would be closed on the morrow. He requested that reticence be maintained regarding the day's occurrence until the guilty person should be apprehended. Suspicion had been directed toward a mendicant who had entered the kitchen for food, but very little was known as yet.

One minute later, in Hautover's chamber, he shook his head at Dr. Gerrish's look of inquiry.

"No," he said, "there isn't a person among the guests now in the house who could by any possibility be fitted into the circumstances. Though the women were, without exception, in one stage or another of hysteria, and might easily do some foolish thing in a moment of excitement, not one of them was capable of the sustained cunning and method of this crime, to say nothing of the motive of it. We must look among the servants. Hautover, how do you feel? Could you answer a few questions?"

"Yes, I think so," answered the sick man, wearily. He was lying on a couch. "It's terribly harrowing," he said, in a feeble voice "and I beg—"

"Well, then, I need only ask you to order all the female servants to assemble in the hall at once."

"Very well." He touched a button and gave his instructions.

In twenty minutes Dr. Gerrish saw Furnivall beckoning him from the doorway. He excused himself to his patient and went into the hall. Furnivall's face was alight with triumph.

"I've seen them all," he whispered eagerly, "and think I'm on the track. I am going after somebody, and, if nothing breaks, I'll give you the greatest surprise of your life inside of ten minutes. Now, I want you to fix it so that you and Hautover can hear all that is said in the boy's room, without being seen. Get him up, give him a stimulant—he can stand it—and have him there in ten minutes."

With that he left Gerrish, who stood with a look of fervent profanity in his face, staring after him, and almost ran down the maple walk, along which he had searched once before on that evening.

At the end of the walk the iron trelliswork of a gate in the wall barred his way, but he had already found that it was unlocked, and presently he was ringing at the door of a well-kept cottage across the road.

"I wish to see Miss Prentiss," he said to the maid who answered his summons. "I can't come in; I am a doctor from the Hautover place. Please ask her to step to the door, I have only a word to say to her."

"I am Miss Prentiss," said a timid voice, and a woman took the maid's place as she stepped back.

"Good evening, Miss Prentiss. I am Dr. Furnivall. I have just come from Hautover's to see if you or your sister wouldn't sit up with the child tonight. They're in such a state there, and it's a matter of trust—"

"Why, most gladly, doctor," sounded a new voice from the hall. "We will both go. Please come in and wait a moment, and we'll go right back with you. Poor dear little Tads!"

The doctor stepped forward and took the hand that was offered him by this second speaker.

"You are Miss Helen, I'm sure," he said, "They told me of your love for the little boy. His loss must be a great blow to you. Yet, as for him, if we are to believe in the rewards of the pure spirit hereafter—"

"Ah, I am so glad you look at it that way."

She gave his hand an additional pressure, looking up at him brightly through tears. She was a woman in the thirties, with light eyes and hair turning gray, with a placid, genteel expression of the face, which showed strength of character, but as a latent rather than active quality. Mildness and sweetness predominated there, though she was plainly the ruler of the household. The sister, whose features resembled hers so strongly that their relationship to each other could not be mistaken, seemed some years older, but was very evidently the silent partner. She only stood back and meekly smiled at their visitor.

The ladies, moving quickly and methodically, were soon ready, and the three set off together, the doctor walking between them. It was dark under the maples, and by comparing the walk to the dim aisle of a church he turned the conversation easily upon the subject of religion. And after some talk he said:

"I trust that the clergyman who officiates at the burial services will dwell more upon the joys of immortality than upon the sorrow the dead leaves behind with the living."

Miss Helen bent her head in the direction of her sister.

"Why, Hannah, he thinks just as we do, doesn't he?"

"Yes," she answered in her thin, colorless voice, adding, a little more strongly, "I should think everybody would."

"Of course, it's very hard to lose our friends," continued Helen, "but then it must come to that sooner or later with all of us, and it's better to escape the world's iniquities and have it all over while one is young—"

She paused and peered up at the doctor inquiringly. They had come into the glare of the electric lights now, and he smiled down at her. The smile might have meant anything, but she took it for assent, and was continuing earnestly when he cautioned her that they were approaching the house and had better finish the conversation inside.

"Now," said the doctor, as they entered the room where the body, still covered with a sheet, lay in the shade cast by a screen before the electric globes, "we can continue our interesting talk. Let me make you comfortable first. Or, stay. Perhaps you would like to see him again?"

The elder woman glanced at her sister hesitatingly. Helen immediately took her hand and led her to the bed, where the doctor turned the sheet back, glancing at the same time toward the curtained alcove.

"He was a beautiful boy," he said.

Helen bent, kissing the cold brow, and her eyes were dimmed with tears as she rose.

"Wh—why," stammered Hannah weakly, touching the body with her fingers, "they have bathed him, and the oil is all off!"

"Hannah!"

The younger wheeled upon her sister with blazing eyes.

"The oil isn't necessary," said the doctor gently, holding Helen with his gaze. "What puzzles me is how you managed to do it all without being seen. There were so many people about, and, of course, they wouldn't understand, so that it would have been very awkward—"

He paused, the elder sister was weeping into her handkerchief, but Helen stood drawn up with fury in her eyes.

"What do you mean?" she cried. "Do it? Do it? Do you mean to insinuate that we had any part in this? How dare you? Why, I loved that child better than anything on earth, and do you think I could see him grow up in this vitiated atmosphere, where all is dissipation, frivolity, idleness, and the worship of wealth, where money is God and fashion the only church? In such surroundings his soul was doomed. Could I stand tamely by while this horrible injustice was done the child of my dearest school friend? I should be unworthy the name of Christian woman. Am I not the bride of the Lamb? And when the laws of man come in conflict with the voice of God, which should I follow? It was by God's own command that I laid that little innocent at his feet, a holy sacrifice. He went to his Maker pure and unspotted—"

A deep groan and the noise of a fall sounded behind the curtains of the alcove. Jonas Hautover had fainted as the truths of the crime burst upon him.

Dr. Gerrish, pallid of face, stepped hastily between the parted curtains and hurried away for restoratives. Astonishment mingled with the grief in his expression as he glanced at the two women. Nothing further from the fiend he had pictured in his mind could be conceived than the appearance of these sisters, the one meek, retiring, humble faced; the other, though showing at the moment strong symptoms of hysteria, plainly of a sweet and gracious disposition, both of them bearing the unmistakable imprint of good breeding and benevolence.

"Heavens!" he exclaimed under his breath, "Furnivall has kept his word with a vengeance. This is the greatest surprise of my life!"

But his surprise in this direction was mingled with admiration of his friend's powers. He saw behind this strange deposition, which had begun as denial and glided easily into confession, without any apparent recognition by the speaker of the contradiction involved, the same unostentatious force which had wrought the astonishing change in Jack Harwich. It was an accomplishment of surpassing interest to science. What was it? It was not hypnotism in the usual sense, with its claptrap shows and humbuggery. And it had worked so smoothly, so directly to the point, so unerringly. Was it a gift to Dr. Furnivall alone? Or could it be acquired? And these were the predominant questions in his mind, when a little later they started on their midnight drive back to the city, for if it were to be learned, if it were a science, and application would make it his own, it should be his. The importance of such a power as that in his profession would prove incalculable.

Nevertheless he felt that now was scarcely the time to enter into that matter with the doctor, and the first thing he said when they set out was:

"Doctor, I don't at all see how in the world you managed to trace those women out."

"There was never anything more simple," he answered. "You remember that mark on the forehead? It was in the shape of a cross. That and the sacrificial oil satisfied me that it was a case of religious insanity. The rest was easy. I had only to find a person whose character fitted all the circumstances. The police searched for motive, and motive in the usual mind is synonymous with money. Therefore their suspicion pointed to poor Jack. But as soon as I saw Helen Prentiss' picture, and learned from the housekeeper that she was religious, unmarried, and therefore more likely to be subject to hysterical insanity, near middle age, lived down that walk, and had free access to the house, I knew I was on the scent. She was the only being about the premises whose character, as I saw it in her picture and learned it from the housekeeper, fitted all the facts. Both she and her sister have hallucinations, visual and auditory, and they had talked the matter of this sacrifice over for a long while, no doubt, before acting, and were both in it, the younger leading and the elder following meekly. But only the younger had the courage to hold out to the last. It was she who committed the deed, in their own house, where the child often went, and who brought the body home. An insane hospital is the place for them."

Dr. Gerrish was silent for a long while. Finally, as they rolled up to the door:

"Shall you do any more of this kind of work?" he asked, with distaste in his tone.

Dr. Furnivall took his hand.

"Gerrish," he said, "if a dear friend of your own were in trouble, whom would you rather trust his case to, the police or me?"

Gerrish bowed his head.

"Well, good luck to you," he said.

THE MYSTERY OF THE GOVERNESS

Returning to his home one spring morning from a two days' visit in the country, Dr. Furnivall, the physician detective, was met at the door of his study by Dr. Gerrish, who, without even pausing to greet him, cried out eagerly:

"Have you seen the newspapers of yesterday and today?"

"Yes. That's why I am here. I recognized your protégé's name, and hurried, for I expected you would be waiting. Begin at the beginning and tell me all about it."

It was then that, for the first time, Dr. Gerrish experienced subjectively the wonders he had twice seen worked on others by those marvelous eyes. For as he sat on the forward edge of his chair, his nerves thrilling with an excitement he had for hours striven vainly to repress, and looked into them he saw the blue of them begin rapidly to shift from blue to gray and gray to blue, flaming and undulating, so that to follow their swift and subtle changes filled him with strange sensations. A prickling shot up and down his spine, warm waves surged through his body, there was a buzzing in his ears, and his mind was a chaos of broken and jumbled-up images. He had not a sane thought in his head. Then suddenly the blue and gray leaped to a steady, limpid black, flooding him with peace. He forgot his nerves, he saw nothing but those two placid, pellucid, bottomless wells, the confusion in his mind which had left him all abroad as to the proper point at which to begin his story vanished, and he became calm and clear headed, with the tale plainly outlined in his inner vision from start to finish.

It was only by a supreme effort of will, which was most dis-
agreeable in the exercise, that he managed to switch his thoughts
momentarily aside and say deprecatingly, with a faint smile:

"You consider it necessary—for me!"

"For you, as for everybody who is confused and excited," said
Dr. Furnivall. "It's nothing but a sedative. You probably will be
surprised when you are through to find what an excellent racon-
teur you are. If so, it will be only because your mind is concentrated on your story, and does not run off at unimportant tangents.
Go on; I'm ready."

"But—," began Dr. Gerrish, with a last faint flicker of protest,
the protest a man feels against having his freedom controlled by
another in any degree.

Dr. Furnivall smiled grimly.

"I am controlling you, Gerrish," he said, "no more than I have
done a hundred times before without your knowledge. Your attention has been called to the fact now by what I did to those others,
and you recognize it, that's all the difference. And even at that I am
only doing, in principle, what you do when you give your patients
a pill. I'll tell you the secret of it in due season, and then you will see
my justification. It won't hurt you, I pass my word. Now proceed."

"Well, then," continued Dr. Gerrish, submissively, "you remember the young fellow I've been helping through the medical school.
You never saw him, but I've told you about him—Percival Warner.
He was graduated last year. It seems he was engaged to be married to this Blanche Goodwin, and they used to walk together evenings along the river banks. Night before last, Tuesday night, she
left her home at 8 o'clock—she's a governess with the Parkers—to
meet him, as it is supposed, but she didn't return, and in the morning her body was found in the river.

"The papers raised a great hue and cry over it, of course. Naturally the suspicions of the police flew to Warner, though, as there
were no bruises on the corpse and no signs of choking, some
thought she might have been dazzled by the lights where the road
is being repaired and fallen over the rocks into the water in the
darkness.

"Those who knew Warner wouldn't listen to a word against him. He was dead in love with the girl, as she was with him, they said, and the two were bending all their efforts toward the accumulation of an income sufficient to warrant their entering the marriage relation.

"They were bound up in each other. But when it was found that Warner himself had left his room that evening at 8 o'clock and had not been seen afterward, the police were satisfied. They held that there had been a quarrel and he had pushed her overboard, so they began to search for him. That evening, Wednesday, a man came in great fear and trembling to the police lieutenant and said that he was a watchman in the car barn near by, and that on Tuesday evening he had seen Miss Goodwin and Warner, both of whom he knew well by sight, leaning on the bridge railing together. Suddenly he heard the girl say, 'Don't, don't kill me, Percy. You said you would once before.' Upon that Warner struck her and she fell on the roadway. The watchman hurried up and said, 'Mr. Warner, you'll suffer for this.' Warner returned furiously, 'If you open your mouth about it I'll serve you the same,' and threw the girl into the river. Then the watchman, who was a much smaller man than Warner, ran back to the barn and locked himself in, where he remained until his conscience overcame his fear of Warner, when he ventured forth and gave his information."

Dr. Gerrish here paused and produced a large diary, bound in red. His voice had been perfectly restrained, indeed mechanical, as he repeated the grewsome story, and now he continued in the same tone, still held as if unconsciously by Furnivall's gaze, his eyes never straying the width of a hair from those bottomless depths, even when he showed the diary and laid its pages open:

"This volume I found in her room when I went there yesterday. It is a confession of her passionate love, the record of a year and more. She tells how first she met him, where they went, what they did, and so on, for nearly every day during the year. The minutest details are gone into, and the most passionate and intimate passages between them are given with perfect candor. In short, it is the whole love story of two extravagantly fond people. But—"

Dr. Gerrish placed the diary carefully on the table and added:

"It was always in the afternoon, not evening, that she met him, and his name was not Percival, but John."

Dr. Furnivall jumped to his feet and clapped his hands in the air.

"Jove, Gerrish!" he exclaimed delightedly, "you're a jewel! 'Tis the most beautiful complication! The curves and angles are as clean cut and lovely as in a Greek statue, or even in the propositions of Euclid himself. Let me see that diary."

He examined it rapidly, pushing over the leaves from the first page to the last. Then he threw it down. As he did so, Dr. Gerrish said, with returning nervousness:

"Do you remember your last words to me the night of the Hautover case?"

"Why, I believe I asked you, when you seemed to disapprove of my neglecting medicine for detective work, whether if you had a friend in trouble you would rather leave his case to the police or me?"

"Yes, that was exactly it. But I little thought I should ever have to call on you. It was abstract justice I was thinking of when I wished you good luck, justice which you might force when some poor fellow was suffering unjustly. Now—now—"

Furnivall wheeled upon him as he hesitated.

"Do you mean," he said, "that if this young man is guilty you don't wish me to prove it?"

Gerrish remained silent, his eyes turned persistently away from Furnivall's.

"I—I don't know what to say," he stammered finally. "I fairly loved that boy, he was all that is noble and manly. He simply couldn't have done it. I knew his people. They were sound mentally and physically. Yet—yet! That diary—suppose he had found out about this other man—and now his absence—the watchman's confession—"

Furnivall waved his hand carelessly and sank back into his seat.

"All right," he said. "It is a mere matter of weight between the boy's character as you know it, and the evidence against him. With you the evidence is the heavier."

"But isn't it with you?" Gerrish regarded his friend eagerly. "I brought the whole case to you, just as I saw it, in order to get your opinion—to see if—if there wasn't some hope, some way—"

"Of escape for the guilty!" interrupted Furnivall dryly.

Gerrish's fair face colored.

"If I had a noble and manly friend," went on Dr. Furnivall in a matter of fact tone, "I should think it my sacred duty to consider him innocent until he was proved guilty. And I'd fight the whole world for him. But you do not seem to believe, really, that 'noble and manly' describes this friend of yours, though you used the phrase. Or else," he added after a pause, and with sarcasm, "you think it possible that a manly and noble youth, with good blood back of him, could knock down a defenseless girl and throw her body into the river."

"But—but—the evidence—" objected Gerrish helplessly.

"I will undertake to solve this mystery, but only to find the truth," interrupted Dr. Furnivall imperturbably.

Gerrish, with a sudden determined expression, arose.

"Come," he said, "I'll help you—but I'd stake my life on the boy."

"Well, that would have been something like, if you had said it in the first place," grumbled Furnivall, as they hastened out. "Your suspicions should have indicated the other man instead of the one you trusted, as soon as you saw the diary. Why shouldn't it be he? But that's the way with the human mind," he added querulously, as they entered his motor and sped away, "it always jumps to the thing it fears most, like the moth to the candle. It can't seem to see anything else. So it is always biased in the direction of overthrow, like the old woman who was afraid she'd go out over the back of the sleigh every time it struck a cradle in the road, and so finally did."

"That's right, give it to me," said Gerrish. "I know I deserve it, and will accept it meekly."

"Yes—because you think I believe your friend innocent. That eases your mind. But I am not at all sure of that innocence. The whole thing looks bad for him, and the only argument on his side, so far, is his character. If you have read him rightly he would never dream of hurting the girl, even if he found her perfidious. He would rather be glad to get rid of her by turning her over to the happy John. If you have been mistaken in him all things are possible. I don't know him myself, so I rely on you, and must work on the supposition that he could not have done it, as straight against him as the evidence tends. Life is full of coincidences, cases of mistaken identity, and appearances as distinguished from truth. You learned that long ago in your practice. Besides, on the other side, any person who could commit murder should be nabbed and put where he couldn't, even if he had been thought manly and noble. Here we are."

They were now in a small suburb, the scene of the crime, some three miles out, and drew up at the door of the undertaker's establishment where the body lay.

"If you had told me we were coming here I could have saved you the trouble, for I have seen the body, and there are no marks of violence on it," said Dr. Gerrish as they alighted.

Dr. Furnivall did not answer until they had pushed through the mob of men, women, and children around the door of the little place. Then he said:

"I am not looking for signs of violence, but for something quite different," adding, as he motioned for the two or three neighbors, who stood staring awestricken at the corpse, to move back, "I must make the facts my own at first hand as nearly as possible. Different men do not see even plain facts alike on all sides."

Dr. Gerrish, watching curiously, saw his brows knit as he scrutinized the face of the dead. An introspective expression came into his features as if he were making an effort of memory, and for some seconds he remained in an indeterminate attitude, one hand on the marble slab on which the body lay, bending over it, though apparently seeing with the eyes of the mind alone. Suddenly he turned to the undertaker's assistant.

"I suppose she was brought directly here from the river?"

"Yes, doctor," he answered respectfully. He was a callow youth with mild features, who, having been smoking and playing cards with several other men in an inner room, laid his cigar on a shelf, closed the door, and came forward zealously when he recognized the famous physician of the penitentiary.

"Have any of the Parkers, the people who employed her, been here?"

"No, sir. Mr. Parker left for the West last night, and I suppose Mrs. Parker—she's pretty tony, you know."

"Who found the body?"

"The groceryman, Bill Anderson, doctor. He was just coming from the Parker place. The police had her brought here and sent for her relatives."

"Where are her clothes?"

"Here, doctor," pointing. "They were soaked through and about spoilt, but we dried 'em out."

Furnivall turned to them briskly. They were lying on a table in a heap, and he examined several pieces one by one.

"I'll wager you confined your attention to the body, Gerrish," he said. "You never looked at these?"

"Certainly not. Why should I? They wouldn't be likely to show what the body didn't."

"Don't you see anything extraordinary in them now?"

"Why, no. I can't say I do. But stay—they have been cut or torn in pieces—"

"Yes, yes. The name-marks were removed. That is strange, certainly, but is that all you see?"

Gerrish scanned them again and shook his head.

"I am a physician, not a dressmaker," he said, somewhat sarcastically.

"Nor a detective," added Furnivall. "But I am. And I see enough in that pile of wearing apparel to upset my whole theory of the case."

"You had a theory, then?" asked Gerrish eagerly.

"Certainly, and a wrong one, when, but for your stupidity, it would have been the right one—as it is now," he added, rushing from the shop and jumping into the automobile, without paying any attention to his companion's look of amazement and hurt. The next moment they were whirling down the street, and presently drew up at a telegraph office.

Into this Furnivall hurried, telling Gerrish to remain where he was, and stayed a full half hour. Through the windows he could be seen consulting a newspaper and dashing off numerous telegrams. When he reappeared it was with a countenance eminently good humored.

"We'll see the watchman next," he said as they shot away. "They told me in there that they held him up to this morning, and then decided to let him go on the car company's recognizance. He is probably asleep now in his room at the barn, for his work is done at night. As I question him, watch him, for unless I'm most egregiously mistaken you'll see something of curious interest to psychiatry."

"I suppose it's my stupidity," returned Gerrish, "but I confess that your theories seem to me to be made too nearly out of whole cloth. How can you have any notion of what this man is like or what he will do or say, or that he will prove interesting to science? I admit," he added hastily, as Furnivall stared at him, "that you usually hit the bull's-eye, but how?—that's what sticks me, and I ask for information?"

Furnivall threw back his head and laughed.

"Why," he said, "allowing for a few additions and subtractions as I go along, it is the simplest thing in the world. Tell me, now, how many new kinds of crime have you heard of since you were a boy in college?"

"Well," returned Gerrish, thinking slowly, "I used to read—"

"Exactly," Furnivall interrupted, "you had read Poe, Gaboreau, and the others and history, besides the newspapers, and so, even as a boy, you were familiar with all of them, or had heard of all of them. For there are no new ones. They are new only until they are laid bare, when they are seen to be one of a class that has been known pretty nearly from the dawn of time. Isn't that so?"

"I don't know but it is," said Gerrish, doubtfully. The thought was a strange one to him and he couldn't entertain it too readily.

"Yes. We have twenty-six letters of the alphabet only, and out of these 250,000 different words are made to compose the English language. In physics there are some seventy bases, and of these are constituted all the different objects on earth. And you know how it is in medicine, how few at bottom the principles are, and what an enormous multitude of forms they can be made to assume. Schiller and others showed that all the various plots employed by dramatists and story-tellers in all the ages may be reduced to an extraordinarily small number at bottom. I don't recollect how many, but somewhere about the twenties. And it is so with every-thing, even with crime. The principles involved are few, and one who is familiar with the subject, who has digested and co-ordinated all the cases, has only to learn the facts of a crime in order to name the class to which it belongs. The class being determined, the next thing is to find the person concerned whose character would ad-mit of his belonging to that class, as in language, physics, medi-cine, and plots."

"Ah! You think, then, that this watchman—" began Gerrish, excitedly.

"Sh–h!" cautioned Furnivall, "this is the place, I fancy," and stopped the machine before the office of the car barn.

They found, as Dr. Furnivall had prophesied, that the watch-man was asleep in a distant corner of the building. The superin-tendent offered to send for him, but Furnivall declined the favor and asked to be shown to the room. Here the man was awakened without difficulty, and, lying in bed, told his story as the newspa-pers had printed it, and as it had been repeated by Dr. Gerrish.

A thrill of excitement shot through the younger physician as his friend, standing in front of the reclining man and looking down into his eyes, began to question him. He expected some startling denouement, though he had no idea what its nature would be, and he listened and watched with bated breath. The man was a white faced, sandy little Irishman of perhaps 30, with thin, reddish whis-kers and hair, nervous in manner, and his speech, though directly to the point while he was telling his story, was quick and jerky.

But for the frequent short pauses between phrases the words would have tumbled over each other as they shot from his colorless lips and became an incoherent jargon. He was thoroughly in earnest, however, and spoke apparently right from his heart, with spasmodic gestures.

"Let's see, this was on Tuesday evening," said Furnivall. "At what time did you first notice this young couple?"

"'Twas jist tin minutes afther nine, sor. 'Twas sure that toime, becaze why? Becaze Oi go round th' place wanst ivery hour, an' 'tis jist tin minutes Oi am frum th' office t' th' soide dure phwere Oi seen thim. Oi shtart in th' office, sor, an' phwin Oi pass th' dure Oi'm alwuz afther takin' a look out, jist fer t' mind th' weather, sor, an' how bes it out around th' yard, an' 'twas th' nine o'clock thrip."

"Were they on the bridge then?"

"They wuz, sor, lanin' on th—"

"How did you know them? The night was dark, wasn't it?"

"Sure Oi did not know thim at th' toime, sor, but I thought it wes thim, becaze they do be afther walkin' around th' bridge scand'lous frequent, an thin phwin she calls him 'Percy' I knows, an' phwin Oi runs up til 'im Oi sees him, sor, an' Oi shpakes til 'im, faith, an' be th' same token he shpakes back."

"Yes, and the woman? She was lying on the bridge at that moment, wasn't she?"

"She was, sor. An Oi sez—"

"Was she laid straight out, doubled up, or how?"

"Oi c'u'dn't say, sor. Oi jist seen her there."

"Was she moaning, or moving around any?"

The Irishman wrinkled his brows and stared into his questioner's eyes with an expression of dismay.

"Sure, me mind is black dead," he said in astonishment. "Oi can't think."

"Well, and when he threatened you, you ran back to the barn?"

"Oi did, sor, loike a snipe, an' locked mesel' in."

"Isn't the car barn kept open later than 9 o'clock? Weren't there any people about, conductors and motormen, and others, with cars going and coming all the time?"

Again the puzzled expression possessed his face, and he answered:

"Oi don't remember, sor."

"Yes. And you didn't go your rounds after that, but remained locked in your room, this room?"

"Oi did, sor."

"And you stayed here all the next day?"

"Oi did."

"Sleeping?"

"No, sor. Oi c'u'dn't shlape, Oi was that frighted."

"Did you eat anything?"

"Oi—oi don't remimber."

"Where do you get your meals usually?"

"Wid th' Widdy McGuire. 'Tis a boardin' place she kapes."

"Yes. When did you first hear that the body had been found in the river?"

"Siven o'clock, sor, that mornin'. 'Twes Tim Dooley, th' conductor, sor, wes afther tellin' me. Miss Goodwin—"

"Where did you see this Dooley?"

"On th' car, sor, phwin he jumped off an' wint t' th' office, sor."

"Yes, and where did you get your newspaper that day?"

"In th' office, sor. 'Tis there Oi get it ivery marnin'.'"

"Then, I suppose, you went to your breakfast at McGuire's, and afterwards came up here and read your paper?"

"Yis, sor."

"There was nothing about the crime in it?"

"Nor, sor, 'twes th' marnin paper. 'Twes in th' avenin' wan it foist came out."

"And how did you get that?"

"Oi bought it, sor, mesil', aff a b'y in th' shtrat."

Furnivall looked coolly at his friend.

"Well, thank you, my man," he said, "for your trouble. Don't fear that fellow any longer, but go to sleep in peace. I'll guarantee he'll never hurt you."

"What in the name of heaven can you make out of that?" cried Gerrish as the door closed behind them. "That fellow lied right and left, and was as honest as a judge about it. I never in my life saw a case of such glaring mendacity in words coupled with such honesty of manner."

"I told you you'd see something of curious interest, but you don't seem to catch on yet. No matter, you will soon. Ah, here's a door that must be the one he mentioned. Can you see any bridge from here?"

"Great Scott, man, the bridge is on the other side of the barn."

"Yes, but do you see any door on that side?"

"No, and there is none. There are only windows, and they're so high up that it would require a giraffe to see out of them. Of all the liars—"

"Come into the office," interrupted Furnivall, rubbing his hands delightedly. "I wish to show you something."

The superintendent, who was very obliging to the well-known physician, produced the watchman's time card for Tuesday night, at his request. Without looking at it Furnivall passed it over to his friend, saying:

"You understand these cards, don't you? See, this is a flat disk of paper, with the hours marked on it, like a clock. It fits into a machine in the office, and when the watchman presses a certain button on each floor the push is registered here. This is the disk for Tuesday night. If you don't find every floor registered there for every hour of the night—the night, mind you, when, he claimed, he was locked in his room trembling: with fear—"

"It's all here," cried Gerrish in disgust. "On every floor, every hour. He performed his duties that night the same as usual. By Jove, that fellow committed the crime himself, and is trying to—"

Furnivall looked at him quizzically.

"What did he do with Warner, then? Warner could throw that little fellow a rod, couldn't he?"

Gerrish appeared chagrined.

"That's so," he admitted. "Still," he continued, "I thought this hypnotism of yours made a man tell the truth. How could he contradict himself so? And what does it all mean?"

"Ah, it's Pilate's old question. 'What is truth?' And it means that you have just witnessed what I thought you would—a spectacle of extraordinary interest to both medicine and law. Did you see how straight he had his story until I began to question him? It was then that the contradictions began. Do you think those contradictions and those blank spots in his mind would have appeared if my eye hadn't held him? If I had looked another way, or if a lawyer in court had put the questions, those gaps would have been easily and logically filled, and the tale as straight as a string. Even that part about the door, a curious and interesting slip of the mind, yet seen to be common enough, too, when analyzed, he would have doctored up in some way."

"But that time card. How can you explain that? Isn't it strange that nobody has thought of examining it in connection with his confession?"

"Not at all—so far. The first excitement hasn't worn off yet. They swallowed everything he said without question, he was so honest about it, and because he came of his own accord to tell it and give himself up. Later, of course, after a lot of prying around, the defects of his logic would appear. But come—I must return to the telegraph office."

"But the watchman—shouldn't he be arrested—"

"No, no; he's safe. Let him alone. Only," he added, as they whirled away, "it will be a good exercise for you to think his case over during the next few minutes, applying his character and temperament, as you read them, to the circumstances. Perhaps you will be able to get a little light on those strange antics in the witness box that occur so frequently."

At the telegraph office he received a message which seemed to please him, and which he immediately answered. From there he drove back to the undertaker's, and, leaving word that the body should be put in condition for removal within two hours, headed for the Parker mansion.

"Doesn't it strike you as singular, Gerrish," he said, as they rolled smoothly along, "that Parker should have disappeared just

now, and that nobody from his house has called to view the remains?"

Gerrish threw him a startled glance.

"Good heavens," he exclaimed. "Another complication. I never
thought of that before."

"Ah! I told you, you know, in the beginning, that it was a beautiful case."

"It may be beautiful according to your notion," returned Gerrish
disgustedly, "but it strikes me quite otherwise. To me it is grewsome and beastly—an inextricable snarl full of contradictions and
impossibilities, that never in the world can be disentangled."

"Well, yes, it is grewsome from a personal, or even human, point
of view. But in order to serve out justice the mystery must be regarded in a spirit of pure science, as a problem in astronomy or
law. I can't afford to entertain the sympathetic side until justice is
done, for it would warp and bias my judgment, so leading to injustice. As for its being inextricable, so is the mystery of the parallax
of a star, I suppose, but to whom?"

"Well, of course, to the ignorant," responded Gerrish, somewhat sheepishly. "Still," he added, "that sort of thing can be learned,
while this seems to me all guesswork."

"Oh, does it? My dear fellow, the rules of crime are as lucid
and yet rigid as those of mathematics. The expert has only to learn
the facts and then apply the rule. Of course, the difficulty lies in
getting the true facts, and all of them. It is especially hard to glean
the truth from witnesses, for the human mind is so constituted that
a man rarely tells a story twice in just the same way, however honestly he may try, unless he has committed it carefully to memory.
And those who do that, those who tell the straightest tale, are precisely those we should suspect. For plain truth does not think of
preparation, and may, therefore, often be easily disconcerted, while
falsehood stands seemingly invulnerable. But there are rules, rules!
And I know them. I am applying them now. And when this problem is solved you will see the beauty of it as I do."

"Hold up!" cried Gerrish at this moment. "Here's where the
body was found, right there, on the edge, in shallow water."

"That's nothing," returned Furnivall, not even turning his head.

"Nothing! Why, the police and the other detectives rushed out here the first thing!"

"I'm this detective," said Furnivall, with a grimness that passed into a smile as his companion looked his astonishment.

"There's another thing I can't understand," said Gerrish, after, a moment of silence. "From start to finish you have scarcely mentioned this other man, this John, when, as it seems to me—"

"I'll introduce you to him this evening," was the quick response.

Dr. Gerrish was still floundering helplessly in the midst of this amazing idea when the car stopped at the Parker mansion.

The two physicians sent in their cards, and after some minutes of waiting on their part in the drawing-room, Mrs. Parker appeared. She was a woman of 28 or 30, with flashing black eyes, muddy skin, thin, uncurving lips, an angular form that was too plainly padded, and a peremptory manner. She was, however, very gracious in her greeting to her visitors.

"So glad to see you, Dr. Furnivall," she said. "Such a pleasant surprise. And Dr. Gerrish, too! Please be seated, gentlemen. I trust," she added, turning to Dr. Gerrish, "there is nothing more about that—that person regarding whom you called yesterday. It has all been extremely annoying to us—"

"Only," said Dr. Furnivall, "to ask her character, and whether she left of her own accord or was discharged?"

"I discharged her!" exclaimed the lady quickly, and with spontaneous heat. Then her eyes, flashing into Dr. Furnivall's, hesitated, wavered, became fixed there, a slight color warmed her cheeks and she continued evenly: "I should have discharged her in the morning if she had not left, for I simply could not endure it longer. I am sorry she took her life, of course. I do not find any fault with the girl, really, for she could not help being beautiful, but Philip—"

"I think that is sufficient," Dr. Furnivall interrupted hastily, rising. "Jove!" he added to Gerrish as they re-entered the auto, "I couldn't let her go into details of that nature. Besides, it was enough. Now, one more point, only one, and the thing is settled. Oh, but it's beautiful, beautiful!"

"Yes, just like clockwork, isn't it?" said Gerrish with sarcasm. "For my part, I can't see but the whole matter is more hopelessly involved than ever. How did you know the girl's connection with the Parkers was severed?"

"Mrs. Parker told me," returned Furnivall with a chuckle.

"Um—m!" Dr. Gerrish looked meek. He thought he really might have guessed out that part of the riddle without help. Then, the next moment, his face became illuminated with intelligence. It actually beamed as he turned it on his friend and exclaimed:

"J. Philip Parker was the 'John' of the diary—he is missing—it was he who—who—when he found that Percy—"

His voice trailed off and died away as the objections to this theory suddenly struck him. Besides, Furnivall was roaring with heartfelt laughter.

"My dear Gerrish," said his friend when he had controlled his mirth sufficiently to speak, "I always liked you from the first time I saw you, but now I'm beginning fairly to love you. You are so irreproachably innocent and ingenuous! It's a fortunate thing this young protégé of yours is not abandoned to your tender mercies, for you'd have him in jail before morning though he was as innocent as the Great Mogul himself. Medicine, plain and unadulterated medicine, is your line, where the paths of science are straight and pure, and in which you have already covered yourself with glory. Don't risk ignominy by scattering your talents. Medicine—stick to pure medicine, my boy. Take my advice."

"I most certainly intend to do so hereafter," he returned with a good-humored laugh. "What I can't comprehend is how you yourself can stomach this kind of thing."

"Oh, I'm a sort of Apollo, merely glancing at the mist rising from the River Styx, and thereby changing it into a beautiful rainbow," returned Dr. Furnivall lightly.

He stopped at the telegraph office again as he spoke, ran in, and Dr. Gerrish saw through the window that he received a large package of messages which he began to open eagerly. At the seventh he stopped reading, threw the others unopened into a wastebasket, consulted his watch, and, hastily re-entering the car, started it at speed toward the city.

"Another complication?" suggested Dr. Gerrish, not knowing what to make of his companion's manner, which, from the signs, might have been anything from anxiety to amazement, or even suppressed jubilation.

"You'll think so when you see it," was all he could answer.

In ten minutes, to Dr. Gerrish's surprise, they drew up at his own door. Dr. Furnivall made no movement to alight, however, but again looked at his watch and threw a quick glance down the street. Then he sat back in his seat, lit a cigar, and took his ease.

Dr. Gerrish said nothing, for his eyes were on a hack the driver of which was lashing his team as if he had been paid to hurry, and it seemed as if he were about to crash right over the automobile. The next instant the horses were thrown on their haunches, with their noses almost touching the machine; the driver jumped down, wrested the hack door open, and a man and woman emerged, making hastily for the entrance to the young physician's office. He then gave one look and sprang erect as if electrified.

"Good heavens—Percy!" he cried.

"And Mrs. Percival Warner," suavely said Dr. Furnivall, "formerly Miss Blanche Goodwin. Do you see the beauty of the solution now?" he added, with a droll cast of the eye.

"The moment I read of the affair in the papers," said Dr. Furnivall to his delighted friend that evening in the speaker's study, "I suspected accident despite the watchman's story. My theory was based on Warner's character as you had found it to be. I thought as others did, that the girl, dazzled by those lanterns along the road, might have missed her way and fallen in, and that Warner, failing to find her at the trysting place, and led astray for some reason known to himself, was searching for her out of town, which would explain his absence.

"The watchman, as surely as Warner's character was what you believed, was subject to neuropathic hysteria, and after dwelling a whole day on the subject had imagined that scene. We have many such cases on record. It proved that I was right. His hysteria, aggravated by the crime so near by, the loneliness of his occupation, his knowing the girl, too, as he thought, and perhaps a tinge of

266 GEORGE F. BUTLER

that love for notoriety we see everywhere—through all this he had conjured up that vision and seen it so frequently in his mind that he fully believed it. In his confession he stated the truth as he saw it. It was only under my influence and through my examination that the contradictions and gaps showed, for he was unprepared for the questions and could tell only what was in his mind. Many a man with his trouble has shown up as a rascal on the witness stand, and in private life, too, when he was only diseased. So much for him.

"Then, when you informed me of the diary, and showed it to me, I believed I recognized another phase of hysteria in its glowing, often incoherent, pages, and thought of suicide, because, never dreaming that the body was not hers, I could explain the facts in no other way. You recall the Pledgett case, in which the woman kept a diary for a whole year, detailing a love affair, just as in this instance, and there wasn't a word of objective truth in it. I reasoned that Miss Goodwin, with her mind excited by the hallucinations of her disease, subject as she must be to fits of deep melancholia, had jumped into the river. But as soon as I viewed the body and those clothes—why, man alive, where were your eyes? The face might possibly have passed for that of a fairly intelligent woman, but not a cultivated one. Certainly she never could have been the governess of Philip Parker's children.

"I had, too, a dim recollection of a housemaid who was missing, according to the papers, and, as I recalled the description, it seemed to fit. The clothing settled the question. No woman who was sufficiently cultured to be your friend's sweetheart, or a governess either, could dress so tastelessly. I knew it was the lost maid, doubtless a suicide, from the fact that her name had been cut from her garments, so I telegraphed the police and received word that she would be called for by her brother.

"The groceryman who, you remember, was the first to identify the body, had gone to the Parker place for his morning order, without doubt learned that the governess had fled, and then, of course, the rest was natural and inevitable. Any body found near there would be that of Miss Goodwin if it bore even a remote resemblance to her; and the mob, expecting to see Miss Goodwin, when they looked at the body, simply saw her. That is human. It isn't likely that she was well known by any of them, and a body lying dead and nearly naked on a slab isn't expected to resemble very closely the same body alive, erect, and fashionably attired. The identification of a corpse even by intimate friends is often a very difficult matter.

"In the meantime my theory! It was annihilated. Though Miss Goodwin was not dead, as far as we knew, she was missing, and Warner's case was not much improved. I had to begin all over again. Where was she? There seemed to be only one answer. Since her lover also was absent she probably was with him. If with him, then married to him. They had for some cause slipped away suddenly to be married. Where would they naturally go for the purpose? To the home of one of her relatives. These, according to the newspaper, were many. I telegraphed them all, for I had the paper with their addresses in my pocket.

"But why should they disappear so suddenly? Logically, because something had happened either to him or her. The chances were that it was to her, for the Parkers had not called at the undertaker's—a curious fact—and Parker himself had suddenly gone away. While we were waiting for the answers to my telegrams we could visit the girl's employers.

"We did, and in ten seconds learned what we wished to know. Philip Parker preferred the beautiful governess to his ugly wife, had made advances to her, which for some time had grown more and more marked, attracting the notice of Mrs. Parker, until on that evening he had gone too far, she could endure it no longer, had fled hastily, leaving all her things behind, told Percy, and then, she being homeless, there was but one thing to do, and they did it. The next evening they saw in the papers that he was being searched for, and were already on their way to your house, by the 8:10 train, when my telegram reached the cousin at whose home they were married.

"On my receipt of this news we had just time enough to meet them at your door. As for the diary—look here."

It was still lying on the table, where he had thrown it that morning, and, opening it, he pointed to several phrases, one under another, on the margin of the first part. A pen line had been drawn through all but the lower of them, which was, "Love's Depths," and this remained unscratched.

"She has evolved a novel—in the first person," he grinned. "And this is the rough draft of it, with Percival, under the pseudonym of 'John,' for the hero. She had the usual difficulty in choosing a suitable name for it, and finally hit upon 'Love's Depths.' Is everything plain now?"

Dr. Gerrish screwed up his lips, lighting a fresh cigar.

"All but one little item," he answered, puffing.

"What's that?"

"I am wondering what will happen to J. Philip Parker when Percy finds him."

"Not much doubt about that either, in my mind," responded Dr. Furnivall.

THE TIN BOX

The chief of the Centreville police raised his head in astonishment. Just at the moment when he had settled down in his chair for a morning nap the door of the little office swung open with a crash and a great hulk of a man staggered in, collapsing on the settee.

The intruder's hands were pressed to his sides, the breath whistled in his throat, his face burned a violent red through a heavy dark beard, and, leaning with one shoulder hunched against the back of the settee, head hanging, mouth dropping, he presented alarming signs of physical exhaustion.

"Hi—hi there, Bill!" cried the chief, recognizing him at once. "What's th' matter?"

"Ma—matter! Ma—matter enough! It's murder!" gasped Bill.

"What!"

The dreadful word scared the officer into activity as if it had been a bodily danger. He darted around the railing which inclosed his desk and shook the big man, raising his chin roughly and staring into his face.

"It's old woman Snowman—and Ed, too. Both on 'em," the man gasped, recovering a little breath. "I run all th' way."

The officer blinked his eyes rapidly, as if trying his best to concentrate his faculties. It plainly was a difficult task. Out of the chaos in his mind only one thought, as being related to familiar things, evolved itself, and he asked pertinently:

"Why didn't ye harness up and ride, Bill?"

"Harness up!" exclaimed Bill. "Why, goshamitey, Hezekiah, I didn't have no time. I had t' git here!"

If Bill's notions of time-saving on a two-mile journey struck the chief as peculiar, he gave no sign of the fact. The word harness had suggested the first step in his mode of procedure, and in great excitement he rushed to the stable and hitched up his own rig. All of the four members of his staff were away on their beats, so that a legitimate substitute to leave in charge of the police station was lacking, but that was no obstacle to the chief. He cried out to his only prisoner, a vagrant, who could be seen behind the bars in an inner room:

"Hi, you! If anybuddy calls tell 'em I'm over t' old woman Snowman's!" And the next moment, with the reanimated Bill beside him, he was rattling along the dusty road into the country toward Spuzz's hill. Then, invigorated in body and somewhat brightened in mind by the sunlight and fresh air of a clear autumn morning, he began to question his companion about the facts of the case as far as he knew them. These were few, but to the point, and, divested of Bill's peculiarities of narration and speech, were as follows:

Mrs. Snowman, an aged widow, who was considered as wealthy as she was miserly, and her bachelor son, Edward, lived in a little house on their extensive farm on Spuzz's hill. With them stayed a middle-aged woman, Susan, a distant connection, who worked around the place for her board. This woman, who was looked upon as somewhat soft in the head, and seemed of a mild and colorless disposition, had come running in her night gown that morning at daybreak to the nearest neighbor, a Mr. Henshaw, who was the narrator's father, and with an appearance of great fright declared that Mrs. Snowman and her son had been murdered. She said that she slept in the same room with her mistress; that hearing her scream suddenly in the night she jumped up, and, seeing a big man striking her with a club as she lay in bed, ran from the house and hid in the yard. In about five minutes the door opened and two men came hurrying out and went toward the woods. One was a very large man, the other rather small. That was all the description she could give of them, for, although there was a candle burning in the kitchen, where the son slept, its rays were dim, and when the two men came out the morning was only just breaking and their features were invisible to her in the uncertain light. Not daring to venture back to the house she had finally decided to arouse the Henshaws, a quarter of a mile away.

By the time the story was finished they had arrived at the scene of the tragedy. Eight or ten neighbors were already there, and the chief, springing to the ground, made his way through them with dignity and entered at the door. The case called for tactics entirely new in his experience. He had not the least notion of the proper course to take, but he was a man of great confidence of manner, and as he stood on the threshold surveying the grewsome spectacle he seemed to the eager watchers to be perfect master of the situation. The lines of wisdom and command in his face were much more plainly marked than they are in the countenances of Alexander and Caesar as they have come down to us on medals and statues. Stepping in and closing the door behind him, he said to the elder Henshaw, a little old man with a bushy white beard, who stood frightened and helpless in the middle of the floor:

"Put out that candle! We don't need candles now; it's daylight."

Whereupon the light was extinguished and it became dark as night in the room, owing to the fact that there were shutters on the windows, which seemed to be nailed up and could not be opened.

"Wall, why didn't ye say so afore ye blowed the candle out?" said the chief magisterially, when he learned this. "Light her up again. Now, le's see what all this is about."

The kitchen contained a cot bed, and on this was huddled the body of the son, frightfully bruised about the head. The bedding was twisted, torn and stained with blood, part of it on the floor, and one of the two pillows hung over the edge of the sink ten feet distant. Opening out of the kitchen was a door into another room, and in this the mother lay, also in bed and battered in the same dreadful manner. The bed was so nearly the width of the room that there was scarcely space enough in which to walk between it and the wall, but there seemed to be a considerable vacant area at one end, beyond the high head-board. Candle in hand, the chief advanced and found another cot bed on the floor, and in a corner a small bureau.

He stood a moment regarding the scene speculatively. Then he looked toward the elder Henshaw, who was peering timidly through the doorway.

"Whereabouts'd Susan say she wuz when she see him clubbin' her?" he asked in a whisper.

"Why, she wuz riz up in bed," responded the old man, edging back from too close proximity to the ghastly body.

"If she wuz in there," pointing, "how in natur' could she git by him a-standin' here?" demanded the chief. "She couldn't climb up over that there headboard, leastwise I never see a woman yit that could climb like that. An' even if she hed she'd a flopped down on the bed right plumb in front of him, an' he'd a' hed her sure. She couldn't git by him, for th' ain't room enough. Look at here, Henry. I take up the whole width. Could anybody git by me now?"

"No, they couldn't. An' I told Susan so, too. But she says he leaned over on the bed when he seen her comin' an' let her scoot out."

"Now, Henry, that don't stand t' reason," exclaimed the chief, turning on him suddenly. He stood a moment shaking his head dubiously, and then continued: "There's somethin' almighty cur'ous about this anyways. So near's I can make out the' ain't been nary a thing stole from this house, an' it's mighty strange—"

"No, th' ain't!" interrupted the old man, eagerly. "Everything's here jest 's 'twuz afore. Why, there's Ed's watch an' chain that cost his father a clean hund'ud dollars—"

"Where?"

The chief started back into the kitchen. The dead man's clothes hung over a chair, and there in plain sight dangled a valuable gold chain and charm from the vest. In the pocket the chief found the heavy gold watch. But this was not all. A quick search disclosed several dollars in silver in the trousers and in the coat a long pocketbook containing a considerable sum in bank bills.

The appearance of wisdom deepened on the chief of police's face as he eyed these discoveries. He did not, however, communicate to the old man the elucidation of the mystery which, to judge by his expression, was so plain to himself. He merely began to tie up the various valuable articles in his handkerchief. In this occupation he was interrupted by a timid knock at the door.

"Come in," he called sharply, looking up.

A woman, one of the neighbors, advanced hesitatingly toward him, holding a small tin box in her outstretched hand.

"Wal, what is it?" he asked, glancing at the box impatiently.

"This is what she used to keep her will in," said the woman, offering it. "And I found it out by our house, in the path that leads down to the woods, and there was these pieces of burnt paper there, too, and I thought—"

"How do you know she kept her will in it?" he asked, taking it and turning over the bits of paper in his hands.

"She told me so. And I've seen it often, too. It used to stand right there on the bureau behind her bed. See, her name is scratched on it with a pin or something."

The chief stood in profound thought, his chin in one hand and the box in the other, the handkerchief bundle on the floor between his feet.

"Ah!" he exclaimed suddenly. "That's it! It wasn't done for robbery, not to get money that way. They left all the money behind and took the will and then burnt it up. Now the question is, Who is her heirs? Who gits her proppurty now the will is gone? Them is the ones that done it."

"That's so, that's so," cried the old man, excitedly. "It's plain as the pike road. And it's them two scallawags in—" He stopped suddenly, his mouth hung open, and he shifted uneasily on his feet.

"Why don't ye go on, man?" said the chief, sharply. "Do you know 'em? Or what was you goin' to say?"

"She's only left three relations," answered the old man, "and two of 'em's in the city, Willum Henry's boys, drinkin', shif'less critters they be, and she wouldn't have nothin' to do with 'em. And t'other one is—is—wal, she's Susan."

The reluctance with which the old man offered the latter part of this statement was fully equaled by the alacrity with which the chief received it. All was plain to him now. He allowed himself a

grim flicker of a smile as he thought of the weakness of that evasion, when, confronted by the indisputable fact that a person could
not pass another in that narrow space, she had foolishly claimed
that the man leaned over on the bed to let her by. A curious sort of
murderer that would be, thought the elated chief. Even if he hadn't
wanted to put her altogether out of the way he would have grabbed
and bound and gagged her, to prevent her from escaping and giving the alarm. And then, after she had escaped, as she claimed, the
criminals had stayed on in the house five minutes longer! A likely
story, with her running to have them nabbed! The truth plainly
was that, if two men had anything to do with it, they were the nephews from the city, and she was their accomplice. It was still more
probable that she herself had done the deed and alone. She had
had every opportunity, was one of the heirs, and had lied about
the facts. Besides, she was half-crazy.

Therefore, within ten minutes he was on his way to the police
station with his prisoner, Susan Clemmons, a charge of willful
murder against whom he was laboriously formulating in his mind.
It is true that he had neglected to summon a physician to view the
remains and find whether or not the persons she was accused of
murdering were dead.

Dr. Furnivall answered "Enter" to a tap at his office door, and
a young man appeared on the threshold.

"I have not come to consult you, doctor," he said, advancing
with hesitating step. "The truth is, I hardly know—how to—to state
my errand."

He stood nervously eyeing the doctor. Perhaps 24 years of age,
he was of good appearance, with large black eyes and thick, dark
hair, tall and slim of build, and well balanced on his feet. His
clothes were fashionable and immaculate. He took the chair to
which Dr. Furnivall motioned him, and continued with somewhat
more confidence

"One of my chums who is studying medicine has told me of your
remarkable hypnotic powers, which, I am given to understand, have
more than once been employed in the detection of criminals who

were about to escape, leaving the innocent to suffer. Now, a very old and highly valued friend of mine is suffering unjustly, accused of a crime which she was as unable morally to commit as I am physically to carry this house away on my shoulders. And if money—I— I shall have a great deal by and by, though now—"

"Wouldn't it be well for you to introduce yourself, since we are going into a matter of such intimate interest?"

"Oh, pardon! I forgot—let me give you my card."

He produced a modest bit of engraved pasteboard, which the doctor examined.

"Now tell me the story, Mr. Sewell," he said. He reclined in his chair and disposed himself to listen comfortably behind the thick colored glasses.

"It is very good of you, Dr. Furnivall, to accept the case so generously. I wish to speak of the crime yesterday in Centreville. Perhaps you have read the newspaper stories regarding it?"

"Yes."

"Then I have little to add to them, except that the woman is entirely guiltless, and the two nephews, for whom they are searching, as well. But the police in that little last century town are hopeless imbeciles, and as somebody must be caught, and they've caught somebody, they will listen to no other view of the matter."

"Are these nephews the young toughs they are described as being?"

The visitor smiled deprecatingly.

"Nobody could be further from it. Their reputation was given them by their aunt. Of course," he continued, with another movement of deprecation, "one doesn't like to make charges in such a case. But the truth is their father left all his money to her in trust for his twin sons—she was quite a different woman in her younger days—and one night, when they visited her with the smell of wine on their breath, coming straight from their class supper, she was horrified—or pretended to be. She never sent them a dollar afterward, and gave dissipation as the reason. They didn't know this at the time, for Susan, this woman they have arrested, kept up the remittances in the aunt's name—kept them up until all she had was gone, all she had saved and all she had inherited. Then they found out, for their college course was not completed, and after writing and writing for money in vain one of them went home and soon learned the true state of affairs." A choke came into the speaker's voice and he paused. Then, with flushed face, he went on energetically: "I'll save that blessed woman if it is in the power of man to do it. Why, she was only second cousin to them, and she gave them her all. And it left her a pauper. See the life she was obliged to live with those skinflints on account of it! And there never was a word of complaint from her, nor anything but gladness for doing it."

"They never took the case to court?"

"No, sir; they have not done so yet."

"Have you seen the house—the rooms where the crimes were committed?"

"Yes, doctor."

"Is it true what is said about that passageway between the bed and the wall? Is it so narrow?"

"Ah!" cried the young man, shaking his head. "There's where the rub comes. She stoutly maintains that her story is true. She fled past the murderer, and he, in order to give her exit, bent over on the bed. It seems impossible. But she doesn't know how to lie, and if she is in her right mind, and didn't imagine that part, I must believe her."

"How do you account for the facts that so many valuables were left untouched, and only the will was taken and then burned up?"

The visitor threw out his hands.

"It is the mystery of mysteries!" he almost groaned. "I don't pretend to explain it in the least. One thing only I am sure of, and it is that the deed was never done by any of those who would benefit under the law by destroying the will."

Dr. Furnivall removed his spectacles and looked the young man in the eye.

"Mr. Sewell," said he, "tell me why you do not believe in hypnotism?"

The youth started and flushed.

"Why, doctor, I—I—" he stammered, "why—that is why I am here." His eyes, which had shone with some excitement, took on a calmer expression, and gradually assumed a look of intentness, as if he were deeply studying something within rather than outside of them, though they were fixed on the doctor's.

"If you had believed in it you would not come to me in just the way you have. You do not believe in hypnotism in the least, do you?"

"No, sir." The answer this time was calm, matter of fact, perfectly assured.

"Tell me why."

"Because I have studied the matter from both sides, at times as the hypnotist and at other times as the subject, and it is only a delusion. When I was at college and in need of money, I hired out to a number of different hypnotists at $2 an evening. There were eight of us who did that frequently. Some of the professors were honestly in pursuit of science, and these we used to fool. Two dollars an evening was a good deal to us.

"Never did any one of us feel the slightest influence of hypnotism, though we pretended to be helpless. We practiced difficult feats in order to do them at command, and suffered a good deal of pain sometimes in the experiments rather than give up our job as good subjects. But other so called hypnotists never attempted anything occult with us at all. They were simply showmen, who taught us funny stunts and paid us for going through them before spectators or before a camera. We were often distributed around through an audience, and at the call for volunteers came up as greenhorns and did the tricks."

"You have looked at the matter on all sides then, haven't you? And all that you have ever seen of hypnotism has been pure fake?"

"Yes, doctor. Either one side or the other is always fooled."

"Why did you come to me?"

"Because I trusted your detective ability and benevolence."

"Why did you say that you believed in my hypnotic powers?"

The youth shook his head slightly, but with surety.

"I did not say that."

"What did you say?"

"I—I can't seem to think."

"Perhaps it was only that you had heard of my remarkable powers?"

"Yes, doctor, that was it."

"Why did you mention hypnotism at all?"

"Because I thought I should gain your interest that way. Every scientist is an enthusiast on his specialty, and is easily led by it almost anywhere."

"You do not think I could hypnotize you?"

"No, sir, you could not."

"You don't think there may be a phase of psychology entirely outside and different from the lines with which you are familiar, and which may be true hypnotism?"

"Oh, I would not say as to that. I only maintain that there is no such thing as thought transference in the commonly accepted sense. I have seen a hundred cases which seemed to be pure hypnotism beyond dispute, but always there was a trick, either by the operator or the subject, or both, which made a farce of the exhibition."

"But you must admit the hypnotic sleep?"

"There is undoubtedly some truth, perhaps a great deal of truth in that. A person may be induced into a sort of half-conscious state, possibly, through sight or pressure. I think I have seen that done, but there are so many things to consider that I would not take my oath on it. What I deny is the possibility of the reception of a thought, projected mentally by another, while the subject is in that state. The thing is absurd. It would be equally against the laws of the soul and those of physics, as unjust as unscientific."

Dr. Furnivall resumed his glasses with a decided movement.

"I do not see that you were far wrong, Mr. Clemmons," he said quietly, "in coming to me under a false name. Of course, I recognized you immediately as one of the nephews by the description in the newspapers and the subject which you opened. Your appearance and words struck me favorably, and I did not wish to pry into your private reasons. All these things we will talk over later. In the meantime I shall hasten to Centreville. The case interests me extremely, on one point at least, and I am sure it will interest you and all psychologists when that point is made dear. Will you go along with me?"

At the beginning of this speech the visitor turned pale and looked swiftly around as if about to flee. But as the doctor proceeded he became gradually more quiet, until at the end the chief expression on his face was that of mild perplexity, and he said hesitatingly:

"It's most curious—I—I feel a sort of—of dual personality, as if I were here and yet not here. And I am sure I had no intention of telling as much as I have told you."

"Oh, that's common enough," said the doctor lightly. "We all of us have a double personality, because one lobe of the brain is educated and the other is a sort of vagabond dunce. And most of us talk too much. But come," rising, "will you accompany me to Centreville? We may dip into psychology some other time."

"You have a theory?" cried the young man, eagerly.

"Certainly. But it is in a fluid state, so to say, as yet, and may materialize in either one of three different forms. The structure requires still a block or two of solid fact. So far it is a sort of arch, with that impossible passage as the corner stone, and the tin box as the keystone, and I must see that woman at once."

"I shall be glad to go, but—they'll recognize me there—arrest me—"

The doctor passed him a motor mask.

"Put that on when we arrive in the vicinity, and don't leave the automobile unless I call you."

Five minutes later they were rushing toward Centreville as fast as the law permitted.

"Wal," said the Centreville chief of police, when Dr. Furnivall had introduced himself and made known his business, "I got the criminal all right, that's sure. An' I guess you can see her, if you want to, but 'twon't do no good. She sticks to that tomfool story spite of all I can do. I've showed her plain enough that 'twas onreasonable, an' only made it wuss for her a-stickin' to it, fer everybuddy knows it's nothin' but a lie, an' if she that was there present 'll lie about the fac's, then she must be guilty some way. But here ye be."

He halted before a cell, through the grated door of which, on a cot in a corner, a woman could be seen seated.

"Susan," he called, "here's a big doctor frum the city come to see ye. Mind what ye say to him, now, fer everything ye tell 'll be used agin ye. All ye gut t' do is speak the truth. I ain't gut no right to gin ye no orders, an' I won't neither, but all I say is, you drop that fool yarn, an' if ye must lie, why do it reasonable. Nobuddy ain't ever gonter take any stock in that one."

The woman arose and came forward timidly. Her figure was very tall and gaunt, and perfectly straight, so that her gait as she walked would have given her a majestic air but for the mild helplessness and bewilderment of her face. That neutralized the effect and resulted in caricature. Her brown hair, turning gray, was parted in the middle, brushed tightly back and piled on the crown of her head, with an old fashioned net over it, which did not prevent a stray lock from dangling into one of her dim, light hued eyes. She was wetting her finger and trying to tuck this into place as she approached the cell door. Dr. Furnivall reached through the bars and grasped her hand, shaking it encouragingly. The chief went back to his desk.

"I wish to ask you," said the doctor, "if those men said anything that night? Did not either one of them utter a single word that you could hear?"

"Land's sake! I dunno," she answered, with the monotonous inflection of voice peculiar to the simple minded. "She's screechin' so I couldn't hear nothin' else. An' I sorter didn't hear that till arterwards, I wuz so frightened an' haired up."

"There was a window over your bed—why didn't you open that and crawl through? Why did you run toward the man? You knew you couldn't pass him, didn't you?"

"Oh, I dunno, I dunno!" she moaned, helplessly. Then, her eyes fixed on the doctor's, a shade of intelligence flickering into her face, she added: "Th' winders is all screwed up nights, 'fraid o' thieves, an' I couldn't git out that way. I didn't know what I wuz doin'. I jest put her fer th' door."

"The only light in the room shone from the candle in the kitchen, through the doorway?"

"Yes, that wuz all th' wuz. An' 'twa'n't no great. Jest enough t' make darkness visible."

"How were you able to see the man at all?"

"He wuz agin th' light. Sorter like a shadder on th' wall."

"Could the rays strike you as you came around the headboard? Or did they go the other way, toward the foot of the bed?"

"I dunno, the' wa'n't much light. He took it all up, 'cept a little on the bed."

"Did you scream as you ran toward him?"

"My sakes! No, I guess not. I was too skeered. I couldn't open my mouth to save my life."

"Did he bend over to let you pass before you touched him? Did you come against his body at all?"

"I dunno. I run against a good many things. My night gown wuz all tore, an' the' wuz some whitewash on it. I dunno what I gut that off of. But I didn't seem to feel nothin' I hit against till arterwards."

"Whitewash! Is there anything whitewashed around the place?"

"The chicken coops is, an' the side fence, but I didn't go nowheres near them. I run out the front way."

"You say the man was very large. Was there anything else you noticed about him?"

"I dunno 's the' wuz. He run kinder cur'ous when he come out the house. He was lame I guess. His feet seemed kinder funny, th' way he used 'em."

"Should you say he might have been clubfooted?"

"Maybe he wuz. I couldn't tell. 'Twuz the kinder jerky way he run. Paps he had a wooden laig. 'Twuz dark, an' I only see th' men quick-like."

Dr. Furnivall took her hand again between the bars and pressed it.

"Cheer up. We shall have you out of here very soon," he said.

She watched him as he walked down the short corridor to the office, the unwonted intelligence in her face slowly giving way to her normal fatuous expression.

"Is there a negro in the town who does whitewashing?" the doctor asked the chief.

"I dunno of none," he answered. "Can't ye git none in th' city?" He was grinding tobacco between his horny palms and looked up in some surprise at the question.

"I should like to find one here," returned Dr. Furnivall in a matter-of-fact tone.

"D'ye know where the's a coon whitewasher, Jim," asked the chief obligingly of one of his men who was working about the room.

Jim spat, scratched his arm thoughtfully, and came forward.

"I guess th's one over in Sol Weathersby's shanty," he answered. "I see a darky there this mornin', an' he looked like one—hed on white overalls an' his jumper was kinder daubed. Might 'a' been lime, though. Paps he makes mortar fer th' masons."

"You don't know him then—he's a stranger?" asked Dr. Furnivall.

"No, I don't know him myself," the man returned. "But th' Weathersbys could gin ye pints on him, I guess. He's in their shanty. Joe Weathersby wuz with him when I see him."

"Joe is Sol's nephy—used t' work in th' city. He ain't been back long," volunteered the chief for Dr. Furnivall's enlightenment.

"What kind of a man is this Joe?" the doctor asked. "If he should recommend the negro to me, could I take his word?"

"Wal." The chief knit his brows. "I don't wanter say nothin' agin any o' Sol Weathersby's folks. He's a good man, an' 's gut propurty. An' Joe ain't never made us no trouble. He ain't lived 'round here much since he wuz a boy."

The doctor hastened out to the automobile in front of the door.

"I am going to drop you up here in the woods, where you'll be out of sight for a little while," he said to its occupant. "In which direction is the shanty belonging to the Weathersbys?"

And when they were started he continued:

"I accept the woman's story in toto, and must base my theory on it. What kind of a character must be his who, in the circumstances, would allow her to pass—what could be his reasons? I have settled on what seems, so far, the only possible fact, and am looking for a man who is large, for she so described him; brutal, because of his methods; densely ignorant, for reasons that will appear in his confession, probably a foreigner or negro of the lowest stamp. I incline to the negro, because the woman noticed that he had an odd gait—so many of them have great feet and wear ungainly shoes run down at the heel, and walk with visible effort— and also for the reason that she found traces of whitewash on her nightgown. Many whitewashers are negroes. His companion doesn't matter now, for, the big man once found, the other can't escape. The only point that is not clear to me is why the will was taken and burned and the money left behind. But that will appear in the sequel. You would better alight here and hide in the bushes. I shall go to the station for help, which the chief will readily give me if he thinks we're after Susan's accomplices. When we come back from the shanty you can join us if we stop at this spot. But if we drive straight by, our expedition will have failed, and you'll have to wait until I return for you."

A half hour afterward the automobile containing Dr. Furnivall, the chief and one of his men, approached the Weathersby shanty. It was a small, unpainted, weather-beaten structure, sitting a little back from the road on the edge of the dark woods, in use only in haying time, for the occupancy of such itinerant laborers on the Weathersby place as were not desired nearer the farmhouse. Trees and underbrush crept closely up to it on two sides, in front was a small clearing with a well in it, and on the remaining side ran the county road under the forbidding shadows of a forest crowned cliff. The spot was cheerless, sordid, uncanny. Its very countenance suggested vice and crime.

The two officers descended from the machine some rods from the building and crept through the woods toward it, while Dr. Furnivall drove into the clearing. There were shutters on the windows, the door was closed, and no signs of life were visible anywhere about. The premises seemed utterly deserted. But as the doctor rapped loudly on the door a sudden scream of mortal terror arose within, and in a long drawn chattering and jabbering shuddered away into silence.

Finding the door fastened, he rattled the latch noisily and called out, "Hello."

Again the anguished cry sounded, but this time in tones as if the voice were muffled. And finally when, putting his shoulder to it, the doctor burst in he found a burly form shaking and scream-ing on a pallet in a dark corner, its head buried in the rags which answered for bedding.

As Dr. Furnivall threw open one of the shutters, letting in a stream of daylight upon the bed, the occupant started up, disclos-ing a terrified black face, which quickly took on an expression of relief, and he exclaimed:

"'Fo' Gawd, man, I'se glad yo' come; oh, I'se glad yo' come. Git meh out'n yere, W'ere ah cain' see hit, an' Ah doan keer w'ere yo' puts me."

He crept forward on his hands and knees, groveling at Dr. Furnivall's feet.

"Ah done hit, mister, Ah am' gwine deny dat, an' Ah sees hit eber sence. Joe he claim 'twuz de sarven' gal, b't Ah doan know 'bout dat. Ah sees hit eber sence. Ah done t'ought yo' wuz hit."

"Sit up here, take this chair. There, now tell me all about it."

He placed a chair facing the light that entered the doorway, and motioning the policemen, who now stood at the open window, to remain where they were, helped the negro to the seat and bade him proceed with his story.

So thankful was the man, as it appeared, for human company, and relief from the superstitious fears which were driving him in-sane, that he scarcely needed the assistance which Dr. Furnivall's peculiar powers could afford him, and he readily confessed as fol-lows:

"Ah knewed dat Joe Weathersby in de city, mister, an' he say some sarven' gal dat uster wurk en de fam'bly done tol' heem ol'

Mis. Snowmun allerz keep fi' t'ousan' dollars en de tin box on de bureau en de baidroom. He say he gwine gi' meh half dat money eef Ah he'p heem git de box. We done bruk en de house an' gi' de man chlo'form, b't we bungle dat job an' de man wake up, an' we done hit heem wid de club. Den ol' Mis' she bergin' t' scream, an' Ah run en tuh her room for tuh stop her noise. Den—Ah—Ah see de ghos' come a-flittin' right up tuh dis nigger an' Ah drop on de baid, for den Ah knows de man in de odder room am daid an' Ah is a murderer, an' Ah cain' do anodder t'ing. Joe he come en an' git de box an' we run fo' de woods, b't dar wan' no money in de box, on'y ol' paper. Den Ah gibs up. Joe burn de paper for git hit out de way, an' Ah hide ma haid en de leabes an' grass, but de ghos' is dar all de taime an' nebber leabe meh. Joe he say hit de sarven' gal b't Ah knows bettern's dat, Ah see hit offen sence. Ah see hit jes' 'fore yo' comed, mister, right yere en dis plaice. Ah done t'ink yo' wuz hit w'en yo' knock on de do'. Yo' tek meh t' de jail, yo' tek meh anyw'ere, Ah doan' keer, ef on'y yo' tek meh w'ere dat cain' come!"

"Goshamitey!" muttered the bewildered chief as he slipped on the handcuffs, painfully relinquishing the theory which seemed so simple for the simpler truth of which he had not dreamed, "I never'll believe northin' agin as long 's I live onless I see it or hear it myself. Things is dretful queer in this world; that's what they is, dretful queer."

Dr. Furnivall jotted down in his notebook the following:

THE TIN BOX CASE.

Memo—Hallucinations: Classify the negro's. Mento-objective: notify psychical research.

Memo—Coincidences: The (probably vainglorious) lie of the former servant, that there was $5,000 in the box leads to destruction of the will, whereby the strongest presumptions of guilt are directed toward the innocent; circumstantial evidence; classify.

THE TRAGEDY AT THE COLONIAL

It was 4 o'clock in the afternoon of a debilitating spring day. The crowds that thronged the street, surging always to the shady side, moved with a lack of energy peculiar to the time of year. Listless, perspiring, yellow of skin, uneasy in clothes that were too heavy by some pounds, they seemed more like an army of invalids out for a prescribed constitutional, than representative men and women of one of the foremost cities of the world, which they were, bent upon their accustomed round of business or of pleasure. Even the hackmen on their stands, those eternally alert and invincible types of the genus "wide eye," were calmly nodding on their boxes, careless of fares, apparently, wishing for nothing but to be let alone in their shade by the curb.

But in one instant all this was changed. A hoarse cry rang gut on the air. Three of the seeming sleepers tumbled from their boxes to the ground as one man, and at the top of their speed dashed down the street. The crowd on the sidewalk awoke as from a shock of electricity, paused, stared in surprise at the bounding shapes, and then set off after them. In front of the Colonial Hotel the lines of people, running from all directions, met as the spokes of a wheel meet in the hub, with the hackmen in the centre, bending over something on the ground.

"What is it?" excitedly cried a hundred breathless runners.

"A woman fainted!" answered one.

"A pickpocket!" answered another.

"No, it's only a drunk!" contributed somebody else.

Meanwhile the hack drivers were examining the body of a man, which, smashed to a pulp, was huddled in a ghastly heap on the flags.

"Tenth story," said one to the other in a hushed voice; "I seen him when he started, end over end like one o' them 'ere windmills."

"He's gone," said another. "My! Ain't it awful!" He turned away, sick from the horrid spectacle.

"Get a doctor!" shouted somebody in the crowd.

The hackmen straightened up and looked irresolutely around. They had no notion what to do. Suddenly one of them raised his hand, standing on tiptoe, and beckoned. He had seen a policeman pushing into the jam and he called out: "This way—hi! Over here!"

"Now, then, clear the road!" cried the strong voice of the law, and, though the road was not cleared, because it could not be, on account of the density of the human pressure behind, the officer fought in to the central group, taking care not to be too gentle about it. The hackmen began to explain, all together, each relating a little different story from the other, but all agreeing in the essential that the man had fallen to his death from an open window on the tenth floor of the hotel, and that they had all of them seen him do it.

"Anybody here know him?" asked the officer, consulting the nearest bystanders with his eyes. But as the body lay face to the ground, unrecognizable, nobody ventured to claim its acquaintance.

"Well, move back, move back! There's nothing to see here," the officer exclaimed with impatience, and was beginning to enforce his command with a strong arm when his eyes, raised over the heads of the crowd, fell on a man making extraordinary gestures, apparently to him, from a window of the great apartment house opposite. He was on the tenth floor, directly across the street, acting like an insane person, working his shoulders, pushing with his arms against nothing, pointing to the hotel on a level with his window, and then extending both forefingers in the direction of the Colonial entrance. Some in the crowd, following the direction of the policeman's surprised gaze, began to cry out: "There's another one!" "He'll be down in a minute—let's run up there!" "He's crazy!"

And then a youth, in a burst of inspiration, hit the truth. "He's trying to tell us that this man was pushed out of the window, that he saw it done, and that the entrance should be guarded while a search is made for the murderer."

"Run up there, then, and bring him down here," said the officer to the last speaker. "Come down here, you!" he moved his lips as if to say, beckoning to the gentleman at the window. But he shook his head and displayed new motions. He was an invalid and could not walk. He made that plain by his gestures.

At this moment the hospital ambulance caused a diversion by rushing up and depositing a surgeon and his assistant, who took charge of the body, which, as soon as its face was exposed, was recognized by a dozen different men as that of Frederick Seavey, a real estate dealer, who lived in suite 1001, The Colonial, with offices down town. By this time both the proprietor and the janitor of the hotel had appeared on the scene, the one with a declaration that Mrs. Seavey was lying sick in bed, and must not be told of the tragedy for fear of its effect on her, and the other with a statement that rendered the former's precautions useless. Mrs. Seavey must know about it already, he said. In fact, there had been a row in the Seavey rooms. He had heard loud voices, one of which was Mr. Seavey's, and the other that of a man with a powerful bass, this latter replying to some heated words of Mr. Seavey's with, "You dog! You ought to be kicked out of the window!" This occurred in the front room, where the sick wife was lying. She must be fully aware of all that had taken place there, and could throw such light on the mystery as would immediately clear it up.

Upon this the landlord hurriedly volunteered to see the lady, and was turning to go inside when a bright reporter, who had appeared in time to hear this testimony, suggested that though the murderer had had plenty of time to escape, he might not have done so, and the house should be searched and guards stationed at all the exits, who should allow nobody to pass to the street until identified. This was arranged for at once, several responsible persons offering their services to help out the employes of the hotel, and the landlord again started to enter.

The policeman who had so far figured in the case had meanwhile hastened to the apartment house across the way and questioned the excited man at the window. He now reappeared and, taking the landlord by the arm, whispered:

"It's a clear case. Murder! Mr. Daniels over there seen the whole thing. He was lookin' into the room. There was two men; one near the window and the other shaking his fist at him, and the first thing he knew one was tumbling, the window being open, and the other was just pushing him. He seen his hands on him."

The much exercised man turned a troubled face to the patrolman.

"That corroborates the janitor," he said. "Notify your office as quick as you can."

He then summoned the house physician, and together they hurried to suite 1001.

The rap at the door remaining unanswered, they were on the point of turning the knob when a housemaid came running toward them along the hall with the information that a doctor was with Mrs. Seavey and she was not to be disturbed. The doctor himself had given orders to that effect.

This statement, so far from having the effect the maid expected, resulted in an action on the part of her employer that made her fear for his sanity, for with a sudden wrench he tore the door open and, with his left arm bent above his head, as if to ward off a threatened blow, he bounded into the apartment like a tiger on its prey, the physician closely treading on his heels.

But once in, both men stared blankly. There were no signs of disturbance. Nobody was in the room but the sick woman, who lay perfectly still on the outside, of the bed; her face to the wall; and a hasty examination showed that the door leading to the other parts of the suite was fastened, the key being in the lock on their side.

"How long ago was the doctor here?" the landlord asked the maid.

"Why, only a few minutes ago, surely. I didn't know he had gone. He has not had time to make the examination. He said nobody was to enter until he called me."

"Were you to guard the door?"

She hung her head.

"Ye—yes, sir. I—I only went for a drink of water."

"Did you see Mr. Seavey come in?"

"No, sir. He is seldom home till 5 or past."

"Don't y'u know what has happened here?"

"Wh—why, no, sir. Is she worse?"

She threw a startled look toward the bed, and then hastened to it. The doctor and she reached it at the same moment.

"I didn't mean to leave her," she whispered anxiously to him. "She wasn't very sick; and I couldn't have been away from the door five minutes."

The doctor examined the invalid's face and took her pulse.

"Hysteria," he said.

As he spoke, the patient's eyelids trembled open. At sight of him bending over her she screamed and began to cry out incoherently, which brought the landlord, who had been searching the apartments hurriedly, to the bedside.

"What is she saying?" he whispered. "Has she given any clue? What's the matter with her?"

"I can't make out what she says," the doctor returned; "and I can't make out what the matter is, either. If it's hysteria, it's the queerest case I ever saw yet. It's more like raving insanity. Look at her eyes. What doctor did she have?" he asked the maid.

"Why, I don't know who this one was. She's had several. She called him herself on the telephone. She wasn't very sick then. See, she isn't undressed."

"How came you here, anyway?" asked the landlord. "Did Mr. Clark assign you to Mrs. Seavey?"

"Yes, sir. She has no maid of her own just now and asked for me at the office. Oh, dear, I am so sorry—"

She stopped suddenly and her eyes grew wide as the helmet of a policeman was pushed around the edge of the door, immediately followed by the burly body of Sergeant Nulty, who advanced softly to the group looking inquiringly from one to the others. While the physician busied himself with the patient the landlord drew the sergeant aside and told him all that had been discovered.

"An' yees dunno phwat wan the docthor was?" he asked.

"No."

"Well, 'twas him done it."

"Of course. But how does that help us? Mrs. Seavey can't speak, and she is the only person who can give that doctor's name."

"Can't sphake? She can."

"Not intelligently. Listen."

"Man," said Nulty, after giving an attentive ear to the jerky syllables that issued from the patient's mouth, tumbling over one another in a turgid stream, wholly devoid of sense or connection, "man, Oi have wan that c'u'd make the lady sphake. Yis, begob! Sphake? He c'u'd draw language from a pig. He made mesilf shpake wanst." He looked as if he scarcely relished the remembrance.

The landlord eyed him disapprovingly.

"This is no time nor place for joking," he said, "and I don't understand you."

"Whisper! It's no joke. I know me juty. 'Tis the name o' the docther we want, noo, and only the lady can tell thot same, but she can't sphake. But she can sphake! The's wan man will get the news from her, I'll tell you. Whisper! Dr. Furnivall!"

He winked knowingly as he pronounced the word, and shook his head confidently. The landlord, however, was unresponsive. He did not understand yet. But the physician at the bedside caught the name, and nodded to the sergeant.

"Call him," he said. "Tell him I have asked him in consultation. There's more than hysteria here, I don't know what yet, and I should be glad to have his advice."

The sergeant was fortunate enough to get speech at once with Dr. Furnivall over the telephone, and in less than a quarter of an hour he arrived. The patient now lay in comparative quiet, crying out only occasionally, in such an incoherent manner that nothing could be made of her meaning. Indeed, as soon as Dr. Furnivall looked into her eyes he declared that she had no meaning. If she spoke, it was automatically. And he was forced to confess that in this case his hypnotic powers were of no avail. Her mind was in such a chaotic state that he could not reach it. It had no stability. She was incapable of thought. To attempt to force her to concentrate her ideas and bid her speak would be like gazing into a mass of floating vapor and bidding it to body itself forth as a voice.

Sergeant Nulty, who had hailed the entrance of his hero with a broad grin of triumph, scratched his head and grew pale with chagrin, turning a helpless eye upon the man he had so confidently relied upon, but who now disappointed him at the moment of trial. Although he had already, over the telephone, briefly explained the circumstances to Dr. Furnivall, giving him the main points of the case and stating what he wanted, he could not help thinking that the doctor's failure was due, perhaps, to the fact that he did not quite appreciate the great importance attaching to the discovery of that missing doctor's name. When it is absolutely necessary to do a thing, it can be done, even if it is impossible, according to the sergeant. With deference he therefore approached and in an earnest whisper began to go over the story again for the doctor's better understanding. But it was useless. Dr. Furnivall shook his head.

"No power on earth," he said, "can draw sanity from a mind whose organ of expression, the brain, is as defective as that woman's. Repair the brain and she will speak, but not until that is done."

Now, when the sergeant had come up and began to whisper his explanations, the doctor, who was at the bedside, moved away and stood by the wall at the footboard, regarding the invalid's face, which was turned directly toward him, nevertheless listening to the story of the urgent Irishman. He noticed at once that the bed did not lie snugly against the wall, and he saw a small piece of paper on the floor in the vacant space, but thought nothing of it until the necessity of discovering the mysterious physician's identity was so impressed upon him, but at the very instant when the last quoted words were on his lips, he recognized the paper as one torn from a physician's prescription pad, and, moreover, he knew immediately what physician's pad it had come off of! It was that of

Dr. Wellington. In short, one of Dr. Furnivall's own dearest friends was indubitably the mysterious doctor whom the police were hunting for having committed this brutal murder!

In a flash the whole situation was changed in Dr. Furnivall's mind. Heretofore he had accepted the theory of murder without question. All signs pointed to it—the loud words in the room, the fist of one man in the other man's face, the pushing arms, the fall through the window, the condition of the wife which was supposedly brought on by the shock of seeing her husband tumbled to his death, and, far from weakest in the category of strong presumptive proofs, the sudden absence of the other man, who must be the doctor in attendance on Mrs. Seavey. Up to this moment Dr. Furnivall had had only popular grounds on which to base an opinion. He had known nothing of the case beyond what others knew. But now he had first-hand evidence, the evidence of character. Could Dr. Wellington do murder? No. In his right mind murder would be as impossible to him as Greek to a baby.

Therefore, supposing him sane, and granting that his was the bass voice heard in the controversy with Mr. Seavey, no murder had been committed. But if that were so, what had really happened? And why did Dr. Wellington run away? Would such a man shirk the consequences of any act of his? No, no more than he would wallow in crime. He would stand like a man and pay the penalty. Cowardice was as impossible to him as viciousness—always providing he was in his right mind. But the one man was dead and the other was missing. What, then, had really occurred between them? Was Wellington insane? Had he done this terrible thing in a fit of maniacal frenzy? Or was he still sane? And, therefore, had no crime been perpetrated?

All this passed through Dr. Furnivall's mind with the rapidity of a flash of lightning, and his course was determined upon as quickly. Despite the evidence to the contrary, he would start from the supposition that an accident, not a crime, was the real basis of the tragedy. With him known character outbalanced a solid mass of evidence which depended on decisions of the human intellect, made up from the testimony of the senses. He agreed with Bacon

that, though the senses may be true, the intellect is usually incapable of passing on them. It was, therefore, with a firm belief in
his friend's innocence, and a resolution to seek in the direction of
mishap, rather than in that of violence, for an answer to the enigma
before him, that he whispered to Sergeant Nulty:

"Leave the doctor and me with the patient. We will make an
examination. Clear the room. Find out what you can around the
hotel. You can't do anything here now, and I will call you if you are
wanted."

The house physician, who was interested in the medical rather
than the criminal aspects of the case, saw with relief the execution
of this order, and the instant the door closed on the heels of the
last of the departing group he questioned Dr. Furnivall eagerly:

"What is this? I have never seen anything just like it. There are
right hemiplegia and asphasia, shouldn't you say? And word-deaf-
ness undoubtedly, as well as word-blindness. Look at her face. She
is suffering intensely."

"No, she suffers little," returned Dr. Furnivall. "The contortion
of the nerves is a reflex. There is more than fright in this. Still, she
is not insane. She is numb. Something is pressing into that woman's
brain—a tumor, perhaps, invading the superior or middle temporal convolutions."

His colleague looked surprised.

"Do you think so? Well, that would surely account for it all.
But in that case—" He paused meaningly.

"No," answered Dr. Furnivall; "not necessarily fatal, I feel assured. An operation—"

"But such an operation never has been done!"

"True. But it is the only chance. And I am sure it is feasible.
Her constitution is more than strong; it is robust. With good fortune she would bear it well. Get the consent of her relatives; call
in Myers and Whewill and let's hear what they say."

The young doctor's face brightened.

"Good! I'll do it at once," he answered with alacrity, and started
for the door. But he had scarcely disappeared when Dr. Furnivall,

"Why?" asked Dr. Furnivall.

"It never has been attempted, for one reason."

Here ensued a long technical discussion, the result of which was that the balance hung so even between the arguments for and against that no positive decision could be reached. Then Dr. Furnivall played his last card.

"Gentlemen," said he, "we must admit all the reasons that have been given here why this operation should not be attempted. We must admit all those likewise on the other side; and we find the chances of success and failure so nearly even that, speaking generally, the weight would be thrown on the negative, and all thoughts of the knife abandoned. It would be too full of risk, But, aside from the fact that I myself feel strongly that an operation is the only means of saving the patient's sanity, if not her very life itself; aside from the fact that I am willing to pledge my professional reputation on the success of an operation performed by me with your assistance, on the tumor or whatever it is that I believe is invading this brain, either in the superior or middle temporal convolutions—aside from all this, I have another reason to offer, which, I feel sure, must appeal to you. It is this: The fame, and even the life itself, of one of our number, depend on this patient's sanity. Without the surgery she certainly never can recover, and she may die. In that case a man you all know well and highly respect must, as far as I can see into the future, pay the penalty of a crime of which he was innocent, and the penalty is death. With the surgery she will recover, I firmly believe, and will save him by her evidence. Even at the worst, she will be as well off after as before the trial, unless undreamed of conditions prevail. There is the case, gentlemen. The affair of our friend should not bias us to do to this patient what we should not do, but it cannot lack weight in these delicate circumstances, and I for one am obliged to confess that it bears me, all things considered, irresistibly in the direction of the operation. It is not a question of professional ethics with me, for I should advise the trial, though there were no outside influences. I am sure of success. With you it may not be so, but I beg you to consider well what I have said. There is the gentleman you will save by deciding as I have done."

He threw the crumpled prescription on the table before them as he spoke, and as one man the group cried:

"Wellington? Impossible!"

"Yes, impossible, indeed! But it is he who is now filling the role of the mysterious doctor, nevertheless. I called up his house and learned that he had left there for this hotel. In the janitor's description of the voices I recognize his. I found this paper on the floor beside the bed. What happened here we can hardly conjecture. But of this I am certain, as I know we all of us are, that our friend and comrade, Charles Wellington, the tenderest, warmest hearted, most upright of men, never wantonly or in anger or maliciously pushed a man from a ten-story window. The mystery in the case is where can he be? What is he hiding for? Or is he hiding? Perhaps some accident has also overtaken him. These matters, however, I engage to clear up later. At present our duty is to our patient."

It was a long struggle. Each of these men with his professional honor at stake stood to the last ditch for his opinion. But finally Dr. Furnivall's counsel prevailed. The operation was performed with perfect success, a dot of blood being found on and removed from the superior temporal convolution, and the patient was pronounced sane and out of danger.

When she was strong enough to relate the story of the tragedy she said, in the presence of several witnesses, including Sergeant Nulty, her eyes on Dr. Furnivall's: "I called Dr. Wellington for my nerves. I did not know there was anything else the matter with me, but he saw at once that it was something more than nerves. While he was examining me, my husband came in. He had been drinking. He knew nothing of my having a doctor, and when he saw us he flew into a passion, not understanding the case, charging me with horrible things. Dr. Wellington resented the tone Mr. Seavey took, and cried out to him that he was a brute to talk so to his wife, and that he deserved a kicking. My husband was standing by the window, which was open, and suddenly he pitched over—"

"One moment," Dr. Furnivall interrupted. "Was your husband being treated for any disease?"

"Yes, Meniere's disease."

"Gentlemen," said Dr. Furnivall to the listening circle, but without moving his gaze from the invalid's eyes, "remember the symptoms of Meniere's disease—intense and paroxysmal aural vertigo, coming suddenly—Proceed, madam."

"My husband fell in such a way that he pitched through the window. Dr. Wellington, with a cry of horror, rushed forward with outstretched arms to save him, but could not get a good hold on him. This is all I remember. I must have fainted then with the terror of it."

Dr. Furnivall turned to the witnesses. "The only thing that seems to be lacking," he said, "is the reason why Dr. Wellington ran away—"

At that very moment the door opened and in walked a bearded man, who said, calmly: "I will tell you that."

"Wellington!" cried Dr. Furnivall, grasping his hand.

"I have come to give myself up now, if I am wanted, since my wife is out of danger."

"Ah," Dr. Furnivall exclaimed, as if enlightened at once. "Give us the details."

"As I came down my steps yesterday on the way to answer Mrs. Seavey's summons, a message was handed me informing me that my wife, who had been in the country for some days, was down critically with pneumonia. Of course, I should drop everything else to go to her. But knowing that the next train would not leave for over an hour I saw that I should have time to come here, and I did so. When the accident happened and I hurried down to the sidewalk, finding the crowd, I should have waited and explained, and have willingly given myself up, but for one reason. It would prevent me from hastening to my wife, who was at death's door. I could not bring myself to that. Seeing that I could do no good I simply went away—to her. She is safe now, and seeing by the papers that I was wanted—"

"Is he wanted, sergeant?" smiled Dr. Furnivall.

"Not be me, not be me, not be me!" repeated Sergeant Nulty, awakening from the trance of disgust in which he had listened to

the evidence. "Begob," he muttered, as, with an air of injured virtue added to his usual dignity of deportment, he marched out of
the room, "begob, men is all goats these days. Goats wid whiskers!
Accidents, accidents, accidents! They have none of them the shtuff
in thim to kill a man. The good old times is gone. No chanct for
promotion! I'll die a sergeant. Well, well, well!"

MRS. WORTLEY'S SECRET

Through the driving snow blizzard in the early morning the milk boy plowed his way up the steps of the dilapidated Wortley mansion, opened the outer door, stepped into the narrow vestibule, and rang sharply the old-fashioned bell. Ordinarily he then would have deposited a bottle of milk on the floor, picked up the "empty" that had been set out over night, and departed with the cheerful bang and clatter that has been anathema to good sleepers since the days of Aristophanes; but this time there was a variation of the program. He waited. Handling his basket of unstable bottles with as much care as if they were eggs, he placed it silently in a corner, and with hunched shoulders, ear to the keyhole, a determined expression on his blowzy young face, he appeared to be listening intently to the gradually diminishing jingle jingle of his summons away down in the basement kitchen.

Refraining, for reasons of his own, from advertising the fact that he was still on the spot by a second pull at the knob, he crouched in this attitude long after the tongue of the bell had ceased its musical clangor. It was fully five minutes before he moved as much as an eyelid. Then he suddenly gathered himself, held his breath, and, as the door opened a crack, pushed it wide, and stepped triumphantly in.

"There!" he exclaimed with satisfaction.

"Lord a massy! What's all this?" cried a thin, cracked voice.

The hall was dusky, but the boy could see that an old woman of untidy appearance stood staring dazedly at him, her hand on the knob of the door which he had closed on entering. He gave a short, sneering chuckle. Then he began laboriously to unbutton his many layered wrapping of heavy clothing.

"This here little bill," he said, producing and handing it to the woman, "has run three months, an' every time the old man comes round for it it's twenty-three for him. Skiddoo! Nobuddy t' home. See? I want th' money. I want it now. An' I'll get it, too, afore I'll leave, or I'll h'ist out th' furniture."

"Well, good Lord!" exclaimed the woman, who, though plainly of a meek disposition, was roused to some degree of self-assertion by this open attack. "If you want your money I guess you can have it. You needn't tear my head off. I don't owe you anything. It's Mrs. Wortley, and she's worth a million dollars. You step over here away from her door and I'll tell her."

The boy jeered at the mention of this magnificent sum. It was easy enough to call anybody a millionaire. Anybody. She might call him one if she wanted to. But her manner presaged success for his mission, and, somewhat mollified, he stood back by the stairs while the woman rapped gently at the parlor door.

"Mrs. Wortley!" she cried, not too loudly. There was no answer.

"Mrs. Wortley! Mrs. Wortley! The milkman is here and wants to see you!" This time the voice was stronger, but there came no sound from within. She waited a moment and then rattled the door knob. Still no response. "She must be fast asleep. She doesn't like to be woke up—can't you come again when—"

"Oh, sure!" he interrupted, with a world of expression. All his doubts and determination were rearoused by these signs of tricks, with the winding and complex patterns of which he was on intimate terms. "Oh, sure, I'll come agin'. An' I'll stay right here till I do, too. You sure got a lead pipe cinch on me in this deal, mommer. Me? Why, you never see me out when the dew is falling. Some rude creature might accost me."

With the explosion of this bomb of sarcasm, picked up last night at the dime museum, he grinned delightedly, sat down on the stairs, and leaned comfortably against the wall as if he would be happy to remain there for any indefinite period.

"If that ain't killin'!" muttered the woman in disgust and indignation. She stood irresolutely, looking at him. "Well," she said, after a moment, "I'll go in through the other room and wake her up, but you won't get any thanks for making me do it, I can tell you. And it's the last milk you'll ever bring into this house in the bargain."

"Huh!" he sniffed. "Good thing, too! Swappin' milk fer wind!"

He watched warily as she went down the hall to a sort of cabinet built against the wall, with a set washbowl in it, put her hand in, and from a corner of a high shelf produced a key, with which she let herself into the rear parlor. Then he rose and softly followed her. Rolling back a little one of the great folding doors between the two rooms, she thrust her head into the spectral gloom beyond and again called "Mrs. Wortley!" and still there was no movement or sound in response. Suddenly she began to sniff.

"Why, that's chloroform!" the boy behind heard her exclaim in a startled whisper.

He crept forward, a vague sense of something strange impelling him, and with eyes younger than those of the woman searched the dim interior over her shoulder.

"Kinder topsy-turvey, ain't it?" he commented under his breath.

She did not resent his presence staring there into her mistress' bedroom. On the contrary, she flung her hand with a quick, backward movement on his arm, as if to reassure herself that she was not alone. Then she went in swiftly, paused, and with a sudden low cry threw herself down upon the bed, clasping in her arms the still form that lay there.

The boy gazed a moment with wide eyes, taking in the significance of the scene. Then he withdrew, set the spring lock on the front door, and at the top of his speed splashed and floundered through the drifts to the police station a block away.

The woman still lay in speechless grief on the body of her mistress when the officers arrived, and they found considerable difficulty in removing her, so that an examination of the corpse could be made. Finally they succeeded in placing her in an easy chair, where she sat with every sign of despairing sorrow on her wrinkled

[

face, and without appearing to take any interest in what was going on answered apathetically such questions as were put to her.

As soon as the shades were raised, letting daylight into the room, the first thing the officers noticed was that the dead woman was bound, and in a most curious manner. Instead of being lashed together with cords the limbs were carried, each wrist and each ankle to its side of the bedstead, and there tied firmly with strips torn from the upper sheet, the remains of which hung over the foot rail with the other bedclothing.

"That is what I call queer," whispered one of the policemen to the other, who nodded, staring. The ambulance surgeon came hurrying in at the moment, and the three stood gazing an instant without a word at the singular spectacle.

The body was that of a beautiful woman of 30, of the pronounced brunette type, with full lips, great black eyes, wide and glazed now, the form of a sylph, and a wealth of lustrous black hair that lay tumbled over the pillows. The skilled glance of the physician, however, immediately detected signs of dissipation in the lovely face. He saw, too, that one of the eyebrows was scorched as with recent fire, and that the forehead and left cheek were marked with slight burns, which must have been inflicted within a few hours. An eight ounce bottle containing a little chloroform lay without a stopper on the bed by her side, its neck raised on the pillow.

"Beats me," whispered one of the policemen.

"It looks like asphyxiation by chloroform," said the physician. "But we'll see about that later. She's gone, any way."

The officers then began a search of the premises.

The upper drawer of the bureau had been pulled out, ransacked, and thrown on the floor, the jewel boxes on the dressing case were empty, an oil painting had been cut out of its frame, and the gold watch which, the woman said, always hung on the bedpost at night, was missing. This seemed to be the extent of the property loss, though there was a great roll of bank bills in the second drawer of the bureau, which had not been opened, apparently, a closet was half filled with beautiful and costly gold and silverware, a clock covered with jewels, small enough for easy removal, still ticked on the mantel, and the two rooms were crowded to profusion with all sorts of elegant and expensive nick-nacks. The officers were comparing notes on this unexpected state of affairs when a surprised exclamation from the physician, who was bending over the body, brought them hastily to his side.

"See there!" he said, pointing to the bonds where they were fastened to the bed.

The policemen scanned them interestedly.

"They're surgeon's knots," the doctor said: "the kind a surgeon ties. No common burglar did this job."

The officers looked at each other quickly.

"There's ain't a winder or door on this floor," said one, "that ain't locked, except the way we come in. And the milk feller says that was locked, too, and the woman got the key to it out of this cupboard here. It looks queer, Jack—this body tied in here alone and everything locked up all snug."

"It sure does, Cale. The housekeeper says nobody lives here but Dr. Wortley and his wife and her, and the milkman swears there wa'n't no signs in the snow of anybody's goin' out. Not a track before his. And it snowed all night."

"Dr. Wortley!" exclaimed the physician. "You don't mean—you can't mean, that this is the house of Dr. Brownall Wortley—that this was his wife?"

"That's just what!" returned Cale, shaking his head as if he were sorry for it.

The younger physician scrutinized the face of the dead with a new interest. So this was the woman! Lying there! Well, well, well! He had never known Dr. Wortley personally, but his history was one of the traditions of the profession in the city. A millionaire bachelor, famous for his surgical skill, enjoying an enormous practice, and, of an old New England family, welcome to the innermost circles of society throughout the land, he had thrown his glove in the face of custom and tradition and turned his back on the obviously correct thing by marrying a shop girl. He was 50, cultivated, handsome, rich; she was 20, uncultured, fascinatingly beautiful, and squalidly poor. The act plunged him into such a hornet's nest of surprise, detraction, and downright abuse, especially from the mothers of marriageable daughters in his own set, that he was sorely stung, and, at first bewildered. He could not see why his marriage with anybody should interest the world, and when one day a newspaper reporter called to interview him he told him so. But, he added, since the world, for some reason or other, indubitably seemed interested, he begged to inform it that this young gentlewoman, who was now his wife, had been brought into this life by him, as the attending physician; that he had followed every phase of her existence from that day to this; that he knew her to the soul; found her so superior to every other woman, in any class of society, whether it were a question of character or body, mind or heart, that for him she was the one woman; that they loved each other; and, finally, that, since the fact that she was poor while he was rich appeared to form the nucleus around which the storm of disapproval howled, he should gladly remove it—in short, he should this day make over all his property to his wife, so that now the conditions were reversed, and it was a case of poor man and rich wife. Perhaps his solicitious friends, the smart set, would care to express their exceedingly valuable and interesting opinions on that sort of a union!

Whether this attitude of his closed the hitherto widely opened doors of society against him, or whether he had already, before the marriage, resolved upon his course, certain it was that he threw up his practice immediately and accompanied his young and beautiful wife abroad. For five years little was heard of them in their native city, except that now and then some wanderer far afield brought tidings of them from out of the way places—now a little village in Switzerland, by and by a modest hotel in Italy, a farm house in Scotland, one of the islands of Japan, or, in India, a villa in the hill country. They evidently traveled extensively, yet wherever they were found it was always in the peace of seclusion, undisturbed by the fret and hurry of gregarious humanity, their life streams blended into one happy, flowing river of love and content.

Then suddenly, in a night as it seemed, the rumors changed ominously. Something mysterious had come between these ideal married lovers. It was now only the husband who lived apart from the whirlpool of society, while the lovely young wife threw herself into the swirling current with extravagant abandon. The polish which, in their five years of intimacy, the accomplished man of the world had been able to impart to his girl wife, the wealth he had lavished upon her, his name, and her own beauty and vivacity, opened the doors of social recognition to her on the instant she tapped for admittance, and, entering with a dash, she disported herself in a manner so reckless that her name was soon on everybody's lips. Her flirtations were uncounted, scandalous, audaciously open; her style of living ruinous even for a possessor of ten times her wealth; she dressed loudly, looked frequently on the wine cup, and, while the doctor remained strictly in the privacy of his own room, she never appeared at home except for the few hours of sleep she was obliged to steal each morning in order to recuperate for the feverish dance of the day and night. Her husband she seemed to hate. Of him and to him her speech was invariably contemptuous, and the flash of her black eye in his direction was like the savage cut of a sword. On his part he paid no attention to her any longer. Her fierce glances seemed to impress him not at all. He answered no sharp word of hers. He never even looked at her, or seemed conscious of her existence, all his interest apparently being confined to his pipe, his food, his bed, and the scientific literature of the day.

These were the reports which for several years came from Europe, chiefly from Paris, and then suddenly the scene shifted back to America. The doctor, looking like a feeble octogenarian, though he was under 60, had been seen through the window in his old homestead. In various ways it soon leaked out that the strange couple had returned and, with an old housekeeper, taken up their abode in the decaying mansion, living in a relation to each other that was nothing short of preposterous. Rumor declared that the wife occupied the two great rooms on the ground floor and never stirred out of them; he lived in the back attic and never stirred out of that, while the housekeeper slept in the basement, carried them their meals, took what little care of the house that was taken at all, and stood as the buffer between her mistress and the insistent duns who, in due season, began to clamor at the front door. And the explanation was that, the million having taken wings, the foolish wife and deluded husband had finally immured themselves here to drag out the remainder of their days in self-sought oblivion. A few of his former friends had called at first, but were turned away without a sight of him, and from that time on nobody but the aged servant and the tradesmen had been observed going to or from the house.

This story flashed instantly through the physician's brain as he sat there with his eyes on the woman who had caused it all, now cold in death, her earthly pilgrimage with its strange mystery ended suddenly forever. What that mystery was never would be known now—ah, but now it most certainly would be known! The doctor would tell it in palliation of—palliation? Yes, or justification, what might seem justification to him. For there was but one explanation of that murder. The evidence all pointed to it—the locked doors, the key whose hiding place could be known only to an inmate of the house, the professional knots, the chloroform, the large number of valuables left untouched and the few taken as if to send suspicion astray, the absence of footprints in the snow, the couple's attitude toward each other, and, above all, the great secret of the estrangement! There was no other way out of it. It was written as plainly in the circumstances as if it had been carefully set down in black and white. Driven to desperation by the misery into which she had plunged him, and most likely unhinged in mind, he had done this terrible thing. And this was the end of him as for her! What a finish for a career that had begun and for twenty years continued so brilliantly.

Dr. Furnivall was eating his breakfast when the news of the crime, coupled with the request from the prisoner that he would call upon him, was brought by an officer of the police station; and a few minutes later he sat face to face with the man he so highly honored for his early achievements, and whose domestic tragedy had long been known to him in the version current in the profession. He found him, as reported, an old man in appearance, with hair and beard perfectly white, a stoop in his shoulders as of care, a trembling hand, and the pallid, wrinkled skin of fast approaching decrepitude. The eyes, however, were undimmed. Black, steady, full of fire, they might have been those of a person of 30, but, hidden behind gold rimmed spectacles, and their power somewhat veiled by curiously puffed lids, which gave him the appearance of looking downward, they took nothing from the effect of age, unless one looked directly into them.

"I requested you to call, Dr. Furnivall," he began, speaking evenly, as if it were a matter of every day business, "because I have heard of your notable successes along the lines of hypnotism, and in the interests of justice—" He paused, and then asked abruptly, "Do you believe I am guilty?"

"No," said Dr. Furnivall at once. And added: "I may say that I know you are innocent."

"Your reasons?" The question shot out in the tones of an alert man of affairs, and the black eyes examined Dr. Furnivall's face with suddenly awakened interest.

"Because you are not a bungler. According to the story the officer told me on the way here, every sign points to you, and you only. If you had committed the crime it would not be so. Not a single sign would indicate your hand in the tragedy. Besides, had it been in you to do it at all you would have done it years ago, quietly and skillfully."

"Ah!" the old man exclaimed. "It really seems as if others might have thought of that. But no matter. What I wished to say is this: I have no notion who the criminal is; not the least. But that woman at the house, Mrs. Partridge, may be able to tell something if you can make her talk. There was some bond between my wife and her. I don't know its nature, but it was very strong. They used to weep in each other's arms every day, I should think, beginning some five years ago, and I never knew why, but it was evidently something terrible to them. The fact may have bearing on the case. It is the only thing I know, at all events, and I would suggest inquiry in that field. If you could hypnotize the woman and question her about that secret of theirs, maybe her answers would throw light on the murder—if it be a murder."

"What! You think—"

"Those women were capable of any bitterness toward me. She might have died a natural death. I don't know. But she had trouble with her heart. And this other woman would not hesitate to make it look like murder and throw the appearance of guilt on me. But what upsets the theory is that I am sure she knows nothing of tying surgeon's knots."

"She might have had help."

"Yes, that may be. Perhaps that is it. She has no initiative of her own, but would do what she was told to do, and it is quite within the possibilities that all this was arranged between them long ago, in case Mrs. Wortley should die suddenly. Her health was in a very delicate state, and I fancy she had for two years expected to go off suddenly at any moment. Yes, they were quite capable of arranging beforehand to make it look like murder and directing suspicion toward me, for they seemed to hate me most rancorously, both, of them, and tried in every way to humiliate and degrade me. The strangest part of it is that I haven't the faintest shadow of a notion why they felt so."

"You don't know the cause of Mrs. Wortley's estrangement from you?" said Dr. Furnivall in surprise.

"No," he answered wearily. "All in an instant, quick as a flash of lightning, like the discharge of a cannon it came. Her love for me turned to bitterness and downright loathing." He ran a trembling hand over his brow, and after a short pause, as if to gather fortitude, continued: "One day, in France, after more than five years of happiness with me, or what I would have sworn was happiness, she received a cable message from America. I handed it to her myself. She read it standing, and remained motionless so long that I looked up from my newspaper, and there she stood glaring at me so fiendishly that I shouldn't have known her. Her face resembled a frenzied animal's more than a human being's. Her cheeks were like chalk, her lips were drawn back from her teeth in a snarl like that of a wildcat, and her eyes fairly blazed. Startled terribly, I jumped up and ran to her, when she shrieked out that I had ruined her life, struck me with all her force in the face, and fled from the room. I thought she had suddenly lost her mind. And, indeed, I believe she had. I followed her, of course. But she would have nothing to do with me, would explain nothing, listen to nothing, accept nothing that I proposed. She raved, swearing that she hated me and always had. But I can't go into all that. I tried everything, in vain. I offered her her freedom, offered to leave her and allow her to obtain a divorce, at last, but she would not consent even to that. I suppose she wished to drag my name in the mire and remain near to torment and humiliate me."

Again he paused, drinking a glass of water.

"In a few weeks this woman, Mrs. Partridge, arrived," he went on with effort. "They were plainly old friends, having some secret bond of sympathy. And they have remained inseparable ever since. I don't understand their relation. Years ago I gave up trying to understand. That my wife had all along deceived me, hated, rather than loved, me, was all I wished to know. It made an old man of me. I lost interest in life; gave it up. Nothing was left for me this side of the grave but a waiting. And I am waiting, patiently as I may. But I should rather not do it in prison."

Dr. Furnivall rose abruptly. He had been present at the unfolding of too many tragedies not to realize the impotence of words of condolence in such a case as this. Confining his attention strictly to the subject of the crime he asked a few questions regarding visitors, and the relations on which the three inmates of the house lived with one another, and after a word of encouragement hurried away to the Wortley mansion.

He found it in the possession of the police officers, one of whom, at his request, showed him immediately in to the housekeeper, who sat in stony silence at her mistress' bedside, never removing her eyes from the rigid body. She neither answered his greeting nor seemed aware of his presence there. The officer, who had heard great things of Dr. Furnivall's occult powers, and remained in the room curious to see for himself some starling exhibition of them, touched his arm, and shaking his head whispered:

"She was all right a little while this morning, and answered everything we asked her. But she won't say no more—took stuffy! Won't open her mouth, no matter what you do."

"Oh, yes, she will!" the doctor returned somewhat grimly. "Mrs. Partridge," he said to her, "did you ever see me before?"

She looked up quickly and peered at him with some show of interest, but immediately moved her head as if to return her gaze to its former direction. She moved it only slightly, however. Then it remained fixed. Her weak eyes, staring into his, took on an expression of concentration wholly new to them, and she answered in an emotionless voice: "No, sir."

"How long have you known Mrs. Wortley?"

"Most all her life."

"What relation do you bear to her?"

"I ain't any relation. Only she was engaged to be married to my son."

"Married? She was already married. What do you mean? Tell me all about it. Begin at the beginning."

"My son James and her worked in the same shop and was goin' to git married when they could afford it. Then Dr. Wortley wanted her, and they thought she better take him, for she said he was an old man and—and would leave her a lot of money and then she could have James. But he was only 50. She thought that was old, but it ain't. And he's alive yet. But James died five years ago. That broke her heart and mine, too, and she sent for me and we've lived together ever since."

"My God!" burst involuntarily from Dr. Furnivall. This, then, was the great secret! He thought he never had heard so ironical a tragedy put in so few words. This was the girl whom Dr. Wortley had watched from infancy, and found to be the one woman in the world! The young lover's death, which was undoubtedly what the cablegram had announced to her, upsetting her plans, destroying her hopes, showing that all her duplicity and sacrifice had been in vain, had maddened her, and with the one sided logic of an intensely materialistic mind, she attributed her failure and despair to her devoted victim. Had it not been for him all this never would have occurred. And he should pay for it! Yes, he should pay for it to the last tittle—with his honor, his happiness, his money, the very decencies of life!

The policeman, who knew only enough of the story to blame Dr. Wortley's lack of perspicacity in choosing such a woman for his wife, sniffed cynically. Dr. Furnivall resumed his questions.

"Have you any idea who committed this crime?"

"No, I haven't."

"Who besides Dr. Wortley and you knew where the key to the back parlor was kept?"

"Nobody. And the doctor didn't know, either. It wasn't ever there till yesterday. I stuck it in there myself."

"Why?"

"It was loose in the lock and fallin' out all the time. I had to go in that way a good deal, and first I used to leave it in the door daytimes, and then I kept it in my pocket. But I lost it yesterday, so when I found it I thought I'd better hide it in the cupboard."

"When did you put it in there last?"

"It was 9 o'clock last night. She wasn't feelin' well and went to bed about 8."

"And there was nobody but you three in the house at that time?"

"No, not a soul. And there ain't been anybody but us in the house sence we lived here, except the water inspector."

"You have groceries and such things brought here, don't you?"

"Not often. I go to the store myself mostly. And when anything is brought I take it at the door. The milkman got in this morning, but he's the only one."

"You have no callers, any of you?"

"No, nobody I let in."

"Who calls and is not let in?"

"Only Fred now. People used to come for the doctor, but I always told 'em that he didn't want to see 'em, and so they don't come any more."

"Who is Fred?"

"My son."

"Another son! Does Mrs. Wortley ever see him?"

"No. But she gives me money for him. People think we're poor, but we ain't."

"Has he been here lately?"

"Not for two weeks. I told him not to come again till he was sober. Mrs. Wortley wouldn't give him any more money to buy liquor with."

"What is your son's business?"

"He drove a hack last, but I guess he ain't working now."

"What did he do before that?"

"Oh, different things. He took care of horses in a stable, and worked in a grocery store, and was a bartender once. Then he was a waiter. But mostly he drived horses for somebody."

"He hasn't ever had anything to do with medicine, has he? Did he ever work in a drug store?"

"No, not that I know of. The nearest he ever came to it was driving the hospital ambulance. He tried nursing, too, but didn't like it, and went back on the team."

"Where does he live?"

"22 Prospect street."

Dr. Furnivall scribbled a note and gave it to the officer.

"That man fits all the circumstances," he whispered. "As soon as you find him call me up on the telephone and then take him to your station."

At 3 o'clock that afternoon Dr. Furnivall, responding to the summons, walked into station 15 and found a short, clean shaven, red faced, shifty looking fellow, about 28 years old, protesting to the lieutenant that, by all that was holy, though he was Fred Partridge, and lived at 22 Prospect street, this was the first time he had ever heard the name of Wortley. He knew nothing of any murder. These officers, he said, had gone to his boarding place, and not finding him there, had searched the whole neighborhood for him, which was enough to give a man a bad name for life, and finally coming on him in a saloon, among friends that knew him, had snapped the darbies on him for murder. Nice way to treat an honest man who was trying to earn his living without sponging on anybody for it! He didn't even know what street the murder was done in. And here were two friends, Con and Ed, who were with him when he was arrested, and could swear he hadn't been out of their sight since yesterday noon. He slept with them last night in their room, three in a bed.

Two men standing near nodded.

"That's right," said one of them to the lieutenant. "We had a free lunch yesterday noon over to Tim Nagle's place, an' we been together ever since, lookin' for a job."

The lieutenant's face wrinkled derisively as he glanced into the watery eyes of the friendly trio, picturing in his fancy the kind of job they were undoubtedly looking for. Then he nodded to Dr. Furnivall, who came forward and stood by the railing close to Partridge.

There were several police officers in the room, and, their curiosity sharpened by their comrade's story of the marvelous results obtained by Dr. Furnivall that day from the woman who wouldn't speak, they watched his every move with absorbed interest. But when, without any spectacular waving or stroking of the hands, such as they had always associated in their minds with hypnotism, without the production of any mysterious machine, or even a globe of magic crystal, he simply, in an ordinary tone, asked Partridge, "Where did you learn to tie surgeon's knots?" they were plainly disappointed. If this was hypnotism, hypnotism was no great shakes.

The man turned quickly at the question.

"Surgeon's knots?" he cried. "What's surgeon's knots?"

"Didn't you ever nurse in a hospital?"

His face grew hot and then blanched.

"No," he answered huskily.

"Never drove an ambulance?"

"No."

"What do you know of Mrs. Wortley?"

"I tell you I dunno nothing of her," he began heatedly. "I never heard the name till this minute. My mother is her housekeeper."

Before the circle of listeners could digest this grotesque contradiction the doctor asked evenly, repeating his first remark:

"Where did you learn to tie surgeon's knots?"

"City hospital," he answered readily now, in a mechanical voice, his eyes intently on his questioner's.

"Tell me all about the Wortley affair. What did you go there for? Go on. Begin at the beginning."

"I went fer some money. Mother said last week she wouldn't give me no more till I quit the booze, and I had been on it a little that day, but I thought maybe she might cough up some. I was bound to try it anyways. But when I got over there I seen the ketch on the winder wasn't fastened, and I thought maybe I could git more myself, if I went in, than they'd give me. So I h'isted the winder and crawled through. There was a candle lit on the table and I could see that the key was on the inside of the door, so I shet the winder and fastened it so nobudy'd notice outside, and then unlocked the door, so I could git out quicker. While I was at it she woke up and started in to scream, and I grabbed her and shut her mouth. She sorter fainted then, and I tied her up so she couldn't fall out of bed when she come to and wake up mother downstairs. Then I begun to clean out the room, but she laid so still I went over to look at her. She looked so bad I was rattled and grabbed a bottle of something I thought was water that stood on the table and threw it in her face. But then I found it was chloroform. That rattled me more'n ever, and somehow I dropped the candle on her. But I picked it up again and put it out and run into the hall. But before I could git out mother was comin' up from the kitchen, and I hid on the stairs, I thought she'd heard me, but she hadn't; she only went into the back parlor for something. When she come out I see where she put the key, and I thought I could stand it better to search that room than the one where the woman was in the faint, so I got the key and went in. But it was dark as pitch. I couldn't find anything. I remembered that her watch hung on the bedpost, and I thought I could stand it to git that, so I opened the foldin' doors easy. Then I got the watch, pulled the foldin' doors to, locked up the back parlor, and put the key where I found it, and come out the front way."

"Do your friends here, Con and Ed, know all this?"

"No, they don't know nothing about it. They was waitin' round the corner, and thought I went to see my mother a minute, that's all. I only showed 'em a diamond, and said she give it to me."

"What time was it when you came out of the Wortley house?"

"Somewheres about 9 o'clock."

"That agrees with the woman's time," said Dr. Furnivall to the lieutenant, "and clears up the question of footprints. It had only just begun to snow then."

"I didn't hardly touch her," said Partridge, following out the trend of his thought. "I didn't mean to hurt her. I couldn't 'a' hurt her—much."

"It will be found to be heart failure accelerated by fright, I think," said Dr. Furnivall.

The lieutenant motioned to the now thoroughly astonished men, who led the prisoner away.

"If it hadn't been for you," he said to the doctor, "we never would have got this Partridge. Dr. Wortley would have to stand for it. Say," he continued, earnestly, "I'd give a year's salary to learn how to do a stunt like that one."

"Well," remarked Dr. Furnivall, soberly, drawing on his gloves, "it cost me as much as that would come to—in one way and another!"

THE WETCHELL JOB

One of the most extraordinary cases that ever came under the observation of Dr. Furnivall, and which, as it turned out, could in all probability never have been solved in any other way than through his peculiar method of hypnotism, was what is known in police circles as "The Wetchell Job." The truths of this unique crime as brought out by him are as follows:

In a large, barnlike old house of three stories, of brick, painted yellow, sitting in a yard of its own, surrounded by high board fences, amidst new tenement buildings filled with an element utterly incongruous with its air of old fashioned respectability, lived Miss Wetchell. She clung to the ancient homestead as to her one friend on earth, to the everlasting disturbance of the clamorous neighbors, who, in their congested quarters, resented in six languages the occupation of a whole house of fourteen rooms by one person, and that one an elderly, single female of oily manners and a good income, who pretended to be what she was not. For this woman, by her smile, which was ostentatiously gentle; by her voice, which was ostentatiously tender; and by her ostentatious acts of kindness, which consisted in feeding stray cats and allowing children of the tenements to play in her great back yard one hour a week—this woman, by all these signs advertised herself as a person of good nature and benevolence, when she was very far from being that. It did not require many days of observation on the part of any one of the interested observers to force the conclusion on them that all this, while done by the lady with the view of exalting her reputation, was in reality the expression of cowardice. In fact, this benevolent woman was afraid. She wished to conciliate these rude ones; she wished to be on good terms with her neighbors for fear of them. Too miserly, they said, to sell her property at the low price which it was now worth, on account of its location, so near the heart of the slums, she held on with a grip comparable to that of death alone, fawning and smiling lovingly when she felt only dread and hate, in order to save the few dollars she would be obliged to sacrifice from her plenty in selling out and going to more congenial quarters. The bases of this opinion were many, spread over a large area of observation by the onlookers, who were shrewder than she thought, but one of these bases flared out like a beacon light from among all the others and was observable, perhaps, once a day for every twenty-four hours of the year.

It was the distinction she made between the value of men and that of cats, and upon this distinction as she made it rests the story of her strange misfortune.

Up the street towards this lady, who was sweeping the steps of her domicile in the morning, a man advanced. He was not a nice appearing person. His clothes were greasy and ragged, his nose was blooded, his gait was halt, as if there were sores on his heels, and his skin was exceedingly dirty, and grown over with thick, black hairs. He saw the busy sweeper all at once, and immediately began his preparation. These consisted in a smoothing down of the heavy beard, a pull at the brim of his old slouch hat, a straightening of the shoulders, a sidling movement of the body, and a deprecatory eye. He coughed, and with his hand on the gate post spoke:

"Hm'm! Lady, c'd yer help a poor man that fighted fer yer in the war?"

She turned upon him like a tigress. She was not handsome, and the distortion of her coarse features, the baring of her strong yellow teeth, and her sudden raging at him, took him completely aback.

"You!" she hissed, "You, a man 6 feet tall, and healthy, asking help! You ought to be ashamed of yourself. Why don't you go to work? There is plenty to do. You are lazy. Don't you dare ask me for assistance, you—you—ugh!"

In a fever of virtuous wrath she gave an extra swish of her broom, stamped her foot, threw a last indignant glance toward the abased mendicant, flew into the house, and slammed the door.

Hobus leaned on the fence wearily. He had not been in the war, and he wondered if she, by some occult power known only to the higher classes, had found him out in his lie. Was that the reason why she was so fierce? He believed so. He did not know how it was, but the world was down on him. The whole world! He looked up at the house wonderingly, smoothed his beard with a trembling hand, and tried to think. Where should he go next? He was hungry, he was wretched, he was impotent, and he could not see that all this was his fault. It appeared to him that he had been born so—hungry and wretched and incapable, and never could be anything else.

Listlessly he moved away across the street to the scant shade of a straggly tree, and considered. Presently another man, with the soil of several states on his person, hardly distinguished in appearance from Hobus himself, though he was smaller and younger, and his beard was of a fortnight's growth only, slouched around the corner, examined the Wetchell house a moment, and then crept into the yard. Hobus began to grin, and, hobbling hurriedly to a position of advantage behind the great square fence post, pricked up his ears to listen.

"Lady," said the young tramp to Miss Wetchell when she had answered his ring, "could you please feed a poor man that was in the Spanish war and got broke down fightin' fer yer?"

Hobus shook his head solemnly as he heard this form of address, so closely resembling his own. In the mouth of another it took on a new meaning. It seemed like attempting to establish a right to alms rather than a bid for charity and kindness, and Hobus, without understanding the philosophy of the case, felt intuitively that it was a wrong move. Condescension is a necessary concomitant of charity with many givers, and to remove the possibility of their enjoying that comfortable emotion by asking help of them as a right, not as a favor, is unwise. He resolved to remodel his own formula after this. In the meantime he shook with wild laughter to hear Miss Wetchell's address. It was exactly, word for word, the same answer she had given him, and not knowing that it was a familiar form to her, beaten into her mind by the constant repetition of it during fifty years or more of resistance to the horrible evil of pauperization, he wondered how she remembered it so perfectly.

"You!" she hissed. "You, a man, six feet tall (he was 5 feet 2), and healthy, asking help! You ought to be ashamed of yourself! Why don't you go to work? There is plenty to do. You are lazy. Don't you dare ask me for assistance, you—you—ugh—"

She slammed the door in his face.

Hobus, peering around the post, preparing to meet the rejected applicant with a facetious grin, was startled by the sudden deathly pallor of his skin, and quickly drew back to his hiding place. The young man slowly left the yard and started in the direction whence he had come, walking weakly, staggering a little, and keeping near the houses, against which he frequently leaned to steady his tottering steps. At the corner he paused, looked dazedly around, clapped his hand to his side, and then sank in a heap on the sidewalk.

In an instant there was a crowd around him, which Hobus joined, hovering on the outskirts of it with morbid curiosity. A doctor came hastily from his office near by, knelt over the huddled body, and presently announced that it was death, due to a weak heart and starvation. Hobus waited until the ambulance arrived and closed its doors on its ghastly burden, and rattled away. Then he returned to his former position by the tree, and stood eyeing the old house opposite with a queer passion struggling for expression in his weak face.

In a moment up the sidewalk came a little girl with a cat in her arms, and, turning into Miss Wetchell's doorway, rang the old fashioned bell, expectancy in her bright eyes, the flush of enthusiasm in her round cheeks. Miss Wetchell opened the door, the tramp looking on in curiosity.

"Oh, Miss Wetchell!" cried the child, "here is a kitty—and she is lost—and I found her and—and—do you—do you want her?

Mamma said you belonged to the—the—oh, something that takes
care of kitties!"

"Oh, the dear little thing!" observed Miss Wetchell loudly, with
a cast of her eye up to the windows opposite, as if addressing them.
"Come right in, darling, and I will give the poor thing some milk.
And I think that is very nice of you to bring the poor, little kitty
here. I will give you a piece of nice candy for it. Come."

It was one of those idiosyncrasies of character which only the
profoundest philosophy can explain, that while she hoped and believed that the neighbors would become cognizant of her goodness
to cats, and would applaud it, thinking it was abstract goodness,
she at the same time never thought of their becoming aware of her
harsh treatment of men, and resenting it, though the evidence she
gave of the latter was at least four times stronger than that of the
former. She always looked at the surrounding windows with self-
conscious benevolence when she took in a cat, but when she drove
a human being away from her house in a voice of strident power
she never dreamed of anybody's hearing it, except the person she
addressed.

The door closed behind the two as the child accepted the invitation with the delight of her years and innocence.

A great man has said that so subtle are the springs of conduct
there is for every person, even the lowest, some one action at least
in the external world that will infuse him with courage and all the
passions which the highest can feel. Hobus, the moment he saw
that transaction, became another man. He straightened up, his
flesh seemed suddenly to grow less flabby, his eye brightened, and
a look of intelligence flashed into it, though it had long been devoid of that excellence. And, this time without smoothing his beard,
or coughing or arranging his hat, he started across the street to
the big house, entered the yard, and put a dirty hand to the bell.
When Miss Wetchell appeared he pushed in, took the little girl,
who had, childlike, followed her hostess at the sound of the bell,
by the arms, gently lifted her to the outside, and closed the door.

"Now, sizzle ye!" he said to the bewildered Miss Wetchell, "arter
you've fed the cat give me something to eat."

He grasped her arm as he spoke and shook her, scowling and masterful. "Sizzle ye!" he reiterated. It was the first time in his life that he ever could have been called masterful.

The horror of her situation nearly overcame Miss Wetchell. She was alone in that great house with an ugly tramp. To call out would be foolishness. Nobody could hear. And even if anybody could hear she would be murdered before help could arrive. But Miss Wetchell was not one to remain overwhelmed. She knew exactly what to do in the circumstances, once she had time to collect herself. A thousand times had she practiced her perspicacity on the neighbors in exigencies which, though they never any of them had been as urgent as this, were still of strategic importance. She had a principle and she would employ it now. It was oilyness. Therefore "Oh!" she exclaimed, as if to a dear friend, "come right in. Now, what would you like for breakfast? Lay off your hat. Here, let me take it. Should you like some strawberries and cream? I like them. But you can have just what you want."

She bustled away through the sitting-room and thence into the kitchen, where the table was kept continually set. Hobus followed her closely.

"Anybody else in the house 'sides you?" he asked.

"Oh, yes," she answered with emphasis. "There's a family up stairs. I expect Mr. Wockwell down every minute."

He laughed boisterously. Her manner convinced him. They two were alone. He sat in a chair, put his feet on the table, produced a cigarette and said:

"Give us a light, old girl."

She brought it to him obediently, with an exaggerated show of condescending hospitality.

"Do you enjoy smoking?" she asked in a desperately friendly manner, working about the range.

He threw his head back and laughed, blowing blue clouds. But he said nothing except "Hurry up! I'm hungry—" and then, "Sizzle yer!"

"I'll give you some nice ham and eggs," she volunteered with a broad show of happiness. "Should you like that?" She paused, with a fork in her hand, over the gas range, and looked inquiringly at him. There was fear, deadly fear, in her eyes and face, and in all her manner, which she strove with all her might to hide, vainly, and this man, who, ten minutes before, had cringed to her, saw that fear, and the seeing made him her slave driver.

"'Ham and' is all right," he said, changing his legs, "but hurry up, sizzle yer!"

"Oh, yes," she cried, "I'll hurry." She ran here and there in the kitchen, now for this thing, now for that, and presently the fumes of the frying meat filled the room. She started to open one of the windows to let the smoke out, but he leveled his forefinger at her from where he sat, and said simply:

"Don't!"

"Oh, wouldn't you like the window open?" she said. "I thought you would. But there, I rather like the smoke of frying ham myself. Only I thought you wouldn't, and—"

She finished with a gasping cough, the commingled stenches of gas, cigarette, and meat nearly strangling her. He looked at her cynically and blew acrid puffs and badly made rings toward her shrinking nostrils. The stray cat was lapping milk out of a saucer in the sink, and Hobus, putting his legs down, scuffled his feet on the linoleum covered floor suddenly to see her jump. When she answered his expectations by spitting and scuttling beneath the stove he grinned delightedly.

"Say, old girl," he called in a loud voice, in order to make himself heard above the sputtering and sizzling of the ham, "it's cheaper to feed cats 'n what 'tis humans—ain't it?"

She was so fully occupied with her fears for her property and her bodily safety that she did not take in the sarcasm of his remark.

"Oh, I don't mind that," she said automatically. "I am sure you're very welcome to this!"

"Yes," he sneered, and then, "Ain't yer gonter give the pore little kitty none? Say, yer oughter give the dear little kitty the ham and eggs, arter keepin' 'em away from that young feller jest now. She's more importance 'n what he was! Yer know what 'come of that sick boy yer sent away hungry, on top of a tongue lashin'?"

She was not following him in the least. Her mind was deeply intent on turning over various plans of escape or calling help, but his words set vibrating within her certain chords of argument which, from long use, acted mechanically when touched, and she said, hardly conscious that she was speaking:

"A man has free will. He can take care of himself. If he doesn't it is his own fault and he doesn't deserve help. If a human being is destitute, look back into his or her record and you'll find the reason for it. But the animals are helpless, they—"

With a howl of rage Hobus threw himself upon her, and, seizing her wrists, bent and twisted her arms back until the joints cracked and she sank to her knees on the floor.

"Humans has got free will, has they? Oh, yes, humans can do jest what they want to, I'll bait. I'll bait you can do just what yer want to now! A lot you know about what humans c'n do! I wish you had to go through what I had, that's all—yer ign'rent old cross atween a rhinoceros and a jackass! You stand up and fry them aigs, and when you say anything, talk sense, or I'll know the reason why."

He flung her hands down, and as she rose quickly, stood glaring at her. Then, as she spaded out the ham into a plate, setting it on the range to keep hot, and broke the eggs into the griddle, he resumed his seat, muttering and scowling. She went on with her work as if nothing had happened, perfectly cowed, anxious to conciliate him.

"Do you like your eggs turned?" she asked, looking up and hanging on his answer as if it were a matter of international importance.

"Give 'em here jest's they be!" he growled, hitching his chair to the table. He ate voraciously, leaving not a scrap behind, while she waited on him assiduously. Once she started to another room, ostensibly for the sugar, but he scowled and motioned, and she returned instantly.

"You, got any more cats in the house?" he asked abruptly, when he had lapped his plate clean.

"Yes, I have seven," she answered promptly. "I expect a man from the animal home to call for them any moment. I sent for him yesterday."

He examined her narrowly.

"Yer sech a liar that I dunno how t' take yer. Yer said there was fambly up stairs, and there ain't. I dunno whether there's a man comin' er not, but you show me where them cats is. I wanter see 'em."

"They are in the cellar," she said.

"Wal, come on, show 'em to me," he commanded rising.

She was greatly perturbed over the thought of being alone in the cellar with this horrible vagrant that she forgot the lamp which was necessary to dispel the gloom of the windowless place, and with shaking hand withdrew the bolt to the door, which opened on the stairs directly from the kitchen, and started down, with him close on her heels. He did not proceed farther than the door at the foot. Gazing into the damp, gloomy beyond he grunted with satisfaction.

"Say," he growled, as he stopped, "seems to me this is just about the kind of a place an old addle-head like you oughter live in— along with yer dear little kitties. Yer ain't fit fer human society, that's straight. So I'm agonter leave yer here. And when yer mind runs out of other pleasant things to think of—how yer c'n do jest as yer wanter, bein' human, not a cat, and all that—yer can jest remember that that sick young feller yer turned away is dead. He died jest down to the corner. It was starvation. You killed him— yer high minded, lovely gentle-woman."

He shut and hasped the door as he spoke and hobbled upward to the kitchen,

This was on Monday. On Thursday morning the neighbors notified the police that Miss Wetchell had not been seen around her home lately, and, after a conference at the station, it was decided to force an entrance and investigate the suspicious circumstances. Then Miss Wetchell was found in the cellar cowed and frightened, but in good bodily condition, for the cellar was well stocked with food and water. The moment she was released she rushed into her sleeping room, and no sooner had entered than she uttered a shriek of anguish and terror. A board had been removed from the side of the disused fireplace, revealing a cavity behind, which was now empty. All her ready money and all her jewelry had been taken, she lamented, and she had nothing left to live on.

Then she told her story, and the police, spreading the net for the criminal, had Hobus in charge inside of twenty-four hours.

But the story of Hobus differed materially from that of Miss Wetchell.

In the first place, he declared that he had not taken a thing out of the house except the dinner she had given him. Moreover, it was only for an hour or two that she was confined in the cellar, not three days, for somebody had come and let her out. He had been there at the time and it was the arrival of this somebody that had frightened him away.

Of course he was not believed. But, though he was given the "third degree" in the endeavor to sweat the truth from him, he stuck to his original statement and would not change a word of it. He said that after locking the woman in the cellar to frighten her, he sat down in the kitchen and smoked, intending to release his prisoner when he had rested and was ready to leave the house. He did look around a little after a while, to see if there was anything worth appropriating, but he saw nothing very desirable, and besides, he had so much contempt for the lady that he was afraid it would bring him bad luck if he should steal from her. She had just the same as killed a man. She was a hoodoo. So he went back into the kitchen and smoked and read an old newspaper that lay there. Finally he fell asleep, and some time afterward was awakened by the ringing of the doorbell, which was right above his head. He jumped up and peeked through the window. He could just see the elbow of a man standing on the steps, who remained there a moment longer, giving the bell another pull, and then started off. Hobus, supposing he had gone for good, resolved not to risk staying there after that. Somebody else might come.

He had just about shot back the bolt on the front door, ready to go out, when he thought of the prisoner. She must not be left there, locked in. But before he could take one step to release her he heard a footfall on the walk outside, the bell rang again, and the doorknob rattled. He sprang into the front room just in time to avoid facing the newcomer, for the door swung open as he shook the knob and he entered, crying out:

"Do you keep your doors unlocked here?"

At the same moment there came a vigorous thumping on the floor from underneath, as if it were being pounded with a stick of timber. The stranger exclaimed under his breath and hastened down the cellar stairs, when Hobus, knowing what he would discover there, softly slid into the street and hurried away. That was all he knew about it. He had not intended to hurt the woman; only to scare her and show her how sometimes the best of us cannot do as we would; and he had not seen any money in the house, to say nothing of taking any away. The man, whoever he was, had certainly let the woman out, for he knew she or somebody was down there, and Hobus had heard him descending the cellar stairs.

This story was ridiculed by the police; yet they could not account for the fact that no money was found on the prisoner. He was sober, too, which hardly would have happened if there were any cash where he could get hold of it. They took him to Miss Wetchell for identification, and when she declared him to be the guilty one he repeated his yarn over again.

"I heard the doorbell ring," she said, in answer, "and I thought I heard voices. So I knocked on the floor with a stick. Then somebody came down the cellar stairs, and I ran to the door and cried out that I was locked in there; but, as the person turned around and went up, I supposed it was you and that nobody had come in. Indeed, how could anybody get in with the door locked? I didn't suppose you would open it for anybody."

"Wa'al—he rattled the knob, and the door come open—" began Hobus, when she started up and stared at him, crying out in agitation:

"Did you say he shook the door knob?"

"Yes," said Hobus, sullenly. "I've said it fifty times. Ain't that enough?"

She sank back on the couch, where she had been lying, with a pale and troubled face.

"What is it, Miss Wetchell?" asked the officer of police who had the prisoner in charge.

"It can't be anything but a coincidence," she said in a low voice, "but it is very strange, very strange."

"But what is strange?" he urged gently. Miss Wetchell was a person of property, and as such entitled to the respect and deference of the guardians of the city's peace. They were all of them very polite when they came in contact with her.

"Well," she answered, "you know I am alone here, and I don't like to answer the bell unless I can see who is ringing it, especially at night. So usually I go upstairs and look from the window down onto the steps. But to save me that trouble with my own folks—I haven't many, you know, only two or three distant relatives—it is understood that when it is one of them at the door, she will pull the bell and then loudly rattle the knob, so I'll know. That is all. If the person of whom this man speaks rattled it it was—was very—" She looked at the officer and he looked from her to Hobus, with a subtle change of expression flitting over his face.

"Are all your folks women?" he asked her. "You said 'she' would rattle—"

"No, they are not!" Miss Wetchell cried, sitting up. "And if you can find out that any of them did this horrible thing, and if you get this money back—"

"It was him done it," interrupted Hobus, nodding his head wisely. "'Twan't me."

The officer again glanced at him and back at Miss Wetchell swiftly.

"Miss Wetchell," he said, "do you suspect anybody?"

"Yes, I do—now!" she answered, with emphasis. "One of my folks is not a woman. He is a man, or a small part of one, and it would be more like him to do it—" She stopped speaking and lay back on the couch as if exhausted. But she no sooner had touched the pillow than she bounded up again. "His name," she almost screeched, "is Ferdinand Bostwell, and he lives at 41 Pearl street, in Wentonville. If any man rang that bell, and at the same time rattled the doorknob, he is the one. I always knew he wanted my money, and would do anything to get it—the wretched person! You come here!"

The last phrase was addressed to Hobus. She seemed to think she had done him an injury by suspecting him of the theft of the money, and, overlooking his treatment of her in the past, she sought now to forgive him for this, as a kind woman would do, and make honorable amends for her suspicion.

Hobus stood where he was.

"You go sizzle," he said, disgustedly. "There's people that's low, 'n' there's people that's high, I s'pose. Folks says go, anyhow. I never seen no low people but you. You say 'come here!' You say it to me. Waal, I say to you, 'You go to hell!' Yore a Jonah. You killed a man. I seen yer do it. There ain't nobody no lower 'n what you are. You got a plenty, an' 'twas all give to yer. Yer never earned a cent 'n all yer low life. Yer didn't have ter. But I had ter, 'n' I couldn't. Who'd give me a job? Nobody. How c'n I git work? The's too many folks like you in the world for me to git anything to do. Yore one of them twenty-five that looks inter a man's record, yer told me so, and if it's bad—why, yer fool! Whose is good, when yer come ter know it? Is yore's? How is it, then, that all yore money is stole, and yer ain't got nothing ter live on? Yore human, ain't yer, not a cat? Yer can do as yer wanter! Why didn't yer keep yer money? Sizzle yer! You pertend charity, and yer give it ter cats, and let better folks 'n what you be starve! I'd like ter—"

The police officer, looking up from his notebook, held him back when he started for her as if he would throttle her.

"Don't mind him, Miss Wetchell," he said. "He's only a hobo—harmless. He dunno what he's saying, and he wouldn't hurt a flea."

Without ceremony he took Hobus by the arm and walked him back to the station.

Then Mr. Ferdinand Bostwell, the man whom Miss Wetchell had named, was brought in. But, having been questioned, he at once made out what seemed to be a perfect alibi. He kept a job book, and in it were noted all his movements for practically every moment of the fateful day. He had not been within six miles of Miss Wetchell's residence on that Monday, he said, had not called at her house for three years, and, if he had his way, would never call at it. He admitted that it was not in the best of taste for a man to run down any member of his own family, and therefore he would not give any particular reasons why he had stayed away and why he would always stay away. He was a blacksmith by trade, an honest appearing, sturdy, open mannered man, and his evidence seemed conclusive. The police were perplexed. They believed Hobus had told the truth, for there was something about him, an entirely new air, never seen in him before—an air almost of dignity, which carried conviction with it; and this other man, Bostwell, not only appeared sincere in his declarations of innocence, but he had in his notebook the names of men who, he took his oath, could and would testify to work he had done for them which would show that he had been in his shop on Monday from 6 in the morning until 7 at night, with an hour for dinner and a pipe. It was just as he was finishing his denial that Sergeant Nulty came in.

"By gob!" he whispered to the lieutenant, "there's wan man will get the thruth from him. Phwat! Lave him loose on him onct. He'll make the fur fly, I'll bet you! Dr. Furnivall! He c'u'd bore holes in the sea wid thim eyes of his, and make the fishes shpake. Aha!"

The lieutenant's face brightened.

"That's right," he said. "It will save us a lot of trouble. I wish I'd thought of it before. Ring him up, Nulty, and see if he can come here right off."

So Dr. Furnivall entered a few minutes later and questioned both the tramp and the blacksmith. But to no purpose. They both of them stuck to the stories they had already told, and nothing new was elicited, except the reason of the blacksmith's dislike for his wealthy relative, which was, he said, because, among other inhuman atrocities, she had refused to furnish the money to send her young niece to Colorado for her health, a move which the doctor ordered, and she had died with lingering consumption, a martyr to her nearest kindred's penuriousness. She had no belief in ill health. Work, she declared, was the remedy for all so-called sickness. People were lazy, not diseased, and pretended to be suffering only to escape the common portion of labor. She claimed all this, the blacksmith asserted, in order to furnish herself with sufficient reasons for never helping anybody out of her abundance.

As for wanting her money, he stated that though all her property would at her death come to him and his sisters in the absence of any will, it had already been decided among them that they would devote every cent of it to charity, to human charity, in order to repair as far as possible the wrongs this ignorant woman had inflicted on countless wretched strugglers. Charity to animals was good and necessary, but inferior to charity for human beings, even the lowest, and should not be allowed to supersede it. A woman, he said, might have a perfect right to do as she pleased with her money, and never spend any of it on others, whether men or cats, if she felt that way, but she had no right to judge always harshly of those human beings whose chief fault might easily be that they were born weak minded and in low conditions, and send them away with revilings and condemnation. Somebody whom she had treated thus was probably the thief. There must be countless persons who hated her and would seize the slightest opportunity for revenge.

Dr. Furnivall turned to the lieutenant.

"These men, both of them, have told the truth," he said, "and I am persuaded that the key to the mystery lies somewhere within the woman herself. I must see her."

Accordingly, Sergeant Nulty accompanied him to the home of Miss Wetchell and introduced him to the lady. While he was making the presentation the bell rang, and the sergeant, as soon as he had finished speaking, turned, and, taking two or three steps into the hall, opened the front door. There stood, with a large covered basket on his arm, a young man, who, on sight of the officer, started and flushed.

"Well," he said, "I didn't expect to see a policeman here. It kind of startled me. Is Miss Wetchell in? I've come for the cats."

From where Miss Wetchell was lying on the couch she could hear these words, and she immediately cried out:

"Why, step in here! Is that you? Where have you been all this time? You should have come Monday morning."

Dr. Furnivall, at this statement, threw a quick glance at the newcomer. Then he removed the thick, colored spectacles, and as the man entered, hat in hand, leaving his basket in the hall, he addressed him, looking him in the eye.

"Do you come from some animal home?" he asked.

"Yes, sir," he answered. He was a somewhat mild appearing youth, smooth of face, rather slouchily attired, small in stature, and not overclean.

"Are you a regular employee there?"

"Well, no, sir, I ain't. Dr. Blagden is laid up with a cold and they're short of hands, so they got me for this kind of work."

"Have you ever been here before?"

"No, sir, never—"

"Yes, you have, too," exclaimed Miss Wetchell, indignantly. "You came here once—I remember you—and I gave you two cats—"

"I mean—not lately," he hastened to interrupt. His face, which had been flushing and paling alternately, grew calm as he spoke, and his watery eyes, fixed on the doctor's, having passed through the stages of furtiveness, mildness, peacefulness, and earnestness, took on an expression of deep introspection.

"Now," said Dr. Furnivall, "tell me when you were last in this house?"

"Monday morning," he replied.

"Describe that visit."

"I came for the cats. Nobody answered when I rang, and I started away, but as I was going out of the yard I thought I heard the doorknob turn, so I waited a second, and then came back and rang again and rattled the door. It swung open and I walked in. Somebody began pounding on the floor under my feet and screaming and I started down the cellar stairs to find out what the matter was, as there didn't seem to be anybody else around, and I knew Miss Wetchell lived alone. I heard a woman calling out that she was locked in the cellar, and just then I felt a draught of air and heard a noise that sounded as if somebody had opened and shut the front door. I was rattled and didn't know what to make of it. The neighborhood was bad and the house was alone. I ran back to the hall, but saw nobody, and then the pounding below got louder than ever. It shook the floor and knocked down a board over the fireplace, and a zinc box fell on the bricks and burst open, letting out a lot of money and jewels. I couldn't help taking it. I was all worked up and hardly knew what I was—"

Miss Wetchell sprang upon him with clinched hands and flashing eyes.

"Wretch! Give me back my money!" she screamed. But he did not hear her. He was intent on his story, and finished calmly with "—doing. And going over on the ferry I lost the box overboard, so I didn't get anything out of it, after all."

"Villain! Lost? Lo–lost?" shrieked Miss Wetchell, and sank back in a swoon on the couch.

THE MISSING BRIDE

There was a rap on the door and a maid put her head in.

"Here's a man—" she began, but as she spoke a large gentleman with a red face, white mustache, and an excited blue eye pushed in past her.

"Dr. Furnivall, pardon me!" he said hastily. "It is a matter of more than life or death. Name your own price, but I must have your assistance at once."

The maid laid the visitor's card on the table before Dr. Furnivall, but he had no need to read it. He knew the man by sight as one of the multimillionaires of the city, George B. English of banking fame. Mr. English took the seat pointed out by Dr. Furnivall and rushed on:

"My daughter was kidnapped last night on the eve of her marriage, and I have good reason to believe that she is at this moment in the hands of a villain whose object is—is—not money!"

He paused, his red face growing almost purple with anger and excitement, queerly mingled with fright, and looked into the colored spectacles of the doctor as if expecting some demonstration on his part. But he said merely:

"Go on."

He braced himself and, with an evident effort at calmness, in which he did not succeed too well, continued:

"Everything was ready last evening for the wedding ceremony, which was to be celebrated this noon. The whole household retired early—by 10 or a little later—and not a suspicious sound was heard, not a namable thing out of the common happened, that anybody noticed, during the night. There were no guests—only my two daughters, one of them a child of ten years; my sister who is a maiden lady; myself, and the servants, fourteen of them. This morning the first thing we discovered was that the house had been robbed of all the smaller and more valuable wedding presents; and then we learned that Evelyn was missing. Her bed had not been occupied, and the only clothes of hers that the women couldn't find were those she wore last evening. Her wardrobe was intact. She did not even take a hat—disappeared bareheaded! And there isn't a trace of her. The police and detectives have been scouring the city since early morning, but without avail. The loot the miscreants got is nothing; I don't care for that, and would say nothing about it. They are welcome to it if only they would bring back my daughter. The idea of her being in the power of that—"

He stopped, overcome by his feelings.

"You spoke of suspecting somebody?"

"Yes, yes; that is why I am here. They told me at the police station that you, by your hypnotism, could make the man talk. The trouble is that there are no grounds on which to make an arrest; and even if there were, how could he be induced to confess his guilt and give her back to me?"

"He could be shadowed—"

"Oh, yes! And that is what is being done. Three men are watching his every move. But in the meantime what will happen to Evelyn? And they won't catch him. He is sharp as a fiend. He will outwit them. All his plans were laid long ago, of course, and, knowing very well that he would be suspected, he has provided for everything."

"We are getting a little ahead of the story. Who is the man? What does he do? And what are your grounds for thinking him guilty? And then the robbery—do you lay that to him also?"

"The robbery I don't understand—unless it was a blind. The police gave me that notion when I told them whom I accused. But to begin right—the man is Baron von Castle. He once courted my daughter—"

"What, he who has just inherited so many millions?"

"Yes, the same. He is a rascal—the degenerate son of an old German house, cast off long ago as a good-for-nothing spendthrift, but now made rich through the neglect of his late uncle to leave a will behind him at his death. He asked me for Evelyn two years ago, but I had looked him up and I seized the opportunity to tell him what I thought of him. He had the unparalleled impudence to laugh in my face. Afterward I heard that he had sworn that he would have her at all costs; and, to tell the truth, being somewhat shaky—er—I—somewhat—about Evelyn—"

He paused, gnawing his mustache.

"I suppose I must go into all the details, however distasteful," he went on, after a moment. "Evelyn liked the fellow and took his part—said that he had been grossly misrepresented to me, and all that—the way girls always talk in such cases! So I sent her abroad to separate them from each other as widely as possible. But what did he do but borrow money—from my own bank, too—and follow her! Under an assumed name he courted her in the very face and eyes of the chaperon to whom I was paying high wages to keep her away from him! What do you think of that? It was four months before I found out what was going on. Then one day in a hot temper I dropped in on them suddenly—it was in Paris, in a hotel parlor. But was he disconcerted? Not in the very least. He laughed at me again—in my face! The man is Satan himself! Nothing disturbs him. He seems to enjoy being put in difficult positions, in which other men would cringe with mortification and shame. He walks out of them with the air of a conqueror, as a victor who disdains to profit by the advantages he has gained, holding the vanquished in too much contempt even to notice him. When I ordered him from the room this time he threw himself down, on the sofa, smiling, without giving me the least notice, and began talking gayly with two or three women there, and when I led my daughter out he hurried to open the door for her, begging her not to forget her engagement for the evening.

"Those are a few among many details I could give you of the man's conduct. He stops at nothing. And he has pursued her ever since in spite of every precaution I can take. But he is careful not to overstep the law. He is too shrewd for that. He has sworn that he will have the girl, and now, since she has been stolen away on the very night before her wedding day, what can be thought? He has got her, of course. There is no other possible explanation of her sudden disappearance."

"This man whom she was to marry—does she care for him? Or is she in love with the other yet?" asked Dr. Furnivall. "Was the match made by you, or did it come about in the usual way?"

"Well." He coughed and hesitated. Then he went on. "It was I who wished it in the first place. He is the son of one of my business associates, and his father and myself had long entertained the idea of their marriage to each other. As soon as I broached the subject to Evelyn she seemed pleased, and has, at least, never made any objections. They get along well together. And since the engagement she has never mentioned Von Castle's name. In fact, there is where my greatest fear comes in. I think that after he heard of the betrothal he met her somehow and frightened her—vowed revenge, perhaps. It would be just like him to do it. And there was something strange in her manner. If he should get possession of her after that, Gods knows how he would act! Not honorably, you may be sure! It is a thousand times worse than if I had allowed them to marry in the first place."

As Mr. English began his answer Dr. Furnivall removed his spectacles and looked him steadily in the eye, continuing to hold his gaze for some seconds after he had finished, and when he saw the various changes pass over his face—nervousness, running into hesitancy, into earnestness, and finally into calmness, accompanied by a deeply introspective expression of the eyes, he asked:

"What is your real objection to Von Castle as a son-in-law, Mr. English?"

"I dislike him," he answered at once. "I feel a sense of inferiority when I meet him. I have money enough to attract the kind of a husband for my daughter that I want—one who will defer to me, respect me, consult my opinions. Von Castle I never could move in any direction. He despises me because I wrung my wealth, as he puts it, from the hearts and souls of the poor, and has regard neither for my opinions nor my personality."

"Is he really a good-for-nothing?"

"He is very far from that. He has great abilities, and in time will make his mark. He is a naval architect, and has produced more than one work of genius—has just taken the prize offered by the Emperor of Germany for the best model of a warship."

"The complaints you made against him to your daughter were wholly unfounded then?"

"Yes."

"Why do you wish her to marry the other man?"

"He wants her, in the first place, and I am under obligations to his father, who also wishes her for his son, which I cannot deny. Besides, I can rule the boy. We shall live together and the union will be harmonious all around. I shall have my daughter with me, as before, and she will be as much subject to me as she always has been."

"Hm—m!" Dr. Furnivall cleared his throat and put on his glasses. "I don't think you need fear for your daughter," he said, as Mr. English, released from the power of his gaze, began to rub his eyes and look about him perplexedly. "She has undoubtedly gone with Von Castle of her own accord, partly, perhaps to escape the rigorous control which, it is plain, you hold over her, as well as for love of the man. They are probably safely married by this time, and soon you will receive notice to that effect—perhaps today. The burglary I do not understand yet, but her apparently willing acceptance of the man you wished her to marry—"

At this instant the office door opened without ceremony and a young man appeared on the threshold, the maid's face, gathered in an expostulatory scowl, showing at his shoulder.

"Von Castle!" exclaimed Mr. English.

The newcomer, who was a self-reliant looking young fellow, dark and big and handsome, cast one glance at the speaker, and then, giving him no more attention, addressed Dr. Furnivall.

"You will forgive me, Dr. Furnivall," he said, "for this rudeness on my part when you know the reason of it. In extremities all rules

of deportment may be broken. The fact is that my betrothed wife
has been either kidnapped from her home or shut up in it illegally
and hidden from her friends, and I—"

Dr. Furnivall, the instant the newcomer's name was cried out
by Mr. English, threw a swift glance at the two men. What he
thought it would be impossible to conjecture from his face, which
was immobile and, apparently, disinterested. But as the young man
hurried on in his speech he rose, and motioning to the maid, said:

"I am busy. Show this gentleman to the reception-room."

"Ah!" the gentleman breathed. He regarded Dr. Furnivall
haughtily. "I am not accustomed to this sort of treatment—"

"Laura!" said Dr. Furnivall.

The maid came forward.

"Show this—man to the reception-room."

The young man stood scrutinizing Dr. Furnivall. He had large
black eyes, a high, square forehead, and a strong nose and mouth
and his manner was forceful. He plainly was used to having things
his own way. Mr. English sat with his eyes rolled up at him as if
prepared to dodge a missile which he expected him to throw.

The maid touched the young man's elbow. Dr. Furnivall stood
looking at him. He finally bowed low to the doctor.

"I beg your pardon," he said. "I was wrong—I admit it. The ur-
gency of—but I will wait. I only add that I suspect her father!"

With that he bowed again and, without a glance at English, followed the maid.

As he left, Dr. Furnivall, who had held his spectacles in his hand
while speaking, laid them on the desk, and fixing Mr. English with
his eyes, said:

"Sir, if you come to me for help in this crisis you must tell the
story as it is. All this shilly-shallying and subterfuge is useless,
and worse than useless. It retards the investigation." By this time
the subject was again under control, and Dr. Furnivall added: "Do
you know where your daughter is?"

"I do not," he answered automatically.

"Had you any fear that Von Castle would attempt to get possession of her before the marriage?"

"I had a general fear of what he might do. I did not suspect that he would try to take her by force, of course. It is only since her disappearance that I have considered him capable of that—capable of succeeding in doing so, at any rate, for Evelyn had given up all thought of him. It plainly would be against her will to go with him, and without her consent what chance had he for her?"

"What do her maids say about it? Did they attend her to her room last night? When and how did they leave her? At what time did she go upstairs?"

"The last that was seen of her was at 11 o'clock. Bettine, her maid, who had got her ready for bed, left her at that time to go to her own room. Evelyn was at her table writing a note—"

"Has this note been found?"

"No, there is no trace of it."

"Go on. She was not seen by anybody after that, and that was at 11 o'clock. Who discovered her absence in the morning?"

"Bettine. She was waiting to be called by Evelyn, who had not rung at the usual hour, when the burglary was discovered, and she ran in to inform her of it. She was not there, and could not be found anywhere."

"You say that she was prepared for bed, yet this morning the clothes she wore last evening were missing with her, and those only?"

"Yes."

"Of course, then, she must have dressed of her own accord. What was the nature of the costume she wore?"

"I don't know."

"You can't say whether it was a walking suit or a ball gown?"

"Well, it was something—er—medium. I don't know what the things are called. An everyday affair, you know."

"How did the burglars get in?"

"Through a window in the dining-room. They must have sprung back the lock somehow, for the butler takes his oath it was fastened last night; but it was unlocked this morning and open."

"Mr. English, sit where you are and listen to what Von Castle will tell me," said Dr. Furnivall suddenly, and, having pressed a button, he waved Von Castle, who was immediately ushered in by the maid, to a seat near him.

The young man seemed not to be aware of Mr. English's presence in the room.

"Doctor, I have come—" he began, when Dr. Furnivall interrupted him.

"I must tell you, Baron Von Castle," he said, "that we are not alone here. Whatever you say will be overheard by another. Moreover, you will be compelled to tell the exact truth regarding your connection with this matter. If you consent to these conditions I will hear you, but unless you are willing that Mr. English should know, as well as I—"

Von Castle bowed and waved his hand.

"I see you are prejudiced against me," he said, smiling. "Well, no matter! And as for Mr. English, I came here for the very purpose of asking you to interview him and wrench the truth from him. Nothing could have fallen out more appropriately than his presence here. I am told on the very best authority that you are able, by some occult or scientific process, to force a man to relate things as they are. Question this man, then, and you will learn that his daughter is being illegally restrained of her freedom by him. She is her own mistress, and not a minor, in the eyes of the law— has been since yesterday morning. He has no right to incarcerate her."

"But I have already questioned him and am positively certain that he has no notion where she is."

Von Castle picked up his hat, looking ironically at the doctor.

"In that case," he said, rising, "I congratulate you on your extreme perspicacity and the value of your occult powers. No doubt they are great—to the vulgar! I wish you good day, sir."

He did not go out, however. He remained as he was, standing in front of his chair, his eyes fixed on Dr. Furnivall's, his strikingly handsome face undergoing several marked changes of expression, beginning with perplexity, running through irresolution to calmness, to earnestness, and finally ending with deep intentness. Then Dr. Furnivall said:

"Tell me at once if you know where Miss Evelyn English is."

"I do not, sir," he answered. Mr. English made a quick movement of protest, but Dr. Furnivall put out a warning hand, and he subsided in his chair, eyeing the young man with a singular mixture of wonder, fear, dislike, and incredulity in his face and eyes.

"Are you willing to state before witnesses where you were last night?"

"Perfectly."

"Be seated, then! Now, begin with 11 o'clock. Where were you at that hour?"

"At the Athletic club."

"Had you any engagement for a later hour anywhere?"

"Yes."

"Where and with whom?"

"At the home of Miss Evelyn English, and with her!"

"There!" almost shouted Mr. English, starting up.

"Interrupt me again and you leave the room," said Dr. Furnivall to him, without removing his gaze from Von Castle. Mr. English now sat forward on his chair, his eyes bulging at the young man, his face apoplectic, his hands trembling on his knees, his thick lips working under his white mustache. "Did you keep that engagement?" Dr. Furnivall said to his subject.

"I kept it, yes."

"You saw Miss English, then, after 11?"

"No. I did not. I was in her house, and searched it for her, but she was not to be found, though she had agreed to—"

"In my house! Searched! Good heavens! I'll have a policeman here in three minutes!" ejaculated Mr. English, and ran from the room. Neither of the two gave him any attention. Von Castle kept right on:

"—meet me in the library at 12 o'clock. We were to go away and be married at once. Everything was arranged—the minister, the passage for Europe in the morning, some necessary clothing which she had bought ready made, in the baggage-room at the wharf—everything. When I came—"

"But you are getting ahead of the story," Dr. Furnivall interrupted. "Answer my questions. First, when did you make this arrangement with her?"

"A week ago tonight."

"Her apparent willingness to marry this other man was a blind?"

"Yes. I had suggested it to her."

"Why?"

"She was afraid of her father, who domineered her, and I was in no position to marry until very recently. Besides, my family would have objected to an American girl as my wife. But we were settled upon it. Nothing can part us. I advised her to appear docile, and then at the last moment, if no better way could be found, we would elope."

"Yes. And was the burglary planned as a blind also?"

"I know nothing of any burglary."

"You don't know that the wedding presents have been stolen?"

"No."

"You say you searched the house. How could you search it, or get into it even?"

"Evelyn was to unlock the front door as soon as she could, after the family and servants had retired for the night, and I was to come into the library, where she would be waiting for me. She is timid in the dark, and I would not have her stay outside. Besides, something might happen to detain me. I don't have much luck with motor cars. They go back on me often. We thought the best way for her would be to sit in the library, where there are inside blinds, which would prevent the light from showing in the street. I found the door unfastened all right, and went along the hall to the library, turned the knob, and looked in. But, though the room was lighted, she was not in it."

"Then you went over the house?"

"Over the lower floors—yes."

"And you saw nothing of the wedding presents?"

"No."

"What did you do then?"

"I went outside, and after waiting a while returned to the library. I thought she might have forgotten something and gone to her room for it. Or—a number of reasons for her absence occurred to me. But she did not come. I spent the night waiting, stealing back and forth between the front vestibule and the library. Then I gave the case up and resolved to appeal to you. I believe her father somehow got wind—"

"But if he had done so he would not have allowed the door to remain unlocked all night, nor would you have been allowed to enter and depart as you did, freely. Did you unlock a window in the dining-room?"

"No. Why should I? I touched nothing that I was not obliged to touch in my search."

"Was a window of the dining-room open when you were in it?"

"I did not see any open, though one might have been. I was not looking for any such thing, only for her."

At this moment the maid tapped at the door and opened it. Her face was flushed.

"There's that other man and a policeman outside," she said. "Shall I let them in?"

"Outside?" questioned Dr. Furnivall, releasing Von Castle from his gaze and arching his eyebrows a trifle humorously.

"Yes, sir, if you please, sir, outside. There's nobody else will get in this house today in them unceremonious ways," said the girl, folding her wrists and putting her head up at Von Castle. She was a Yankee farmer's daughter, loyal, and had not to be told anything twice, and seldom once.

"Bring them here," said Dr. Furnivall. "They have come to arrest you," he added to Von Castle, who was at the moment looking dazedly around. Instantly he arose.

"Not while Miss English's fate is unknown," he said calmly. With one movement he turned the key in the doorlock and with another he pulled out a revolver. Dr. Furnivall sat in his chair and laughed. His laugh was wholesome and free, and the young man regarded him in some surprise. But he cocked his revolver at the same time.

"Dr. Furnivall, you will not attempt to interfere with me, will you?" he said. "You are not like these other—these animals. You are a gentleman. And you are wise, I know that. Advise me. But do not counsel surrender. I tell you plainly that Miss English is more to me than my life, and I absolutely refuse to give myself up before I know what has become of her. She is crying out for me at this minute—"

"Unlock the door, put away your foolish pistol, and sit down," said Dr. Furnivall. "That sort of thing may do in German universities, among your light-headed students, but not here. How much chance would you stand? The whole world is against you when you resort to firearms. It is both cowardly and ignorant. Unlock the door!"

"Dr. Furnivall," he said, with a calmness that was visibly forced, and looking him in the eye, "I should be sorry to proceed to extremities with a man like you. But the woman I love is in danger, some sort of danger, I don't know what, and by the good God above us—" leveling his revolver, "if you make one move to deliver me to these men, or to help them in any way to capture me, before I learn what has happened to her, I will shoot you like a dog—dog—d—d—er—er—"

His voice trailed away to silence. His eyes took on a deeply introspective expression, the hand that held the revolver dropped to his side. He stood like a tree, firm rooted, strong, handsome, but helpless. His gaze seemed to turn in upon itself as the leaves of the tree curl inward blindly.

"Unlock the door!" repeated Dr. Furnivall.

He complied at once, feeling unerringly behind him, his eyes in the doctor's.

"Now, sit in that chair! Give me that revolver, young ass! You have everything your own way, but haven't the sense to realize it. You would spoil all if you could. It will cost you some fifty years yet to learn that though everything in this world is gained by force, it is by force of merit, not by force of the brute—by the force of wisdom and knowledge, by love and intellect, not by force of arms! If I didn't know that it would do you no good I would give you a lesson on the asininity of that confident way of yours, and make you grovel! But you wouldn't learn: The shears of experience, not vicarious but personal, always have to clip the wings of a person like you, and the act is accompanied by great suffering. My object now is to get at the bottom of this mystery. Come in!"

The phrase was addressed to somebody who was fumbling at the door knob. In walked a policeman, and behind him, not very confidently, came Mr. English.

The officer, at sight of Dr. Furnivall, stopped short.

"Sure, I was not afther knowin' 'twas yezsel', docther!" he said in singular confusion, his helmet in his hand. "Excoose mesel'! Coom on noo," he added, turning suddenly on English and taking him by the collar. "Oi arrist yez!"

"M—Me!" gasped the astonished man, who had summoned him. "Wha—what for?"

"On suspeecion! Coom on noo, or Oi'll—"

"Wait a moment."

Dr. Furnivall spoke, and sat forward in his chair.

"What's your name?" he asked the policeman.

"Soolivan, sor—r!" he answered somewhat doggedly.

"Do you know me?"

"Oi saane yez onct—at th' station," he returned with hesitation, keeping his eyes persistently away from the doctor's, turning them on English, on the floor, on the walls, on Von Castle, out of the window.

Dr. Furnivall looked at Mr. English.

"How did you happen to run across the officer whose beat takes him past your house?" he asked.

"Sure th' mon is th' divil! He knows arl things!" muttered the policeman dazedly. "Me own bate, an' arl! Coom noo, out of this wid yez!" he cried with a sudden forced show of authority, flourishing his club and shaking English by the shoulder.

"Wait a moment, Sullivan!" said Dr. Furnivall. "Mr. English, how is it that you bring here this officer, whom you know because your house is on his beat, instead of one of the several others you must have passed between here and there?"

"Because, Dr. Furnivall, it was he for whom I went, for the very reason that I did know him. I did not wish to stop for a warrant, and I knew he would act for me without one. I don't understand his sudden change of attitude toward me at all."

"Neither do I," said the doctor. "For some reason or other he wants to escape my eye. Sullivan, look at me!"

The policeman broke away for the door. But Von Castle, who had watched with extreme interest the little drama since the two entered, was there before him, big, smiling, facing him. He stopped.

"Sullivan," said Dr. Furnivall, "there is something in you that is wrong, and whatever it is has got to come out. You can't get away from it. I don't know what it is yet, but I shall know, at least, if it has to do with this missing girl, which is all I am interested in at this moment. If the guilt which you show as plainly as if it were written in black letters on your forehead, does not relate to her, look at me and say so! Does it?"

The policeman, with sudden bravado, looked directly into his eyes.

"Sor–r, docther," he said, with the air of one making a candid confession. "Oi knows nowthing at arl about th' case. Yez says Oi'm guilty lukin', an', begob, Oi am that, fer 'twas kissin' Sadie McGuire, Oi was, th' cuke at Stacey's, behindt th' dure, an' Oi tort yez had me on it. 'Twould be afther raisin' throuble wid th' ould woman onct she heard of it! Oi was frighted, jist! B't Oi knows nawthing at arl at arl about yez case. Th' gintlemun forninst, Misther English, he comes rhunnin' oop to mesel' an' he says, sez he, 'Sooliван, coom arrist a mon that shtole me dochter!' 'Hov yez found him?' Oi says, 'Oi hov that!' says he. 'Begob!' says Oi t' mesel', 'that's dombed funny, jist, becaze Oi am th' mon mesel', an' bedam if Oi'm found be youse—'"

Two excited ejaculations issued simultaneously from two separate mouths, but Dr. Furnivall put his hand up and Von Castle and Mr. English sank back upon their seats, hanging with breathless excitement on the words of the policeman, as without a break he went on, being now under full control:

"'—ixcept to arrist mesil',' Oi says, 'an' how th' divil can Oi be afther doin' thot same annyhow,' Oi says, 'an' who is he?' says Oi. An' thin—"

"Sullivan," Dr. Furnivall interrupted, "do you know where Miss Evelyn English is at this moment?"

"Oi do, jist! None betther! She's wid me woife, Bridget Soolivan, that calls hersel' Beatrice since Oi was ilivated t' th' foorce, at twinty-siven and a half A, Falmouth shtrate!"

The door whirred open. Von Castle was out of it like a streak of lightning, with English a hopeless second.

By aid of a few additional questions Dr. Furnivall learned that the policeman had overheard the agreement between the lovers, which was made at night in the darkness of the park in front of her father's house. At the time he was interested only in the fact that the door to that rich house would be left unfastened, with all the costly wedding presents within easy reach. On the given night he secreted himself in the dark vestibule, trusting to his uniform for explanation should he be discovered, and a moment after he heard the lock and bolt click softly back he opened the door and stole along to the dining-room, the location of which he knew well, where the wedding presents were displayed in readiness for show in the morning. He unlocked the door with a skeleton key, lighted the gas, and helped himself to the jewels and silver. While he was busy the girl, attracted by the light through the keyhole, opened the door, and he grabbed her to prevent her from crying out. What to do then he did not know, but she must be kept quiet. Luckily for him she fainted at once, and seeing that he was in for it, for she knew him, he bore her in his arms through the deserted streets to his home, which was only two blocks away, determined to hold her for ransom, hoping to get enough to take him out of the country.

Von Castle, however, got the girl, and, it is whispered, with her father's full consent after all. For one reason, perhaps, he knew he might as well give it; for another—

But what is the use of considering other reasons!

When we must, we must, and that seems to be all there is to it.

THE STRANGE SICKNESS OF
MR. WHITTAKER RANSOME

A middle aged man with a freshly shaved red face and a short clay pipe in his mouth came rolling burlily up the street, his hands in his jacket pockets, cap pulled over his brows, his eyes darting here and there, taking in all the sights of the great city that came in his way. A good student of character would set him down at once as an English sailor ashore in a strange country, his wages securely stowed away in some secret part of his painfully new and ill-fitting suit of blue serge. Short of stature, but bulky and solid, after the fashion of his native oaks, with features whose natural stolidity was enlivened startlingly by the unexpected brilliance of his eyes, which, though gray, were of so dark a shade that the effect was nearly that of piercing black, and with the assurance of well considered and unshakable opinions in his manner, he was plainly no sort of prey whatever for the landsharks. If he had his roll in his clothes he was able to keep it there, as far as they were concerned. And the proof was, if one had needed other proof than his appearance, that here he was two miles up from the wharves, safe in the heart of one of the best residential districts, having passed under the very noses of the longshore barkers, runners, heelers, and strong arm men, like a sturdy old battle-ship among river pirates and mudscows. His build and gait were enough to inspire respect, even seen from a distance, and the fiery glitter of his eyes as he approached would be nothing less than appalling to a person with secret intentions toward him.

Arrived at the entrance to the public garden the sailor turned his back upon it, spread his legs, took his pipe from his mouth with his right hand, and, blowing a cloud of smoke upward, with a lift of the chin, ran his eyes over the buildings across the way. Then he lowered his gaze to the hurrying crowds on the sidewalk, glanced swiftly at the street signs, put his pipe back into his mouth, re-lieved the congestion of his nose between his thumb and finger, wheeled and rolled into the park. On an empty bench he seated himself, fitted the tin stopper to his pipe, thrust it into his coat pocket, and drew forth a small piece of paper lined with diagrams. This he studied for ten minutes, his face gathered in a perplexed scowl. Then, "Dang!" he burst out, crashing his great fist down upon his knee. He looked at the diagram again for a long moment, again said "Dang!" and repeated the pounding of the knee.

From a little flat pin cushion which he fished from his pocket he selected four pins, picking them out with a sureness and grace that no ordinary landsman would believe possible, after a glance at the enormous thumb and awkward appearing square fingers, and with these he fastened the small paper to the slats of the seat. Then, following the lines with a careful forefinger, he traced out certain figures, muttering his calculations as he worked them.

"This 'ere's a bloody purty how-d'-do, this is! As how? Why, then, here's the ship, and here's the park, and here's yore Com-monwealth avenoo. But then agin here's yore Arlington street, and here's yore blessed Church street, way off up here, no'theast by east, and yore Park street clean away down here sou'east by halfeast, and here is Summer street, running the same tacks iden-tical as Winter, and on the chart Summer is west and Winter is east, and blarst my bloody eyes if I didn't heave out o' there a minute back, and they're the other way about or I'm a landsman. And here I lay, up here, by Park street—here's the church," casting his eye at the tall spire over the way, "but the sign says Boylston. And the' ain't no Boylston on the chart! And here's Beacon, only a little furder on its Commonwealth, and not Beacon, and here's Beacon 'way off sou'cast agin, and Park street church becalmed under her lee, when it oughter be layin' up alongside about where I be this blessed minute. And, shiver me! here it is, too, on Boylston street, right in hall, but stern foremost, at the wrong end of the park!"

He straightened up with a jerk and cast his eye toward the heavens as if in search of the sun, by which to get his bearings, but it was a gray day and there was no sun in sight. He pulled out his pipe with a surly growl, lighted it, and sat puffing stolidly, now and then glancing at the map, and occasionally looking up and down the mall and into the near by paths among the trees. Presently, as a young man and woman entered the gates, strolling slowly along, he gathered the map up with a hasty movement, folded it in his hand out of view, and turned his head away from the advancing couple. Three other persons passed immediately after these, without gaining from him more than a quick glance as they approached. But the fourth, who was in the yeoman's uniform of the United States navy, he accosted.

"Mate," he said, "where's this here Arlington street?"

"Right here," he answered, pointing to the street behind them.

"Right here!" he growled, throwing a suspicious, menacing eye at the bluejacket. "Why, ain't that there Park Street Church?"

The bluejacket laughed.

"So you're up against the curves of this town, too!" he said. "Well, we've all been there! The streets is sure crooked, that's a fact. This church is the Arlington street. Park street is at the other end of the common—a mile up there! You've been sailing in circles, likely. Where you from, mate?"

But the sailor's only answer was to get up and, muttering anathemas against landsmen's charts, and everything else that belonged to them, or was related to them in the remotest degree, walked off, puffing his pipe, his hands in his pockets, his eyes set straight ahead as if in search of some known light.

At the corner of Commonwealth avenue, two blocks beyond, he stopped short at sight of the long double rows of trees stretching away into the distance, with the graveled walk between them, and pulled out his map. A moment's scrutiny of it elicited a grunt

of satisfaction from him, and he set off along the sidewalk, looking at the numbers of the houses as he went.

At length he paused before a brown stone front, tucked his pipe
away, settled his cap on his head, coughed foggily, mounted the
steps, and was hunting for the bell when he saw a printed notice:
"Sickness; don't ring; please walk in."

"This here is what I call a rum go!" he muttered, standing back
a step or two and throwing a calculating eye up and down the fa-
cade. Then, "Well, anyhow, if I c'n board him without nobody's
seein'—" He softly turned the knob, and, greatly to his surprise,
stood face to face with a footman over six feet tall.

"Lud!" he exclaimed, thrown off his habitual poise, and doubtless awed by the servant's gorgeous livery.

"Did you wish to see anybody?" the footman said, with a super-
cilious glance at the visitor's ill-fitting clothes.

"Not to say as how I don't, shipmate," he answered, dryly, having
immediately regained his accustomed stolidity, "seein' as I've sailed
twelve thousand miles to meet up long er Cap'n Whittaker Ransome. Does he live here?'

"Yes, but he's sick, on his death bed, and nobody is admitted—"

A girlish figure, with pale face and large brown eyes, beneath
which dark semi-circles showed, came forward softly.

"Are you an old friend of Mr. Ransome's?" she asked of the
sailor. "You said you had come so far to see him—"

She paused, her childish, innocent, but unattractive face upturned to him, seeming almost spectral in the darkness of the hall.

"My father, Miss, was Stephen Parker," he answered, pulling
off his cap, "and I—"

"Oh, I have heard my father speak of him frequently. Please
come this way," she said. "But nobody can see him," she continued,
when she had led him up stairs and into a little reception-room. "I
am so sorry! How he would have liked to meet the son of his old
friend!" She put her handkerchief to her eyes, while he sat uncomfortably on the edge of a sofa and twirled his cap in his hands.

"So he's goin',' is he?" he said, as she finally, brushing the tears
away, raised her head.

"There is no hope," she answered. "The doctors have given him up. It is only a question of time—a very short time."

"Well, of course," he condoled, "it's hard. But he's an old man—and—and—of course, ye see—but there, that ain't what I come to say! It's particl'er unfortnit—it is, all round—that's what it is. Because, d'ye see, my father, who was great friends long of him when they was cap'ns together, and afterwards, too, when Cap'n Ransome gut rich in tea, in Ceylon, leavin' the sea, though my father kept it till he died. You knowed about that, didn't ye?" he asked suddenly.

"Oh, yes! He often has told me of Captain Parker and what great friends they used to be. But I thought—I thought—"

She stopped in confusion, arresting her glances which were straying over his face and general appearance as if she were surprised that a son of Captain Parker should show so little refinement.

"Ye see, I runned away!" he said, as one replying to a criticism. "No colliges for me! The sea, d'ye mind? I was all for that. 'Twas agin the old man's will, but he was a kind sort, the old man was, and when he died he didn't hold it out agin me. No, he left me everything. So there ye are. And among other things he left me somewhat to say to Cap'n Ransome, a somewhat that's important." He paused and glanced at her face, which was anxious. Then he proceeded. "It has to do with a thing long gone by—to right a great wrong, to say it above board, and it can't be done onless I can see him. Jest two minutes alone with him—"

"But, sir, Mr. Parker!" she cried in agitation, rising and standing before him, "he can't meet anybody. The least exertion wears him out. The doctors say—"

"Miss," he interrupted, "yore his adopted daughter, ain't ye, not his real one?"

"Yes, sir, I am; but he has been more than a father to me, and—"

"Well, it's for yore sake that I want to see him!"

He crossed his knees and sat back confidently. But the girl, with a wan smile of relief, answered:

"Then, sir, no matter about it, if it is only for me. I certainly should not have him disturbed on my poor account. If it were for another—"

He seemed taken aback for an instant.

"Well, there is another," he said, after some hesitation, "but I didn't want to speak of him. I don't know him, not even his name, but you do, lady. It will make all the difference to him. Whoever he is, he is yore promised husband—"

Her face, a moment before pale, and determined as a face of its meek character could well be, now flushed to a real beauty, the set lines softened, the lips quivered, and the mild eyes flashed into eagerness. Her whole small form took on a womanly coyness almost impossible to imagine in her until it was seen, and she spoke with an excitement which she tried in vain to hide, interrupting him:

"Mr. Parker," she said, "if you will wait here one minute I will see what I can do. The doctors are with him now, and I will ask their advice. If it is possible for him to receive anybody in the world, you shall be that one."

She ran out hurriedly, blind to the expression on his face, whatever it might be, scarcely seeing him or anything, recognizing no logical gaps in the situation, intent only on one thing—the thought of *him*.

The sailor jumped up and softly followed her down the dim hall, his face grim, his eyes glittering. Four doors beyond she stopped and went in. The sailor stole on to the next door, turned the knob stealthily, peered into the vacant room, ran to a cabinet of ebony, inserted a key, pushed the slide back, exchanged for a long envelope he saw there one which he took from his pocket, locked the cabinet, and inside of one minute was back in the reception-room, sitting as he was when the girl left him.

Presently she returned, regarding him strangely.

"My father says that he was under the impression that his friend's son was an Oxford university man, and that he was no longer living, she said hesitatingly.

"Oh, well, ye see," he answered, readily, "I runned away from there. Yes, that's it; I runned away. No college for me! And so 'twas give out that I was dead. That's it. D'ye see?"

His words were far from reassuring her, innocent as she was of the world's ways, and she still regarded him with eyes in which some undefined fear lurked.

"Are you sure it is about HIM that you wish to see my father?" she asked, anxiously, "Because if it isn't—" She hesitated.

"Well, I'll tell ye what," he said, as if suddenly arrived at a satisfactory conclusion. "I'll go git the papers—I didn't fetch 'em along this time, d'ye see—and I'll come agin. Then ye'll see for yerself, for I'll show 'em to ye."

He picked up his cap and arose.

"But, sir, my father wishes to see you!" she exclaimed. "Though the doctors do not approve, he wishes it, for he cannot imagine what the important thing is—"

"Well, I'll git the papers and come agin," he interrupted, moving toward the door. She stood well away from him, but her anxiety regarding his message overcame her fear of his person, and she asked hastily:

"Couldn't you tell me the nature of the communication you wish to make to him? He cannot imagine what it may be, and I, you know—you said that I—that it was for my sake too. I have a right to know."

"Well, I'll bring the papers, that's all," he growled, glaring at her. With that he passed down the stairs and out, the footman opening the door for him stiffly, while she followed him with troubled eyes.

"What a strange man! What could his message be?" she murmured. Then she hurried softly back to the sick room.

Dr. Furnivall, seated in his library, drew a breath of relief. He had had a hard day and was tired. What with his prison duties as resident physician, his private practice, and, recently, since the fame of his hypnotic powers had spread so widely, the grind he had been called upon to undergo in police circles, he was pretty well worn out. But this evening there was nothing on the tapis and he would—

The door opened without ceremony and in walked Dr. Gerrish. He was flushed and excited, and held a paper in his hand. Though he was privileged to burst in upon his friend in this sort of way if he so wished, he began an apology.

"If it weren't so important—" he began.

"Oh, yes! Everything is important with you young fellows. But to tell you the truth, there hasn't been an important happening since 6,000 B. C. That is according to Usher's chronology. Adam and Eve were born then. My own notion is, plagiarized from Rabelais, Montaigne, Mr. Shakespeare, and others, all equally unknown today, except in name, nothing ever happened that was or is or in any way can be important. Well, go on!"

He smiled affectionately at his younger friend, leaned back in his chair, put on his spectacles of colored glass, and looked attention.

But Dr. Gerrish was in earnest. He did not respond to his friend's banter, except by a fleeting smile. Then he began:

"Three of us were in consultation this afternoon over a case that will puzzle even you."

"Who were they?"

"Whewell and Hersey, with me."

"Good men! What was the case?"

"That's it. What is it? Listen now." Dr. Gerrish leaned eagerly over the table toward Dr. Furnivall and continued: "Take a man 60 years old, hale and strong—never been sick in his life. Gradually he becomes weak; no apparent disease; organs intact; no bad habits; just sinks, and goes to bed. For a long time no physician called because not considered necessary; just a weakness which, with ordinary care, will pass away. But it doesn't pass away. On the contrary, it grows greater, and keeps on growing greater, he refusing medical advice, until a whole year is gone by. Then the daughter will wait no longer, and calls in Hersey. Hersey can make nothing at all of the symptoms and calls in Whewell. Whewell is all off, too, and calls in me. I also am all off. Now I want you, we all of us want you, and I am here to get you; and," he added, thrusting the paper he had held in his hand since he entered, under Dr. Furnivall's eyes, "here is the document that will fetch you."

Dr. Furnivall put out his hand for it, but Dr. Gerrish withdrew it.

"It is a record of symptoms," he said, "filed down to the last analysis. You need not know them all. This will be enough for you, or I am much mistaken. Listen."

Searching here and there in the written diagnosis, leaving out the minor details, he read, eagerly, the symptoms of a disease so strange that it never had been heard of by merely practising physicians in the United States of America and by but few of the best physicians anywhere. Yet these symptoms sounded so simple! The following is all Dr. Gerrish read:

"Almost utter muscular weakness—breathlessness upon least exertion—palpitation of heart—puffy face—enlarged spleen and lymphatic glands—slight fever—badly defined reddish patches on body—profound mental lethargy; all this, with no mania, no delusions, but of course with no optimism, no hope. Lethargy the predominating feature. Patient's age 60 years or so."

Dr. Furnivall arose at once.

"Is it far from here?" he inquired, his hand on a push button.

"Whittaker Ransome's!" replied Dr. Gerrish succinctly.

"Indeed! Then we'll just walk around the corner. We shall need no conveyance."

The patient lay a massive ruin in his great bed, like a giant tree stricken down. The flesh over his ponderous bones had shrunk until the corrugated skin, except over his face, which was puffy, resembled thick bark more than the cuticle of a man. His great hands, pale and thin, lay like skeleton claws outside the quilt, the veins showing large and knotted, but filled apparently with some lighter hued fluid than good red blood. The eyes were closed wearily, the whole body expressed weariness in the last degree, and the man seemed even to breathe with the reluctance of one over a hard and painful task. It was a ghastly spectacle.

But Dr. Furnivall cast only one glance at the patient himself. His attention was all concentrated on a vase and its accompaniments on the mantel from the instant he first saw it. Long necked, of well levigated clay, it was gilded without and within with a dull, golden colored mica. By the side of it stood a glass jar containing a brownish red powder, and close to that was a forked stick, one fork of which was split and filled with chicken feathers, while inside hung a little clay pot containing a number of chicken bones.

Dr. Furnivall, having finished his examination of this unique curio, looked from it interestedly to the patient, and then beckoned Dr. Gerrish.

"I did not know he ever was in Africa," he said, motioning toward the patient.

"It was not Africa, it was India—there is where he made his money—in the tea business."

"Yes, but this vase and these—"

"Oh, his nephew gave him those. He is a surgeon, a young Englishman, his sister's son, and his heir, out somewhere in the Anglo-Egyptian Soudan."

Dr. Furnivall threw him a quick, singular glance.

"Do you suspect nothing?" he asked.

Dr. Gerrish shook his head, with a quick glance in his turn.

"No. Why?"

Dr. Furnivall stepped to the bedside and looked down earnestly at the slumbering patient. He took his pulse. Then he whispered to Dr. Gerrish:

"I am going home to refresh my memory with an authority that occurs to me. Bring me some of the patient's blood as soon as you can. If we haven't run up against the most subtle, fiendish crime—"

"Crime!" gasped Dr. Gerrish, taken wholly by surprise.

"You say this nephew is his heir—is there a likeness of him of any kind in the house that you know of?"

This seemed to Dr. Gerrish to be exceedingly irrelevant, but he answered readily by pointing to the wall, on which was hung a fine oil painting of a young man in uniform. Dr. Furnivall stood back and examined it. His mental processes as he did so were somewhat as follows. The interpretation has become so famous among physicians and phrenologists that it would be supererogatory to introduce here any more than the striking points of it:

"The brain is large at the base, as compared with the upper superior convolutions of the cerebrum, especially in the upper frontal lobes at the seat of the faculties of benevolence and veneration. The development immediately over the eye shows perception in a marked degree, and the fullness of the eyes themselves means a flow of language—words, words, words, to such an extent that a superficial observer, or one who loved the speaker, would believe him much deeper and more accomplished than is the case. The forehead, in the abrupt recession of the upper superior convolutions, indicates also this same lack of benevolence. Causality, comparison, and veneration are largely deficient. His most striking faculty is that of human nature. The head, through the regions of the ears and the temporal lobes, is extremely broad—it means destructiveness, acquisitiveness, secretiveness. There is great energy and executive ability, love of money and power, active slyness and cunning. Roof shaped at the vertix, sloping toward the parietal eminences, the head here indicates a lack of conscientiousness. The still, small voice in this man is so very small and still that he never heard it. His self-esteem will give him absolute confidence in his ability to carry out whatever scheme his selfish propensities may concoct, and he has the determination and steadfastness of the bulldog. His cerebellum is abnormally developed, which indicates muscularity, and he is doubtless strong and vigorous. Caring primarily for his own feelings and wants, sly, surreptitious, yet at the same time forceful, he is a dangerous type of man, one in whom it would be difficult to find any natural quality of a gentleman—neither love, honor, trust, nor conscience."

Dr. Furnivall turned to Dr. Gerrish. "What uniform is that in the picture?"

"I don't know. But he is a surgeon, in the Egyptian medical service, until recently working with the Soudan commission."

"Until recently? Where is he now?"

"On his way here. He was sent for three months since, and is expected daily."

"How long ago was this vase received?"

"Oh, he brought it himself when he was in the city last year."

"Ah, he has visited here himself! Do you know if the patient has been out of the United States lately?"

"Not for eight years, certainly, for I have known him for that length of time."

"Well, bring me the blood."

Dr. Furnivall straightened up from his microscope and, putting on his spectacles, looked at Dr. Gerrish.

"It is as I thought," he said. "Bacteriologic culture of trypanosomes!"

"Good heavens!" ejaculated Dr. Gerrish, stepping quickly to the microscope. "How on earth did you ever come to suspect such a thing?"

"In the first place, the symptoms of the patient indicated it. And as soon as I saw that odd vase in his room I was practically certain. For vases of that sort, as I see by my authority here, are made only in the Bahr-El-Ghazal province in the southern Soudan, where trypanosomiasis, or 'sleeping sickness,' is common."

Dr. Gerrish, who was eagerly studying the culture, raised his head quickly.

"But," he said, "the patient was never there—and how could he contract—"

"The disease is spread in two ways, first by the bite of the tsetse fly. That is the common way."

"Well, there are no tsetse flies here!"

"No, there are not. But there is the second way—direct inoculation of the parasites into the blood—and we have hypodermic needles here."

Dr. Gerrish stared at him blankly for a moment. Then he comprehended, and his face paled.

"Good God! Can he be such a subtle fiend!" he murmured.

"The disease proves fatal, you understand, always—not until a long time subsequent to inoculation, however, anywhere from three months to three years after decided symptoms appear. And there is no sign of poison—only general paralysis, or chiefly that."

"But why should he wish to do it? He was his uncle's heir, and would get his property anyway, or most of it. And, indeed, all of it, in effect, for he is to marry the adopted daughter, who is the only other living person likely to be thought of in the will."

"The reasons we may leave until we interview the nephew. Rest assured he had good ones in his own estimation. I'll get a warrant for him, and as soon as he arrives he and I will have a little chat together on the subject."

The next day, accordingly, found Dr. Furnivall face to face with the young Englishman, who had reached his uncle's house that morning. The portrait which the doctor had studied was a good likeness, and he shuddered inwardly as he looked into the pitiless gray eyes and felt the atmosphere of brutal selfishness that enveloped the man beneath the cultivated suavity of manner, which, to the casual observer, was very far from uninviting. Stout and florid, of the pure English type, in the traditional slouchy suit of gray tweed, he conversed with the doctor as one of his uncle's physicians, manifesting much sorrow over his condition. He said that he supposed they had abandoned all hope of his recovery.

"Yes," answered Dr. Furnivall, looking into his eyes. "You have just seen him, I understand. What, in your opinion, is he afflicted with?"

"Oh, I haven't examined him, don't you know. Not yet. You have very fair physicians in this country, and I fancy everything has been done for him—er—properly, and all that. I don't say what might have been if I could have seen him in time. Er—too late now, and all that—er!"

"You have no idea what his disease is?"

"I fancy it is—er—old age, don't you know—er—general paralysis—er—er—"

His face having shown several remarkable changes of expression as he talked, his eyes in the doctor's, beginning with perplexity, running into vacancy, into stolidity, and then earnestness, now settled into deep introspection; and his voice, trailing away to silence for an instant, began again without hesitancy, but with a mechanical intonation.

"What did you ask me?" he continued.

"What disease is your uncle afflicted with?"

As Dr. Furnivall put the question this time the door of the room, which had been slightly ajar up to this moment, swung wide, and Dr. Gerrish and another man came in. The subject gave them no attention, but answered at once:

"Sleeping sickness!"

"How did he contract it?"

"I inoculated him with trypanosomes fourteen months ago!"

"How did you manage to do that without his suspecting it?"

"I put enough arsenic in his food to give him violent pains in the stomach and bowels, and followed with hypodermic injections to relieve the suffering, one containing the trypanosomes, the other morphine. For the arsenical poisoning I gave him hydrated sesquioxide of iron."

The man in plain clothes with Dr. Gerrish stepped nearer, but Dr. Furnivall put another question.

"What was your object in inoculating your uncle with this fatal disease?"

"He was a strong man, likely to live long, and I wanted his money as soon as I could get it. Besides, he had made conditions in his will that did not suit me. By its terms I am to marry his adopted daughter or else give up half the property to her. I was present when the will was made, and pretended to agree to its provisions, knowing that with a man like him it would be useless to do otherwise; he would have his way. I had a duplicate key to his cabinet made while I was here, and when, some months after my return to the Soudan, I learned that he was too sick to be up and around, I sent here a man, a sailor, who is in my power, with the key. I coached him up on a cock-and-bull story that he was the son of an old friend of my uncle's, and on some pretext or other he was to get into the room, which I described to him, where the cabinet was kept, and change the real will, which was locked up there, for one I had forged myself. All this was done while I was thousands of miles away, so that no suspicions could attach to me should occasion of suspicion of anybody arise. Even that was not likely. There is nobody interested but the girl, who will accept meekly whatever happens; and, you know, I didn't want her, but I did want the money."

"And I want you," said the plain clothes man, stepping up to him as Dr. Furnivall turned away in disgust. "I arrest you for the poisoning of your uncle, Mr. Whittaker Ransome. Later the charge will be murder. Come! Step lively!"

With a look of the deepest astonishment on his usually self-satisfied face, the young man was hustled from the room, not too gently.

THE MAN WITH THE GLASS EYE

"Friendship," said Delancy, lighting his briar root, "consists in overlooking faults."

"One would have to overlook quite a few in you," returned Sewell, sourly.

Delancy grinned and blew rings.

"You're my friend, aren't you?" He crossed his knees and crowded down the tobacco in his pipe with a knife handle.

"Not when you want money—not by a blessed sight!" retorted Sewell, also crossing his knees.

"There's one thing I like about you, you most humble apology for an old chum," said Delancy, blowing clouds of smoke debonairly, "and that is you are rich but honest. Most men would be ashamed to confess to your principles."

Sewell snorted smoke.

"How much do you owe me now?" he burst out, leaning forward, his pipe in his hand, his bald head glistening in a ray of sun that lay across the corner of the room, his white mustache lifting up and down over his thin lips, his black eyes shooting sparks, his face full of condemnation.

"What's that got to do with it? It isn't what I've had, it is what I want, that bothers me. And you've got enough, more than ten times enough. Come, shell out! Lend me a thousand—ha, ha, ha!" He threw himself back in his chair and laughed boisterously at the astonished expression on the other's face. "Anybody would think you were surprised," he added. And then ruminatively, "What a queer devil!"

"It's you who are the queer devil!" exploded Sewell, hitching excitedly around in his Morris chair, and, his pipe in his fingers, the stem pointed at Delancy, scowling thunders. "I can't keep going on forever lending you money! What do you take me for? An ass! You must! Or else you wouldn't have the gall—"

"Well," grumbled Delancy, his fresh face, smooth shaven and rotund, crinkling lugubriously, "I can't live the way you do. It's disgraceful! A man with $10,000 a year income, with nobody but himself to look after—it's disgraceful, it is, spending only three thousand! What is money for? Why, if I had as much as you have—"

"You wouldn't be worth a dollar in two years," interpolated Sewell with spirit.

"Very likely not. But other people would be—the people on whom I would blow it. I can take care of myself—they can't! And there you are! I should be a philanthropist."

He laughed again, pleasantly, kicking a hassock end over end.

"You are the most inconsequential ass I ever saw in my life. See here! If I should lend you a hundred, what would you do with it?"

"A hundred? Oh, a hundred! Well, I'd take Mattie out and give her a supper. We might get a fairly decent one for that. But what should I do tomorrow?" He examined the toes of his patent leathers, twisting them about to get the view on all sides. Sewell thumped the arm of his chair with a strenuous fist.

"That's what I thought—or something like it—an actress—and at your age—br-r-r!"

It would be a good thing for you yourself to do 'something like it!' A girl, any kind of a girl, is an education. But you? Why, man, did you ever in all your life get a fluffy lot of lace and feathers and soft, rolypoly in your arms and hug it and kiss it? Not you, you crustacean! You don't know what it means. But look at me! I know!"

"Never mind about what I ever did!" he answered, querulously. "And you can't shove me off like that, Dick! I know you! You're trying only to run me off on an infernal tangent, chinning about

366 GEORGE F. BUTLER

something else, and before I am on to you you'll have me good natured and forking over the rhino! But I won't do it—again, I've given you enough. What you think I'm made of gets me. Why, confound it—here!" He jumped up and ran to the desk in the corner of the elegantly furnished room and pulled out a ledger. "There! look at that date! Only two weeks ago I gave you $500, and here you are again gunning for a thousand."

"Why," said Dick, eyeing the book in amazement, "you don't mean to say you set down what I borrow, do you?"

"Set it down! Set it down! Of course I set it down. How else can I remember how much it is when you come to settle?"

Mr. Dick Delancy lay back and roared.

"Well, of all the queer Willies!" he chortled. "I knew, of course, that you were fool enough to lend it to me, but I didn't suppose you were fool enough to expect ever to see it again!"

Sewell slammed the ledger upon the desk and resumed his seat.

"That's enough, Dick!" he said in a tone of exasperation. "You know you'll pay it in time, when your pictures go! You have honor, anyway, I know that."

"Honor! Honor! What has honor to do with it? Did honor and money ever yet meet? It's a simple matter of business with me. I get all I can, the same as you do. You grind your tenants, I grind you, somebody else grinds me, and it's that somebody else that you grind. And there you are—the vicious circle! If God put me into this world with beauty and brains, and put you into it with nothing but money, why, then, I'll be generous with you—I'll allow you to feast on my good looks and sample my gray matter, as displayed in the facility with which I grind you, and all you have to do is to stand the grind. If that isn't generous in me, what could be? That's what I want to know."

He reclined in his chair with a self-satisfied expression on his face, threw his leg over the arm, ran his fingers through his thick chestnut-colored hair, tousling and mauling it fantastically, and blew a cloud of smoke ceiling-ward.

"Well, I'm aware," said Sewell meekly, "that I never could have taken my degree at college but for you, Dick, old man. And I'll not soon forget that. I owe you a good deal, no doubt. But I don't owe you everything—not all my money. And sometimes it seems as if you thought I did. I've coughed up six thousand for you in the last eighteen months. It isn't business. It's worse than unbusinesslike—its downright tomfoolery in me. How have you got on all these years without me—over there in Paris, and Rome, and Venice, and those places?"

"That's just it!" explained Mr. Dick, starting up. "How did I? Ask my creditors, but don't give me any such conundrum as that. Why, Neil, I'm a wonder to myself! I don't know how I managed to pull through. You ought to see the cribs I've been obliged to sleep in—barns and old snaky ruins! And the grub! Man, it was frightful, the whole experience! I used to think of you and the dinky feeds we laid in together, and the soft mattresses in the dormitory, and the glad clothes, and—sometimes I felt like chucking the complete thing—Art and all her relations—and going in for groceries or coal or dry goods—in them there are food and raiment, at all events! Or I could put on my natural face and pose as a born idiot in a dime museum—a hundred plunks a night—what!"

"I don't see how it is that you have to use so much now, after running the gait on nothing so long, Dick," Sewell grumbled. "I'd do anything for you, in reason—"

"Why, man, don't you know that the greatest spenders are those who never had anything until they made their strike! It's natural, of course! Begin with nothing, finish with satiety; begin with satiety, end with nothing! There you are! It's law, the law of compensation, which is universal, working in all things; and do you suppose I am going to sit still and see you break the law, a law as big as that, spread everywhere? Why, no, I am too much your friend, old man! You've always had enough, and never would throw anything. Don't you see what the gods are doing for you? They are sending you a clean cut young fellow like me to do the blowing which you owe to the law, but which you refuse to do yourself. It's perfectly simple. And it's your only salvation. Good heavens, Neil, think what would happen to you if you should deny me money, trying to buck all by your lonesome against a universal law—hello!"

The exclamation was called forth by the sudden appearance of a woman in the doorway.

"I knocked," she said apologetically to Sewell, "and the gentleman was talking so loudly that I couldn't tell whether you said 'come in' or not."

She was a tall, handsome, somewhat faded woman, very dark, svelte, and stylish in a tailor made gown, and as she finished speaking she glanced at Delancy with a curious expression in her large black eyes. There was distrust in them, and a little fear and a glint of indignation.

"Mrs. Dillingham, my old friend Delancy! Mrs. Dillingham is our new lodging mistress, Dick," said Sewell. "She makes it very pleasant here. Is there anything, Mrs. Dillingham?"

She acknowledged the introduction with a conventional nod and smile at Delancy, and then answered:

"The man has come about the automobile."

"That's good! Ask him right up; and thank you, Mrs. Dillingham. Too bad you should have to come away up here, three flights! I must have some sort of a bell arranged—or a speaking-tube, or something."

"Oh, it is nothing! I am sure you are very welcome," she returned, and with another nod and smile that included both men she went out, closing the door behind her.

Delancy glanced slyly beneath his lashes at Sewell, and, as he met his somewhat sheepish eye, burst out laughing.

"Pretty stylish rig, isn't it, for a lodging mistress—and before noon!"

"Oh, rot!" Sewell threw one leg over the other impatiently. "You always think every woman in the house where I happen to be is after me—or my money! It's low, Dick. Quit it! This is a good woman, and does all she can to make me comfortable—"

"Even to dressing up in her glad rags and mounting three flights of stairs to tell you you have a caller, instead of sending him right along, or deputing a maid!"

"Dick!—"

"Well, well, no matter! Say no more. What did you begin the argument for, anyway? It's useless to give you advice. You'll fall into the trap whatever warning you may have. You never could look out for yourself in any but money matters. In those—great Scott! You make up for all the rest! And that brings me back to my mutton. What are you going to do about that little matter—at once, before your man arrives?"

"I'm not going to give you a dollar!"

"Really, Neil?"

"Really, Dick!" Sewell looked at his friend with a determined eye. "In the first place," he went on, "I can't spare it now. Everything is tied up so tightly that I can't lay hold of what I need myself. All the ready cash I've got is in that desk, two thousand, and that is going for the auto tomorrow, providing the machine suits—as I have no doubt it will do. I shall be terribly short for three or four days—"

"'Caterwauling calamities cannonading come
  Dealing death's devastating doom—'
The man is to be broke for three days!" uttered Delancy in great horror.

Sewell waved his hand impatiently.

"And there's another thing, Dick. I feel sure that you will sell your pictures—in time. And then you'll pay up. Of course! But it may be a long time, and I don't feel like lending—er—er—"

He paused, puffing his pipe uncomfortably. "Proceed," said Delancy, eyeing him wonderingly.

"Well, hang it, you're always slipping into the poor old uncle so! Of course, I am aware that he was a grinder, piling up all he could get hold of in any old way, denying himself everything, and 'doing' everybody that he could, and all that. I'm reaping all the good of the harvest he sowed, and it doesn't seem the square thing in me to give or even lend his money to a man who despises his memory, loading him down with all the opprobrious epithets in the book of slang. He wasn't a good sort at all, I admit, and there is something in your point of view that appeals to me a little—that poetic justice is being done when a high roller like you gets hold of a skinflint's money and distributes it all over the world that he skinned. I suppose that is one great reason why I have let you milk me so. But I'm through now, Dick. At least I can't do anything for you today. I must think it over. You have always had a better time than I have, anyway, if I am the prince and you are the pauper, as you so often have said. Look at my bald nut and white hairs—and you haven't a sign of age about you, though we are both 35. You don't look 30!"

"Aha, so that's it—jealousy!" exploded Delancy, immensely pleased. "Why don't you cut out worrying, you poor old addle headed hippopotamus? That's what's the matter with you—"

A rap at the door interrupted him. Smiling, he arose as the automobile agent appeared, winked at Sewell, clapped on his hat, and departed, humming a gay air.

"Dick! Dick!" exclaimed Sewell in an excitement of contrition. "Yell at him, will you, Mr. Burbank! Tell him to come back—I want him!"

Mr. Burbank shot into the hall, crying, "Mr. Dick! Mr—er—Dick! Hi—hi!" No answer! He ran down the stairs, the three flights, and even opened the front door, looking up and down the street. There was no sign of Mr. Dick Delancy, and he returned with the declaration that it was curious that he had disappeared so suddenly, but he was gone. There was no doubt about that. It was one of the most singular things that he had ever heard of!

"Why, Mr. Sewell," he said, with bulging eyes, "I passed him right here in this doorway, and immediately he vanished! Where did he go? Up stairs—"

"There's only the roof up there," interrupted Sewell, perplexedly, "and at the head of the stairs is a trapdoor locked with a padlock. He couldn't get out that way—and what the nation would he want to for?"

"But he didn't go down, that is certain! He wouldn't have had time even to drop bodily down the stair rail well!"

Mr. Burbank was a small man of sandy complexion, with nervous light eyes, which were now dancing in excitement.

Sewell sat with wrinkled brows. He had not moved from the chair in which he was sitting when Delancy left him.

"I'm not going to talk 'automobile' today," he said, suddenly. "I don't feel like it. But I'm inclined to ask a favor of you, Mr. Burbank."

"You are welcome, Mr. Sewell, whatever it is," answered Mr. Burbank, with the readiness of a salesman dealing with a good customer.

"I've done my best friend an injustice," Sewell went on, rising and putting his pipe in the rack. "I want you to help me right it. Take me in the auto to his rooms, the Fenwag, will you? That will be as good as a longer spin, and we'll let it go at that. I am sure I shall accept the machine, anyway."

"With pleasure. Let me help you with your overcoat—why, what's the matter?"

Sewell was standing, his light overcoat on his arm, before an open drawer in his desk, his face as pale as ashes. That instant he tottered and fell weakly into the chair he had just vacated.

"Good God!" he gasped. "Why—why—what is it?"

"Good God!" Sewell muttered again, dashing his hand against his forehead. "Oh, Dick, Dick, Dick!"

"Mr. Sewell, if there is anything I can do " began Mr. Burbank, anxiously.

"For heaven's sake keep still, and let me think!" cried Sewell distractedly. "Somebody has stolen two thousand—let me think—let me think!"

He dropped his coat on the floor, sank back in his chair, and covered his face with his hands. The automobile agent stood embarrassed before him, not knowing what to do. The situation continued some moments. Then Sewell roused himself.

"Burbank," he said, with a business-like air, which, though plainly forced and with the greatest effort, was determined, "will you step down to the front room on the first floor and ask Mrs. Dillingham to come up here?"

And as the automobile agent hurried to do his bidding he again buried his face in his hands.

"Dick, Dick, poor old Dick!" he groaned. "Oh, why, for heaven's sake, couldn't you wait until this poor fit passed away from me! I'd have given it to you, Dick! You knew I would! Why, Dick, we're chums! How could you forget it! And you'll be famous some day, with your art—I know it—I've always said so—you're a genius—and to think that you could stoop—. But, by heavens, if it is you, I'll prosecute you to the—. Come in!"

Mrs. Dillingham entered, Burbank holding the door for her, and stood waiting while Sewell gazed at her undeterminately.

"I—I thought I would ask you, Mrs. Dillingham," he hesitated, "whether you could say—. But please take this seat! Sit down, Burbank! I wish you both to hear."

He jumped up and offered his chair to the woman, who accepted it with grace. Mr. Burbank sat on the couch, looking from the one to the other anxiously. Sewell walked over to his desk and put his hand on it.

"Mrs. Dillingham," he said, "it is unfortunate—but—but—and you are so recently come here—I shouldn't wish you to receive the opinion that the neighborhood is bad—but the fact is, $2,000 have been taken from this desk this morning. I was out of the rooms for only an hour, and—and was there anybody in here, besides the maid, during that time?"

His manner was strained. It would not require a superlative degree of insight in a listener, certainly no greater degree than this woman possessed, to see that he was fighting against a conviction in his own mind, and that even to him the question was irrelevant.

"Mr. Sewell," she answered, with dignity, sitting straight in her chair, "I hope I conduct my house properly—"

"Oh, I beg you a thousand times to pardon me!" Sewell exclaimed, "I did not mean that. It is very far from my intention to charge the maid or anybody connected with your—"

"I should think not," the lodging mistress interrupted, with curved eyebrows, and rising. "And," she continued, with contracted lips, "if you want to know who got your money I can tell you!"

Sewell shivered. He felt what was coming, and he dreaded it horribly; but his code of ethics, which taught him to hold honesty, business honesty, above all other qualities in a man, and to punish its lack implacably, inspired him with bravery, or at least with bravado. He straightened up, clutching the desk to steady himself.

"That is what I wish," he said, and his voice caught in his throat so that it seemed as if a frightened child were speaking.

"Mr. Sewell," she answered, holding her head high, "there has been nobody but me in this room today, except that rowdy—that friend of yours, Mr. Delancy. I made up your apartments myself, while you were out, and if you care to know what I think—"

Sewell made a gesture of denial.

"I feel extremely obliged to you, Mrs. Dillingham," he interpolated, hastily, "for all your trouble regarding this trifling matter. Allow me!"

He opened the door for her and stood politely waiting. She moved to the threshold, and then turned her flashing eyes on him.

"I have always known that man was robbing you," she hissed, "and I have been afraid, because I was sure that sooner or later you would lay it on me, or on the house in some way. I have been here only three weeks, but I have heard and seen—"

He began closing the door. She stepped over the sill, and then discharged her Parthian shot:

"And I heard him say to you this very morning that something terrible would happen if you refused him money today—"

The door closed and her voice ceased.

The automobile man looked at Sewell curiously.

"Did he threaten you?" he asked.

"No, no, nonsense! He was chaffing about a universal law, and my bucking against it. He said something about things happening to me if I did so, jokingly, in his way, and this ignorant woman—"

"Do you know what I think?" cried Burbank excitedly. "She took it! See the way she acted—tried to be dignified under her paint—and was the only one in here—and tried to lay it on somebody else—"

Sewell groaned.

"Burbank," he said in a low voice, "to me stealing money is the meanest, the lowest, most abominable thing a man can do; and my heart is broken. I had that vulgar woman brought up here only in hope of something—something impossible! I knew—I knew! Yet I wished to evade the knowledge. And hoped against hope that she would give me some reason to do so. But she only added to it. Good heavens, Burbank!" he almost shouted, starting toward him with hands stretched out, "think of it! A man you love—a man who is your dearest friend—a man for whom you would do anything in reason—a man who has done things for you, too, even beyond reason, who has given his time to you, time that was worth money to him, while you had all, the money and he had none—"

"There, there, calm yourself, Mr. Sewell!" exclaimed Burbank soothingly, putting his arm around Sewell's shoulders and guiding him to the Morris chair, "Come, it's a small matter to you, and, besides, you are not sure it was he. How can you be? There are lots of ways out of it. I should sooner suspect the woman. She looks like it, fast enough!"

"Man!" cried Sewell with sudden energy, "it is not a small matter—the principle isn't! And I know—I know—See here! I put that package of bills into that drawer while Dick Delancy was here, observing me do it! Nobody comes in until he leaves, and the next moment I find that the money is gone—at the same time he goes! Not a soul in the room besides us two in the meantime! And he was all over the place—ten times at the desk, as well as at every other spot in the apartment! What can I think! What can I but know?"

"If I can do anything, Mr. Sewell—"

Sewell arose, walked to the pipe rack, put his hand on a pipe, a great meerschaum with a figure supposed to be that of Lief, the Norseman, on it, and, as if inspired by contact with the image, turned with sudden rage on the agent.

"Get out of here!" he howled. "Never let me see you again! Confound it, can't a man be let alone in his own place!"

"Why, Mr. Sewell"—began the man, startled.

"Leave the room!" commanded Sewell, fiercely.

Mr. Burbank looked at him an instant. Then, with raised eyebrows, he picked up his hat, and, an expression of injury in his face, opened the door, bowed with dignity, and withdrew.

Sewell stood looking after him with the gaze of a blind man. Then he fumbled at the pipes, taking up one and putting it down, repeating the operation with others, finally turning away altogether. As he did so his eyes fell on a morning newspaper that lay on a chair, with the following headlines staring at him:

DR. FURNIVALL'S MYSTERIOUS POWER AGAIN!
ANOTHER CRIMINAL FOUND BY ITS AID!
SCIENTISTS AND POLICE ALIKE PUZZLED
BY THIS OCCULT FORCE WHICH COMPELS
A MAN ALWAYS TO SPEAK THE TRUTH!

"Jove!" he cried. "The very thing! Why didn't I think of him at once!"

In less than a quarter or an hour from that moment he was telling his story to Dr. Furnivall.

"As I understand it, then," said the doctor, regarding him through his colored spectacles, "you can't believe that this rather frivolous friend of yours is guilty, while at the same time you must believe it because all the circumstances indicate his guilt."

"Yes, yes, that is it!" cried Sewell. "And I was hoping that, with your hypnotism, you might force him to confess—privately, you know! We would have no publicity about it, and all that. The confession would be punishment enough for him—and I would let him keep the money, and he could go away. For I can't have him around any longer—"

"It appears to me," said Dr. Furnivall, sitting back in his chair, "that you have begun at the wrong end of the matter. It is true that from what you say your friend is a spendthrift, altogether too light of mind for his own material good, but that does not make him a thief. If it did most all our artists would be thieves. And to steal from his own best friend, too! Isn't that an enormous charge to make—"

"But the circumstances! the circumstances!" Sewell burst forth, excitedly. "I tell you I put that money into the desk while he was there—he saw me do it— and not another soul was in the room from that moment until I missed it—"

"There was the lodging mistress, and there was Burbank!"

"Oh, but they don't count! How can they? Dick and I, both of us, had our eyes on the woman every instant she was there—"

"No matter if you did have! Human affairs take on strange twists sometimes. The money might not have been in the desk at all— might have rolled to the floor, where she could kick it behind her out of the door as she entered, under cover of her skirts—a dozen different ways might—"

Sewell shook his head hopelessly.

"No, no it is useless," he interrupted. "It was there in the drawer, and the drawer was open, so that I could see it all the time. I did not move from my chair, except once, when I went to the desk for a ledger, after putting the package of bills into that drawer, and I was facing it every instant until I suddenly missed it, nobody having approached it in the meantime except Dick."

"The other man, Mr. Burbank, he—"

"Oh, he passed Dick in the doorway. Burbank drew back to give Dick room—hadn't entered at all before I sent him to call Dick back."

"You sent for Delancy to come back? Why didn't he come, then?"

"Burbank couldn't find him. He had disappeared like a flash of lightning, and that is one of the counts against him, He must have started down those stairs three at a leap the instant he reached them. Now, why should he do that unless he were guilty?"

"Do you mean to say that you asked Burbank to call out to Delancy, who had just passed him in the doorway, that Burbank had not entered the room—so short a time as that had elapsed— and he could not make him hear?"

"I do. And, further, he ran as fast as he could safely go down to the front door, and looked up and down the street, and even then could see him nowhere."

"After Burbank came back didn't he enter the room?"

"Certainly, but not until I had missed the money. He stood right on the threshold while he told me that Dick had vanished. I am positive of that, for I thought at the time it was queer. It was as if he felt timid about coming in—I couldn't understand it. It was just at the moment when I discovered my loss that he first stepped on the rug, coming forward with the offer to assist me with my overcoat."

Dr. Furnivall gave a long look into his face through his spectacles. He then with an ophthalmoscope examined his eyes.

"Of what firm are you buying your automobile?" he asked suddenly. Sewell told him. He went into the telephone closet, and after a few words with station 16 put on his hat, saying:

"I am about to show you something so strange that you wouldn't believe it possible until actually compelled to do so! Come, let's go for a short walk."

"Shall we call on Delancy now?" asked Sewell, as they reached the sidewalk.

"Delancy! Oh, no, we have nothing to do with him at present! Quite another person! And if the experience teaches you to accept the evidence of character against circumstances—but there!" He stopped, with an amused glance at Sewell. What did he know about reading character! No more than a child who, because he can see nothing beyond appearances, must be swayed by them, and them alone! "I am unacquainted with Delancy," he continued, "and can judge of him only by your description, which was meager; but I should say he is careless rather than dishonest. He is more fool than knave, but unless I am greatly mistaken he is not fool enough to rob you surreptitiously, knowing that the act would cut his supplies off, when he has so little difficulty in doing it openly through loans, which might go on indefinitely. We must look in quite another direction for the thief."

Sewell shook his head. He had gone over all the details in his own mind, and he could imagine no possible chance of Delancy's being innocent. But he said nothing. There was something in the doctor's manner that inspired confidence, and Sewell felt an undercurrent of satisfaction in the view the celebrated scientist took of the case, though he could see no reason for it, and his mind rejected at the same time that his heart accepted it. In a few minutes they arrived at the police station, and, to Sewell's surprise, Dr. Furnivall took him by the elbow and guided him up the steps and

in. There stood Mr. Burbank talking with the desk man, a policeman on each side of him. The officer, by a look, invited Dr. Furnivall
forward, and he, removing his spectacles, gazed into Burbank's eyes
steadily, saying:

"Mr. Burbank, what do you know about this robbery?"

"I know nothing about it!" Burbank exclaimed angrily. "It is
monstrous to bring me here in this way and put these questions to
me. There is Mr. Sewell himself, who will testify that I was not in
the room at all until—" He started to turn his eyes in Sewell's direction, but did not do so. The head moved slightly, but the eyes
remained fixed in Dr. Furnivall's. His face at first showed quick
surprise, then the expression changed to bewilderment, from that
to earnestness, and then both face and eyes became deeply introspective. It was not ten seconds from the time of Dr. Furnivall's
first glance into the eyes to the moment when it became evident to
the hypnotist that he was under control. He then asked at once:

"Mr. Burbank, who took that money?"

"I did!" he answered without a hint of inflection in his voice. It
was as if a machine were speaking. Sewell started forward with an
exclamation of astonishment and disbelief, but Dr. Furnivall waved
him back.

"How could you do it? Start at the beginning and tell me all
about it."

"I came up the stairs, and was just going to knock on the door
when I heard Mr. Sewell say he had $2,000 in the desk. I waited a
moment and then rapped. A man came out, singing, and I entered
the room, saying 'How do you do, Mr. Sewell?' He did not seem to
see me—sat in a sort of trance, gazing after the man who had just
gone out. I thought instantly of the money in the desk, and, glancing over there, saw it in an open drawer. I looked at him again. He
still had that far away light in his eyes. I remembered the peculiar
expression—my grandfather used to be that way, and many a time
I had taken things right out from under his nose without his being
aware of it. It's a sort of disease, I suppose, with old people, but I
never had seen it in a young man before. I was almost too much
afraid to risk it, and, in fact, I spoke to him the second time to test

him. As he did not answer, I gained courage and in three steps snatched the package of bills, slipped them into my overcoat pocket, and darted back to the door. Then I spoke again, and still again, but he did not hear. His mind was too busy with its own thoughts. I couldn't help thinking of the story Mark Twain tells of the woman. He was sitting on the piazza when he saw her coming up the walk toward him, and suddenly she disappeared as if the ground had swallowed her up. He found that she had passed right by him, rung the door bell at his side, and been admitted to the house without his seeing her. I explained that by absent-mindedness. He was thinking so deeply of something else that he had no room in his memory for her. My grandfather had been that way, I have seen drunken men that way, and Mr. Sewell was that way. It didn't last long—perhaps a minute. He suddenly woke up, and, as if his friend had just left, sang out to him; and as there was no answer he asked me to yell, too, and I went down the stairs even to the front door. But, of course, the man was clean out of sight by that time."

"Where is the money?"

"Here!"

He produced it as he spoke, and Dr. Furnivall passed it over to the bewildered Sewell.

"You are diseased," he said to him, "afflicted with cerebro-vacuisitis, otherwise ophthavitreousitis, otherwise the glass eye. But, seriously, you are suffering from amnesia, and you were near to making your friend settle dearly for your sickness. Go home now and take care of yourself. Call in a physician. He will tell you, among other things, to quit your eternal smoking, exercise more, choose your food, not for its daintiness and the taste of it, but for the good, honest blood it will make; and, above all, to occupy your mind with some useful avocation. Then you will be able to see what is going on—or what is going on under your very nose at least!"

THE KLEPTOMANIAC

A little old man with a warty face, hooked nose, wide mouth, stooping shoulders, small beady black eyes, and a generally inferior presence, but nevertheless with decision of character in his manner, to one who could see beneath the surface, walked swiftly up the steps of police station 16 and accosted the first man in uniform he met.

"There has been the most unheard of crime—" he began.

"Speak to the lieutenant!" the officer interrupted, nodding toward the desk behind the high network iron railing.

The ugly little man advanced to the pigeonhole window, through which he could see the upper part of the night desk man.

"I have just been robbed in the most monstrous way," he said, speaking rapidly, but with no sign of excitement, "and I wish no publicity—"

"I'll take care of that. We don't need any advice from you—" began the lieutenant. But he stopped there to glance at the visiting card which the little man placed before him, and when he raised his eyes again to his caller's face he also raised his body from his chair and bowed, touching his round silk office cap.

"Excuse me, Mr. Emmons," he said, "I didn't know it was you. We have to be pretty short here with strangers, or they'd ride right over us. But with the richest man in the district— Step in this way, sir, please!"

He swung wide the gate in the railing. The richest man in the district walked in and seated himself in the chair that the officer drew up for him in a retired corner.

"Now, sir, no publicity, you say? Very well! We'll do all we can."

He waited with respectful attention for the story.

"It's a queer matter," began Mr. Emmons at once, in the incisive voice, which, coming from such an insignificant appearing personality, always excited surprise in a listener and drew his attention. "In the first place I must tell you that a few days ago our firm became possessed, in the way of business, of one of the most valuable diamonds in the world. It has a name famous in history—but no matter about that. The chief thing is that it is worth—well, say—er—" He paused with the shrewd glint in his eye that was known among his business acquaintances as the sure sign that he was not going to commit himself, and then added, "thousands," as evenly as if the word were "hundreds." The lieutenant could not restrain an exclamation.

"Ah!" he breathed, his face flushing with the thought of fat rewards.

"This diamond," went on the great jeweler, with no hint, either in voice or manner, of the terrific surprise he was about to give his listeners, "was swallowed this evening by my wife's pet monkey, and in less than two minutes afterward the monkey was stolen!"

The officer's full, round face became almost apoplectic.

"A mo—monkey!" he stammered.

"I will give you the main points of the case so that you may know how to start the investigation intelligently," continued the jeweler in a clear, rapid, matter of fact tone. They were odd traits, this clarity of head and speech, this iciness and poise, which nothing could melt or disturb, in a man of such an inferior aspect, never failing to evoke in a stranger, and often in every-day acquaintances as well, the same stare of wonderment with which the policeman was now regarding him as he went on:

"For reasons of a strictly private nature I took this valuable diamond home this evening. Two other men, well known diamond cutters, were the only living persons who knew I had it in the house. It was to show it to them, and consult with them about it, that I brought it there. We three had been examining it for ten minutes, perhaps, and I was holding it up to the light between my thumb and finger, when the monkey leaped in at the door like a flash of lightning, snatched the stone, and swallowed it. It nearly choked him, and, jabbering and twisting in pain, he ran to his mistress four doors away. I followed him immediately and found him whimpering in my wife's arms. I thought at first of giving him an emetic to make him vomit it up, but Mrs. Emmons suggested that it would be safer to call a physician, and then I decided on doing that. We might have to cut the animal open. So cautioning her to hold on to him and not let him escape, I hastened to the telephone closet, but before I could get the physician's number I heard my wife scream, and, hurrying back to her room, I found her collapsed on the floor, crying out that a woman had suddenly rushed in, grabbed Bruno, and fled out of the door with him in her arms.

"That is practically the case. Of course, we searched the premises inside and out at once, but to no purpose. The stone, the monkey, and the thief had vanished as if by spontaneous combustion. Now ask your questions, for I suppose you have some to ask?"

The lieutenant indeed had; but he was almost too much astonished to speak. If the narrator of this queer story had not been the richest man in the district he would have thought him either a practical joker or a lunatic. Finally he found his voice.

"There was no chance for either of those men you were showing it to—"

"Not the slightest. I was always between them and my wife's room, even when I was at the telephone. In fact, in the telephone closet I stood facing them, and could see them all the time through the doorway. Until Mrs. Emmons screamed they never moved from their seats, though then they ran with me to her room. Besides, the thief was seen, and was a woman."

"Is the telephone fixture near Mrs. Emmons' room?"

"Yes; but the walls are circular in shape, rounding outward into the hall, so that a person coming from the rear of the house, keeping close to the north partition, might enter her door without being seen by one in the telephone closet."

"Hm—m!" The lieutenant cleared his throat. "Why do you wish to keep the matter quiet, Mr. Emmons? It seems to me the more publicity that is given—"

"To the loss of a monkey, doubtless the better—yes. But nothing must be known about the diamond. We should be sure never to see it again."

"Yes, yes—of course. We will work quietly. Every night man in the city shall be notified as soon as possible to be on the lookout for the monkey. If you will write a description of him I'll see that it is given to the men. A little reward, now—"

He looked inquiringly at Mr. Emmons, who nodded.

"A hundred dollars," he said. "Great family pet. Worth nothing to anybody but the owners. I think it should be put that way."

"Could Mrs. Emmons say how the woman looked?"

"She saw her very plainly. She was short, plump, red cheeked, with black eyes that seemed to strike out sparks as she snatched the animal, and with hair so white that the contrast between it and her fresh face and youthful form was nothing less than startling. We knew nobody of that description, neither among our friends nor among the servants and tradespeople. Her dress, too, was the oddest imaginable—a yachting cap of blue, with a small visor worn sidewise over her ear, a short Eton jacket, and flowing out from under it a voluminous train of salmon colored satin, over white, high heeled shoes. This train she threw over her arm, covering Bruno completely and hiding him from sight as she rushed from the room. Her appearance was so wild that Mrs. Emmons took her for a crazy person who had escaped from some hospital. That is what frightened her so. An ordinary woman coming in on her in that manner would not have got off so easily, for Mrs. Emmons is brave enough and quick enough to act. But this nondescript fairly scared her strength away. In fact, she never in her life came so near fainting."

"You saw nothing of the woman?"

"No, the door was beyond my view. She must have come and gone like a flash of lightning, as Mrs. Emmons said. She didn't know she was in the room until she saw her eyes sparkling into her own and felt Bruno being pulled out of her lap."

"But where could she have come from and where could she disappear to so suddenly?" said the lieutenant, staring at him. "It sounds like witchcraft. What guess can you make, Mr. Emmons?"

384 GEORGE F. BUTLER

Mr. Emmons threw out his hands.

"None at all," he said. "She simply could not get into the house by the back way, through a gate and two doors, all of which were fastened, pass among eight servants at least, mount two flights of stairs, and appear on the scene at the very instant of time necessary to accomplish her purpose. And if she couldn't get in she couldn't get out. By the front way she would be obliged to pass me."

"None of the servants saw her?"

"No. That is, one of them, a half imbecile, came to the conclusion that she had distinguished what looked like a dark shape running down the back stairs to the basement; but she did not reach this conclusion until she had found out that something mysterious was going on and that she would be regarded as a heroine if she had seen anything of it. I am convinced that her first denials were undoubtedly the real truth. The rest was a vivid fancy."

"Hm—m!" The lieutenant, who had made a number of notes, now put down another one, coughing deprecatingly as he did so. "Every little straw shows something of the wind's direction, Mr. Emmons," he said. "However, we will come to that later. Were the gate and the doors found fastened all right after the theft as before it?"

"Yes; all locked up tight, and the servants running around all the time between them and the stairs, with plenty of light on—lighter than in the daytime. There was absolutely no chance for even a mouse to leave the place unseen in that direction—or enter it, either."

"And the roof?"

"I should certainly have seen anybody who should start up that way. The foot of the stairs was not ten feet away from the room in which the crime was done, and I commanded a full view of them every instant I was absent from my wife."

The officer looked up from his notes quickly. Then he scratched his head. He did not like to contradict a man worth so much money as Mr. Claggett Emmons was, but it was certain, from the description already given of the rooms and halls, that if a person in the telephone closet could see the two men in the front room, in order to do so he would necessarily turn his back on the stairway in the rear. A thrill of exultation shot through the lieutenant's breast as he realized that this stairway must be the key to the mystery. The foot of it was only ten feet away from the door of the room in which Mrs. Emmons sat; while Mr. Emmons was walking to the telephone his back must have been turned on it; while he was in the closet his back must have been turned on it also if he could see the men who sat in the front room; and, without a particle of doubt, the woman, who had been waiting above, seized this opportunity to accomplish her purpose. She would have plenty of time if she had acted as quickly as she seemed to have done. It was perfectly plain. She had escaped as she had entered—by way of the roof. It was strange that a man with Mr. Emmons' perspicacity should over-look so palpable a truth; but he had done so, and it was a matter of warm self-congratulation to the officer that he should prove so much sharper than this man of heavy affairs, and that, too, regard-ing the arrangement of his own house. But he would say nothing about it. It was a case for action rather than words, and after he had made the capture and received the reward—

At this point in the jubilant flow of his thoughts he was struck with a sudden chill. Reward? What was it? A hundred dollars! He had been dreaming of thousands!

"I suppose," he ventured, tapping his book with his pen handle carelessly, "that if any one in the secret—er—er—who knew about— the diamond, I mean—should find and return it, the—reward—"

The little old man glanced keenly at him.

"Of course," he said, nodding. "I understand that. A thousand— eh? And influence—supposing the finder needed it. Oh, of course— all that sort of thing."

The lieutenant breathed freer. A thousand! It was not so vast a sum as his dreams had pictured, but it would do very well. There were ways he knew of making it all his, dividing only the hundred for the monkey with whomsoever he might be obliged to call upon for assistance in his search. He could already feel the crisp, de-lightful crinkling of the bank notes in his fingers. That woman was simply a lunatic—he was sure of it—who had escaped from her home in some neighboring house by way of the roof, entered by the scuttle—oh, it was all plain. A few minutes searching among the families in the block— But he must not let it be seen that he was getting his money too easily. He would explore the Emmons mansion first, to give some color of labor to his easy task, pretend then with much scientific figuring to evolve a solution of the great mystery, the only solution that could be possible under all the conditions, walk out with the declaration that he would return in ten minutes with the diamond, according to the most approved methods of detectives in the fiction thrillers, and then would keep his word, just as they do; and the next morning he would be in all the papers, just as they are, with $1,000 in his inside pocket—which none of them ever yet got, except to give away, being too delicate of soul to work for mere money!

But when in company with Mr. Emmons and a man from the office, he entered the hall of the Emmons house, a few minutes later, he grew pale green with chagrin. In his mental plan of the floor he had figured on straight walls and staircases, while in fact there was scarcely a straight line in sight, and circles, semi-circles, ovals, and spirals predominated to such an extent that there seemed to his unaccustomed eye to be a perfect witches' dance of them, turning topsy-turvy all his ideas of interior architecture. He stepped into the telephone closet, and saw that, owing to these surprising shapes, Mr. Emmons had really been right about facing both the back stairway and the front room at the same time, if the ability to see one of these objects out of one eye and the other out of the other eye might be called "facing." It was near enough to it for practical purposes, at all events, for the walls were so deeply concave on the telephone side, and so highly convex on the other, that the closet, while it was between the stairs and the room, was far enough back from a straight line between the two points to command them both.

"I never see such a built house!" he growled in the anger of his great disappointment. In this mood his mind was rich soil for the seeds of suspicion, and, from the certainty that he could in no way explain the robbery, he passed at one bound to the doubt that any robbery had been committed. It was a foolish thing, come to think of it, to say that a monkey snatched that diamond and swallowed it! Who ever heard of such an absurdity? It was a lie on the face of it. And even granting that absurd lie, it was a bigger absurdity still to suppose it possible that a crazy woman from outside, or any kind of a woman, could be there at just the opportune moment—that all these various queer things could happen at the same time. In short, Emmons had that princely stone himself, and for some reason wished it believed that it had been stolen. The great mystery was that a man of his known shrewdness should have invented such a clumsy story to explain its disappearance.

Having reached this conclusion, the lieutenant assumed a magisterial expression of countenance and asked to see Mrs. Emmons. The lady received him with an eager smile on her keen old face, in the expression of which the officer saw at once a close resemblance to that of her husband, and invited him to be seated.

"Oh, dear!" she exclaimed, "I do so hope you will find out about all this! It is so trying—and such a queer thing! I never heard of anything like it in my life."

He would not sit, but stood before her, asking every question touching the case that he could conjure up. All in vain! Emmons had told him her story already, and the most searching cross-questioning failed to elicit anything new, or alter the facts as already given. She was much more prolix than her husband had been, going into every detail with volubility and minuteness. But the sum of her testimony was that the strange woman had pounced upon her, snatched the monkey, and disappeared apparently into nothingness.

The two visiting jewelers during all this time had remained, after their first hurry into Mrs. Emmons' room when they heard her scream, where they were sitting at the moment the monkey seized the diamond, locked in. This was by their own request, Mr. Emmons said, for in the circumstances they felt that to leave would invite suspicion of collusion on their part with the thief, and that they would better remain until the diamond should be found, or some definite course decided on. These men the officer now questioned as closely as he had Mrs. Emmons, but with no better result. They had seen a black thing shoot in the door, snatch the stone, swallow it, and scamper out, and almost immediately, hearing a scream, and seeing Mr. Emmons running across the hall from the telephone, they had jumped up and hastened with him to his wife's door, where they heard her story of the thief. They acknowledged that the whole matter had a queer look, and they wished they were well out of it. But they could not give any information. It certainly would be impossible for anybody to pass along the hall toward the front of the house without their seeing him, and they had seen nobody. The thief must have gone to the rear, and if she were not one of the servants disguised, and in conspiracy with all the rest of them, they could not imagine how she was able to escape that way. There was, in fact, no possible chance for a person to do what, it seemed, had been done. The problem was too big for them.

The suggestion of a disguised servant infused a little hope into the officer's mind. He had now become convinced that it was as absurd to suspect Mr. Emmons as he had formerly thought it was to suppose that the beast should swallow the stone. These men vowed they had seen the swallowing, and honesty and distress were too evident in their words and manner to be disputed. Besides, even if this very rich man were not above secreting the diamond his intellect was above concocting such a paltry scheme for doing it. On the notion of a servant in disguise he based his last hope, and asked to have them every one, men and women, summoned before him.

But at the very first view of them this last hope vanished. The thief was short and stout, and by the same accursed spite of fate which seemed to have met the lieutenant at each turn and crossing of this case every man and woman among these servants was thin and tall! The butler, it seemed, who hired all the help, was a lath in shape himself, and, maintaining that short, stout people were usually drinkers and always slow, if not downright lazy, he would have none of them. The officer in disgust motioned them away. A short person may by the exercise of skill and taste be made up to resemble a taller one, but the reverse metamorphosis is out of the question. Monsieur Lecocq himself never could have turned a tall spindle shanks into a chunky sawed-off.

With this wise reflection the officer made a few notes, ostensibly of great importance, but really only for appearance sake, and promising Mr. Emmons that every effort should be made for the apprehension of the thief was about to take his departure with his assistant, when he thought of the servant who claimed to have seen the dark shape gliding down the basement stairs. So he had her brought back to him, and put her through such a rigorous examination that she suddenly burst out crying, supposing that he was charging her with the theft. It was plain that she was a woman who could see shadows anywhere. He gave her up for a fool, and then it occurred to him to explore the back way and see things down there for himself. He did so, but learned nothing except that it would be absolutely impossible for anybody to come in that way unseen by the servants. Finally he searched Mrs. Emmons' room, she giving him full liberty to do so, pulling out drawers for him herself and moving tables and sofas around, till not a square inch in the apartment remained unseen by him. Then he went away. Though he left encouraging words behind him for the benefit of the husband and wife he felt that as far as he was concerned the case was closed.

"Docther Fur–rnivall, sor–r," said Sergeant Nulty, with red face and bulging eyes, "c'n a monkey swally a rooty bagy tur–rnip?"

"What's that?" said Dr. Furnivall, wheeling around in his chair. Seeing Sergeant Nulty's head, helmetless, sticking around the edge of the door, he smiled a welcome. "Come in, sergeant," he invited. "What's up now?"

"Well, noo, 'tis wan shtrange thing," answered the sergeant, stepping carefully over the polished floor to the chair the doctor indicated. "Here's wan mon cooms rhunnin' t' th' shtation wid blood in his eye, an' he says, says he, 'B'yes,' he says, 'here's a tousan' dollars,' he says, 'fer a woman an' a monkey, an' she swalleyed it,' he says, 'b't 'twas a dimont,' he says, 'an' th' woman swiped it off me,' he says, 'an' 'twas not me own, b't me woife's,' he says, 'an',' he says, 'Oi'll give,' he says, 'a tousan' dollars fer her, an' she's th' soize of a rooty bagy tur–rnip, or mabbe a car–rtwheel,' he says."

"That is rather strange," said the doctor dryly. "Aren't you somewhat excited, Nulty?"

"Well, mebbe!" The sergeant, with a deep breath relaxed himself, and proceeded more calmly: "Has a monkey a t'roat on him like a whale, an' c'n he swally a dimont, jist, as big as himsel', an' walk off wid it unbeknownst, an' thin swally himsel' forby an' dhrop out of th' wor–rld at wanct, loike thim moving picthures off th' shtage? Becos, af he c'n do that same, he's a wondher, an' af he cannot, the's a t'ousan' dollars in ut, an' ayther way aboot he's afther bein' a val'able craythur, whativer, an' wort' th' throuble, jist, or Oi miss me guess intirely."

It required some minutes of hard work on the doctor's part to arrive at the excited sergeant's meaning, but finally he succeeded, and was in possession of the strange tale of Mr. Emmons' loss. The sergeant had a theory, and wished Dr. Furnivall's aid in working it out. He believed that Emmons had the diamond, that the whole thing was a conspiracy between Emmons, his wife, and the two jewelers, and that Dr. Furnivall, with his hypnotism, could get at the truth of the matter in two minutes by interviewing Emmons. He based his conclusions on two facts—the impossibility of a monkey's swallowing such an enormous stone, to say nothing of the beast's miraculous disappearance, and the self-evident truth that no thief could have escaped in the circumstances as this alleged one had done. As for the first, Dr. Furnivall asked him:

"Did Emmons say how big the diamond was?"

"He did, begob—'twas wort' t'ousans of dollars!"

"Oh, I see! Because it was worth thousands it must be as big as a cartwheel?"

"Sure! Phy, me woife has wan wid twintysiven pearls set roond ut that cost $4, th' soize a pratie ball, an' phwat wud a fifty t'ousaner be loike?"

He was deeply chagrined to learn his mistake—that the value of precious stones depends on quality as well as size; that the capacities of different monkeys' throats vary as widely as those of the human family, some members of which cannot take a pill, while others can swallow a handful of swords; and that therefore it was quite within the bounds of belief that this animal had done as represented, or could do so. The second point of the sergeant's theory Dr. Furnivall admitted. But, then, what of it?

"Why should I mix up in this affair?" the doctor said. "Nothing is at stake, no innocent person is accused; it is a trivial affair, of no interest whatever to me. What is the philosophic or scientific value of the fact that a rich jeweler has lost a diamond, or has stolen one?"

The sergeant looked disappointed. He moved uneasily in his chair, and ruffled his mustache with a quick rub of his hand. Then a shrewd beam flicked into his blue eye.

"Shure, docther," he said, deprecatingly, "yez wud not lave thim say yez is bate, an' th' job is wan too much for yez!"

Dr. Furnivall regarded him tolerantly through his colored spectacles.

"Nulty," he returned, with just a hint of sharpness in his voice, "no doubt you have set many persons by the ears in your time by that sort of an argument! A 'stump yer' or a 'dare' may work with children and imbeciles, but I didn't suppose you were ass enough to think it would have any effect on me."

"B't docther! Jist luk at it, now! How th' quare woman wint oop in air—an' th' monkey, jist—phwere wes th' chanct fer him—"

"Nulty, out with it now, and no more evasions! What is the real reason why you wish me to take up this matter?"

The sergeant's face grew violently red, and he looked sheepishly at the floor.

"Well, thin, docther dear," he said slowly, "Oi knows Oi c'n kape nothing at all fr'm yez—b't—'bt t' tell th' trut', me woife is ailin' an' nades th' counthry air, an' shure Oi'm near broke, phwat wid wan thing an' anither, an' this an' that, an' I tort th' reward, or me own share of ut—"

"You should have said so at once. That adds just the touch of human interest to the case which alone makes anything worth while—"

"Will yer take it, docther?" cried Nulty, jumping up with glistening eyes. "Faith, I'll rhun out t' th' tilephone an' tell Maggie t' pack oop fer t'ree mont's in th' counthry tomorry mornin' on th' tin-twinty that laves at noon—"

"Don't get rattled again, Nulty. I thought something was wrong with you when you came in, and I am sorry to learn that it is your wife's sickness that troubles you. But say nothing until you get your money. We haven't found the diamond yet—"

Nulty curled his lip in disdain.

"As good as—as good as!" he said. "An', begob, Oi hov th' reward all spint! 'Tis something fine, Oi tell yez, docther, t' spind ut wanst before yez git ut an' wanst afther, an' thin, av yez do not git ut at all, phy, thin yez hov lost nothing, an' av yez do git ut yez c'n put in th' bank."

Dr. Furnivall, during this lucid formulation of a philosophy as old as the beginnings of poverty, was selecting an instrument or two from his surgical case and preparing an emetic. With these in his pocket he took his hat and told Nulty to lead the way to the Emmons house.

"I won't venture any theory yet, though I have the threads of one in my mind," he said as they walked along. "I know nothing whatever of the characters of these different persons who figure in the case. I have never seen any of them even, that I am aware of. The right beginning, however, is with Emmons, and if we find him at home—"

"Shure we will thot!" said the sergeant. "'Twes wid an eye fer his hours, jist, that Oi coom fer yez. Oi knows thim well. He's wid his woife this minute."

And so they found him. Dr. Furnivall talked with them both a few moments and then drew the husband aside.

"Mr. Emmons," he said, regarding him through his spectacles, "have you no theory of this matter?"

The little man stooped forward, his beady black eyes growing even smaller and more brilliantly black, and crossed his wrists over his waistband.

"I had none—but on thinking it all over I—believe I have," he answered, incisively.

"I understand that there is a reward, offered by you, of $1,000 for the recovery of the diamond."

"This is correct," he returned, in the same tone.

"No matter who is hit by the detection of the guilty person?"

"None whatever. If you are the great Dr. Furnivall, the hypnotist, who can read men's souls like an open book, you should have no need to ask that question."

"I can read no man's soul. Neither would I care to do so if I could. But I can read some things, and one of them is that you would sooner see this person of whom we both speak humiliated than any one else. In fact, you know well who has the stone, and you are irritated almost to insanity because you can't force the possessor to give it up."

Mr. Emmons bowed coldly.

"I honor your perspicacity," he said, ironically. "Perhaps if you had my reasons you would feel as I do."

"I have no doubt of it. Still, you are wrong. The whole difficulty is as much your fault as hers. Kleptomania is a disease, and should be treated as such. It sticks out all over her."

"All I want is the diamond," he said, adding quickly, "and to know how she managed the business."

"We will arrange that on one condition—"

"The $1,000?" he interrupted, with irony.

Dr. Furnivall went on:

"It is that when you have received this information and recovered the stone you will call in the physician for your wife that I shall name to you."

The ugly little man hesitated. A bright color flowed into his cheeks, as of burning anger, but he still held to his coldness of manner

"Very well; I agree—on condition that you fulfill your promise," he finally said. It was plain that he was doubtful of this alleged hypnotic power; and, indeed, he added, as Dr. Furnivall removed his spectacles and started toward Mrs. Emmons: "I think you'll find your match there."

She would not have been a promising spectacle to one who fondly looks upon softness and lovability as the distinguishing characteristics of the sex. Small, wrinkled, pettish, with nerves of fire, and a will that lay cold in her glittering little beads of eyes, unbreakable, not to be bent, and merciless as fate, she resembled her husband so strongly that one would say they were brother and sister, rather than husband and wife. But Dr. Furnivall was interested only in her disease, the indications of which he saw in her eyes and around the homely, quivering mouth and pointed chin, as well as in the shape of her head. The strength of her will would be a help to him in his hypnotism, rather than an obstacle; and with Sergeant Nulty standing a little behind her on one side of her chair, scarcely able to refrain from dancing in jubilation over the coming fruition of his hopes; and Mr. Emmons on the other side, darkly attentive, the doctor looked her in the eye and talked with her easily a moment or two about the strange robbery. And when he saw the various inevitable changes pass over her keen, hard, nervous face, surprise at first, then excitement, running swiftly into earnestness and ending in fixed introspection, he asked:

"Mrs. Emmons, where is the diamond?"

"In Bruno's stomach!" she answered, at once, in a voice like that of a deaf person who cannot hear himself speak.

"And where is Bruno?"

"In the closet."

"What closet?"

Mr. Emmons darted up to her upon this, and probably for the first time in many years, if not the first in his adult life, a look of wonder crept into his usually steady eyes. "Closet!" he repeated as one stupefied, "Closet!"

She gave him no attention, did not even see him. Her eyes were on Dr. Furnivall's, and she answered:

"The closet where I keep my things—the things I take."

"Where is it?"

"In the corner of this room, down low, in the wainscot, by the large table."

Emmons and the sergeant stared in amaze. The corner was as bare as a wall could be. There was not the slightest indication of any closet there. But Emmons, after a moment's thought, seemed satisfied and bestowed his attention again on the examination.

"It is plain now," said Dr. Furnivall to him, still holding Mrs. Emmons' eyes with his own, "how the monkey was made to disappear so suddenly, and unless you wish to hear more we will find the closet at once—"

"Let her tell the whole story," he interrupted grimly.

Dr. Furnivall therefore went on:

"Mrs. Emmons, how did it happen that the monkey should seize the diamond?"

"Why, you see, I suppose it was this way: There is a kind of bon-bon that he is very fond of, and I always hold it up for him to leap for. It is astonishing how far he can jump and how swiftly, when he sees one of them in my fingers, or indeed anywhere. They are round, and sparkling like rock candy, and I suppose he thought the diamond was one of them. So he snatched it and swallowed it. But it hurt him and he has been sick over it."

"You had no idea of his doing such a thing until your husband told you it was done?"

"No, indeed, of course not!"

Emmons' face softened the merest shade at this. He had evidently believed that in some way the theft had been premeditated.

"And when you found that he had swallowed the diamond you resolved to hide him?"

"Yes, I did not propose to have my pet cut open, or even given an emetic."

"Was that the only reason?"

"No, I wanted the diamond. Diamonds are so pretty! I always take them wherever I see them, if I can do so unobserved. I have a lot of them in the closet."

"And you made up the story of the strange woman in order to send suspicion astray?"

"Yes!"

"I think," said Dr. Furnivall to Mr. Emmons, "that that is all we want to know, isn't it? It was the description of the alleged thief's appearance that put me immediately on the track. Such a description could emanate only from a mind disordered in some way, and, considering all the circumstances, I at once suspected kleptomania."

But Mr. Emmons was already pounding the wainscot in search of the closet. When finally it was laid open it was found to be a small cavity behind the sheathing used to round the corners of the circular room, the door of which was perfectly hidden, and fitted in tightly without lock or spring. The floor was littered with many valuables, stolen by the kleptomaniac, among them a good handful of diamonds of various shapes and degrees of beauty.

Stretched in the midst of the glittering array the poor monkey lay dead, suffocated.

The diamond was recovered, and Sergeant Nulty received the reward from Dr. Furnivall, to whom alone Emmons would pay it.

THE LODGING HOUSE MYSTERY

Mrs. Foster glanced out of her kitchen window as she went to the sink for water. Up were thrown her hands, down crashed the tea kettle on the floor, with a screech of terror, she rushed from the room, and, gathering her skirts above her knees, flew up the stairs—three flights of them—with the agility of an acrobat and banged with her fists on the door of the "second floor back."

"Murder!" she screamed. "Murder!—in the next house—look—look out the winder—"

A thump of bare feet on the floor within sounded and was followed by a startled voice:

"I see her—I see her!" And the next moment the door opened hastily and a young man, clad only in undershirt and trousers, shot out and down the stairs.

"Here—gracious! You ain't going out without your clothes?" she gasped after him.

But the young man never heard her. His mind was absorbed by the terrible spectacle he had seen. He dashed down the front steps, along the sidewalk, and into the police station just around the corner.

"Murder!" he gasped. "Thirty-eight Boise street—in the yard—hurry—he's doing it now—"

There were but two officers in the room and they looked at each other. The man at the desk nodded quickly to the other, who, coatless and hatless, cried, "Come on!" to the young man, and together they raced up the street. It was raining torrents, and therefore, though it was 11 o'clock in the forenoon, few people were abroad to wonder at the singular sight of a policeman in his shirt sleeves and a man in shirt and trousers running neck and neck at the top of their speed, the officer clutching a revolver, the man's suspenders flying, his bare feet bleeding from their rough scuffling over the bricks. But some saw, and as to see was to follow, when the runners arrived at the house six or seven men and boys were close on their heels, despite the soaking downpour.

"This the place?" the officer panted.

"Yes, in the back entry."

"The gate is locked—I'll ring."

The officer ran up the front steps and sent peal after peal tumbling through the house. But there came no answer, so he climbed over the high gate, unlocked it, letting the young man in, and with him sped toward the back door, which stood wide open.

"She was right here when I saw her," said the young man as they reached the step landing. "She was covered with blood and screaming. She staggered, seeming to try to get out into the yard, but a man's hand pulled her back—I could see his coatsleeve—there!" He pointed to a gruesome daub on the door. It was the print in blood of a human hand.

The officer, his revolver ready, rushed into the entry. There was a pool of blood on the floor, and the walls were spattered, but nobody was in sight. He entered the kitchen. A pot of potatoes was boiling on the range, the fire was blazing merrily in the red-hot stove. Preparations for dinner had evidently been interrupted suddenly in their very midst. Vegetables strewed the floor, chairs and table were overturned, dishes lay broken and scattered about. A rack of freshly ironed towels were blood daubed. The dark trail led from the kitchen through the hall, where, at the foot of the stairs leading to the upper floor the carpet was saturated.

"There's nobody down here," said the policeman rapidly, "that's certain. She must be up there."

"How is it there's no blood on the stairs?" wondered the other. "The stains stop right here."

"I dunno—come on!" cried the officer, and he ran up, two steps at a leap.

Across the threshold of the front room lay the body of a woman. She was breathing faintly, and they carried her to the bed.

"They'll send help and a doctor from the station right away," said the policeman. "We'll leave her here and hunt for the man."

The house seemed to be deserted. It was a lodging-house, the young man explained. Occupied by men alone, and they were all away at work. What puzzled him was that the woman victim was not the one who ran the house, whom he knew. This woman was a stranger to him. Somebody plainly had been getting dinner ready in the kitchen, yet Mrs. Doane, the mistress, the only woman belonging on the premises, was missing, and here was this unknown female being murdered! From kitchen to garret there was not to be found another living person. What was the meaning of it?

Soon the officers from headquarters arrived and began their investigations. The woman was found to be in a critical condition, with numerous knife cuts on her face, head, hands, and arms, and a stab wound near the heart that promised to prove fatal. Delirious, moaning inarticulate phrases, the only words of which they could understand being "Oh" and "Don't," repeated over and over again, she was good looking, buxom, of 35, with black eyes and hair, dressed in a morning wrapper, and, to judge by her face, of mild and amiable disposition, though not of cultivated intellect. The room across the threshold of which they had found her lying was in some disorder, though there were no blood stains in it, except near the door where she had fallen in the endeavor, apparently, to reach the bed and lie down. Two chairs were upset, the lambrequin hung half torn from the mantel, a drawer of the dresser was open, and a lot of small articles of feminine wear, its former contents probably, littered the carpet. Otherwise the apartment was in the normal condition of a room in a third rate lodging-house, grimy, with cheap furniture, sleazy window curtains gray with use, and a worn wool carpet.

"What I can't understand is who is she?" said the young man, whose name was Miles, to Detective Mullen. "She doesn't belong in the house, and the woman that does belong here is missing?"

The detective looked at him quickly. "How do you know?"

"Why, it's Mrs. Doane—she runs the place—I know her well by sight. She's sixty years old, with gray hair, and slim and tall. And I know all the people that room here, and there isn't a woman among 'em. I never saw this one before in my life. She doesn't live here. Where could she come from?"

"Man, she was getting dinner in the kitchen!" said the detective. "Of course she belongs here!"

"Well, if she does, it's funny I've never seen her before. I'm a printer by trade, working nights, and so I sleep days—right up here," pointing. "That's my window, in the next house. I sit there every forenoon for several hours before going to bed, and I can see everything that goes on down here in the yard, and mostly in the kitchen, too. Mrs. Doane is in and out a dozen times a morning, but I never clapped eyes on any other woman around here."

"If she was merely a lodger, occupying a front room, you wouldn't be likely to, would you? What would she be doing down in the back yard? You're way off, man!"

"If you knew anything about women in lodging-houses you wouldn't say that," retorted Miles. "They are always bothering around in the kitchen, ironing and working little messes of candy, or steeping tea or gossiping. Why, they are a nuisance in a house for that very reason. In fact, that is why Mrs. Doane won't have 'em room with her. All her lodgers are men, same as lots of other places round here. And that's what gets me about this woman! Who is she? Where did she come from? And where is Mrs. Doane, the owner?"

"Hadn't you better go home and put on your clothes?" said the detective somewhat sharply. He felt competent to handle the case— at any rate he did not relish instruction coming from this inferior looking person in trousers and undershirt.

"Well, perhaps I had," returned Miles, who in the excitement had forgotten how nearly naked he was. "But, anyway," he added as he started for the door, "you'd better see Mrs. Foster, in the next house. She knows all about things here, and perhaps can tell you something. Besides, she saw the murder going on before I did. Maybe she saw the man that did it."

"I'll go in there in a moment," the detective replied; and as the young fellow departed he began a thorough investigation of the victim's room, presently pulling from beneath the sofa a light colored overcoat stained and daubed with blood all up the front and over the arms.

"Aha! What's this?" he muttered. He searched the pockets and drew out a blood stained knife, such as butchers in provision stores use for light work, and a small leather change purse containing a few cents and a key. On trial the key was found to fit the lock on the front door of the house. The coat was in fairly good condition, of ordinary ready made structure and material, but there was no mark on it, either of maker or owner, by which it might be identified.

"It is plain now how she got up the stairs without leaving any blood on them," he said to his partner detective, Price. "He carried her in his arms and got the whole of it on his coat."

"Then how is it that there's blood up here in the bathroom and farther down the hall?" answered Price. "What do you calculate happened, anyway?"

"Why," returned Mullen, "I can't say yet. Guess we better see that woman in the next house before going on. She saw the thing first, the printer says, and knows the people here."

So Mullen, leaving his partner at the scene of the tragedy, went in and questioned Mrs. Foster.

"No, I don't know the woman," that lady responded. She was lying on a sofa in her parlor, having been nearly prostrated by what she had seen of the crime. "Mrs. Doane runs the house, and her husband works on water wheels—goes all around the country. She has no women lodgers, nor I don't either. Men is the least trouble. I'd ruther—"

"When did you first see this woman?"

"I was looking out the winder into their back yard, standing at the sink. The sash was down a little at the top, and I heard somebody scream, I thought, but couldn't be sure, it was raining so, and making such a noise, the water running down the spout and over the bricks to the sewer. The voice sounded kind of faint, too. But I looked again, and just then I saw her come out the door—it was wide open—and stagger against the railing, and she screamed again. It wasn't a scream that said anything. She didn't say any words that I could hear, but just gave a terrible frightened screech. Her face was all bloody. I was scared into conniption fits. I didn't have anybody in the house but Mr. Miles, that sleeps here days, and his winder is on the back, over their yard, so I run up and knocked on his door and told him to look out into the next yard, for there was murder going on. He was just going to bed, and he jumped up and saw her down there, and he says a man was pulling her back into the entry—he didn't see him himself, only his hand and his arm. But I didn't see any more than I've told you. Mr. Miles run out, and I thought he was going into the place to save the woman, but he didn't. He skipped for the police station and got a policeman. I didn't know that till afterward. I just come and laid down here sick. It was a terrible sight, and I couldn't stand it to look out again."

"Have you any notion where Mrs. Doane can be?"

"No, I ain't. I ain't seen her since yesterday forenoon. She was around then, all right, same as ever."

"And you never saw this other—this victim—before?"

"Never! Who she is beats me. Mrs. Doane won't have a woman in the house—not to live, I mean. Of course she has folks, women folks, and they come to visit her sometimes, but this ain't none of 'em. I've seen 'em all, and know 'em all, and they are all different looking from this stranger."

"Do you know the address of any of her relatives?"

"Yes, two or three of 'em." She gave them to him and he set them down in his book. Then he returned to his partner.

"I've figured it out about this way," he said to him. "Whoever the man and woman are, they don't belong here, and they made way with Mrs. Doane, and then disagreed over the loot. There's no money in the house, that's sure. We've looked everywhere but in the cellar. Nobody has been down there yet, and I guess, we'll find the landlady there, when we've knocked off that almighty big lock on the door. Did you notice it? It's the old fashioned kind, on the outside the door, made to stand pounding with sledge hammers.

We can't find the key to it, and that's why we—but don't hurry! Hold on a minute—"

"If she's locked up in the cellar the best thing we can do is to let her out, ain't it? Then she can tell us all about it."

"Not about the cutting, because it was done after she was tied up and chucked down cellar—"

"How do you explain it that this woman was wearing a wrapper, if she doesn't belong here?"

"Well, that's so!" He was puzzled over this. But not for long. "We can let that go," he said. "Later is time enough for that."

"I am going to get into that cellar," interrupted Price, and hurried to the door.

This was not as difficult a task as he had expected, for in fact he found that it was not locked at all. The knob turned hard, the works being rusty, no more than that; and in a moment he was calling down the stairs:

"Mrs. Doane! Are you down there, Mrs. Doane? Is anybody down there?"

It was pitch dark below, and receiving no answer he lighted a lamp which he found on the kitchen mantel and descended into the black depths. There were several partitions—for laundry, furnace room, coal bins, and ash boxes, and he searched all the compartments, but in vain. Nobody was there.

"That knocks out your theory," he grumbled to his partner.

"Not by a jugful!—not the theory, only that part of it. They've put her somewhere else. That's all. But you can bet it's as I say. Now, look at it this way: A man and woman come here on some trumped-up business, say looking for a room. They know Mrs. Doane is alone and that she has money—the rent money anyway, if no more, for this is the last day of the month—"

"People pay from the date they moved in, not always on the first—"

"Never mind. You listen! Say that as soon as they get in the man grabs Mrs. Doane and gives her chloroform. Then the two goes through the house—it's cleaned out, there's no valuables in it, anyway, you can see that—"

"How many valuables would you expect to find in a house of this sort?"

"We are only on a theory. Of course, we can't get everything right all at once. You ought to know that. This is the only way I can explain the crime. Well, they loot the place. Mrs. Doane has dinner under way, and they, knowing the custom of the house, are sure nobody will interrupt them, so they decide to eat here. The woman hunts up one of Mrs. Doane's wrappers to work around the kitchen in, and somehow they fall out with each other, probably over the loot, and—"

At this instant the bell tinkled feebly. Both detectives started for the door. There stood a youth with a scared look on his face, who said:

"I've just heard what has happened here, and I thought I'd tell what I know."

"Come in!" they exclaimed together, and he entered, hat in hand, glancing fearfully around.

"Now, then, what do you know about it?" asked Mullen, eyeing him so sharply that he was almost too much frightened to speak. He glanced back at the door as if he repented and wished he had stayed away. However, he finally mustered up courage to say:

"I room across the street. I saw Frank Leavitt, who boards here, come home about half past 10, and go out again soon after. I didn't think anything of it at the time, of course, though he never comes here till 6 o'clock—that is, I didn't think much of it. But I thought a little, because when he came in he was wearing his overcoat and when he went out he had left it behind, though it was raining hard and it seemed as if he would need it more than ever. But he had an umbrella—"

"The coat!" exclaimed Price, glancing at Mullen. The latter, who had found the coat under the sofa in the room where the victim lay, frowned silence to his partner and motioned the boy to go on.

"I don't think anybody else can have come into the house this forenoon, that's all. I sit at the window studying my lessons, and can see everybody that goes into any of the houses along on this side for quite a distance. I can even hear the door shut here."

"Who is this Frank Leavitt?" asked Mullen.

"He's a motorman on the elevated."

"Wasn't there a woman with him?"

"No, he was alone."

"How long did he stay in the house?"

"Only a few minutes—not more than ten or so, I should say."

"Have you ever seen a woman around here—except Mrs. Doane?"

"No, sir, never."

"I guess we need Leavitt," said Mullen. "Give me your address, young feller, and I'll set it down. We shall want you again."

Not many minutes were required to find the young motorman. They took him from his car as he drove it into the barn.

"Murder!" he cried, growing pale. "I know nothing of it—what do you mean—who's murdered?"

"That's what we want to find out," answered Mullen. "It is a woman at 38 Boise street."

"What! Why, that's where I room! Is it Mrs. Doane?"

"No, somebody else—it was done at about 11 o'clock this morning."

"Good God! Why I must have been in the house myself at that time, or near it."

He was warned, according to law, that what he should say might be used against him. He paid no attention to the warning, but went on excitedly, as they rode toward the station, giving an account of his forenoon. He said that he left his car at 10 o'clock on his regular lay-off of two hours, and as he was going to the theater with his girl that evening, he went home to change his clothes and leave his overcoat, which was not good enough to wear to the theater. He put on his best suit because he was to go from his car directly to the playhouse, and he had a rubber coat at the barn which he could wear over it during his trips, the day being rainy. He saw not a soul in the house while there, heard no noise, not even any sounds of work down in the kitchen. He thought nothing of that. The place was practically empty during the day always. He knew of no other woman lodger—was sure there was none, there never had been, and he could tell the names of all the people in the house and what rooms they occupied. The first floor front, where the strange woman lay, was Mrs. Doane's. And all the rooms were let. There were no vacant ones. He had no notion who the newcomer could be.

That was the story he told. He was perfectly straightforward and lucid in his speech, and grew calm after his first excitement, seeming to feel more wonder that he should be concerned in such a case than fear for himself.

In the meantime the victim of the assault had recovered sufficiently to be removed to the hospital. Though she was able to speak, she refused to give any account of herself—would not tell how she happened to be in the house, where she lived, who had stabbed her, or who she was, saying that she only wished to be left alone to die in peace. When, later, they informed her that her assailant had been captured and was now in a cell awaiting the outcome of her injuries, she showed some interest.

"Don't hurt him," she said. "He didn't know what he was doing."

When informed that he would be convicted of murder if she died, and be compelled to suffer death himself, she appeared greatly disturbed, and said:

"But I don't want that—I won't testify against him. They can't hurt him then, can they?" They replied that they certainly could and would. Therefore, if there were any extenuating circumstances she would better mention them. She asked then how they knew it was he and how they captured him. So the story was begun; but before ten words of it had been spoken she gasped, cried out something unintelligible, and fainted. When she regained consciousness she refused to say another word about the case. All their efforts to gain some information from her were futile, and finally they were obliged to leave her in the peace she desired.

The young lady stepped forward timidly as Dr. Furnivall rose to receive her.

"Are you Dr. Furnivall, sir, the great hypnotist?" she asked, with a stare in her light gray eyes partaking of both fright and appeal.

"I am Dr. Furnivall," he answered. "Will you be seated, Miss—"

"My name is Johnson, Esther Johnson, sir," she said, sitting on the edge of a chair, "and I came to ask you if—if—" She paused, blushing, and drew forth a small roll of bills. "I have only seven dollars, sir," she continued, holding it tentatively toward him, while the appeal in her eyes grew, "but if that isn't enough I can pay you more later—"

There she stopped and could get no further. The tears began to roll down her cheeks. She was a pretty, earnest looking girl of eighteen or nineteen, plainly American born, of Scandinavian parentage, slight of form, and was dressed in good taste, very inexpensively. She plainly had the faculty of making a little money go a great way. Dr. Furnivall regarded her approvingly through his colored spectacles.

"Whether or not seven dollars are enough will depend on what you wish in return for them," he smiled.

She brightened up at once, encouraged by his friendly manner.

"I have heard so much about your—your making people speak the truth," she said, forgetting herself now in her errand and becoming natural and earnest. "I am in great trouble through a woman that will not tell what is right. My friend—he is a young man—we shall marry some time—and he is in jail because they say he stabbed a woman. And she says he did, too, but he did not, and he never saw the woman before they took him to the hospital where she is sick. And she said, 'This is the man!' And she will not change that saying. So I came to ask you, sir, to make her change it and tell the truth. Then they will let him out of jail. But I have not much money. My father and mother laughed when I told what I was going to do. 'Child,' they said, 'the great doctor will want more money for doing that thing than you will ever have in all your life.' But I said, 'Not so, because it is right to make her tell the truth, and it is a good action. He will not charge too much for doing it.'"

She laid the little roll of bills on the table and smiled at him in perfect confidence.

"Is your friend's name Frank Leavitt?" he asked, gently.

"Oh, yes, doctor," she cried, eagerly. "Do you know him? If you do you are sure he could not do such a thing as that. He would not hurt anybody. Oh no! He is good and kind and very handsome!"

She uttered the last adjective as if it were conclusive proof of his innocence.

"I don't know him, no," answered the doctor gravely. "But I have read about the case in the papers. So they took him to the hospital and she identified him? Did she say what he did it for, and how he did it?"

"She said only, 'That is the man!' Not another word would she speak. And they took him back to the jail, and he will have to die unless you, sir, will make her take those words back and say what is true."

"Have they found out who the woman is?"

"No, sir. She will say nothing, and they can't find out. They do not know how she came there in the house. And Mrs. Doane is not found—nobody knows where she is. It is very strange. I do not understand any of it, only he did not do it; it is foolish to think so. How could he, when we are going to get married sometime? It is impossible, and I would laugh at it if I did not feel so frightened of the jail where he is."

The eyes grew moist again and resumed their appeal. The doctor handed her back the money.

"I don't accept pay in this way," he said. "But," he hastened to add, seeing her look of alarm, "I'll call on the woman, and if I can do you any good I will let you know how to make it right with me. And I'll go immediately. Will that satisfy you?"

"Oh, I thank you so much, doctor!" she cried, flushing with happiness. "Now I will go home and laugh at my mother and father, who said you would not do it. And how can I know at once what she says—"

"Do not think any more about it until morning," he advised her. He knew that the matter would be settled one way or the other in a few minutes, providing the mysterious woman was awake and able to talk, but he was far from sure how it would turn out, and did not wish to raise a hope in her breast that might prove futile.

A quarter of an hour later, in company with one of the hospital doctors, a policeman, and a justice of the peace, he was standing at the bedside of the victim of the assault. Looking at her at first through his spectacles, he asked:

"Madam, will you tell me your name?" She shook her head wearily.

"I only wish to be left alone," she answered.

"But other people—they have rights, haven't they? When one is in trouble wouldn't you even speak a word in order to relieve him? Think of that young man and his sweetheart! Do you still assert that he is the person who attacked you?"

"Yes." She said it coldly, and with a flash of her black eyes despite her weakness.

"I don't understand why you were so tender of him when they told you he had been caught, and yet now show so much animosity towards him."

She gazed obdurately up at him and said nothing. He then removed his spectacles and looked her in the eye.

"Tell me now," he said, "who assaulted you?"

Her eyes remained a moment in repose. Suddenly they sprang to life, dilating as with surprise, then perplexity shone there briefly, passing into earnestness and finally into concentrated introspection; and she answered in a wooden voice:

"John Merrill!"

"Who is John Merrill?"

"The man I love!"

"Yes, but what does he do?"

"He is a hypnotist."

"Where is he to be found?"

"I don't know. I suppose he has run away."

"What is your name?"

"Ella Frost."

"Where do you live?"

"In Middleton."

"How happened you to be at Mrs. Doane's?"

"I came to tell her that her husband had met with an accident. He was at her sister's in Middleton and wanted her to go there at once. It was late at night, just in time for the 10:45 train, and she asked me to stay in the house for a day or two and take care of the rooms. I said I would, and she left me in charge, for she knew me."

"Now tell us how he came to assault you."

"Mrs. Doane let him sleep on the folding-bed in the parlor that night. Along in the forenoon I had a terrible headache, and I went up to my room and lay down on the bed, and John gave me a hypnotic treatment for it. He had often done this. It never did me any good, but it pleased him to think he could control me and put me asleep, so I always played that I was sleeping, and that his treatment cured me. But I never was affected in the least. When he believed I was under control he walked over to the bureau and began to open the drawers. I had taken all my money, about $1,200, out of the bank in Middleton to bring to the city, and he knew I had it. I opened my eyes and watched him. I knew he was searching for it, still I couldn't believe it. Just as he found it he turned and saw me looking at him, and his face grew so terrible that I was scared and ran from the room. He chased me, and when we got into the kitchen he grabbed me, and pulled me toward the table where the butcher knife was, and caught it up and tried to stab me, but I dodged and fought, getting cut all over my face and hands. I tried to get outdoors, but he pulled me back, and I ran again through the hall, but fell at the foot of the stairs. There was an overcoat hanging on the halltree and he put it on, and then took me bodily in his arms up to the bathroom, and left me there. I suppose he thought he had finished me, but I came to and started for my room. That is all about it. Only, I don't see why he did it. I would have given him the money willingly if I had known he wanted it. Now he has done such a terrible thing I want to die. I don't care what becomes of me."

"You thought to shield him by accusing the other man?"

"Yes. I fainted with joy when I found they had got the wrong man."

Dr. Furnivall turned to the policeman.

"Go get a warrant for John Merrill, hypnotist. He will be exhibiting this evening in Allie's hall, where he causes a woman to hang suspended on nothing in the air. That is the kind he is!"

It was Frank Leavitt himself who, a little later, was the bearer of the joyous news of his release and exoneration to his sweetheart.

The hypnotist was arrested that evening and the money was found on his person. He was given fifteen years. The woman recovered, and to this day carries flowers and dainties to the man who tried to murder her.

THE SPIRIT CLUB

Through his colored spectacles Dr. Furnivall regarded the excited man before him calmly.

"Dr. Gerrish has already consulted me about your wife's remarkable case," he said, "so I know the salient points of it. But, of course, before seeing her I should be glad to learn its history from you, as you suggest. But be brief, for—"

His companion put up his, hand suddenly. A series of screams, laden with the mortal terror of a human being, burst upon them from somewhere above, seeming to fill to its farthest reaches the lofty and splendid hall in which the two were standing. There was but one light visible among the shadows, which, as it gleamed softly here and there on a marble statue, scintillated evilly on some gilded picture frame, or sullenly burned on a polished bit of ancient armor, served scarcely more than to exaggerate the somber gloom of the place and amplify in the imagination its already huge dimensions. In such vague, mysterious surroundings the screams, startling enough in themselves, were awesome, and with a cold shudder Mr. Harish hastily drew the doctor into one of the reception-rooms and switched on the lights.

"She has been that way at intervals for months," he whispered excitedly. He was a fresh looking man of fifty, of light complexion and regular features, in whose face the dominant expressions were those of the acumen and reserved force which we associate with the highly successful captain of industry. The gray eyes held the possibility of a merciless glitter in their uncompromising depths, the narrow brow seemed always just about to gather in a frown, the lips beneath the thin, bristly brown mustache were firm to rigidity, and the chin, square and solid, was relieved from an appearance of downright brutality only by a vertical cleft in the middle, resembling an overgrown dimple. Some slight suggestions of softness lay in that, and, of all his features, in that alone. But at this moment it was evident, despite his normal atmosphere of impassivity, that he maintained a fair degree of composure only by great effort of will, and as he spoke he sank heavily into a chair as if in urgent need of its support for his trembling body.

"It won't take two minutes to tell you what I wish to," he continued, in a low, hurried voice, "and it seems necessary to your understanding of the case. It is as a hypnotist only that you can be of service here. Medicine we have tried in vain. The trouble began one night last summer. She had been ailing for some time, and we couldn't find out what the matter was, except that it was of a nervous nature, when on this night she startled me out of a sound sleep by screaming suddenly. I thought at first that it must be an attack of nightmare, and began to shake her; but she shrieked louder than ever. So I sprang up and turned on the lights. Then I saw that she was cowering down in bed, with staring eyes, screaming as you have just heard her doing and flinging her arms about over her head as I have seen boys fighting bees. When the light flashed up she threw me a terrified look and dived under the bedclothes, still fighting and shrieking. It was terrible, terrible! To be afraid of *me*—"

"What explanation did she make—then or afterward? Any?"

"Only that she was frightened and felt a pain, as if a nail had been driven into her brain. When the doctor came he pronounced it a case of clavus hystericus—nothing so very serious, he said. But it has proved serious enough. Two or three nights out of every week since then she has had one of these spells. I have called in the most famous physicians. No use." He shook his head despondently. "Though all of them say the same things about the disease and prescribe much the same treatment, she doesn't improve. They do not reach the malady, whatever it is. It was Dr. Gerrish who told me of you and your hypnotic power, which he said was marvelous, and advised me to call you. He said he was convinced that at bottom the trouble was mental rather than physical, and that if a cure were possible you were the man to work it."

"Does she talk with you freely about her case?"

"Ah, that is one of the incomprehensible mysteries!" he cried, rising excitedly and pacing a few steps rapidly back and forth. Then he stopped with his hand on the doctor's shoulder. "She won't talk about it with anybody," he whispered. "She altogether shuns the subject; will not listen to a word of it. It is the strangest thing in the world. The most that can be drawn from her is a 'no' or a 'yes' in answer to some insistent questions put by the doctor who happens to be in attendance. But me—she seems afraid of me! She shrinks whenever I approach her. I—I can't understand it. Why, Dr. Furnivall, I love her. She is all I care for on earth. She has always looked to me for everything. Our married life has been ideal, but now—now—"

He broke off suddenly. In order to hide an emotion of which he was apparently ashamed he presented his back to the doctor, and, motioning over his shoulder for him to follow, mounted the wide staircase to the floor above, without another word.

The doctor found the sickroom, a large and magnificently appointed chamber, blazing in the splendors of a cluster of electric lights which depended from the ceiling in the center. In answer to his questioning look Mr. Harish whispered:

"She insists on that. The least sign of darkness frightens her, even although she tries to keep her head under the bedclothes, as you see now. It is strange. She must have either full sunshine or those lights. I don't dare to go in with you. I'll wait out here."

A trained nurse and a helper were in the room, whom the doctor, after a few words with them, motioned to leave him alone with the patient. Then, removing his glasses, he advanced to the sumptuous bed, in which he could see the outlines of a human form beneath the coverings, which rose and fell slightly with the spasmodic breathing of the sufferer. The screams had ceased, and the only sound to be heard was the melodious ticking of a small gold cased clock on the mantel.

"Mrs. Harish!" he said, touching the counterpane where it was drawn smoothly over the bowed head.

She sprang up with a low cry. He caught the gleam of a white, pretty face, with lines of weakness around the mouth, a pair of blue eyes, the normal expression of which must be extreme mildness, but which were now fixed on him in a glare of fright, and a tangle of blond hair. Then she turned frantically and sought to crawl farther down into the bed, but he put out his hand quickly, gently restraining her.

"They can't hurt you any more," he said.

"Who? What do you mean? What do you know about them?"

Her voice was quavering and high, and, flashing a swift, scared look at him, she tore at his supporting arm with her hands. "Let me alone! Oh, let me alone, or I shall die!" she gasped.

"I know all about them. I have met and overcome them more than once before this, and I can do as much for you now." He held her as gently as he might, but firmly, and began moving around so that he could gaze into her eyes. "I am here to help you," he continued when he had accomplished this. "You are suffering persecution; a persecution, too, that is easily stopped. I will stop it for you. Look at me, Mrs. Harish! Do you know me?"

His gaze held her. The staring eyes grew less wild, a momentary wonder crept into them, then their natural mildness reasserted itself, and finally this mildness was replaced by a rapt fixity of introspection. With a sigh of relief she put her hand into his, saying:

"You are a physician, I suppose. No, I don't know you. But I feel better. Thank you."

He withdrew his arm, and, still holding her eyes steadily, arranged the pillows so that she could recline comfortably, facing him as he sat at the bedside.

"Now, Mrs. Harish," he said, "carry your mind back to the night on which you were first seized with these attacks. Why did you scream?"

"The room was full of spirits who were beating me with clubs," she answered, without emotion.

"Are you what is called a spiritualist?"

"No; but my husband is, and he wishes me to believe, too; and these spirits, I have always thought, beat me for my obstinacy."

"Did anybody ever tell you that they would do so?"

"No; but I have heard of such things. Nobody knows anything about their coming to me. I have never dared tell even my husband. I had endured everything since Mr. Jellipherson died. For a long time I was horribly tormented, and at last, when he himself came to me in the dead of night at the head of a host of frightful shapes, all of them armed with clubs just like his, I could not stand it any longer. I think I lost my mind—"

"One moment. Who is Mr. Jellipherson? Begin at the beginning and tell me all about it."

"Mr. Jellipherson was my husband's friend—a spiritualist. He had an uncanny look and a harsh, rasping voice that made me shiver with fear whenever I heard it. I could not bear him, and used to hide from him when he came here, as he often did. He brought mediums, who got messages from the spirit world, and that frightened me. I could not endure to think of being surrounded by an army of invisible shapes who were watching me, influencing me, knowing all my most secret and sacred thoughts. I cannot tell you how the fancy of such things preyed on my mind. It was maddening even to hear them talked about. But I loved my husband, and, knowing that he believed, and most earnestly wished to continue doing so, I would not pain him by confiding my trouble to him. It might estrange us; and, besides, something—the spirits, I thought—prevented me from speaking of them to anybody. So I hid my fright and pretended that I had no objections to the meetings; that I found them merely amusing.

"But Mr. Jellipherson saw my antipathy and resented it, not openly, but in various covert ways. Once he had a toy club made of some rare wood, inlaid with jewels, and gave it to Mr. Harish for a watch charm, telling him it should typify his spiritual attitude. It was no use, he said, looking at me, to try to talk sense to unbelievers.

People were so stupid that the only efficient argument was a good club. With that, he said, one could silence opposition by knocking brains out, even if one could not convince by knocking brains in. Though this was said jestingly, it seemed very wicked to me. I knew he half meant it. My own creed was love. I said nothing, but it made me wretched, for I saw that my husband agreed with his friend in his aggressiveness rather than with me. It was as if a something of evil growth had been planted between us by Mr. Jellipherson, and I dreaded him more than ever. Then one evening, during a discussion, Mr. Jellipherson, who was nearly seventy, solemnly promised that if he should die before my husband, which he was likely to do, he would prove indubitably to him and the world that a dead man's spirit can return to earth. In what manner he should do it he could not tell, but it should be in a way that must destroy all doubt forever. And that promise was the real beginning of my trouble. I saw that he really believed, and somehow it made me believe, too. From that day I began to fancy shapes in the air, hear ghostly whispers, and feel the presence of evil spirits crowding me in my room, not only at night, but sometimes in the daytime as well. My health suffered, and soon we went abroad for change of climate. Scarcely had we arrived in Paris when we received a letter from home informing us of Mr. Jellipherson's death, and, more than that, that his last words had been a message to Mr. Harish telling him he would surely keep his promise. Then, to cap the climax of horrors, the toy club disappeared from my husband's watch chain!

"What I began to suffer then no words can describe. It was the spirit of the dead man that had removed the club, that was certain; we agreed on that, and all that had gone before was as nothing. But I still managed to conceal my fright from Mr. Harish. For two weeks we remained in the hotel, never ceasing to search for the lost club, expecting all the time we knew not what, when one day my husband in great excitement burst in upon me with an open letter in one hand and the little club in the other. The letter was dated and postmarked 'New York.' It was this—every queer word of it is burned into my brain:

"'My Dear Harish: It was me that got your club with my spirit hand, and it's me sending it back to you to prove what I promised. Now do you believe and know? Because you got to, and can't help it. Go to the medium that sends you this, for you ain't strong enough to meet me in the spirit world yet, but he is, and I will tell you many strange and glorious things through this great medium. Don't mind this grammar. There ain't none here; we have greater things to think of.' The note was signed, 'Yours in the spirit world, Jellipherson.' Below was the medium's address, with an explanation by him of the conditions under which the message was received, and an urgent invitation to Mr. Harish to call upon him.

"There was but one possible meaning to all this now. Mr. Jellipherson had kept his word! It was proved beyond all doubt. Nobody but we three had ever known of the promise, of the gift of the club, or of its strange loss. And it was returned to us from America only two weeks after having disappeared in Paris! Perhaps that man even at that moment was watching me, close at hand in the air, hovering, malevolent, on the point of revealing himself to me in some unearthly shape! How I controlled myself is a constant surprise to me, but I did so; and, seeing that Mr. Harish was in a fever of desire to consult the medium, I proposed that we return to New York in order that he might have his wish. I felt better at home, I told him, than anywhere else; and I knew I should feel safer. So we came back. Mr. Harish hastened at once to the medium, and was more than satisfied. He told him many things which nobody in the world or out of it knew, except Mr. Jellipherson. Still, I made no sign of the torments I experienced. I managed to refrain from shrieking out as my husband gave me these positive proofs, but from then on I grew worse and worse. The slightest noise sent me nearly into hysterics. I saw plainer than ever horrible shapes in the air. They came to me and gibbered, making threatening gestures, leering at me, and touching me with their shadowy fingers; and finally, when one night Mr. Jellipherson himself appeared, as I had always known he would do, at the head of a legion of others like him, all of them with great clubs after the pattern of the toy one, and began to beat me, I knew I must give up. I could suffer no longer in silence. Something in my brain snapped, a sharp pain pierced my head, and at the top of my voice I screamed and hid beneath the bedclothes. But they followed me even there, and continued to beat me. They follow me always now at night, so that in the morning I am literally covered with black and blue spots from their clubs. See! My body is like that all over."

She bared her arms to the shoulder, holding them up pitifully for his inspection. They were beautiful arms, rounded, white, perfect. He was not obliged to remove his eyes from her own in order to see that, of the bruises mentioned, there was no trace throughout their lovely length!

"And you never told your husband a word of all this?" he asked, evenly.

"No. I could not. The subject distracts me. I have tried to speak, but the spirits prevent me. All I have been able to do is to try to call his attention to the bruises by showing him my arms; but he does not even see them. I don't understand it. It makes me afraid of him. It is as if he were against me, on their side, not on mine, and refused to accept any evidence of their hostility to me—would resent my accusing them of this thing."

He arose and rearranged the pillows. "That is enough, Mrs. Harish," he said. "Lie comfortably down again and free your mind of all uneasiness. You shall never be troubled in this way any more. The persecution shall be stopped at once. I am going to bring you a visitor, and, when he comes in you must not cover your head, but, on the contrary, you must listen to every word that passes between him and me. Will you do this?"

"But you are not going to leave me alone? Doctor, I can't—"

He was not holding her eyes now, and she started up in fright.

"No," he reassured her; "you shall have all the company you want, and all the light. Feel no fear whatever. I know just what to do in this matter, and from this moment you are safe."

He called in the nurses, and, after giving them his instructions, sought Mr. Harish, who was in the hall. At sight of the doctor he ran forward eagerly.

"I heard her voice," he whispered. "It is wonderful that you could get her to speak. What did she say? Can you do anything for her?"

Without a word Dr. Furnivall led the way down stairs to the reception-room. Here he resumed his colored spectacles, motioning his companion to sit facing him.

"Mr. Harish," he said, "I can certainly restore your wife to sanity and health, but only on condition that you aid me, at no matter what cost to your sentiments or hopes or even beliefs."

"I—I don't understand," he faltered anxiously. "Certainly," he continued, "I would do anything in the world for my wife, and as for beliefs, how can one change them? Proof is necessarily convincing, and—"

"It is proof that I am going to give you," the doctor interrupted. "I am merely providing against any shock you may receive in that proof. I might proceed without letting you know what I propose, but as your aid is necessary, I will not ask it of you without warning you of the results in advance. Mrs. Harish is suffering from a not extremely rare kind of delusion regarding the spirits of the dead, and in order to restore her to sanity and health, and make the cure permanent I shall be obliged to convince not only her, but you, of a certain truth which will startle you. It is for this that I wish to prepare you."

"I don't think anything would shock me that will cure my wife," said Mr. Harish, with a touch of resentment in his tones. "And my mind is certainly open to conviction as much as any man's. Proof is all I want, of anything. If it is spiritualism you are hitting at," he went on, rising in sudden excitement, "if you can bring stronger proofs against it than I have for it I'll drop it at once, I promise you. But you can't do it. I know! I know by proofs so perfect that even you, if you only dreamed of them, would be as strong in the faith as I am."

Dr. Furnivall proceeded imperturbably:

"In every walk of life, in every art, profession, science, trade, religion, or society there are some persons who are wise in their way, and some foolish; some honest and sincere, others dishonest and insincere. In most cases it naturally happens that, by outsiders, the class is judged by the lower ranks, by the fools or impostors, rather than by the true disciples, for it is they with whom the outsiders come most in contact, and hear most about. And it is the foolish or the evil, not the wise and good, that the uncultivated delight in spreading, because of their superior qualities of excitement. In spiritualism as in everything these ranks exist of course. But it is not in spiritualism that I am interested now, whether it be true or false, good or bad, or indifferent. What I am intent upon is to cure Mrs. Harish, and as you are sure to be staggered by the very medicine that will effect that cure, I think it right to prepare you for it, rather than to lead you unconsciously on to it."

Mr. Harish seized his hand.

"Forgive me, doctor," he said contritely. "I am scarcely myself. I don't know how it is, but that subject always irritates me out of my normal state. The thing seems so plain and indisputable to me, and its opponents are so obtuse and unconvincible! I thought you were an enemy at first, but I see you are not. Come, tell me what to do. I'll follow your directions to the letter. Shock out of me whatever you will, only save her!"

"That is more like it. Now we can start understandingly. It is all very simple and easily arranged. In the first place it is necessary for me to convince you not only of my ability to hypnotize a man, but also that in doing so I use no influence upon him except to draw from him the truth of the matters about which I question him. I put no thoughts, and can put no thoughts, into his mind, but can and do compel him to speak the true thought which is already in his mind. Do you follow me?"

"That is not the usual notion of what hypnotism is," said Mr. Harish interestedly.

"No, it is not," returned Dr. Furnivall dryly. "It is my notion, and since it is with my notion that we have to do just now, that is the one we will consider. I will tell you the secret of it in two words, as the French say. It is important that you should understand it. It is simply this: A man of good intelligence who will, instead of pursuing mere ends, mere results, as is the usual way of men; who will bend all his efforts upon abstract truth regardless of private gain; who is unbiased by expediency, driven neither by debt nor credit, nor friends, nor foes, nor ignominy nor fame, nor riches nor poverty, must set up in his body a flow of forces unknown to and undreamed of by the ordinary human being. This is at once believable to any good physician, for we all of us know that the thoughts of the mind influence the body more or less, and that the longer or the stronger a certain thought is held and dwelt upon the more pronounced are its effects on the body containing it, especially in the more mobile parts, as the face and eyes. Fear shows there at once, and so do anger and joy and pain and weakness and vigor, and so forth; and any thought persisted in for a sufficient length of time will result in a settled change of appearance there. The eyes, when normal, are the most sensitive, most mobile, most expressive register of the owner's thought that he possesses. It is there probably that every thought of our minds finds its surest and quickest expression. Consequently, to hold continually to the desire and thought of pure, unadulterated truth, never to be swayed from that stand by any possible consideration, is to evolve an eye altogether different from that of the ordinary man, who is continually sacrificing truth to expediency. In fact, as I have learned by research and experiment, an eye so formed becomes, for every human being who looks into it, a sort of physical-mental magnet, drawing from him, even though he tries with all his powers to resist, such truth as he has in him on the subject suggested to him at the moment. He couldn't lie to save his life. That is the kind of hypnotism I possess. Does it seem plain to you? And is it reasonable?"

Mr. Harish, for the first time since the interview began, so far forgot his troubles, in his interest, as to smile.

"I think the theory is first rate," he said, "but can you declare that, in the midst of all your professional cares, from your early struggles onward, up to the famous position you have made for yourself, to say nothing of the necessity of expediency in your practice today, you have held to the pursuit of abstract truth as strongly as all that?"

"Does it seem so impossible?"

"To me, yes, I confess it does," Mr. Harish returned somewhat dryly. "I am certain that in my own case six months' adherence to abstract truth, as opposed to expediency, would ruin me outright. And I must believe it is the same with all of us. I am as upright as anybody, and I feel obliged to think that other people's methods, if they are successful, do not differ materially from my own. In fact, I know they do not."

"That is, you would rather see the eyes and experience their quality than to consider a mere theory about them?"

"Well, yes." Mr. Harish spoke with polite reluctance. "I do not question your theory," he added hastily. "It seems logical and reasonable. But to practice it! If it can be carried out; if any man can succeed as you have done amid all this hurly-burly and wild scramble for dollars, still maintaining a constant desire for the abstract truth of every one of his transactions, refusing even to think of expediency as opposed to that truth, why, then I—I should indeed be glad to receive some proof of the fact that could not be disputed."

"And nothing but that sort of proof would satisfy you?"

"I think not."

He looked curiously into the thick colored spectacles, but could see only an outline of the eyes behind them.

"I wear these glasses," said Dr. Furnivall, observing the scrutiny, "whenever I do not wish to pry into a man's mind and force him to say what he would rather keep to himself. In fact, I wear them always on ordinary occasions, for without them I could not help hypnotizing everybody who should look into my eyes, even despite myself."

As he spoke he removed the disfiguring disks, wiped them carefully, and slipped them into his pocket. Mr. Harish started nervously. But he immediately controlled himself, sitting with a half smile around his mouth.

"I am going to give you the indisputable proof you require," said Dr. Furnivall, gazing him steadily in the eye. "Is there anything in your mind that you would tell nobody, something that wild horses could not draw from you?"

"I don't know. Maybe there is."

"Well, you are going to tell it to me. Not only that, but you will write it down, so that you may be absolutely convinced that you have told it. Will that satisfy you that I do not put anything into a man's mind, but simply draw out a truth already in it? It is necessary for you to comprehend this distinction."

He passed a pencil and a leaf torn from his notebook to Mr. Harish.

The gentleman took these smilingly, but the steely gleam that one always suspected to be lying asleep awaiting occasion in his gray eyes leaped to alert life, the chin grew granite like and squarer than ever, the body stiffened, the breath came hard. He was nerving himself for the trial.

"Go ahead," he said, grimly. "I don't know the game, nor what you're after, but—go ahead."

"The game is to cure your wife. And what I am after is to give you a sample of the medicine that will do it. For you are a man who will believe in nothing without material proofs, and, once having been given what you, in your finite, fallible mind, consider to be proofs, you are convinced beyond all doubt—until a stronger proof to the contrary is forced upon you. It would be of little use for me to raise Mrs. Harish to a condition of health and sanity without teaching you a certain kind of caution of the very existence of which you seem unaware, a caution respecting the acceptance of material proofs as conclusive in all cases; for without this caution you would immediately begin sending her back again. To a man of your self-sufficiency, who has amassed $100,000,000 in twenty years, the teaching will doubtless turn out to be somewhat drastic; but, if so, it is your lookout, not mine. It is on your own demand. Now, what is that thing in your mind that wild horses could not draw from you? Answer and write!"

Mr. Harish had summoned all his energies to resist. His face flushed and paled, his muscles grew tense, he set his jaw like a bulldog and clinched his hands, his teeth gritted like grinding-stones. In vain. It was the old, old struggle—brute force against science, selfishness against love, one against the combined strength of skilled humanity. The conclusion was foregone. His eyes, fixed upon Dr. Furnivall as if nailed by some invisible power, gradually took on a more settled appearance, passing from the steely to a nervous-laughing expression, to soberness, to earnestness, to peacefulness, and, finally, with the doctor's closing words, to deep introspection. Immediately he began to write, awkwardly, without seeing the paper, pronouncing each word slowly as he set it down, conscious only of certain truths in his own soul.

"I—perjured—myself—in—court—yesterday—on—the—Brand—case."

"Very good, to start with! How much did you save out of it—or make?"

"I—may—make—two—millions."

"Charming! That admission would be enough to convince most men; but what you ask is real proof, indisputable proof, something that nobody but yourself could possibly suspect. Of that perjury everybody suspects you. What is the first lie you ever told for money?"

"I—can't—think."

"Too long ago, eh? When you were very young? You began almost at once, probably. What was the first mean thing you did for money after you were twenty-one?"

"I—fraudulently—got—and—foreclosed a—mortgage—on—Widow—Gage's—home—and—made—four—thousand—dollars—which—set—me—up—in—business."

"What is the latest thing of the kind you have done, aside from the perjury?"

"This—morning—I—closed—a—deal—that—will—practically—ruin—my—late—partner's—children."

"There are, besides, many other transactions of yours that you would not acknowledge to a living soul, aren't there?"

"Yes."

"Well, tell me one more, and that will do."

"I—swore—off—three—million—in—taxes—in—the—city."

"That's enough," said Dr. Furnivall, putting on his spectacles. Mr. Harish sat immovable an instant, and then began to gaze around as if just waking from sleep. His eye caught sight of the doctor.

"Ah!" he exclaimed, with a jocularity somewhat forced, "I remember. I didn't doze. It was the hypnotism, wasn't it? Ha ha! How did it come out?"

Without a word, Dr. Furnivall pointed to the paper in his hand.

He examined its appearance curiously at first. Then he read the writing, read it again, then stared at it in unbelieving horror. A long minute he stood with bowed head, his face the hue of chalk. Slowly he tore the leaf into minute fragments, thrust them into his vest pocket, shivered, pulled himself together sharply, and, with the steely gleam in his eyes, looked at the doctor.

"What are you going to do about it?" he said. His voice was as if his mouth were full of sand.

"You are forgetting our business. Still, since you ask—is that Widow Gage yet living?"

"Yes."

"In poverty, of course?"

"Yes."

"No doubt some action in that matter and at once, recommends itself to you?"

"Yes."

"And the children of your late partner—"

"Yes."

"Very well. We will say no more about these things unless it should become necessary. They are for you to settle in your own way. My purpose at present is to restore Mrs. Harish. How long before you can have that medium here—the man you have been consulting about Mr. Jellipherson? Can you telephone to him?"

Mr. Harish measured him darkly. His face was very red now, he gnawed his lip nervously, his mustache bristled, his fingers opened and shut, and he breathed heavily.

"I can get him here very shortly, if you wish it," he answered at last. "But is it necessary to bring him into the matter?"

"It is. He must come at once. Mrs. Harish's cure depends on him. I am going to her now, and when he arrives show him up immediately, for it is there that I wish to see him."

"Ah, that's it, is it? I suppose I now know what you want. But you can't do it." He shook his head, with a touch of a cynical smile around his mouth. "You can't do it," he repeated. "I know." But as the doctor turned and without a word looked at him he added, "Well, if you insist." And he went to the telephone.

A half hour later a tall, slim man of 30, with curling black hair, staring eyes, in which a wild gleam flitted furtively, and dark mustached face, came into the sickroom with Mr. Harish. Dr. Furnivall immediately removed his spectacles.

"Business looking up?" he suggested pleasantly to him.

The other returned his gaze with a stare, and then seemed inclined to shift his regards in the direction of the bed, where Mrs. Harish lay peering fearfully above the covers. But he only moved his head slightly. His eyes remained fixed on the doctor's, staring harder and harder. After some hesitation he answered:

"No, we don't do much. Truth is too high for people. They won't come for it. They don't want it. Money is what they want, and fashionable clo'es—the women anyway."

He gave a little, hasty, deprecating laugh, and moved his feet about awkwardly, as one unused to conventional society. But his eyes never left the doctor's.

"Yes, but aren't there ways of starting people up, attracting their attention, making them wish to come to you and pay for your services?"

"I dunno what you mean." He said this grievedly, as if he took it as a reflection of some kind on himself; but even as he spoke Dr. Furnivall saw the familiar, introspective expression pass into his eyes. He asked at once:

"Where did you get that little ornamental dub which you sent to Mr. Harish?"

"My sister gut it for me," he replied readily.

"Where?"

"She took it off'n Mr. Harish's chain one night in Paris."

"Who is your sister? How could she get it?"

"She is Mrs. Harish's maid, and is with 'em all the time."

There was the sound of a startled movement in the bed.

"Keep perfectly quiet, Mrs. Harish," cautioned the doctor. "All you have to do is to listen and understand. Mr. Harish, go to your wife. Sit on the bed and take her hand. Now," he continued to the medium, "tell me about that transaction. Why did you do it? And how did you do it? Begin at the beginning!"

"Wal," he answered, "of course I try to git the names of all the people I can that's anyways interested in spiritualism, 'specially the rich ones and them that's well known, and find out all about 'em that I can, so's I can answer their questions if they come to me. I keep a list of 'em, and all about 'em, and have their pictures so's I'll reco'nize 'em and can tell 'em things they thought nobody knowed of. When my sister said Mr. Harish had mediums come here I told her she must git him for me, so she listened to everything they said, and read their letters, and found out a lot of things, and all about that club and Mr. Jellipherson's promise to come back from the spirit world, and I told her to git the club and send it to me if Mr. Jellipherson died—"

Another hasty movement, and an ominous exclamation, rose from the bed.

"Keep perfectly quiet, Mr. Harish," said the doctor. "And you, Mrs. Harish, listen now attentively. Have you," he continued to the medium, "ever known spirits to beat anybody?"

"Tha ain't no such thing, but it's cur'us—a lot of women think they do, women that's nervous, and them that's jest begun to b'lieve, but don't want to, and fight against it. They git scared and see things that ain't there, and think the spirits is mad at 'em and hurting 'em. I've had 'em come and show me their arms and necks so I could see the bruises, but tha never worn't no bruises there. They imagined 'em, 'cause their minds was set that way."

"Do you believe that the spirit of a dead person can communicate with the living?"

"I dunno. I never had none communicate with me; but great men, college perfessors, say they can, and I s'pose they know better'n what I do."

"In fact, then, while you believe there may be honest mediums, who possibly receive communications, you yourself are a medium for business only, and all these messages which for years you have pretended to receive from spirits, including those you gave Mr. Harish purporting to be from Jellipherson, were made up by you for the purpose of getting money?"

"Yes, sir."

Dr. Furnivall turned to the bed, to a singular tableau. Mrs. Harish, the light of a great joy in her face, her eyes streaming with happy tears, was reaching out her arms to her husband, while he, plainly torn between two powerful emotions—great love for his wife and bitter, overwhelming anger toward the medium—stared first at the one, then at the other, and finally at Dr. Furnivall.

COACHWHIP PUBLICATIONS

COACHWHIPBOOKS.COM

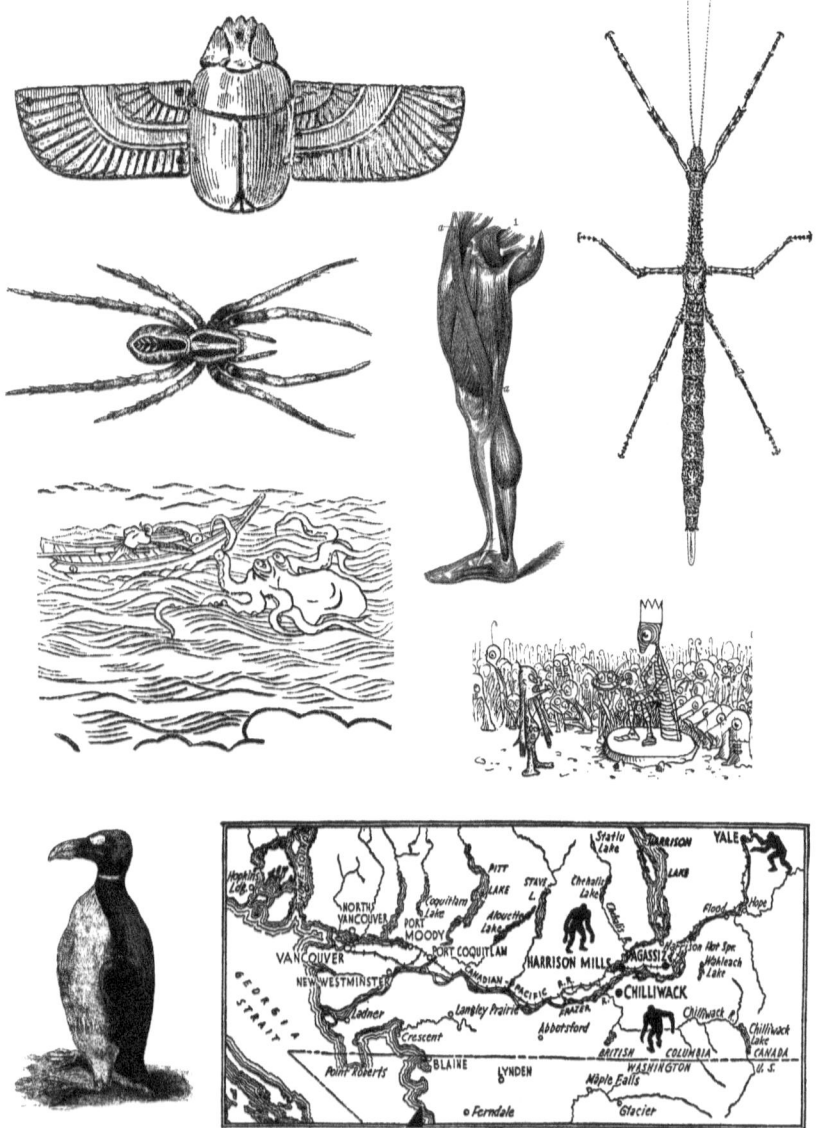

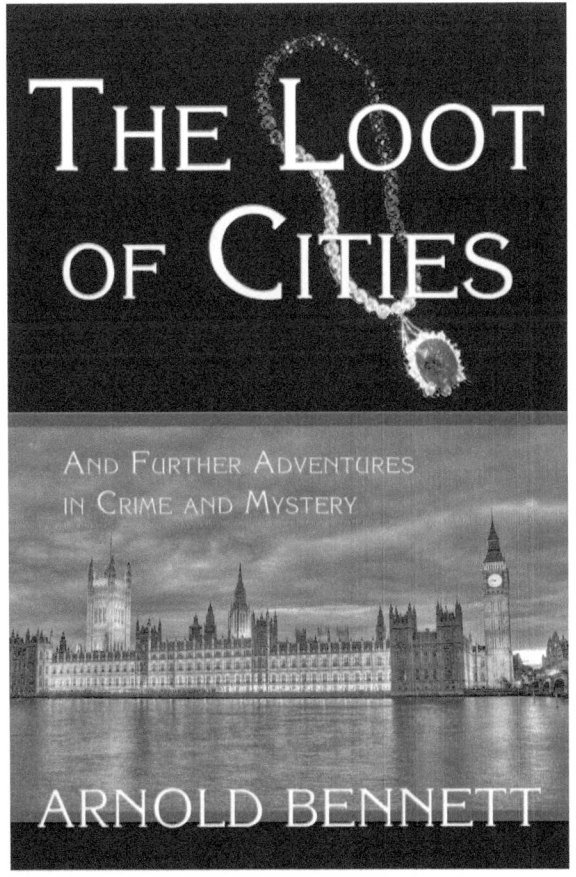

THE LOOT OF CITIES

ISBN 1-61646-060-1

THE COMPLETE ADVENTURES OF

ROMNEY PRINGLE

R. AUSTIN FREEMAN &
JOHN J. PITCAIRN

(AS BY *CLIFFORD ASHDOWN*)

THE COMPLETE ADVENTURES OF
ROMNEY PRINGLE

ISBN 1-61646-090-3

CRIME'S NEMESIS

LUKE S. MAY

CRIME'S NEMESIS

ISBN 1-61646-083-0

WWI ADVENTURES IN CRIME-FIGHTING AND SPY-HUNTING

True Adventures of the Secret Service

Adventures of the D. C. I.
(Department of Criminal Investigation)

MAJOR C. E. RUSSELL

WWI Adventures in
Crime-Fighting and Spy-Hunting

ISBN 1-61646-096-2

MELVILLE
DAVISSON
POST

THE LEGAL EXPLOITS OF
RANDOLPH MASON

THE LEGAL EXPLOITS OF
RANDOLPH MASON

ISBN 1-61646-061-X

www.ingramcontent.com/pod-product-compliance
Lightning Source LLC
Chambersburg PA
CBHW021843010726
47493CB00005B/1522